W9-BYN-454

FOUR BELOW

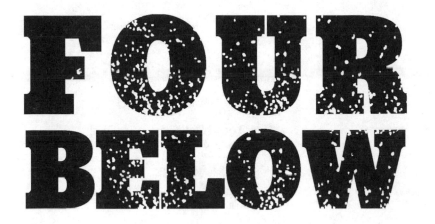

An Inspector McLusky Novel

Peter Helton

Constable • Robinson

Constable & Robinson Ltd
55–56 Russell Square
London WC1B 4HP
www.constablerobinson.com

First published in the UK by Constable,
an imprint of Constable & Robinson Ltd, 2011

First US edition published by SohoConstable,
an imprint of Soho Press, 2011

Soho Press, Inc.
853 Broadway
New York, NY 10003
www.sohopress.com

A copy of the British Library Cataloguing in

Publication data is available from the British Library

UK ISBN: 978-1-78033-143-0

US ISBN: 978-1-61695-082-8

US Library of Congress number: 2011030236

Printed and bound in the UK

1 3 5 7 9 10 8 6 4 2

MIX
Paper from
responsible sources
FSC
www.fsc.org   FSC® C018575

Thou strong seducer, opportunity!

John Dryden

If you think dope is for kicks and for thrills, you're out of your mind. There are more kicks to be had in a good case of paralytic polio.

Billie Holiday

Acknowledgements

Many thanks to Juliet Burton, and to Krystyna at Constable for all the chocolate. Thanks also to Mike and Martin for the excellent music, keep it coming. No thanks at all to Asbo the cat for sitting on the remote and recording *Antiques Roadshow* over my *Rebus*. What were you thinking?

He couldn't believe it was back to this. Back on the bloody night shift by himself. Constantly looking over his shoulder. It wasn't as easy as it had been either, especially being half-blind now. In the dark, having just one eye really made a difference. It stood to reason: only half the light went into your brain. And his left hand still hurt when he put pressure on anything. Lifting things the wrong way made his shoulder scream. He'd nearly dropped a whole bunch of stuff off a roof the other night. He'd get compensation eventually, they'd said. As a victim of crime. Quite ironic, if you thought about it. Of course he hadn't said that to them, about the irony and that. He hadn't said anything worth mentioning to them. You just didn't. Assailants unknown. If he'd said anything else, anything more, and the big man had got wind of it, he'd have sent Ilkin to finish the job. He was lucky to be alive as it was, they had said so at the hospital. He knew they were right, too. Got away with losing one ball and one eye. The pain of it, just the memory, could still make him sweat, even on a freezing night like this one. They'd done it on purpose, too. The testicle, not the eye. They'd taken great care to punch his balls in. As a warning to others. Ilkin threw the half-brick that took his eye. Good at throwing stuff. When they tied him up, he was sure they were going to kill him this time.

Should leave Bristol, really. Much safer, in case the big man changed his mind. Lying low now, back on the night shift. The cushy life was over. But kind of relieved, too. Okay, it was easy money working for the big man, but he was a scary fucker. His cold, trembling rages were enough to turn your hair grey. Better off out of there. Better off on your own, working. While all the idiots slept.

Chapter One

McLusky knew he should get back to the station, but he wasn't entirely convinced he could move. It had been a tedious morning of meetings and paperwork and his eyes just wanted to stay fixed on this painting of snow-capped mountains. Certainly an improvement on the canteen walls at Albany Road. They should get whoever painted this to do a mural at the station. The painting reminded him of the Swiss Alps – not that he had been to the Swiss Alps – though this being an Indian place, it was probably a scene from Kashmir. He hadn't been there either, but if this was what it looked like, he wouldn't mind going. There were several of these mountain scenes hanging around the walls, and all were pleasingly, luxuriously empty of human life. It looked clean and sane. Restful. Unlike the place itself. If the owner was being nostalgic about the wilds of Kashmir, then a noisy fast-food restaurant in the shadow of a railway bridge had to make him feel a long way from home.

McLusky tried to burp but couldn't. Shouldn't have had the enigmatically named 'meat curry'. He never dared ask what kind of meat went into it, but it sat in your stomach like a hot rock. He pushed his cleared plate away from him with too much emphasis and had to make a grab for it before it shot off the Formica table. He got to his feet with a groan. As he walked to the door, one of the men behind the counter gave him a nod of acknowledgement. He nodded back. McLusky was on nodding terms with the city now, but this was his first Bristol winter. A fierce blast of it swept down the

Cheltenham Road as he stepped outside, threatening to freeze-dry the film of curry sweat on his forehead. And it was only November. Two in the afternoon, and already everything felt grimy and grey. It had never properly got light in the first place, with the sky hanging over the city like a dirty tarpaulin. Which reminded him: he'd have to buy a few light bulbs on the way home; two of the bulbs in his flat had blown this morning. This morning already seemed a long time ago.

Traffic didn't look too bad today. By which he meant it was actually moving. As he vainly looked for a gap to cross the street, a man in a white T-shirt ran right-to-left on the other side, behind traffic and parked cars. He was running fast. McLusky didn't like the look of it. The man was running too fast. And what was it he was carrying? Shouts followed him up the road. Now he took a sudden rabbit-hook right into the street, angry horns blaring as cars braked sharply to avoid him. McLusky could see it now: the man was carrying a samurai sword, sheath in his left, naked blade in his right, stabbing the air as his arms pumped to the rhythm of his feet. McLusky thought he saw blood on the blade. Damn. He reached for the radio in his leather jacket just as a harsh and familiar voice approached. PC Hanham came running across lanes of traffic, shouting breathlessly into the radio clipped to his vest. McLusky left his own where it was; Hanham would already be calling for armed response. If he had enough breath to get the words out, of course. The constable jogged heavily past him, giving no sign that he had noticed DI McLusky standing there with his much-needed unlit cigarette between his lips. Leave it. Hanham was the man to catch the swordsman, McLusky thought. He was the one wearing a stab vest, after all.

Rapid response. In this traffic? Oh, what the hell. At least it would warm him up. He started after the burly constable. Hanham was running fast. McLusky speeded up, then found he needed to speed up again. He only caught up as Hanham followed the suspect into Zetland Road. By then, a jabbing stitch in his side was making it hard going.

'He ... attacked a man ... at the bus stop near the girls' school ... a leg wound. Ambulance en route,' Hanham got out.

'By the school? That's miles back.'

'I know ... miles ... I don't think ... I can run ... much further ...'

One look at Hanham confirmed it: his face was slack with exhaustion, his eyes were rolling like those of a panicked horse. He slowed, stopped, sank to his knees. 'All yours ...'

McLusky kept going. He could still see the suspect ahead. Just then the man turned to check behind him and spotted his new pursuer. Civilians shrieked and shouted, jumping out of the way of the dancing sword.

Running in the street now, sweat was pricking McLusky's skin, despite the cold. He realized why he had so easily caught up with Hanham: the constable must have already been slowing from exhaustion. The swordsman was pulling away from him, fuelled by adrenalin, madness and drugs no doubt. And probably unencumbered by a mystery curry.

McLusky ran on. The pain in his side got worse. He'd go vegetarian. Perhaps even give up smoking. Again. Now all he could do was keep running, without the foggiest idea what he was going to do should he ever catch up with the suspect. Without stab vest, baton or pepper spray, he'd have little chance of disarming him. As a last resort, he could always threaten to throw up on him, which he'd do anyway if this went on much longer. The rattle of a diesel engine behind him made him glance over his shoulder. Never had a scruffy cab for hire looked more welcome. Suicidally he ran into its path, scrabbling in his pocket for his warrant card.

'Follow that man!' He threw himself into the passenger seat.

'What man would that be?' The cabby spoke and moved with agonizing slowness, setting the meter. He filled every available inch behind the wheel and looked like he hadn't left his cab for years. Far ahead of them, the swordsman had now sheathed his weapon and was crossing Zetland Road, trotting into a side street.

'Just drive! There, the young man ...' McLusky was still struggling for breath. 'With the light jacket, jeans and ... trainers.'

'Righty-ho.' The driver pulled away at last. 'What's he done?'

'Never mind that, just catch up with him.'

'Only asking. Taking an interest.' He turned the cab into the side street. They could both see the suspect a hundred yards or so ahead. The man was either out of puff or thought he had lost his pursuers. He stepped off the pavement and stood at the edge of the road as if waiting to cross once the taxi had passed.

'Keep closer to the left. I'll tell you when to stop.'

Half a second before drawing level with the swordsman, McLusky popped his seat belt and threw the door wide open. The man had no chance to react before the door caught him a thudding blow on the side, breaking his elbow and flinging him hard on to the tarmac. McLusky could hear him scream as they passed.

The cab driver braked indignantly. 'You never told me to stop!'

McLusky jumped out and ran back the few yards to where the young man was still on the ground, groaning. He had dropped the sword. The DI kicked it under the nearest car, then thumped a heavy knee into the suspect's back and twisted his unbroken arm back.

This wasn't popular. 'Ah! Get off me! You broke my arm! You broke my fucking arm! You fucking arsehole broke my arm! Get off me! I need an ambulance!'

'You need to shut up. Of course it may harm your defence ...' McLusky rattled off half the caution, but stopped when he felt a wave of nausea travel up from his stomach. He thumbed the orange button on his airwave radio. 'Alpha Nine, can I come in please ...?' He gave his position and asked for backup, while the suspect kept up a rich mixture of pleading, insults and threats. Feeling in danger of losing his supper and with no handcuffs to secure the suspect,

4

McLusky was extremely grateful when he saw PC Hanham, who had got his breath back, come marching up the road.

'You can't cuff the other wrist; I think he broke his arm in the fall,' McLusky explained.

The swordsman twisted his head back and yelled his protest at Hanham. 'He ran me down with the fucking taxi, that's what broke my arm, you wankers!'

'Good effort, sir. Did you see what he did with the sword?' the constable asked.

'Under that car. You'd better arrest him properly; I may have burped a few times during the caution. Better make sure.'

'Will you take him in?'

'Me? I got a taxi waiting with the meter running. No, he's your man, Constable.'

Hanham loudly cautioned his blaspheming prisoner while watching the DI get into the cab. Half-arresting suspects, then swanning off in a taxi all casual. *McLusky.* Where on earth did they find him?

McLusky made the driver stop at a convenience store so he could stock up on light bulbs, mineral water and indigestion tablets before letting himself be driven back to Albany Road. By the time he was carrying his purchases along the corridor towards his office, he no longer felt sick, but the curry still sat acidly right under his solar plexus. Definitely the vegetable biryani next time.

DS Sorbie watched McLusky come past the CID room. He checked his watch. If he himself were to take lunch breaks this long, he'd soon get an earful from DI Fairfield. The man had been shopping too, by the looks of it. Unbelievable. And that could so easily have been, should have been, him. If Avon & Somerset hadn't seen fit to import the DI from Southampton, there might have been room round here for long-overdue promotion.

McLusky firmly closed the door of his office behind him and let himself fall into his chair. He didn't have far to fall.

5

The office they had found for him at the very end of the corridor was minute. At first he had suspected it to be a converted cupboard, but he had been assured that it was DI Pearce's old office. Sometimes McLusky thought it had probably been responsible for driving Pearce to retire early. With a large haul of drugs money. Not that 'renegade cop Pearce, 46' (*Bristol Herald*) had enjoyed it for long. The Spanish police, with the help of DCI Gaunt, had scooped him up before he had a chance to spend much of it.

The only good thing about the office was that the enormous radiator under the window, obviously designed for a much larger room, heated the place to tropical temperatures. Not quite the only thing, he reminded himself now. The fact that his window opened on to the back of the station, away from the prying eyes of colleagues and punters, meant he could afford to smoke the odd cigarette without attracting attention. Albany Road, along with every other police station, of course, was a no-smoking area. A recent decree issued by Superintendent Denkhaus had also strictly outlawed the 'abhorrent practice' of smoking near the entrance or in the staff car park.

McLusky opened the window. It looked out over roofs and the neglected backs of nearby buildings. McLusky preferred the backs of houses. He invariably found them more revealing than their better-kept fronts. The rear was not just where illicit cigarettes were smoked. It was where suspects tried to leave when the heavy knock came at the front. The rear of a house was the natural hiding place for drugs, money, weapons and the occasional body.

An illicit cigarette was exactly what he needed now. Last one in the packet, how annoying, and he'd been in the shop not ten minutes ago. Smoking was said to aid digestion, and he could do with all the help he could get. The scarcity of tobacco made the first drag even more luxurious.

It had been a quiet week, apart from the endless paperwork, of course: report-writing, form-filling, box-ticking, assessments and memos. Earlier in the year, Atrium, the anti-drugs operation, had taken Ray Fenton out of circulation, a major drugs baron who would never again see his naff sports car, ostentatious penthouse or tasteless motor yacht. But even in the midst of the celebrations, they all knew what it meant, what the next few months would bring: a vicious little war fought in the resulting power vacuum. In supply-and-demand economics there would always be drugs barons as long as there were customers for his wares, and Bristol was the hub that supplied drugs to much of the West Country. The business was so ridiculously lucrative that new dealers constantly tried to move in, at the risk of all-out war with Yardie and Asian gangs and established dealer networks. Over three hot summer months there had been stabbings and shootings; one drive-by shooting had injured two innocent bystanders while completely missing the target. Yet there was nothing concrete; there had been plenty of hints and rumours, but all had failed to solidify. By autumn, everything had gone quiet. A new kingpin was securing the hub now, only so far McLusky had no idea who he was. There were rumours, of course, and the rumours weren't good. Give it time. He knew that the quiet was deceptive, the short lull before business as usual resumed. Like a quick illicit cigarette break before the return to work.

He flicked the fag end out of the window towards the wheelie bins below. The phone on his desk rang and he answered it. On the other end was DS Austin. McLusky had been right.

They were back in business.

On the night shift, planning was important. Without a plan, you ended up like an opportunist junkie thief, climbing into houses and then staggering along the road carrying some crap that was enough to get you put back inside but not enough to buy you a kebab. Tricky, of course. All the good stuff sat where there was tons of security. Neighbourhood Watch, those were the days. Now it was all high-tech; no one needed to twitch their curtains, they all got security cameras, CCTV, SmartWater, alarms. If you strayed into the wrong neighbourhood, they would have you taped before you'd got your tools out. Taped? What an old-fashioned expression. It was all electronic now. At least in the old days they'd record over the same cassette a million times so when something worth seeing happened the quality was so crap it could have been anyone ghosting through the frame. Either that or they'd already taped over it. Morons. Now it was hard drives and crisp images and as much recording time as you liked.

Not in your league, that, anyway. Not on your own, either, not with one eye and one ball and an old motor that stuck out like a sore thumb. Mind you, he always made sure he looked after the van, and there was nothing the rozzers could pull him over for. Tax, MOT, insurance, all the paperwork. No point in drawing attention to yourself. Clean driver's licence, too. As for housebreaking, it was the lower-middle ground you wanted, the up-and-coming, upwardly mobile, what they used to call yuppies. Thirty-something couples just starting out together, twenty-five grand a year each, first house. Lots of money for stuff and gadgets to plonk on every surface but not enough for a five ninety-nine window lock. Lava lamps. Digital photo frames. They're the ones. Hard-working morons. Not a care. Pick one. Clean them out. All insured. Come back three months later and lift all the brand-new replacements. Nine out of ten still hadn't fitted any security, even then. Idiots. He was the lightning that struck twice. Of course most of the junk people had in their houses was worth next to nothing. All the usual stuff was now so cheap to buy in the first place that it wasn't really worth pinching. You hardly got a thing for it, especially if you used a fence. After all, why spend a hundred and fifty on a netbook you know is probably stolen when you can get a new one for two-twenty? With a year's guarantee?

But at last he had struck it lucky; not a bad haul, this. In fact it was so good he had made two trips to the van, breaking his iron rule not to get Aladdined. Getting greedy and hanging around too long gave people time to notice you, to get on the blower and arrange nasty surprises. But it had been worth it. Not a load of catalogue showroom rubbish this time. Top-of-the-range equipment, this. Professional gear, all photography stuff. Two digital SLR cameras, long lenses, two printers – he'd lifted the bigger one – all the chargers and a laptop. State-of-the-art laptop. Top spec, latest model. Must have cost a fortune. He flicked on the ultraviolet bulb. Not one item was security-marked.

He used to quite enjoy taking pictures. Never had a decent camera, though, just happy-snappy things. Send the pics off to Prontoprint and get them back a week later. Most of them went straight in the bin, but some were good. Some were priceless. No idea where they'd got to. Lost in one of the endless moves or disappeared when his last girlfriend ran off. Took a few good ones of *her*. He had quite an eye for taking photographs. Let's hope it wasn't the eye he'd lost. Ha. First eye joke that made him smile, good one. Might take a bit longer for the first ball joke, of course. He was tempted to keep one of the cameras. And the printer. But perhaps not the laptop. Too expensive, he could never explain that away. Flog it, then buy a cheap one and keep the receipt. That'd unnerve the rozzers if they came calling. A *receipt*.

Of course, before you could sell a knocked-off computer you had to wipe everything on it or whoever bought it in a pub car park wouldn't be able to pretend that he didn't know it was nicked. A shame with this one, because the pictures on it were fantastic. Really good. You could tell the last owner knew what they were doing. Folder after folder. This lot, for instance, the pictures in the woods in autumn. Taken at the crack of dawn or else just as it got dark. Some of the shots were amazing. Mind you, some of the pics had a weird mob in them; the bunch this photographer hung out with didn't half look nerdy. All with little cameras. One of them in a wheelchair, even. How did they get *him* into the woods?

But the pics without people in them, the atmospheric ones, he'd keep some of them. These ones with the lights in the trees looked spooky, like from a fantasy movie. And the pictures had so many pixels you could probably have them blown up big as posters. And you could zoom right in on the spooky lights … and keep zooming in … and …

It was difficult to believe what he was seeing. His mouth had gone dry and his heart was hammering. His palms were sweaty. And this was just a picture of the bastards. It must have been taken with a long lens. Or did he mean long exposure? The big man must have stood still, because he wasn't blurred at all. Neither was the car. The very Merc he sometimes used to drive him around in when he was drunk, he was certain. But the figure with the bag over his head was a bit out of focus, and so was Ilkin. Though you'd recognize him if you knew it was him. He was hard to forget. However much you'd like to.

He got up and started pacing the room, leaving the image on the screen. How was it possible that he had found this very picture? Or was it the other way around? Had the picture found him? Whoever took this picture couldn't have known what they were photographing. The big man couldn't have known, or this photographer would already be six foot under. What he needed now was a drink. And time to think. This could be it, his one chance of revenge. This picture could be his ticket. He would have to move house first, of course, no question about it. The big man would pay a lot to keep this picture out of the papers. Of course he would also happily have him killed – slowly – by Ilkin while he watched from the comfort of his car.

Chapter Two

'This could turn out to be complete nonsense, of course. Bound to, in fact.' McLusky was possessed of a profound cynicism where the observational skills of the public were concerned. 'Once we're across the bridge, you'll have to give me directions.'

DS Austin made himself taller in the passenger seat and craned his neck to catch a glimpse of the river below. 'Okay, will do. It's a great view from up here.'

McLusky, who didn't like heights much, gave an all-purpose grunt and kept his eyes to the front as they crossed the Clifton suspension bridge going west. 'Someone moves their dustbins out of alignment and we get a detailed description of the perpetrator, but you can carry a headless corpse through town and no one sees a thing. I can guarantee it.'

'The woman was quite adamant. A fox with half a human face in his jaws. Or words to that effect.'

'Half a cheese sandwich, more like.'

'She was walking her dog early this morning. Turn right when you're past the sports club.'

'Where would we be without dog-walkers?'

'Back at the nick in a warm office? No offence, it's a stylish car and all that, but the heating is pathetic.'

McLusky knew Austin was right. The old Mazda had been an impulse buy, and the longer he drove it, the more faults showed up. Terrible suspension was one of them. A

11

feeble heater another. But he liked it and felt defensive about it. 'It gets warm eventually.'

'I'll have to take your word for it.'

McLusky turned on to what looked like a forester's track into the bleak woods they had been skirting for a while. 'What is this place, anyway?'

'Leigh Woods. Have you not been here before?'

'I'm not the outdoorsy type. And look at it, why would anyone?'

'Because, it's great in summer, lots of people come here. It's quite big, runs all the way back to the gorge. Streams, ponds …'

The afternoon seemed set to become even gloomier. '*Ponds*, Jane?' DS James Austin was broad, darkly hairy, with an Edinburgh accent, so naturally everyone called him Jane. If the DS minded, he never let on. 'Not bleedin' *ponds* in November, Jane.'

'Yes, okay, it'll be a bloody nightmare place to search.' For someone. It wasn't as if they were personally required to dive into ponds and lakes. Ahead, two vehicles, one a patrol car, came into view, parked across and beside the track. 'This should be it.'

McLusky pulled on to the soft verge beside the patrol car. The woman who had made the call stood by her silver hatchback. She was in her fifties and sensibly dressed in thick boots, padded jacket, hat and gloves. Very sensibly, thought McLusky, whose leather jacket wasn't putting up much of a fight against the cold. Further along, among the stark and practically leafless trees, two police constables in high-vis jackets used sticks to poke half-heartedly at the wet leaf litter. Winter mist hung in the woods, cutting visibility to less than a hundred yards. All around them the place dripped with icy moisture. McLusky acknowledged the civilian with a nod, turned up his collar and waited for one of the constables, who was making his way towards him.

DS Austin approached the woman. 'Are you the lady who called us?'

12

'I am. You must be Inspector McLusky, I was told to expect you.'

'Erm, no. I'm Detective Sergeant Austin; that's DI McLusky over there.'

'Oh, I'm sorry, I heard the Scottish accent and just assumed ...'

'The inspector will be with you shortly. I think he first wants a word with the constable.'

McLusky did. It was PC Pym. He was a slim six foot four and had a habit of folding himself at the hip so as not to tower over superior officers. 'What have we got, Pym?'

'Well, erm ...' The PC looked across to the woman. McLusky walked them away from the cars to get completely out of earshot. 'The lady reported seeing a fox carrying what she believed to be human remains, sir.'

'Part of a *face*, is that right?'

'Imagination may play a part here, no disrespect to the lady. Yes, what she is quite sure about, she says, is flesh, hair and what *looked* to her like a human ear.'

'Bits of rabbit?'

'That may account for the hair, but what about the ear? Rabbit ears don't look much like ours.'

McLusky shrugged heavily. Cold air crept under his jacket as he did so. 'I don't know. Rabbit and *mushroom*, then.'

'Rabbit marengo,' Pym said helpfully.

'What?'

'Sorry, sir. A rabbit dish. My mother used to cook it. It's got mushrooms in it.'

'Please don't mention food, Pym. Whatever it was they put in my lunch refuses to go quietly. Right, let's have a quick chat with that woman. I don't suppose you saw any foxes' lairs, if that's what they have?'

'Holes, I think, is what they have. Not a one. Aren't they nocturnal, though?'

McLusky waved his hand as he walked away. 'Carry on here for a bit, anyway.'

Back at the cars, he introduced himself to the woman. On the other side, Austin was walking between the trees, eyes down.

'I did tell your colleague the fox went *that* way.' She pointed irritably in the opposite direction.

'How long ago did you see the fox?'

'This morning, as I said. About nine thirty. I was walking my dog when I saw it running. Ziggy must have startled him. He ran after him but lost him, predictably. It took me half an hour to get Ziggy to come back to me, he was so excited.'

'And the fox was carrying human remains?'

An impatient intake of breath. 'How often do I have to repeat it? *Yes.* I clearly saw a human ear. There were bits of hair and flesh. It was quite … well, I shouldn't say disgusting; quite shocking, I suppose.'

'And naturally you reported it straight away?'

'Well, no, I didn't. I went home. I reported it later.'

McLusky nodded. 'You waited till the afternoon.'

'I only saw it for the briefest of moments. And it was such a strange thing to have seen. I wanted to be clear in my mind that I really had seen it. And then I decided. Not many things look like human ears. Do they, Inspector?'

McLusky squinted into the mist. Not many things a fox would show an interest in. 'We'll look into it. We have your details, in case we need to speak to you again.'

'I can go, then?'

'Mm? Yes. Yes, thanks, you did the right thing.'

'I know, Inspector.'

McLusky was already walking away. 'We'll let you know if we find anything.'

Sitting in the driver's seat, the woman wiped condensation from the windscreen with the back of her glove. She wouldn't be holding her breath on hearing from them again. And she wouldn't be surprised if they got themselves lost in there; they all looked like they'd never actually seen a tree before, the way they were behaving. You reported a murder

14

and they sent four bobbies up to search Leigh Woods. And they didn't even have the sense to bring a dog.

McLusky hurried to join PC Pym before he disappeared completely into the mist. His colleague was already barely visible between the slick boles of ash trees to the north.

'What was your impression of the witness, sir?'

'Not easily flustered. If she says she saw an ear, then perhaps that's what she did see.' He kicked at the leaf litter. It had to be centuries deep. Things had lived and died in this place since the last ice age. It felt like the next one was on its way. Not a bad place to die, probably. If it was your time, of course. Not if some other bastard decided it was. And as long as it wasn't November.

Austin crossed the track and came over to join them. 'I thought there were two of you,' he said to Pym.

Pym looked around. The mist was turning to fog; there was no sign of his colleague. He cupped his gloved hands round his mouth and called, 'Becky? You fallen down a hole yet?' Almost immediately, the form of PC Becks appeared from the mist, making his way back towards them. 'Now you see him, now you don't,' Pym said. 'So much for high-vis jackets. We'll have to tie ourselves together with string. The fog's getting worse and it'll be dark soon.'

'Are we searching the area, then?' Austin asked.

McLusky nodded heavily. 'Yes, we'll do a bloody search. But first: do you have a cigarette on you, DS Austin?'

'I gave up, don't you remember?'

'So?'

'You mean it would help my promotional prospects if I carried cigarettes of a certain brand at all times?'

'Definitely.'

McLusky turned to Pym, who shook his head. 'Don't smoke. But sir, if we are to do a real search, we'll need a lot more bodies up here.'

McLusky wrinkled his nose in distaste. 'Would you care to rephrase that, PC Pym?'

*

15

Sisyphus, that was it, she remembered the name now. It wasn't a Bible story at all, silly, it was a naughty Greek man who was condemned to push a boulder up a hill and then it rolled off again and he'd push it up again and so on for ever. The Greek myth of Sisyphus this was like, only was Polish myth of Anastazja. You push the trolley first along one floor, then next floor, then other floor again. Every day, a job without happy ending, there was always more where that came from. Only, if you push cleaning trolley through shopping centre you become invisible also. The landlady says: with name like Anastazja you should be on stage. What can invisible woman do on a stage? Play the ghost perhaps. *Excuse me.* Excuse me was what she said mostly all day because of course, when you are invisible woman, people don't know to get out of your ways. *Excuse me.* English people do not notice other people, only notice shopping. Excuse me while I clean up vomit from teenager drunk in middle of day. Of course at night the whole shopping centre was made clean with machine. A *man* with machine. But you cannot clean toilets with machine. For toilets we use Polish woman. Excuse me while I mop up orange soft drink your child spills on floor because he wants attention but you are too busy making eyes at things in shops windows. The English have a saying: where there is muck, there is brass. Well, is completely wrong. Where there is muck there is Polish woman with mop. Cleaning it up.

'And another thing …' Superintendent Denkhaus signalled McLusky to sit down while speaking forcefully down the phone to a civilian IT technician who hadn't got a word in for the last five minutes. Denkhaus even managed the ghost of a smile to go with his nod, without letting up on the tirade he was pouring down the receiver. That was part of management skills, McLusky thought, pretending anger you didn't feel, beaming with enthusiasm at boring stuff, smiling encouragingly at people while thinking of other matters. '… for the past two weeks under the heading "Offenders

Brought to Justice" there was not a single example posted.'
Denkhaus began lifting his coffee cup but set it back down
on its saucer with dangerous emphasis. '*I know*, but what's
that got to do with it? It makes us look like we never get any
bloody convictions *at all*! The public don't fart about on our
website for information; they're just looking for
reassurance.'

McLusky looked stealthily at the superintendent's coffee
tray for evidence of anything skinny. He'd been warned
more than once that Denkhaus, who carried at least four
stone of spare weight, turned ogre as soon as he tried to give
up sugar. A reassuring sugar bowl sat next to the little jug of
cream on the tray, together with a small saucer displaying
telltale signs of recent biscuit consumption. That was as far
as indulgence went in this room, he noted. Not only was the
desk devoid of any clutter; the rest of the office was as functional as could be contrived. Not a picture, plant pot or
ornament softened the starkness of the room, one wall of
which was taken up entirely with a large-scale map of the
city.

'Public confidence is the watchword here, as ever,'
Denkhaus continued. 'From now on I want at least four
mugs on that page for our force area at all times … Well I
don't care if you put your *own* picture up as long as it makes
us look good to civilians browsing the site. If we told them
what really went on, they'd soon start throwing rocks at us.'
Denkhaus hung up without bothering with formalities.

'They're doing that already, sir,' McLusky offered.

'They're doing what?'

'Throwing rocks at us. When we closed down the crack
house in Knowle West last Monday, a rock and a bottle were
thrown at officers, just for doing their job.'

'By some local yobs. Not by your average citizen, not yet,
and that's why public relations is half the battle. A reduction in the public's perception of crime is as important as
reduction in crime itself. No point in eradicating crime if
people are still frightened in their beds.'

17

'A bobby on every street corner.'

'Quite. It would only take an extra million officers. As it is, cuts are now inevitable. Enough.' Denkhaus waved away the distraction. There was no point in discussing issues like these with junior officers. 'How reliable is your witness?'

'Hard to say, but she was no airhead and was quite sure of herself. She did take her time reporting it, though. She waited several hours before making up her mind that she had in fact seen human remains being carried around by a fox. Now she's adamant.'

'And you turned up nothing at all?'

McLusky pointed out of the window. 'It was already getting dark and it's very misty up there, too. '

'Tomorrow, then, at first light.'

'How many officers can we deploy?'

'I can let you have four. With you and DS Austin, that's half a dozen.'

'Half a dozen? Sir, have you seen the size of the place? Leigh Woods is two hundred hectares, give or take. In old money that's probably—'

'Five hundred acres, thanks, McLusky, I'm fully decimalized. There's a big football match on tomorrow; we can't possibly spare dozens of officers to poke around in the woods on the strength of some vague sighting. Find some evidence of foul play and you can have all the officers you want. Until then you'll have to make do.'

Football. Why couldn't they play football in summer, when it was nice and warm? 'There's at least one pond in there as well.'

'Forget the damn pond. It was a fox she saw, not a beaver. Leave the pond alone. Underwater search costs an absolute fortune. Now if there's nothing else, DI McLusky ...'

DI Kat Fairfield turned the heater up. Then she turned the music up. She loved her little Renault. It was quick, it was fun. Come to think of it, it was more comfortable than her flat. Quicker to warm up than her flat, too. And it was paid

18

for. She could play music as loud as she liked without the neighbours complaining, and the view from the windows was ever-changing. There was no one to tell her that heavy metal was rubbish. If Led Zeppelin was rubbish, then fine, she liked rubbish. Mind you, there was no one at home to tell her it was rubbish either. Not since 'the break-up', and that was years ago now. Before the flat and before the Renault. Why aren't we all living in cars? she wondered. She'd probably still be with Paul if they were. Just meet from time to time, park up next to each other for a while, then drive through your own life until you felt like parking up again. She'd hung on to the name, another thing her mother couldn't forgive her; the first had been marrying Paul in the first place. Somehow DI Kat Fairfield seemed an easier name to work with on the force than Katarina Vasiliou. *What's wrong with Vasiliou, Rina? It's a fine Greek name!* And all her own fault for not marrying a nice Greek boy with prospects in the first place. Unfortunately she'd never been completely *one hundred per cent* sure about the boy thing either. But opportunities for the girl thing seemed even rarer than the other.

She liked driving, especially on these back roads, but it was getting quite misty and would be dark soon. And the trip out to Yatton had been a complete waste of time. She'd gone to re-interview the victim herself, hoping to get a handle on a violent reoffender, aka the victim's ex-boy-friend, but the woman had begun by contradicting her first statement, then completely withdrawn the charge. It would have been good to take the man out of circulation for a while. Otherwise not a CID matter. He'd punched the victim to the ground then stomped on her a few times for good measure, breaking her collarbone and several bones in her hand. What counted as *losing your rag* in some circles. Well don't come running to us next time. The next time, of course, it might not just be a couple of teeth and your collarbone.

'What can I do, I *love* him,' Fairfield mimicked in a squeaky voice. Not that the woman had actually said it, but it was the refrain she heard in her head when she came across women in abusive relationships who every time went back for more. He's always so sorry afterwards, so *contrite*. And there it was, that tiny illusion of power, the joy of forgiving. That girl could do with a bit of heavy metal in her life rather than the boy-band crap she listened to. Perhaps it would give her enough backbone to get out of there. Mind you, these lyrics weren't exactly written by a feminist either. Fairfield quickly forwarded through the song to the next track.

Her frustration had made her speed up too much, and she had to slow down quite hard for the bend ahead. Nothing in her mirrors. A speeding ticket was the last thing she needed. Superintendent Denkhaus did his nut last time one of his officers was caught speeding, and she wasn't in the super's good books as it was. Never had been and had no idea how to get into them. To make matters worse, DCI Gaunt was in hospital having 'his operation'. He'd been waiting for 'his operation' for so long, she'd forgotten what it was for. She got on with Gaunt, no matter what others thought of him. Popularity wasn't important in this job; you could do well without it. It was results that counted.

The road was empty now, and Fairfield speeded up again. How she'd love to drive a fast car on a race track one day. Still nothing in her mirrors. She checked her speed. Sixty. It seemed like nothing, but it was idiotic in this mist. She slowed down a little. It was the end of her shift anyway, no need to hurry anywhere. She might not even check in at Albany Road nick; drive straight home instead. Her speed crept up again. It was getting dark now, but it was a familiar road; it felt like she knew every bend, and she swung the car through them in an easy, one-handed rhythm. There was food in the freezer; she'd stop at the off-licence near her house, buy a bottle of wine. Best get two, one for tomorrow. She really ought to try and make two bottles last three days.

The deer jumped gracefully into the beams of her head-lights and froze as Fairfield stood on the brakes. Her car snaked towards the animal while her tyres shrieked and

Fairfield held her breath. Then the deer was gone. She released the brake and straightened the car. *Damn it, Kat, you never know what's around the corner*. She drove on. Then stomped on the brake again, making the car squeal to a complete stop while two more deer followed the first one across the road.

And you never know what the hell is going to happen next.

Chapter Three

Leigh Woods, first light. McLusky was reluctant to leave the car, which had just begun to warm up a little. It was perishing cold out there. Last night, knowing this cold moment would come, he had gone through his entire wardrobe, what there was of it, looking for warm things to wear. He appeared to have no winter clothes. He couldn't understand it. Of course it had been Laura who, back in Southampton, had packed up all his belongings and dumped them at the section house so he would have no excuse to come back to her flat. Finding them there all boxed and bagged after he'd left the hospital had been a clear message: no negotiations. And yet. And yet she had moved to Bristol only a couple of months ago to start a course in field archaeology. She lived somewhere out there in the city now; he didn't know where.

But Laura was far too efficient not to have packed all of his clothes. So it was either thieving bastards at the police section house or the sad fact that his wardrobe was as inadequate as the rest of his domestic arrangements. One thick black sweater, a pair of black leather gloves and this ridiculously cheerful scarf was what he had found. PCs Pym and Becks were also still sitting in their car. He'd told them to wait until the rest had turned up. When they had learned there would be a grand total of six officers available to search the woods, they'd simply exchanged glances and nodded. They were used to idiotic numbers games.

First light it may have been, somewhere up there above the clouds; down here it was dark enough to make the search difficult, if not impossible. Headlights appeared now in his rear-view mirrors, announcing the arrival of a second patrol car, carrying PCs Purkis and Hanham, and behind theirs the tiny blue Nissan of DS Austin. McLusky quit the dubious comfort of his old Mazda and waited for everyone to come to him. Austin parked opposite, beyond the track. He looked wide awake and full of energy as he unfolded himself from the little car.

'You really need to get a different car, Jane,' McLusky mocked, not for the first time. 'For a big hairy DS, a baby-blue Micra is the wrong accessory.'

'You've not met my fiancée, have you?' Austin countered quickly. 'Eve can be very persuasive. They also come in pink, you know.'

'So you're saying you got off lightly.' The four constables converged on the inspector's car. McLusky tuned his voice to upbeat. 'Morning, gentlemen. Oh, and gentlewoman,' he added when he recognized PC Ellen Purkis behind the broad shape of PC Hanham.

'Gentle, *her*?' Hanham scoffed. 'You've not seen her make an arrest then, have you, sir?'

Purkis shrugged happily inside her high-vis jacket and slapped her hands together for warmth.

'Okay, welcome to the Avon and Somerset survival course. There's six of us and we have five hundred acres of woodland here.'

'Four hundred and sixty, I looked it up,' Austin supplemented.

'There you are, thanks to DS Austin here, that's forty acres done already. Visibility is worse than yesterday, we only have six officers and a couple of dragon lights and the whole thing is a total farce. We're now at the spot where the woman saw the fox and she says it went that-a-way.' McLusky pointed west, into the mist. 'We'll form a line … yeah, okay, a very *loose* line, and sweep up and down on this side of the path. Pokey sticks at the ready. Let's go find a dead body. You'll recognize it when you see it; they say it has one ear missing. If you find one with two ears – ignore it, we don't want any of those.'

As senior officer, McLusky could easily now have returned to Albany Road, or at least sat in the car and waited for results, but he'd have felt cut off. He preferred being outside or on the move, only he liked his outside paved and tarmacked and twenty degrees warmer. He took the extreme left of the line next to Austin so he could talk to him without instantly broadcasting every word to the rest of the officers. The six of them walked ten paces apart, leaving plenty of scope to miss all but the most obvious clues. Short of stumbling into a recently dug shallow grave that had been uncovered by foxes, they had little chance of finding the body. If there really was one.

'How long are we keeping this up?' Austin wanted to know.

'Don't ask. I'm trying not to think about it. If we could be sure about the sighting, then we'd simply go on until we find the body.'

'That's if the rest of it is here. Perhaps it's been dismembered and distributed around several sites.'

'That's what I like about working with you, DS Austin, your cheerful optimism.'

Austin checked his wristwatch. 'It's twenty to eight now. Sun sets at sixteen twenty.'

'We'll have perished long before that.'

'Yesterday you seemed quite certain the witness was reliable,' Austin reminded him.

'It wasn't that cold yesterday. I must buy some warm clothes; one jumper is all I found.'

'I'm wearing my thermals for this.'

McLusky directed the sweep up and down in what by necessity was an arbitrary area on the west side of the path. Each time he called the line to a stop and moved it across, he was aware that the body could easily lie just six feet further

25

on into the trees. The strong beams of the dragon lights the PCs were using stabbed thick milky fingers into the mist but after two hours had failed to illuminate anything significant. Cigarette packets, the odd drinks can, faded packaging of biscuits, of condoms. McLusky poked a stick at another bump in the leaf litter, uncovered nothing more interesting than a nest of stones and stopped. He straightened up. They were nearing the lower end of the area, getting closer to the cars again. He was about to order a break when control called him on his radio. He cheered up as he listened, and waved Austin over.

'Enough of this, we're wanted elsewhere.'

'Oh yeah?'

'A bona fide dead chap with both his ears in place. We're even on the right side of the river.' He called the officers over and delivered the news. 'And then there were four. Don't get lost, don't get hypothermia. And don't fall into any ponds, because we can't afford the Underwater Search Unit, I'm told. Pack it in by lunchtime.' He waved his hands, palms skywards, as though shooing along chickens.

'Why don't I drive us in my car?' Austin suggested as they walked towards the collection of vehicles.

McLusky grunted non-committally.

'I'll drop you back here again later. It's got a decent heater. And I've got a flask of tea.'

McLusky hated being driven, but the thought of warmth managed to override his anxieties. 'You talked me into it.'

'So what have we got?' Austin asked once they were on their way. 'Unlawful killing?'

'Apparently not. Chap died in an old-fashioned road traffic accident.'

'Great, now they have us doing RTAs. I must tell my dad. When I first joined, he said I'd probably make it as far as directing traffic.' Austin pushed the Nissan along the country lane as fast as he dared. Not that this was exactly an emergency.

McLusky sipped at the tea the DS had furnished him with and felt content. A corpse you could see, you could work with. 'Slow down a bit or you'll land us in a ditch. More immediately you'll land tea on the windscreen.'

Austin slowed down. A diversion had been set up down an even narrower lane. He ignored it. Further on, a constable stood by a Road Ahead Closed sign. McLusky drained his tea and replaced the cap on the flask. 'That's us.' The constable waved them through. 'Park here, we'll walk the rest.'

'What for?' Austin stopped the car. 'You really are embarrassed about my car, is that it?'

'Nonsense. It's just that I could do with the exercise.'

'You hate exercise.'

They were only a few miles out of town, yet it was markedly colder here than in the city, colder even than Leigh Woods. Against the grey of the frosted countryside the police vehicles and technicians' cars looked bright and almost cheerful where they stood in the lane that led to the scene of the accident. A grey BMW 3 Series, what was left of it, had come to rest against the trunk of an ash tree in the midst of a thick hedgerow that divided the lane from the pasture beyond it.

'His aim was good, I give him that,' Austin said. 'It's the only tree on the whole stretch.'

'Yes,' said Sergeant Lynch. He had been watching their approach from beside the wreck. 'Though it looks like the car had already rolled by the time it hit.'

'Any other vehicles involved?' McLusky asked.

'We think not, at this stage.'

'Who reported the accident?'

'The farmer who owns those fields. He was out early and saw the wreck from the other side of the hedge.'

Accident investigators were already busy photographing, marking sections of tarmac with chalk, measuring distances. There was a sharp scrape across the road surface where car metal had gouged it. McLusky ducked down to get a first look at the interior through a crumpled, glassless window opening. The body of the driver looked grotesquely twisted, as only corpses could. 'So who's the bod?'

'We don't know. White, male, mid-twenties. No identification. But fingerprints will tell us, I'm sure.'

'Oh? You think he's a customer, then? Go on, what's interesting about this one.'

'Ah, where to begin, Inspector,' Lynch said with relish. 'False number plates for starters. These plates weren't stuck on properly.' He pointed to them where they lay beside the road inside a clear plastic bag. We checked and they don't match the chassis number. Cloned, we think.'

'Okay, good. That'll keep you busy. What else?'

'Come and take a closer look.' All three of them scrambled into the ditch to get near to the driver's side. The wreck was tilted at an awkward angle, close to forty degrees. It was hard to believe that this had once been a fairly luxurious, even stylish vehicle. Inside, the driver's body lay broken and twisted over the wheel.

'What am I looking for?' McLusky asked.

Austin saw it instantly. 'No airbags, sir.' Austin was scrupulous about calling the inspector 'sir' in front of other officers. In exchange, McLusky never called him 'Jane' within earshot of others. 'It should have deployed airbags; this one's got side-impact bags as well, but there's nothing.'

McLusky turned to the sergeant. 'Are you suggesting that someone deliberately disabled the airbags to kill him?'

'No, not really. It was most likely the driver himself.'

'What for? Oh, I get it. Didn't pay off, though, did it?'

'No. They do that in case of a chase. If they get rammed by a police car, the airbags could deploy. Makes things tricky, especially if you want to get out quickly and start running.'

'This one won't be running much. Airbags might have saved him.'

'Even a seat belt might have done it. He wasn't wearing one.' The hand of the twisted right arm was closest to them, palm upwards. The fingernails were well kept and clean.

'It's the Darwin principle at work,' Austin shrugged. In his book, if you were that stupid, this was what you deserved.

'You mean the unfit don't get to pass on their genes? If only that were true.' McLusky turned away. He had seen enough. For some reason it was always the *hands* of dead people that affected him most. It was the thought of all the things they had touched and never would again. 'Okay, Sergeant, I'm still bored. What else?'

Lynch nodded. He'd come across DI McLusky before and liked him, despite the man's odd reputation. Or perhaps because of it. 'Just a second, Inspector.' He walked to the nearest patrol car and returned holding aloft an evidence bag. Through the clear plastic showed a dark rectangular metal object. He handed it to the inspector.

'Magazine for a semi-automatic.' McLusky handed it on to Austin.

The DS scrutinized the magazine through the bag. 'Nine millimetre?'

'Correct,' said the sergeant.

'And the gun?' McLusky wanted to know.

'Missing.'

'I want it. Keep looking. Could it have been thrown out of the car?'

'That's entirely possible. If it was, then we'll find it. Though I have another theory.'

'Let's hear it.'

'Come round the back, sir.'

The boot of the car was open, its lid distorted. Inside the boot itself sat an open travel bag. It was black, made from waterproof man-made fibre, and rested on top of accumulated rubbish of empty soft drinks bottles and sandwich cartons.

'What's in the bag?'

The sergeant, who was wearing latex gloves, held it open for him. 'Not a lot now. Some old shirts and T-shirts and a crumpled bin liner. Can you see how the rolling and the impact of the crash has moved all the contents of the boot into one corner? There's a first-aid kit and a big torch right in the back there. But not this bag. The bag is as we found it.

Sitting on top and open. The way the shirts are placed suggests to me that they were surrounding something that sat in the middle of the bag.'

'And someone had it away,' McLusky said.

'That's robbing the dead.' DS Austin's allegiance shifted slightly. The man was almost certainly a criminal and most definitely stupid – the two naturally went hand in hand – but he'd been robbed while dead, or worse, still dying, and it offended his sensibilities. 'I'd like to get my hands on the scrote.'

McLusky looked grimly thoughtful. 'Any chance there were other occupants?'

Damn, thought Austin. I hadn't even thought of that.

'I think we can rule that out,' Lynch said. 'There's no sign anyone crawled out of that heap after it crashed.'

'Right, you have got my attention. We'll need to wait for a complete forensic examination of the car, of course, and a close search of the surroundings.'

'We've got it in hand.'

'When forensics is finished, tell the coroner the body can be moved.'

'Anything else, sir?'

'I want to talk to the farmer who reported it.'

'Okay, I'll get you the details. The farmhouse is just over there. Well, somewhere hidden in that mist, anyway.'

Excuse me. Yes, I know is shocking, letting cleaner use same lifts as the pretty folk that come to spend the money. But you must not care too much, is good remind for you that life can be much more worse than what you are complaining about on your mobile. Ah, lost signal now, poor lady, *going down.* Gents' toilet next, low point of day. One of many low point. At least today Anastazja has cold and cannot smell. Gents' is for gentlemen's toilet. Is not full of gentlemens. Is full of people who cannot piss straight. Who do not use soap and water after. Who do not flush after shit. Leave condoms, rubbish, hypodermic needles.

Excuse me. Cannot see Jez. Jez is nice security man who checks gents' toilet for her sometime and tell people is time for cleaning. After drunk man tries to chase her away with dick out and pissing at her. Not funny. There, put up sign to say 'Cleaning in Progress'. Two more men come out, one more want in. *Sorry, sir, other toilet please or else wait.* Leave trolley in doorway since some English gents not good for reading signs. Still somebody in last cubicle. Dark shadow under door. Start other end and hope man is finished when all is done. Sing song to myself quietly but loud enough so man hears is woman cleaning. English mens embarrassed when fart many times then open door and see Polish woman with mop.

Cubicle before last now. Is man's hand sticking out through gap under wall from last cubicle. Looks funny colour. Hand should not be blue.

Excuse me.

Chapter Four

'I thought you said Goosefoot.'

'No, Gooseford Farm,' Sergeant Lynch corrected him.

'Shame, I liked Goosefoot better.'

'If you look through the gap in the hedge there, you can just make it out, Inspector.'

McLusky peered through the hedge. 'Is that it?' He could see a vague outline of buildings in the mist, a few fields away. It didn't look too far. The road was still blocked and the turn-off was just a few hundred yards down the road. 'We'll walk.'

The lane curved away before getting to the turn-off. When they reached it, the buildings had once more sunk back into the gloom. They walked for another five minutes and still there was no sign of any farm entrance.

Austin quite enjoyed the walk. It beat sitting at a computer, typing pain-in-the-arse reports. Of course that pain would still be there, waiting. The sound of their footsteps seemed unusually loud. 'It's quite spooky in the countryside with all this mist. Well, if I believed in spooks.'

'Don't you?' McLusky wasn't so sure himself. Not ghosts, he didn't believe in ghosts. And yet. A bloke with a baseball bat, a samurai sword or even a gun he hoped he knew how to handle. It was the stuff you couldn't square up to. Where you couldn't call for backup. The things you couldn't see were the ones you couldn't fight so easily. Unease, doubts, premonitions. It trotted alongside you in the dark, in the mist, just beyond your grasp, just beyond reason. Not covered in the manual. Ever since his 'accident', when he'd been deliberately run over, he'd had flashes of unease he had never experienced before the incident. Not driving, not people, not running after suspects. But crossing the street. Being a passenger. Tall structures. He was okay as long as he was doing things; 'being proactive', as the counsellor had put it. It was the empty places, the unexpected moments, the quiet stretches that sometimes produced the strangest feeling. Keep busy, in other words, and he was fine. 'The farm could be one of those ghost things that only appear every hundred years or so.'

'You mean like paid overtime? Or promotion?'

McLusky nodded gravely. 'Exactly like that.'

They heard it before they saw it, the quad bike pulling a trailer full of hay bales that came bumping out of what had to be a track leading to Gooseford Farm. The quad disappeared away from them into the mist, driven by nothing more defined than a huddled shape under some kind of hat. By the time they reached the track it had vanished and the dark loom of buildings had solidified into a squat 1920s farmhouse and assorted outbuildings surrounding a yard of much-repaired concrete. A fairly new Land Rover provided contrast to a dented green Volvo estate near the gate.

They aimed at what they took to be the front door of the house. From the yard a large mongrel of a dog on a retractable chain shot towards them with a rattle and a growl. Austin tried soothing the tethered animal by telling it in unconvincing tones what a *good dog* it was.

Neither the dog nor McLusky was convinced, but the DI didn't care as long as the beast was firmly tied up. He was not keen on farms. He remembered isolated scenes from a childhood holiday where his father had lifted him up and set him on the back of a milk cow in a dim and evil-smelling shed full of enormous animals pissing on the concrete floor. The unimpressed animal had twisted its horned head back and swivelled an enormous eye at him and he had wet

34

himself with fear. Since then he had given cows all the respect they deserved. But it wasn't childhood memories that made him wary of farms. It was the way they sat in their own world, their own realm, and seemed to be governed by different rules than city dwellings. Usually their denizens had seen you coming from a long way off. It was difficult to surprise a farmer. Perhaps that was why they never had any damn bells on their doors. Or maybe that was what they kept dogs for.

'Can I help you, gentlemen?' A middle-aged woman in green plastic dungarees and black wellingtons called from across the yard where she had appeared from one of the sheds.

McLusky introduced himself and Austin, with IDs held aloft. The woman nodded, though with the entire width of the yard separating them, they might have been showing their library cards. 'Could we speak to the farmer?'

'Is it about the car wreck?' she asked without showing any inclination to close the distance between them.

A good answer, thought McLusky. Perhaps there were other questions she expected. 'Yes.'

'You just missed him.'

'Was that him on the quad?'

'Yes.'

McLusky had enough of shouting already and made a move towards the woman. The dog sprang fiercely forward again, renewing its barking. McLusky stopped and shouted some more. 'Where has he gone? Will he be long?'

The woman reeled the animal in and tied off the tether. She met them halfway, in the centre of the dank yard. 'He's gone to the upper paddock. Putting extra feed down for the sheep. Then he'll see to the fencing on Ten Acres.'

'Does he carry a mobile we might call him on? We'd really like to speak to him.'

'He keeps it turned off.'

'We'd best walk up there, then. Ten Acres, where is that exactly?'

She looked dispassionately down on their wet shoes, then nodded her head back towards the shed. 'Other side of the ford.'

There it was. Everything in the countryside was difficult. 'Is there a definite time you expect him back here, Mrs ...' McLusky consulted his notes. 'Murry?'

'Definite? Sunset. Though he'll have lunch here when it suits him.'

Having been given directions and turned his back on the farm, McLusky was about to make the difficult admission that taking the car, even the long way round, would have been the better choice when the quad bike came bumping back towards them on the unmade track, pulling the now empty trailer. 'Thank God for small mercies,' he said instead. He flagged down the driver, since he showed no intention of slowing down. 'Mr Murry?' He showed his ID.

Mr Murry's stout figure was made even more voluminous by many layers of clothing topped by a green quilted waist-coat. The farmer's face failed to show even a flicker of interest. He seemed quite content to sit astride his mount and wait.

'Could we have a quick word? About the accident.' McLusky hitched a thumb over his shoulder in the general direction of the crashed car.

'If you want.'

'Perhaps you could turn the engine off for us,' Austin suggested. The exhaust note of the bike had an irritating edge to it.

'Thanks,' McLusky said as silence fell. 'Just a few quick questions. Did you actually see the accident?'

'Nah. I saw nothing.'

'Did you hear the crash, perhaps?'

Murry shook his head. 'Too far away.'

'You couldn't say what time the accident took place then, Mr Murry?'

'I haven't the foggiest,' he said without apparent irony.

'So ... what time did you make the call?' He made a show of consulting his notes.

'I'd say about seven.'

'Is that when you first spotted the wreck?'

'Just about.'

'And the driver was already dead?'

'I didn't see the driver. I didn't go near the car.'

'Why not?'

'I wasn't on that side. I was in the field. I saw a BMW stuck in the hedge. Called a couple of times but heard nothing. So I dialled 999. That's all.'

'You didn't go to see if you could render any assistance?' Austin wanted to know.

'I'm a farmer, not a doctor. If an animal is sick, I call out the vet. Or else I shoot it to save the expense.'

'How soon after that did the ambulance arrive?' McLusky asked.

'Oh, they took a long time to come. We're used to that here in the country. You don't want to have an emergency in the country. Especially now that no one can read maps any more.' He waved an arm towards the road. 'They drive around following their sat navs into every field and ditch before they have the sense to ask directions.' The farmer looked away from them as though the question had deeply offended him. 'If that's all,' he said after a moment, reaching for the ignition.

'Yes, thank you.' McLusky laid a hand on the man's arm to delay the starting of the engine. 'One more thing. Do you still keep geese?'

Murry nodded without looking up. 'The wife does.' Then he started the engine and pulled away.

McLusky set off back towards the nearest piece of tarmac. 'You see, it's all nonsense, the clichés about unfriendly farmers. He didn't shout or point a shotgun at us. Didn't once say *you city folk have no idea.*'

'He didn't tell us much of use, though.'

'No,' McLusky agreed. 'And what he did tell us was mostly lies.'

*

Ten in the morning and the place was full of shoppers. And it wasn't even like it was half-term. If he had to do some shopping he had to wait till the end of a shift or preferably his day off, but everyone else seemed to have time to saunter round a shopping centre. On a weekday. They couldn't all be shoplifters. And they couldn't all be unemployed; they wouldn't have money to shop. DS Sorbie looked more morose than usual as he kept pace with DI Fairfield. 'Look at all these people. Does nobody have to work? Is it just us?'

'Actually it's just you, Jack. You carry on, I'll be in Topshop if anyone wants me.'

'A dead guy in the toilet. Why do we always get the shitty end of the stick?'

'There isn't a shitty end,' Fairfield said as she marched past her favourite shoe shop, keeping eyes front. 'Both ends are shitty.'

'That explains it.'

Despite its shops and criss-cross of escalators, the Galleries mall always reminded Fairfield of a small cruise ship. One that had run aground. Likewise, cruise ships reminded her of shopping malls afloat. Which was of course exactly what they were. She pointed with her radio. 'It's that way.' The directions she'd been given were very clear. All she had to do was follow the shops the manager on the phone had mentioned.

'You know your way around here, I can tell.'

'*Oh*, yes. Mind you, putting a bored-looking uniform and half a ton of scene-of-crime gubbins in front of the bogs helps as well.' The PC knew their faces and let them pass unchallenged.

Inside, the place was crowded. Sharing the space were a PC who seemed to be simply keeping station there, two crime-scene technicians, the duty doctor and the Home Office pathologist. The addition of Fairfield and Sorbie made it uncomfortably close. Fairfield asked the constable to wait outside. The police doctor, who had been less than enjoying a one-sided conversation with Coulthart, the pathologist, seemed relieved to be able to make his excuses, too, and follow the PC.

Coulthart turned his bespectacled gaze on the new-comers. 'Ah, the beautiful inspector.' The pathologist was in his late fifties, carried two extra stone in weight around his middle and had what looked to Fairfield like a suspicious amount of dark and static hair.

She took his fleshy outstretched hand and shook it. 'If I'm the beautiful inspector, then what does that make DS Sorbie?'

Coulthart gave a perfunctory glance at Sorbie over his rimless glasses. 'What indeed?' He released her hand. 'You are wondering why our paths must cross in these clean yet somewhat insalubrious surroundings?'

Fairfield felt tempted to say something on the lines of 'Indeed I do, good doctor.' She always found Coulthart's deliberate archaism strangely infectious. 'Enlighten me,' she said instead.

The crime-scene technicians withdrew and made way for them in front of the last cubicle. Inside, the body of the dead man lay collapsed over the toilet bowl, with his head almost behind it. His jumper and T-shirt were pushed up to his chest, revealing pale, mottled skin. His trousers were hanging loose. The centre of his narrow face, what Fairfield could see of it, had turned an inky dark; his fingers, too, had turned blue from the effects of lividity. The sleeve of his left arm was pushed up high.

Fairfield leant around to get a better look at the dead man's face. His eyes were wide open. 'Is this how you found him?'

'No, we had to move him a little to take a rectal reading,' explained Coulthart. 'He slumped over into the corner a bit more during that.'

'This is how he was found.' A crime-scene technician with a blond walrus moustache lifted up a large digital camera and offered her a view of the screen. The body had been in a kneeling position in front of the toilet bowl. A black zip-up jacket lay on the floor beside him. Some of the paraphernalia

39

of heroin injection could be seen on the floor. The technician zoomed in on a syringe stuck in the dead man's arm just below the crook of his elbow. 'The syringe fell out when he was moved.' With a nod, he indicated evidence bags on top of his aluminium case by the sink. 'Plunger depressed.'

'It's a dead junkie.' Sorbie shrugged. He tried not to let his impatience get the better of him but couldn't resist adding: 'Case closed. Especially for him, of course.'

Fairfield shot him a silencing glance. 'What's all that discoloration on his arm?'

'I can't tell you yet, though I have suspicions I'm not quite ready to share. I just wanted you here at the beginning in case this turned into anything.'

'Could it be deliberate overdose?'

'With the needle still in the arm like that it is always a possibility. He is definitely a long-term drug user, definitely injecting, too. You don't recognize him as one of your flock?'

'I've seen a lot of them come and go, but not this one. Jack?'

Sorbie pretended to take a closer look, but his eyes remained unfocused. 'Nope.'

'As always, we'll know the deceased a lot better after the post-mortem.' Coulthart picked up his briefcase. 'I'll do it this afternoon. I'll see you there, I hope, Inspector? You may effect the removal of the body with my blessings now.'

Sorbie turned his back on the corpse and waited for the door to close behind Coulthart. 'Well I do feel blessed. We're pretty much finished here, aren't we?'

Fairfield looked thoughtful. 'I suppose so. Nothing for us to do. Coulthart is always careful with what he says, but this time he's being downright mysterious. He seems to think there's something going on here. Other than the obvious.'

'Shame they don't have CCTV in the toilets.'

'I'm not sure people would feel comfortable with that.'

Sorbie shrugged. 'Wouldn't bother me, I've got nothing to be ashamed of.'

'Yes, so you keep telling me, Jack.'

Chapter Five

'Lies? What kind of lies?' Austin asked, a little out of breath from trying to keep up with the inspector.

McLusky was walking away from Gooseford Farm towards the road, marching fast in order to return some warmth to his limbs. 'Are you saying you don't feel lied to?'

'I'm a police officer, Liam, I expect to hear nothing but lies. But what's suspicious about the farmer reporting the accident?'

'Show you in a minute, when we get closer to the wreck.'

'The road's just there; we should be able to see it in a minute.'

'You're getting warmer, Jane.'

'I wish that were true.'

Fifty yards before the lane joined the road on which the BMW had crashed, McLusky jumped the shallow ditch that ran alongside it. He waited for Austin to join him beside the electric fence that surrounded the meadow, the northern edge of which was formed by the hedge in which the car had ended up. 'How can you tell whether these things are switched on?' he asked, putting his index finger close to the wire.

'Why? Are we climbing over it?'

'I thought we might.'

Austin frowned into the mist. 'There's no cattle in the field, so I presume it's not turned on.'

'After you, then.'

'Oh, thanks very much.'

'Go on. Farmers are famously hard up. They'd never run current through it just for the fun of it.'

Austin hesitated for another second, hand hovering, then with the strength of his conviction grasped the top wire. No current. A minute later both of them struggled diagonally towards the hedge, with the wet grass sketching cold streaks of moisture across their trouser legs. They found themselves directly on the other side of the hedge to where the accident took place, confirmed by the landmark of the sole tree. Judging by the noise, a tow truck was just arriving.

McLusky rubbed his gloved hands for warmth. 'What do you see, Jane?'

Austin scratched the tip of his nose. 'I can see the crashed BMW. Well, I can see the exhaust system and bits of the underside showing through the gap there.'

'And you can tell it's a BMW because … you're an expert in car exhausts?'

'Erm, no, it's because I know it's a BMW.'

'And so did Farmer Giles back there. Because if I'm not mistaken, he mentioned BMW before either of us did.'

'I think he did.'

'Seven o'clock this morning in thick mist with no street lighting and Farmer Murry is turning clairvoyant. He would barely have been able to see the bloody hedge, even on a quad or tractor with the lights turned on. Let alone spot a square yard of dark car metal in it *and* identify its make from this side. Yet he did want us to know he hadn't been near the thing.'

'You think our Mr Murry saw the crashed car in the lane, had a nosy round the dead man's luggage and found something he fancied.'

'It's a distinct possibility.'

'Are we going back to have a friendly word about it?'

McLusky sniffed, crossed his arms and blew a white cloud of breath through rounded lips while he thought. 'We'll wait for forensics on the car and luggage and the post-mortem results. Then we might have a better idea what happened here. And then we'll pay him another visit, order a goose for Christmas and scare several types of shit out of him. Now let's get back to your car before we perish out here.'

McLusky worked imaginary brake pedals as Austin drove. The inspector was himself quite happy to risk the odd speeding ticket while remaining utterly convinced that everyone else drove much too fast. The radio had been quiet, which could only mean that nothing had been found at Leigh Woods. By the time Austin once more parked the Nissan near the Mazda beside the woodland track, McLusky felt too comfortable to have much enthusiasm for searching the woods.

'Searching for a dead body is a mug's game. You feel bored and frustrated while you're looking, and if you do find something you invariably wish you hadn't. Especially if it's kids. We don't have any missing children on our books?'

'Nothing recent.' A hundred yards ahead Austin could just make out one yellow jacket ghosting in and out of the edge of visibility. 'Are we joining the troops?'

McLusky felt the persuasive hand of lethargy push him deep into the car seat. He shook it off. 'Why of course we are, my man,' he announced with excessive cheer. 'You try and stop me.' He swung himself out of the car and strode off towards the swaying dragon lights among the trees, calling over his shoulder, 'Why didn't you try and stop me, Jane?'

Half an hour later, feeling as though every last bit of warmth had left his body, and with each sentence uttered among them now littered with swear words, McLusky called a halt. 'Lunch! Go get some! Two more hours this afternoon is all I'm prepared to give this farce, then we'll all go back to policing the city.'

He was the first to the cars and the first away. Driving the Mazda was like driving around in a fridge. Never before had the neon-lit cavern that was the Albany Road canteen looked such a desirable destination.

*

43

To say that she liked going to the mortuary might have been overstating it, but the drive out to Flax Bourton wasn't too unpleasant and the new facilities were a great improvement on the ones they had replaced. From the outside the mortuary looked like a cottage hospital; inside it looked futuristic. Death in the twenty-first century. Inside it appeared highly technical, stainless and brightly lit, though the bodies Fairfield tended to see on these tables often arrived here via bloodstained kitchen floors, glass-strewn pavements or in this case the shopping centre toilets. From this state-of-the-art place of recorded facts and rationality the body would then be moved once more, into the world of ancient beliefs, of procession and candlelit rituals involving earth or fire.

In the viewing suite, separated from the actual body by glass and therefore spared the smells of the operation, Fairfield nevertheless felt she was as close to it as she could stand. Apart from the smell, all other aspects of the procedure were enhanced by the technology; the sound, and not just of the pathologist's voice, was very clear. Details deemed important could be magnified with the aid of the mobile camera that transmitted live pictures to a large monitor on her right. There was no *I'll take your word for it, Doc* here. The pathologist frequently moved the camera or had his assistant do so, to make sure Fairfield didn't miss any of the gore. The doctor's commentary, for the record and sometimes off the record, added a touch of docudrama to the proceedings.

Coulthart had yet to explain why the unfortunate yet utterly predictable death of this junkie should involve CID, and why the post-mortem had been almost instantaneous. Fairfield was about to press the intercom button to ask that very question when something else engaged her attention. Coulthart had moved the camera to give her a close-up view of the dead man's left arm. All along it black and blue bumps and circles formed a hideous chain that made her think of the plague. She pressed the button. 'What *is* that, Dr Coulthart? I've seen plenty of junkies before, but that's unusual, surely?'

44

'Very little escapes you, Inspector. I was just about to draw your attention to this unusual feature and, in a way, was playing for time. I'm expecting a telephone call … ah.' The phone on the wall by the door rang and Coulthart's assistant went to answer it. 'This might be it, quick work if it is, but then I impressed on them the urgency of the matter. I earlier sent several samples off to the lab by courier, and unless the chap fell off his motorcycle or managed to get himself lost in the fog, then this should be it. Excuse me, Detective Inspector.'

Coulthart took the receiver that the assistant held out to him. He listened, nodded, talked, listened and talked some more, from time to time throwing glances in Fairfield's direction. She knew that for him to send samples by motor-cycle courier was unusual, and for a forensics lab to respond this quickly something of a miracle. At last the pathologist terminated the call.

'Okay, enough build-up, Doctor, what have we got there? Tell me it's not another plague that can be spread by sharing needles.'

'No, not a plague, though I fear we may see more dead drug-users soon. Tell me, Inspector, what do you know about anthrax?'

'Anthrax? That's a poison, isn't it? Didn't someone send anthrax through the post in the States a while back?'

'No, and yes. I must say you disappoint me, Inspector. Anthrax is a *disease*, not a poison, and it is caused by the aptly named bacterium *bacillus anthracis*. But yes, some deranged American sent some through the post to express his displeasure at this or that. Not that it matters, DI Fairfield. Somehow, in the past few years, a new delusion has begun to affect the weaker minds, which is that as a means of expressing your displeasure, it is quite acceptable to kill and maim a lot of people you have never met. Because otherwise of course *no one listens*. People used to stand on soapboxes; now they put ground glass into baby food or send diseases through the post. And there are a lot to choose from, believe

45

me. Anthrax, smallpox, botulism, Ebola, plague. Not so easy to deliver, plague,' Coulthart mused, nodding to himself.

'So our customer died of anthrax?'

'Almost certainly.'

'Not an overdose?'

'No. He must have been feeling extremely ill by the time he entered the toilets. He tried to make himself feel better by injecting, but died of respiratory arrest.'

'So how did he get it?'

'He almost certainly contracted it from injecting contaminated heroin. He'd have been feeling ill for some time, high fever, trouble breathing. Probably thought he had a bad case of flu.'

Fairfield felt a shiver going through her. 'How does heroin get contaminated with anthrax?'

'That's a very good question. The same way, I presume, that all the other rubbish gets into heroin. Someone puts it there.'

'You mean someone laced his heroin with it? That means we're looking at unlawful killing.'

'That is for you to decide. But his was no natural death, I can say that much.'

'But anthrax. I mean, isn't that going a bit far? If you want to kill a junkie, you stick a knife into him while he's distracted, which is pretty much all the time.'

'I would agree.' Coulthart paused for dramatic effect. 'Unless of course it wasn't just this *one* junkie you wanted to get rid of.'

Fairfield sat down on the padded bench by the observation window. 'You mean someone with a grudge against junkies?'

'That's entirely possible.'

'So there could be more out there.'

'Oh, that's a distinct possibility. As you said, lacing the man's heroin with anthrax because you wanted to kill him would mean going to extremes of difficulty. Anthrax is lethal and doesn't just lie around for you to use. The lab will

46

try and identify the exact strain, which may help identify the source.'

'So we're going to see more cases.'

'Unless he travelled here recently from elsewhere, carrying his own supply, the city could be awash with the infected drug. The injection sites on his arm suggest he's used contaminated heroin several times. You must find the source of it or we will find ourselves chatting over the cadavers of many more of these unfortunate creatures.'

'Just how infectious is anthrax? I mean, can you pass it on? Can you catch it just from handling the heroin?'

'Person-to-person infection is normally rare. Sharing needles would certainly be efficacious. Infection can be effected both by inhalation and gestation. So extreme caution is advised when handling any heroin. But the surest way to contract it is, of course, cutaneous.'

'Which means …?'

Coulthart zoomed the camera into a close-up of the blackened lesions on the dead junkie's arm. 'Injecting the stuff, Inspector.'

Chapter Six

McLusky scooted into the bathroom. Now that it was definitely winter, he'd have to buy another heater. The Montpelier flat he rented above Rossi's, the Italian greengrocer's, had once had open fireplaces in every room. They had later been replaced by gas fires, and these in turn had been removed and replaced with nothing. The two-bar electric heater he had bought when he moved in couldn't hope to heat even one room, let alone the whole flat.

In the meantime he lit the ancient stove in the kitchen, turned the oven to gas mark eight, put the kettle on the hob and scooted around until he was showered and dressed. He had managed to acquire a few more sticks of furniture, which meant the sitting room could now accommodate three people sitting down, which didn't happen often, and he could breakfast at the kitchen table should the fancy take him. That didn't happen often, either.

This morning ritual of rushing around was made more difficult by the fact that he was required to wear a suit to Albany Road and keep it spotless until he could accompany DSI Denkhaus to a lunch at the Isis.

The Isis was arguably the finest, certainly the most expensive, restaurant in town, where they were to be dined, wined and bored rigid by a few prominent businessmen – definitely all men, Denkhaus had confirmed – who liked to deliver their opinions to the police force in person and in a more congenial atmosphere than even headquarters could provide. All were sponsors of charities close to the Chief Constable's heart.

McLusky had fought hard to try to wriggle out of it. 'Why would they want to meet me? Surely there are more suitable officers around ...'

'For once I agree wholeheartedly, DI McLusky. I can assure you that you were not my first choice, or anyone's first choice, to go to this lunch. Neither was I, for that matter. They didn't really want to talk to anyone below Assistant Chief Constable, but the ACC just can't be ...' Denkhaus breathed deeply, swallowed down his indignation. 'So I got lumbered with it. They are interested in our fight against drugs because businesses worry about the level of drug-related crime in the city. And our hosts want to meet someone who was part of the team that put Ray Fenton behind bars.'

'I only played the most marginal role in that investigation.'

'I'm aware of it. But in the absence of DCI Gaunt, you'll have to do.'

'Claire French distinguished herself in that operation, as I recall.'

'I can't turn up with a DC in tow. Besides, French is quite ... Well, anyway, there we are, stuck with it. What we need to get across is that we are doing all we can, that prevention is better than cure and that progress is being made.'

When H-hour arrived McLusky was glad that he had kept his tie in his jacket pocket and brought a spare shirt, since the one he had put on that morning had acquired a mysterious stain, as he had known it would.

Denkhaus, wearing his uniform, was in energetic, upbeat mode. A large silver-grey BMW with police driver had made an appearance, a sweetener sent by the ACC perhaps. McLusky felt no better about being driven, though by the time the car glided to a stop outside the Isis, he had to admit it had been quite the smoothest journey through Bristol traffic he had experienced without the aid of sirens. For many, lunch at the Isis, especially if paid for by others, would have been a memorable occasion, but no one at Albany Road had envied him the invitation. McLusky himself was fond of good food, though he rarely got it. When he did, he preferred to eat it in relaxed surroundings and in the company of his choice.

The restaurant's designers had achieved an understated opulence that bordered on the minimal and yet managed to instantly suggest privilege. Part of it, he decided, came from the strange sensation that the room swallowed sound. Every table was taken, conversation was animated, yet the place seemed quiet and gave the impression that all was simply a setting for your own entrance. The other noticeable thing about the place was the age of its clientele; with a few glamorous exceptions, the diners were on the whole male and over fifty. Perhaps it took that long to earn enough money to eat here, McLusky thought as they were led to the table by an immaculately groomed creature. With dismay he realized that what he had envisaged as a long dining table full of local businessmen chatting over their food, where he would be required to merely nod and pretend to agree with Denkhaus, turned out to be just three men who now rose to greet them.

In his sixties, the oldest and largest of the three, Paul Defrees appeared to be the mover of the enterprise. 'Ah, Superintendent, I'm so glad you could find the time ...' He had a sonorous voice, very little hair and preternaturally white teeth. McLusky had heard the name more than once in the past but until now couldn't put a face to it. Defrees ran the largest private security firm in the West Country, among other things providing staff for commercial premises, night patrols for wealthy property owners and security for festivals. A lot of his initial money, however, had come from running gangs of wheel clampers, operating mainly on private land. He introduced his two companions. Frank Walden, a disappointed-looking man in his fifties with a hint of dampness in his handshake, was a property

51

developer who had run projects all over the south-west of England and in the south of Wales. The youngest of the three, James Cullip, had tightly curled dark hair and quick, intelligent eyes. His business interest went far beyond Bristol and included holdings in Europe, mainly France.

McLusky had decided to stick to non-alcoholic drinks, which also relieved him of any stress he might otherwise have felt over the intimidating wine list. The lunch menu was difficult enough, since his French was non-existent, but he settled on confit of duck liver to be followed by roast quail. Once the starters arrived, he began to relax. The three men seemed genuinely interested in the policing of the city. Cullip, who owned two bars in Bristol, one in Millennium Square, was particularly worried about the level of street crime and complained about it in a low, scratched voice. 'I like Bristol a lot. I'm from London, you see, but I chose to move here. I believe the quality of life is much better than in the capital. Bristol is going places. But when you have interests in the catering business, then street crime affects it directly. My customers need to be able to walk safely at night and my staff need to get home very late. Two of my bar staff were mugged last month. One of them decided not to work evenings any more. '

Defrees agreed. 'Bristol must clean up its act. It's not enough to tart up the centre. If there is to be sustained investment, then crime must fall. A reputation for drug crime is always bad for a city. Businesses are highly mobile now; there is no reason why many of them couldn't move north or south.'

McLusky soon found that Denkhaus had come extremely well prepared, and that his own role was more or less to agree with him and to provide some colour. The superintendent had the statistics of crime reduction – always reduction – at his fingertips. But time and again the talk returned to drugs.

Mandatory life sentences for drug-dealers was Cullip's solution; compulsory rehabilitation for addicts was Walden's. McLusky was tempted to throw *forced deportation* into the ring but stopped himself in time.

'What I can't understand,' Defrees said as he speared some venison and chased it through the *jus* on his plate, 'is why they can't stop the drugs trade at its source. Why is it so difficult to eradicate the poppy fields?'

'And how would you do that?' McLusky asked.

'Surely a good dose of weedkiller should do it. We've got helicopters, haven't we?'

McLusky wanted to say what a brilliant idea that was and how naturally nobody had ever thought of it before, but instead he said: 'A few thousand hectares of opium poppy are enough for the entire heroin consumption of western Europe. You could grow it in Belgium and we'd be hard pressed to find it.'

Defrees looked unhappily at him, but Denkhaus came to his rescue. 'And heroin is politically complicated. Most of ours comes from Afghanistan. It's grown by very poor people who couldn't make a living from the acreage they are farming if they grew, let's say, wheat or millet. And many are being coerced into doing it anyway, so even if you paid them to grow something else, it wouldn't work.'

'As long as people want to get off their faces on heroin, there'll be poppy fields,' McLusky said. 'Anyway, heroin isn't really our main problem any more. Crack is.'

While a minor squabble broke out over this assertion, McLusky surreptitiously reached for his mobile and activated his get-out strategy. From inside his jacket pocket he sent a pre-prepared text to Austin, the signal to call him. Two minutes later his mobile chimed.

'I thought I asked you to keep that turned off?' Denkhaus hissed.

'Sorry, sir, it's the station, could be urgent.' He answered it. On the other end was Austin, saying: 'A man walks into a bar ...' Keeping a straight face while listening to one of Austin's invariably bad jokes, he gave a few grunts, then said: 'Send someone else ... Oh, I see.' He terminated the call. 'I'm sorry, sir,' he said to Denkhaus, who looked at him suspiciously and struggled to hide his annoyance. 'Something's come up and no one else can deal.' He rose. 'Thank you, gentlemen, for an excellent lunch. I'm sorry about the disappearing act.'

In the taxi back to Albany Road, McLusky mused on how far removed the Isis had felt from the streets where crime and drugs had made their home. His hosts' ideas about how to solve the problems of the city were correspondingly unrealistic. There was no magic bullet, which was what Defrees and his friends were hoping for.

He found Austin in the station canteen, sitting in front of the ruins of a ham and pineapple pizza. 'Thanks for the rescue.'

'How bad was it?' Austin wanted to know.

'Remind me not to seek promotion beyond DCI. At least I could run away. Denkhaus is stuck there. He looked murderous when my phone went.'

'But the food must have been something special.'

McLusky shook his head. 'The confit of duck was okay, but I thought the roast quail was quite average.'

Upstairs he walked into the CID room to make coffee. With the kind of shock a person feels when discovering that their car has been stolen from the drive, he came to a sudden halt in front of the yawning gap where the kettle and tea things had sat.

He looked around to see where they had been moved to. 'Claire, where's the kettle?'

DC Claire French looked up reluctantly from her keyboard, where she'd been busy chasing biscuit crumbs between the keys with a moistened fingertip. 'Gone, sir.'

'Gone where? To a better place?'

'Hadn't you heard?'

'No. Did I miss the funeral?'

'It's not that. We're no longer allowed kettles.'

'What?' McLusky's voice carried quiet menace.

'Health and safety, sir. You should have had a memo.'

'I didn't want a memo, I wanted coffee. What's wrong with kettles all of a sudden?'

French shrugged. 'Water and electricity? Steam? We might give ourselves an electric shock. Or something.'

'Really.'

'Yes. They're quite happy for us to tackle violent criminals jacked up on crack with nothing but a tin of pepper spray, but health and safety draw the line at tea-making. Far too hazardous.'

'*Marvellous.*'

'We're supposed to use the drinks machines.'

'I see. They're not by any chance owned by health and safety, are they?'

McLusky had always assumed that instant coffee was the worst the planet had to offer, but that was before he had tried the drinks machine offering. In his office he sipped machine coffee and brooded over his list of emails and messages. There was naturally nothing from the mortuary on the BMW driver, but there should have been at least something from the vehicle search, even if only to say they'd found nothing. Sometimes police work was like wading through treacle: you had to adjust your stride accordingly or you constantly felt the drag. He picked up the phone to call about the examination of the car when a knock on the door stayed his hand. It was Austin.

'Don't think you're leaving any of those in here,' he told the DS, who was heavily burdened with files and folders.

'All mine, I'm sorry to say.' Much intelligence and information had long migrated to the computer, only no one trusted computers, so half of it existed on paper as well. Making sure that both were up to date was double the work. 'We had a call about the BMW. Preliminary forensics says minute traces of class A, on the seats and in the boot. Also some herbal.'

'Any ID on the driver yet?'

'Nothing so far.'

Sergeant Lynch had been positive their customer had to be known to them. 'Why not? Drugs, ammo clip and a

cloned car? He can't have just dropped from the sky. Hang on, perhaps *that's* how the accident happened; we never thought of that, did we?'

'He's just not come to our attention before. There has to be a first time for everyone. In his case, of course, it was also the last time. Or perhaps he had no previous because he was too clever for us.'

McLusky nodded theatrically. 'Sure. That's why he took his airbags out and drove without a seat belt.'

'Oh, okay, a bit thick but slippery.'

'Let's hope the car can tell us some more. Of course we didn't find the missing gun?'

The files were getting heavy. Austin rested them on the edge of the desk. 'Nope, nothing. The whole surrounding area was searched and gone over with a metal detector. He either didn't have it on him or it was pinched.'

'That's all we need, some opportunist lowlife armed with a gun. What type was the magazine for?'

Austin riffled through some papers. 'I got it here. Beretta 92 FS.'

'Marvellous.' McLusky didn't know much about guns, but this was a common enough model. He knew it held fifteen rounds. Sooner or later the counter staff at a post office, a shopkeeper or a police officer was going to be looking down its barrel.

'Where exactly was the ammunition clip found?'

'In the glove box.'

'Could be a spare.' McLusky nodded inconclusively and took a sip from the plastic cup. The contents had cooled to an unpleasant temperature. 'Oh, yuck. Talking of unsolved crimes, have you heard about the kettle? We're supposed to drink this muck now.' He theatrically dropped the half-empty cup into the metal dustbin.

'I know, it's quite mad. There's always the canteen …'

'By the time you'd carried your cup to your desk it'd be cold. No, Jane, something has to be done. This job's hard enough without jobsworth making it harder.'

Behind Austin, DC French stuck her head through the open door. McLusky quite liked French, though he thought she might qualify as the plainest-looking woman he had ever met. Unless she was in the same room, he could never remember quite what she looked like. She was waving a piece of notepaper. 'We had a call from a member of our adoring public. A dog-walker up in Leigh Woods.' Austin and McLusky's symphonic groans didn't put her off her stride. 'Her dog stumbled upon human remains.' She gently laid the note on top of Austin's pile of files and patted it. 'Control have already dispatched some uniforms up there, but this appears to be yours.'

Austin looked past McLusky out of the window, where thick mist drifted in from the River Avon. 'Great, and me not wearing my thermals today.'

Leigh Woods was, if anything, colder, damper and mistier than before. Not only did they once more find themselves down the same forester's track, but McLusky's heart sank even further when he recognized the dog walker as the same woman who had called them out two days earlier, only this time she was standing by her car wearing a definite I-told-you-so expression. PCs Pym and Purkis had already cordoned off the find, some thirty yards further into the trees. Giving the dog-walker a cowardly berth, McLusky aimed straight for the cordoned-off piece of ground guarded by the officers. The area looked suspiciously small.

'Please tell me you're standing by the very small body of a very old person, complete but for one missing ear. And preferably clutching their bus pass so we know where to send the remains. You're just not, are you?'

'I'm afraid not, sir,' said PC Purkis, keeping a straight face for the benefit of the woman, who was looking across at them.

McLusky stopped at the police tape and looked down on the rectangle of leaf litter. In the centre lay a mangled piece of human tissue. 'What exactly am I looking at, Purkis?'

'You can see it more easily from this side, sir.' She made room for him and squatted down. 'See?' she said as McLusky joined her. 'It's part of a hand. Left hand. Two last fingers and part of a palm.' She seemed unperturbed by the unpleasant sight.

McLusky looked as closely as his breakfast allowed. He could clearly see now that it was part of a hand, dark, dirty and chewed. Ants were crawling over it, and through it. It looked like it had belonged to a man. He thought he could catch a nostrilful of its sickly smell and quickly straightened up. 'You need sharp eyes not to walk straight past that. How does that woman walk her dog, on all fours?'

'Do you want me to ask her?' Austin hadn't bothered to get close to the find; he was happy to take everyone's word for it. Bits of body. He could imagine it, thanks.

'Her dog found it,' Pym said.

'All right, this time we'll get all the manpower we need for a systematic search. We'll go over the whole area, including the part we covered ourselves; there were so few of us, we could have missed it.' He walked back with Austin. 'Get the surgeon to take a look at it and get it bagged up before the ants make off with it.'

'Could still turn out to be just a walker who died of natural causes, of course. Keeled over in the wood somewhere.'

McLusky sniffed the air. Despite the mist and cold he had to admit the place smelled better than the city centre. 'No. It'll be a shallow grave. Somewhere back there.'

The dog-walker stood her ground beside her silver car. Her Jack Russell stared out through the back window of the hatchback. 'Thank you for calling us promptly today, Mrs ...' Did he know her name?

'Walker.'

Appropriate. 'Mrs Walker. Has someone taken a statement from you yet?'

'Yes, the woman constable took a long statement, asking all sorts of irrelevant questions.'

'Then there's no need for you to remain here.'

'I know that, Inspector.'

McLusky walked with Austin to their cars. 'Let's get back to the nick. We'll get a search organized, and you and me can sit this one out until they find the rest of the body.'

The call came through late that afternoon. 'They found the body of a man. Shallow grave, remains disturbed by animal activity.'

Just as McLusky had suspected, they had completely missed the body in the mist and gloom. Things looked different now. The track was choked with vehicles; generators and arc lights had been set up. Despite the mist, the scene was thrown into sharp focus by the lights and the occasion.

'You lot must have walked straight past it,' DSI Denkhaus told McLusky as they were donning protective gear beside the scene-of-crime tape. A white tent had already been erected over the body. 'If you hadn't missed it two days ago, it would have saved a dozen officers a lot of man hours.'

McLusky got on with kitting up, putting on overshoes and face mask. He knew that the less you contradicted Denkhaus, the sooner his lectures petered out. Sometimes he suspected the superintendent simply thought it was part of his remit to harangue junior officers.

Inside the cordoned area a narrow path had been established along which everyone and everything now travelled to avoid further contamination of the site. A suspicious death always invited the professional attention of scores of people: police officers of all ranks, from the bored constables guarding the site against unauthorized persons to the senior investigation officer; crime-scene co-ordinators to manage the site, surgeon, pathologist, scene-of-crime officers, forensics technicians and CID, from freshly minted detective constables up to superintendent. As he followed Denkhaus along the path to the tent, it struck McLusky just how crowded this lonely spot in the woods had become. Many people wouldn't attract such attendance figures at their funerals, especially if they had died quietly of natural causes, and would get shorter notices in the papers, too.

Just then the surgeon dived from the tent, pulled off his mask and took a few gulps of cold, uncontaminated air.

'Is it bad?' Denkhaus asked.

'It's pretty rank, yes, Superintendent. I'll never get used to the smell of human decay, I'm afraid.'

'In that case, aren't you in the wrong job, Doctor?'

'I don't do this all day, you know. They don't pay me enough as it is. Anyway, I'm finished. The pathologist is here, and he's the one with the fat pay cheque. I doubt they pay *you* enough, though,' he added as he squeezed past them.

Inside, the tent was busy. Three scene-of-crime officers were in there, one taking video shots under a glaring light. They made room around the body for Denkhaus and McLusky. Coulthart, who was squatting next to the remains, greeted them curtly. 'Rob ... McLusky.'

Denkhaus remained standing while McLusky squatted down on the stony ground, joining the pathologist, who was using a plastic spatula and tweezers to probe the flesh of the corpse. 'We can safely rule out accidental death, then,' McLusky murmured.

'Oh, quite,' Coulthart agreed. 'Unless he somehow put a bag over his head, then tied his hands together and buried himself.'

The corpse had been mauled by scavenging animals. With the hands entirely chewed away, the first thing that struck McLusky was that the victim had been tied by the wrists with thick, brutal wire. The bag that originally covered his head was made from natural fibres and had been torn open by sharp teeth. The head was badly chewed. The whole area looked a filthy mess to McLusky, who found it hard to distinguish any features. He thought he could glimpse bits of skull where nose and eyes ought to be.

'How long's he been dead, Doctor?'

'A rough estimate would be four to five weeks. Direct contact with the forest floor allowed rapid insect access, but the exceptionally cold weather kept down bacterial activity and helped to preserve the body somewhat.'

If this was what Coulthart called a 'somewhat preserved' corpse, then McLusky never wanted to see a rotten one. In his eight years on the force, he had come across more than one body that had had time to start decomposing, but this was his first disinterred corpse. The sickly, cloying stench was so intense that it made thinking of anything else difficult.

'What kind of a bag is this, do you think?' It had been tied around the victim's neck with what looked like green garden twine, which was now almost completely black from having soaked up many types of fluid.

'It appears to be some kind of shopping bag made of rough canvas or similar. If you look closely, you'll see it had handles once. They've been cut or torn off.'

McLusky's eyes followed Coulthart's pointing spatula to the frayed stumps of twisted rope handles. 'Any idea as to the cause of death?'

'I wouldn't want to hazard a guess at this stage; it is too difficult to establish out here which traumas are pre- and which post-mortem. I heard you found parts of a hand?'

'Yes, it's what led us to him.'

McLusky had kept his breathing as shallow as possible, but all this talking had made it necessary to take great lung-fuls of death, and his stomach was now in revolt. 'I'll take a quick breather, Doctor, if you don't mind.'

'Not at all, go ahead. I don't blame you, Inspector, espe-cially since your boss fled some minutes ago.'

Once outside the tent, McLusky walked quickly along the designated path and ducked under the crime-scene tape. It wouldn't do to throw up inside the cordon. After a few deep breaths in the cold forest air, the danger of vomiting receded. He strove to keep his mind clear of the images from the tent, and memories of the canteen lasagne he had eaten for lunch. He found Denkhaus behind the wheel of his Range Rover, the engine running. The superintendent had shed his protective gear, which meant he had no intention of returning to the locus. He didn't invite McLusky to join him in the warmth; instead he rolled the window down a few inches.

'What does it look like to you, McLusky?'

'Hard to say. We'll know more when they come up with the cause of death.'

'I hope so. How long's he been there?'

'Up to five weeks. SOCO tried to get fingerprints off the partial hand we found, but changed their minds when they saw it. If he has previous, we'll ID him from his DNA; if not, there's always dental records.'

'Good.' Denkhaus put the car in gear. 'Okay, McLusky, it's all yours. We don't expect DCI Gaunt back for several weeks, so you'll report direct to me.' The window slid up as the large engine surged and sped the car along the track. A few press photographers, corralled beyond the police vehicles, flashed their cameras at it, mostly from boredom.

As McLusky ducked back under the scene-of-crime tape, Austin emerged gasping from the tent. He stared hard into McLusky's eyes for a few moments while he greedily filled his lungs with pure forest air.

'Well done,' said McLusky.

'Only because you insisted. I didn't last long in there. Why did they have to put a tent over it? It just concentrates the smell. Coulthart is still happily poking around among the maggots. People like that worry me.'

'Now that you've seen the body – any immediate thoughts?'

'I definitely want to be cremated.'

'Anything beyond that?'

'His end must have been absolutely terrifying. Presumably they didn't put the bag over his head after he'd died. They tied his wrists with galvanized wire.'

'Yes. I think if someone ties your hands with fencing wire, you more or less know you've had it. Whoever has got you has no intention of letting you go.'

62

'I suppose not.'

McLusky heard the pathologist call his name and nodded his head towards the tent. 'I'll go back in for a last look. You go on ahead and set up at Albany.'

Inside, the pathologist was waiting for him beside the corpse. More of it had now been uncovered. 'Do you see this slant? The way the body seems to rise up?' He ran the spatula alongside the body, downwards towards the knees. Here, the leaf litter and earth cover was still undisturbed. He stabbed the spatula into the ground below the knees. 'I expected the legs to continue there under the ground, but they don't. They disappear into the ground at right angles.'

McLusky signalled to one of the SOCOS. 'Right, let's have the chap's legs out. Can we first dig down alongside them to see what's going on there, please?'

The scene-of-crime officer started excavating carefully with a hand trowel, throwing leaves and earth on to a waiting tarpaulin, where it would later be sifted. Nothing would remain unexamined. It made McLusky think of Laura and her archaeology studies. What they were doing here had much in common with field archaeology, and the disciplines shared many techniques. He wondered if right now she was also out in the cold somewhere, on a dig perhaps, or sitting in a cosy lecture hall, taking notes in her neat, always legible handwriting.

'It's very tightly packed around the legs,' said the SOCO.

'What about around the rest of the body?' McLusky asked.

'It's much looser there. As burials go, it wasn't very deep. Or even well done. Not exactly shallow, but very … lumpy. Uneven. Except here. I'm nearing the bottom now.'

The last few scrapes with the trowel revealed stained boots. 'Timberland,' McLusky said. 'Not cheap, those. The jeans didn't come from a supermarket either. Okay, why are his shins in a deep hole? Was that just conveniently there?'

'No. It was dug. The soil layers are disturbed and mixed up and there's a definite cut edge to the hole.'

'It looks to me,' said Coulthart, 'as though someone started digging a grave of a decent depth, then couldn't be arsed to do it for the whole length of the body.'

'Probably underestimated how long it takes to dig that deep a hole. Okay, I'll look forward to your reports, gentlemen.' McLusky had seen and smelled enough. Outside, he shed his paper suit, overshoes, mask and gloves into a waiting bin liner and walked towards his car. A few flashes went off, and two or three journalists shouted questions at him, all of which he ignored. The press office would give a sanitized version of what had been found and the papers would simply invent the rest – *dead men don't sue*.

The car was an ice box. With the heater on full, he bumped over the rough ground and on to the track, then drove off past the reporters as fast as the terrain allowed. Further on, close to the junction with the road, stood a woman in a long black coat, her neck and chin muffled with a silver scarf. She was drawing large clouds of smoke from a hundred-millimetre cigarette without the aid of her gloved hands. As he drew close to where she was standing, she took a step forward on to the track and stuck an ironic thumb out like a hitchhiker.

Between cigarettes Philippa Warren worked as a reporter for the *Bristol Herald*. She was brighter, sharper and more dishonest than most of her colleagues; she and McLusky had made use of each other in the past, in an easy-going atmosphere of mutual distrust.

He stopped and rolled down the window three inches. 'What do you want, Warren?' he asked through the ungenerous gap.

'Lift into town? My car's at the menders and the guy who gave me a lift out here took off without me.'

'Professional courtesy is dead.'

'Thanks,' she said when McLusky cleared papers and cigarette packets off the front seat for her. 'Blimey. It's colder in your car than out there.'

'I can drop you at a bus stop, Warren, if you prefer.'

'You can call me Phil, like everyone else.' She drew her coat closer around herself. 'First his hand, now the rest; tell me about it.'

'Who told you about the hand? That's not supposed to be general knowledge.'

'Responsibly sourced. Like line-caught fish. And we're not printing it until you release it, that's how responsible we are at the *Herald*.'

'Naturally.' McLusky turned on to the road and speeded up. He wondered how Warren had got hold of that information. Pym? Purkis? She probably paid retainers to several officers who sold information to the papers. It could never be stopped completely, not while the rank and file felt undervalued and underpaid. McLusky himself occasionally leaked bits of information to the press, but only if he thought it helped his own investigations. 'It's a dead male. Shallow grave. Hasn't been there all that long. We've no idea who he is yet.'

'Not even a suspicion? Who's missing?'

'Someone's son, that's all I know.'

'Cause of death?'

'That I *genuinely* don't know.'

'Meaning the rest you just told me was lies?'

McLusky didn't bother to answer.

'You're smiling, that's always a bad sign. A body in the woods is what people want to read about. No one wants to know about dead junkies in toilets.'

'You know about that as well?'

'Come on, he was found in a public toilet. Funny thing was, though,' she said with exaggerated carelessness, 'he was rushed off to the mortuary, where he was autopsied immediately. Not normal procedure, is it? Who cares about dead junkies? I wonder.'

McLusky was further peeved by Warren's knowledge of the immediate autopsy, and kept quiet while he mulled this over.

'Hey, talk to me, I'm a journalist. It's my job to know stuff.'

65

'It's your job to help sell advertising. I'm not concerned with dead junkies. Not my department. You're talking to entirely the wrong guy here.'

'I'm beginning to think so myself.'

They were approaching the triangle. 'Where do you want me to drop you?'

'Anywhere near Brown's, actually.'

'Sure.'

'Thanks for the lift, Liam,' she said and waved McLusky off from outside the restaurant. Then she took the first cab she found back to Leigh Woods, where her car was parked.

Chapter Seven

'You won't get much out of him today, I'm afraid,' the doctor said. They were standing in intensive care, separated from the patient by a thick glass window. It reminded DI Fairfield of the mortuary viewing suite, the difference being that this junkie was still alive. Just. His sallow skin was stretched tight across his skull, his arms covered in dark lesions. He was hooked up to heart monitor, oxygen and a drip. The diagnosis of anthrax had been confirmed.

'Will he live?' Fairfield asked.

'We're giving him high doses of antibiotics,' the doctor continued. 'It's a lethal disease. It's not invariably fatal. But close enough when it gets to *this* stage. He has a small chance of pulling through. His chances would be a lot better had he been brought in earlier. That's what I told the girl as well.'

'What girl?'

'The one who brought him in yesterday. She was here a minute ago. Still wouldn't give her name. Or his.'

'Damn. What did she look like?'

'Thin. Mousy hair. Blue tracksuit bottoms, grey hooded top.'

The inspector was already running.

'Like a half-empty sack of potatoes,' the doctor called after her. 'The way they all do.'

Fairfield ran along the corridors and took corners at a skid. If they were to stop the hospitals filling with half-dead junkies infected with anthrax, then they had to find out where the contaminated drugs came from. This was only the second victim they knew about, but across the city there could be hundreds of users infecting themselves. She didn't see anyone fitting the girl's description until she reached the main exit, when she spotted her getting into the passenger seat of an old red Polo, dull with grime. The hard-faced girl looked straight at her as the driver pulled away. Fairfield only got a partial look at him, but thought he was young, with very short hair. She noted the index number of the car, requested a check and waited behind the steering wheel of her Renault for the results. It came back after three minutes.

'Car is logged as having no keeper. No insurance or MOT.'

'Par for the course.' She requested a marker to be put on it and drove off towards Albany Road. What she really needed was a decent coffee.

There was now a permanent incident room at Albany Road station, which for obvious reasons many called the Murder Room. All information regarding the Leigh Woods murder was gathered in the incident room, all actions were planned and most briefings given there. CID officers and civilian computer operators worked side by side. The room had a wall map of the city and one of the county, picture- and whiteboard, printers, phones and desktop computer units, no air-conditioning, strip lighting and probably several miles of cable. There was a gap where, until recently, the kettle had sat. The windows afforded a similar view as the one in McLusky's office, and the beige plastic blinds looked like they were 1970s originals and were permanently at half-mast.

McLusky's desk faced Austin's and the door to the corridor. An internal window beside it allowed the inmates to see anyone approaching from the left; unfortunately the superintendent had a habit of approaching the incident room from the right. McLusky thought it might be a good idea to install a bicycle mirror as an advance-warning system, though he would be the first to admit that the super-intendent was preferable to the universally disliked DCI Gaunt, who was at present safely hospitalized.

In front of him on his desk he had spread out a series of photographs of the body in Leigh Woods, taken before the tent had been erected. They showed the grizzly find from all angles. It was easy to see how the six of them had missed it in the mist; from any distance it looked like so much twig, stone and leaf. Only from certain angles was it obvious what the camera had captured. The pictures of the partial hand were there too, not that there was much they could do with them. He was about to lift the receiver to try and put pressure on forensics when Austin came in.

'Result! We got a preliminary ID from the body. He has distinctive tattoos on both upper arms, dragons of some sort. It's on file.'

'So who have we got?'

'Wayne Deeming. Career criminal and first-class moron. We thought he might have had links to Ray Fenton, but we couldn't find any at the time.'

'Perhaps someone else had better luck,' McLusky said.

Austin brought up the results on his computer screen. 'Born May '83, convictions for theft, blah blah, taking without consent, burglary, ABH, GBH, assaulting police and possession of cannabis with intent to supply.'

'Good riddance,' DC Dearlove ventured from behind the safety of his monitor.

'Less of that,' McLusky said. 'You're allowed to think it, though perhaps you're in the wrong seat if you're thinking it too often. Do we have an address for him?'

'Yup, place he was last arrested, eight months ago.'

McLusky scooped up his car keys. 'Worth having a look, then.'

The address turned out to be an anonymous rented prop-erty in a terrace of narrow houses in Bedminster. The front-room window had dark blue curtains drawn, the front door was locked. There was no answer to Austin's knock, and no one appeared to be at home on either side.

'We can always ask the chaps from the drug squad to come and charge the door for us,' Austin suggested.

'And find the place is now occupied by an old lady who's hard of hearing? Try two doors down.'

Austin was in luck. The slightly crumpled, quiet man who opened the door didn't recognize Deeming from the picture he showed him but was happy to allow them into his back garden. McLusky was hoping to jump the fences into the back of Deeming's place and get a look through a window.

'I pretty much keep to myself here,' was how the man explained his failure to recognize his neighbour from the picture. 'I don't get involved in what goes on in the street. There's a lot of students.'

In the tiny, dispiriting garden, McLusky dragged an empty concrete planter to the fence and, standing on it, vaulted into the garden next door. This was equally bleak but also contained the trashed remains of a kitchen. Some of it looked more modern than his own. He used an upturned black bucket in which plaster had thickly set to get himself over the next fence into what he hoped was Deeming's garden. The kitchen window at the back was obscured with net curtains, but an uncovered chink of glass afforded him a glance at the interior. 'Bingo.' Everything he saw spelled drug-fuelled chaos.

'Do you want me to come across?' called Austin, who had stayed behind.

McLusky waved him off. 'Front door, DS Austin.' He looked around for something with which to smash in the kitchen door. A large mossy rock at the edge of the muddy lawn looked good. Then he changed his mind. He fished out a pair of fresh latex gloves from his jacket, put them on and tried the door. It was unlocked. 'More taxpayers' money saved.'

The kitchen was small and in a mess. He had seen some of it through the window, but what he was looking at now

70

went beyond the usual slobbery. Apart from unwashed dishes, empty cans and pizza cartons, there was disturbance here – the two chairs had been overturned, an ashtray spilled and a mug broken on the floor. It was warm in the house, the heating obviously running. The place smelled stale, slightly mouldy. As he passed an encrusted pedal bin, the smell got stronger. He flipped the lid open and lowered it again. Festering rubbish. He'd leave that to forensics; they always loved a nice mouldy bin. He gingerly made his way from the kitchen into the hall, where he let Austin in. 'Gloves,' he said automatically. Austin wriggled his fingers in mad-strangler mode: he was already wearing them.

'This door wasn't locked or bolted, just pulled shut. Back door was unlocked. I think he left through the front door but not necessarily of his own accord. Drops of blood on the floor.' McLusky pointed to a circular pattern of drops on the carpet, turned almost black with age.

'Could just be a nosebleed, of course.'

McLusky pointed to a brighter spray pattern on the yellow wall. 'This nose also bled sideways. Someone persuaded it to bleed. I've seen enough, no point trampling all over the house. I'll call scene-of-crime; you see if any of the motors in the street are registered to Deeming. We'll wait outside, make forensics happy.'

'Shame, nice and warm in here.'

A blue Ford Focus with a long scrape along the driver's side turned out to be Deeming's. It would be carted off to the pound for forensics shortly. McLusky wanted to cast his eye over the interior beforehand, but it was locked. Back in the house, he went through the front room and the kitchen. 'Have we found any car keys?' he asked the SOCOs. No one had. In the kitchen, he asked the nearest officer: 'Where do you keep your spare keys at home?'

The man thought for a moment. 'In a tin in the kitchen with loads of other stuff.'

McLusky lifted the lid on a china biscuit barrel and emptied the contents on to the counter. Mobile phone batteries, cigarette papers, plastic rubbish, painkillers and keys for a Ford. 'Genius. Gold star.'

The SOCO allowed himself a smile; he didn't get much praise in his job.

The car's interior was as messy as that of the house. McLusky searched while leaving everything as he found it: among the empty cans and food debris he saw plastic wraps for parcelling up class A, a long kitchen knife in the driver's door pocket, cigarette papers, crumbs of herbal cannabis on the seats and in the glove box another knife, a sharpened screwdriver and a blister pack of what looked like Viagra. All as expected.

Traffic was building as he and Austin drove back towards Albany Road. 'The papers are going to call it "another gang-land killing".'

Austin agreed. 'And they'll be right, won't they? Deedee called it "good riddance".'

'So will most people.' They both knew that the citizens of Bristol would echo the sentiment expressed earlier by DC Dearlove: *one less*. 'What they don't see is that if one lot of dealers kill the other lot, all it means is that they've now been replaced with a more murderous mob than the first.'

'Sound capitalist principles. Triumph of the greediest.'

Traffic in the centre was at clutch-burning pace. While stationary in Baldwin Street, McLusky saw her.

Even in an unfamiliar winter coat and with a huge scarf wound round her neck, he recognized her instantly. It felt as though his abdominal muscles had seen her first, so instant was the fist-in-the-stomach feeling at the sudden, unexpected sight. The man she was walking with took her arm as they slipped between cars. He had a mop of dark hair and looked to be barely in his twenties. McLusky was relieved to see him let go of her arm once they had gained the other side of the street. He craned his neck to see past the cars crawling in the opposite direction. Both seemed to be talking simultaneously, and their walk looked more like a dance. Then they turned a corner.

72

'Liam?'

Austin's prompt and the impatient horn of the car behind brought him back to the task in hand. Ahead of them a long gap had opened in the traffic. He quickly caught up to the bumper of the car in front, already stationary again.

'Sorry. That was Laura. My ex.'

'Ex … girlfriend – you weren't married, were you?'

'No, none of that.'

'I remember you saying she was studying here now. Was that the first time you've seen her since …'

'Since we broke up? No. She came to see me once. In the spring. To tell me she'd be coming to study here. At least I think that's why she came.' Back then McLusky had briefly entertained hopes that they might see more of each other, but the meeting, if it could be called that, had not gone well. He hadn't seen her since and he didn't know where she lived. Of course it wouldn't take much for him to find out, but he was sure that Laura would not take it kindly if he used his police powers to track her down. And there were other, less carefully thought out reasons why he hadn't made an effort to get in touch. Louise Rennie, the chemistry lecturer, was one. A suspicion that one more unhappy meeting with Laura might make their separation absolutely final was another.

'Archaeology, isn't it?'

'Oh, yes.' Laura had always been good at digging up things from the past.

With the door closed, the blinds drawn and a dozen people inside, the incident room was warming up. It was the first time since getting up in the morning that McLusky had felt warm enough to take his leather jacket off.

'This doesn't of course come as a surprise to any of us.' Denkhaus, who outside his office was never seen without his jacket on, hooked a thumb over his shoulder at the A4 mug shots of Wayne Deeming pinned to the board in front of which he held forth. 'DNA results have confirmed it, it's him. We knew after we put Ray Fenton away that it wouldn't be long before the remaining groups started to fight it out between themselves. Nature abhors a vacuum. Out with the old, in with the new. Wayne Deeming, it appears, was the old. We know he was involved in drugs. We always thought he was part of Fenton's chain. Perhaps he fancied stepping into shoes too big for him; perhaps he was simply too close to Fenton.'

'Or it could be completely unrelated, sir,' DC French suggested.

'We'll keep that in mind, naturally.' That young DC was forever trying to show that she could think laterally. It hadn't worked for her so far. 'We all heard the rumours that outsiders have moved in to mop up Fenton's old business, but that's all they are so far, rumours. No one seems to know.'

'It took us years to discover Fenton's identity,' French said. 'He had time to make millions while we kept arresting replaceable people. Expendable people.'

'Are you trying to cheer us all up, DC French? In which case, please stop.'

'Sorry, sir.'

McLusky quickly jumped in. 'The Ford Focus we recovered from outside Deeming's house was pretty new. I checked, and he bought it two months ago from a dealer here in Bristol. A car dealer, I should add.'

'When he was last arrested, he was driving a ten-year-old Honda,' Austin supplied.

'So he was definitely moving up in the world,' McLusky continued. 'But I had a swift dekko at the car, and apart from dealing, he definitely had a drug habit himself. It might only have been herbal – there were crumbs all over the place – but no one who smokes pot himself is going to get very far in the business.'

The room murmured agreement.

McLusky thought about it again that night at home as he cracked open a can of Murphy's and sprayed froth across his laptop screen. Earlier he had eaten a bowl of spaghetti at the Barge Inn, opposite his flat in Northmoor Street, and washed it down with a pint. He was glad his stomach was back to normal, since it allowed him to sink a few pints of stout, the only form of relaxation he knew.

Brewers drank beer. Vintners drank wine. Alcohol was a drug, but here lay the difference: the drugs bosses, the ones with the real connections like Fenton, never touched drugs. They despised drugs and the wretches who bought them. McLusky wiped the beer froth off the laptop's screen, double-clicked on Channel Four's view-on-demand site and sipped frothy beer while he waited for it to load. The real drugs bosses drank vintage champagne and age-old brandies and ate at fine restaurants. The more successful they became, the further they moved away from the physical presence of drugs or violence. Their money was well laundered through legitimate businesses and they lived in houses far from drug-riddled city streets.

'A quiet village in Cambridgeshire,' said Tony Robinson on the screen, 'is about to be invaded by *Time Team*'s finest and have its back gardens riddled with trenches. Why? Because last year, a local farmer ploughing his field came across *this*.' The presenter offered up a broken piece of pot to the camera.

McLusky lay back on his sofa, perched the laptop on his stomach and adjusted the screen. It was high time he swatted up on some archaeology.

Chapter Eight

The first surreptitious snowflakes drifted down as McLusky set off for work. Mid-morning, as he looked up from his computer, a shift in the quality of light made him turn around. The view from his office window had changed: the roofs of the houses were dusted with snow. Below, it was settling on cars, bins and tarmac. High up in Leigh Woods, snow would quickly cover all the ground. Had they not found Wayne Deeming's body, their chances of discovering it now would already have been slim. Come to think of it, the partial hand would probably not have been found at all had it snowed a few days earlier. The body could have remained undiscovered up there for a long time.

As it was, the remains had been removed to the mortuary. McLusky had dispatched Austin to be present at the post-mortem that was taking place this morning. He himself avoided the mortuary at all costs. Death – accidental, neglected, forgotten, unlawful – came as part of the terri-tory. Observing the dead where they had died or been deposited was what he owed them as part of his job. It never got easier and he had yet to forget a single one of them. But the insides of the dead he gladly left to others. He was happy to read reports and look at photographs, but he had never learnt a thing at an autopsy that he couldn't have gleaned from the pathologist's report. Austin, he knew, would ask all the right questions and should – he checked his watch – be back soon with some of the answers.

In the meantime, he needed coffee. In the corridor he passed DC Daniel Dearlove. Despite his name, the detective constable had yet to endear himself to McLusky. 'Deedee' Dearlove didn't have a lot to work with. His thin hair barely covered his scalp, his question-mark posture gave him a perpetual air of uncertainty and the static of his polyester suits seemed to attract every cat hair and piece of fluff in his vicinity. Normally McLusky gave him as wide a berth as was politely possible, but just then the distinct aroma of freshly brewed coffee made him stop in his tracks right next to him.

'Snowing out,' said the startled DC.

'Seen it,' said McLusky. 'Why can I smell cappuccino?'

Dearlove sniffed and nodded. The inspector had an obsession with cappuccino, he'd heard. 'DI Fairfield's espresso machine.'

'How come that's not been confiscated by health and safety? We're not even allowed a kettle.'

'Something to do with it being properly wired into the wall, according to her.'

Just then, a little further along, Fairfield's door opened to allow Denkhaus into the corridor, together with a fresh wave of coffee-house smells.

Or perhaps patronage was the answer. To Dearlove he said: 'Properly wired may be right.'

Down in the canteen, coffee was served stewed, but at least it was real and hot and came in china cups thick enough to be useful in a brawl. Drinking coffee always made him want to smoke, but the chances of doing both at the same time had now become rare. McLusky covered his cup with the saucer in an effort to trap the heat and climbed the stairs to his second-floor office, taking two steps at a time while hoping not to meet anyone en route who might want to talk to him.

Safely shut up in his office, he produced a small ashtray with a flip-up lid and his cigarettes from a desk drawer. He opened the window a hand's breadth. He sat the coffee cup back on its saucer and finally lit a cigarette. Civilization, as McLusky saw it, had at last returned to the workplace.

The knock on the door made him stab his cigarette into the ashtray, slam down the lid and sweep it into the drawer, all in one practised movement. 'Come in.' Relief as Austin entered the room and shut the door behind him. He rescued the now crumpled cigarette from the ashtray, straightened and relit it. 'Out with it. What did Coulthart have to say?'

'SOCOs say Deeming was killed right where we found him. Blood spatters recovered from the area around the burial site and on some of the infill seem to indicate that. The place had been raked over, according to them. Coulthart says he had more than eighty separate injuries on his body.'

'The bastards really went to work on him. Is that what killed him?'

'Brain haemorrhage. Blows to the head. Do you remember how stony the ground was around there?'

McLusky remembered thinking it as he knelt next to the body. 'Don't tell me.'

'Coulthart says they definitely threw stones at him as well.'

'Shit.' McLusky thought for a moment. 'Standing in a hole! They buried him up to his knees so he couldn't run. But hang on, someone must have heard him scream; the locus isn't that far from dwellings and—'

'He was gagged and had the bag over his head,' Austin interrupted. 'They found bits of rag inside his throat where he must have chewed on the gag.'

'The sadistic swines.'

'Yes. They really worked him over before they killed him. And they didn't bother to dig him out when he was dead, they just sort of dug behind and under him a bit; that's why the burial was so rubbish, really.'

'That's why we found him so quickly.' He closed the window against the icy draught. 'A couple of days later and we wouldn't have known a thing; look at it.' Outside, from a darkening sky, snow was falling steadily. 'Well, that gives us something to work with, especially the MO. I've not come across it before, but we'll check if there's a precedent.'

McLusky felt upbeat. The stranger the MO, the better. A blunt instrument was only one in a thousand other blunt instruments people cracked over each other's heads each year. As a method, it said nothing much about the perpetrator. Often it was simply the first thing that came to hand when the red mist descended. More than anything, it pointed to a lack of planning. 'It's certainly different.' He had a strong image of the victim, dug into the ground up to his knees, hands tied with wire and gagged under the bag over his head. The terror of it. He didn't care that Deeming had been a thoroughly unpleasant individual who had dished out pain and suffering to others. No one should have to go through that. No one deserved to die like that. 'Let's go catch the bastards.'

City snow. Dirty, unwanted stuff squelched into brown mud by car tyres, trodden into grey slush by inadequately shod feet. Like her own, Fairfield thought. On the way, she had noticed that few people bothered to clear the pavements even in front of their own houses. She remembered helping her dad scatter salt and ashes from the fire on the pavement in front of the house. Not here, though; nobody was clearing snow here.

'This is it.' The narrow terraced house in Barton Hill was neither softened nor prettified by the snow. It stood grey and dispiriting, one in a row of near-identical neighbours with a view of several large tower blocks to remind the residents that life could yet be much worse. DS Sorbie, who had been driving, had squeezed his Golf into a space by the next corner since ambulance, patrol car and the surgeon's Audi were blocking the narrow street. The ambulance was just leaving, soon to be replaced by the coroner's van. The PC guarding the house was sensibly doing so in the hallway of number 11, the house where the body had been found.

'The surgeon is upstairs with the body in the back bedroom,' he informed Fairfield. 'The sister, who found it, is in the kitchen. PC Purkis is looking after her.' He nodded his head backwards towards the end of the narrow hall, where a door stood ajar. The door to the front room was open. Fairfield stuck her head in, quickly summing up the interior. A three-piece suite, framed pictures on the wall, hard-wearing carpet, an old-fashioned sound system. Tidy. It didn't look too shabby, considering there was a dead junkie lying upstairs. To get to it required a quick shuffle of officers in the desperately confined space at the bottom of the stairs.

'In here, Inspector.' The surgeon's voice guided them to the right bedroom, though it would have been hard to get lost. The bedroom was small and in twilight; pink curtains were drawn. There was little here apart from a 1970s dressing table, chair and bed. The woman's body was kneeling and slumped face down on the bed. Fairfield guessed she had been in her late thirties. She was clad in a woollen dress. The furnishings gave out a strong scent of incense, almost masking the smell of escaped urine coming from the body. The air felt damp.

'Cause of death?' Fairfield asked.

'I'd put money on an overdose. I'd say the needle had only just left the vein in her arm. You can see it under her body; she's still holding the syringe with her right hand.'

Fairfield bent to take a look at it, then surveyed the paraphernalia on the bedside table. 'Deliberate or accidental?'

'I wouldn't want to venture an opinion. We'll leave that to the pathologist, shall we?'

'Any sign she might have contracted anthrax, like our chap in the shopping centre?'

'None at all as far as I can see. The autopsy will show it.'

'I don't see the wrap,' Sorbie said, looking closely at the mess on the bedside table. He crouched down in what little space there was and searched the floor.

Fairfield made room for him. 'Nothing's been removed, has it?'

The doctor snapped shut his case. 'Not by me. And not by anyone else while I was here.'

81

'All right. What's the story here? Did she live alone or with others?'

'With the sister, I believe,' the surgeon said, in the doorway. 'I'm finished here.'

'Right, thanks. Sorbie? Let's have a chat with the sister.'

In the kitchen, Carole Maar sat dry-eyed and still, staring straight ahead at a spot on the wall between the calendar picture of a cat and a leaning mop handle. Her hair was a dull straw that matched her eyebrows. She was dressed in washed-out, unfashionable jeans and several layers of sweaters, the top one a light shade of charity-shop orange. She was thirty-nine but looked much older. PC Purkis, who had vacated the only other chair when Fairfield entered, had made her a cup of tea. It remained untouched.

Formalities over, Fairfield pulled the chair opposite the woman, who was still avoiding eye contact, and sat down. She signalled to the PC that she could leave the room. 'Ms Maar … can I call you Carole?'

Maar shrugged. Why not.

'I'm very sorry to have to ask you questions at a time like this, but it's important we establish some facts. It was you who found her, is that right?'

'Yeah.'

'And it was you who called the ambulance?'

Carole hesitated. 'I didn't know who else to call. I knew Pat was dead. I knew they couldn't do anything. But who do you call? I didn't know.' Her voice was hard and flat.

'You did the right thing.' Fairfield looked around the cramped kitchen. 'You were both living here together?'

'Yes.'

'And do you use drugs yourself?'

A nod.

'What exactly, heroin?'

Another nod.

'And … do you inject …?'

A shake of the head. 'I smoke.'

'So what happened here today?'

82

It was a short and simple story. They had quarrelled. They quarrelled a lot. These days mainly about money and drugs. Both had left the house independently in the morning, not speaking to each other, trying to score. Carole had tried and failed to raise money for a wrap and returned empty-handed. She had been home some time before discovering her younger sister in exactly the position she was in now. Her sister obviously had managed to score drugs. Enough to kill herself with.

Fairfield wondered about the arrangement. Two sisters, pushing middle age, living together, using heroin together, waiting for the inevitable to happen. And here it was.

'Had she been suicidal? Was it deliberate, d'you think?' Sorbie asked.

Carole didn't even look up. She shrugged. 'I don't think so. But you can never tell, can you? It's easy to get ... tired.'

'I'll have to ask you to hand over the remainder of the heroin your sister scored today.'

'What remainder?' Carole asked.

'The house will be subject to a drugs search anyway. And you'll be searched, of course, so you might as well hand it over now,' Sorbie said.

Carole dug the wrap from her jeans pocket and laid it carefully on the table.

'Is that all there is?' Fairfield asked. 'It may be what killed your sister, so I think it would be very foolish to smoke it. You don't know what's in it. We have reason to believe there is contaminated heroin in circulation that could make you very ill indeed.'

For a moment the woman did not react. Then she produced another wrap from where it had been tucked into her sock.

'That's all of it now, is it?' The wraps looked different from most Fairfield had seen recently. The bright white powder was contained in small rectangular resealable bags. She thanked Maar and let Sorbie drop the wraps into an evidence bag. 'Is this what your usual supply looks like?' she asked.

'No.'

'Did you and your sister use the same dealers?'

'Mostly.'

'But not today?'

'Look, I don't know, do I?' Carole became animated for the first time. 'I wasn't with her, okay? I come home and she's dead. Is all I know. Junkies die. It happens. If it isn't one thing that kills you, it's another.'

Fastening her seat belt in Sorbie's car, Fairfield echoed Maar's conclusion. 'One thing or another. Let me have a look at the wraps again.'

Sorbie passed them over inside the evidence bag.

'Ever seen one that looked like that?'

'One or two. Little food bags.' Dealers didn't normally bother spending money on bags. Wraps usually came in any old bits of plastic. 'Posh. But I haven't seen it that colour for years.' For a long time now heroin on the street was Afghan stuff, yellow or brown.

'Quicker we get it to the lab the better.'

'Junkies,' Sorbie complained as he drove off. 'I can't believe Denkhaus has us traipsing after dead junkies. Or even live ones.' In Sorbie's book, a dead junkie was a good junkie, one that was unlikely to cause more grief, commit more crime, suck more drugs into the city.

Fairfield's mood turned as bleak as the streets they travelled along. 'Until we nail the source of the anthrax, we'll be chasing every bloody junkie, dead or alive. And all points between.'

'It's useless,' Sorbie insisted. 'We'll never find it that way.' Fairfield knew that users never revealed the source of their supplies. To do so was suicide. Once you ratted on a dealer, you were never safe again, not at home, not on the street, not in prison, not in rehab. In Mexico, dealers were raiding rehabilitation centres, shooting everyone inside. To discourage the rest. It wasn't quite that bad yet in Bristol. But for how much longer? Sorbie was doing nothing to lighten Fairfields's mood. 'Drop me back at my car, Jack, I'll call it a day.'

*

It had been snowing continuously, and the short drive home to her little maisonette in Cotham had taken twice as long as it should have done. Why was it that the British found it so impossible to cope with snow? In Sweden or Canada they had routinely several feet of the stuff and everything worked just fine, roads got cleared and gritted and people coped. Here, two inches of it fell and the headlines read 'Commuter Misery as Big Freeze Grips British Isles'. Perhaps they were just more used to it in those countries. Her own street of large Victorian houses looked softened and seasonal, with every parked car and every tree hooded white. The path to her front door had been cleared and gritted by the couple in the upper maisonette; she was glad, since she was laden with bags of shopping she had picked up on the way. She would make sure she'd do her bit and sweep the path tomorrow.

In the kitchen, she elbowed the radio on even before she had set down her carrier bags. With the cork pulled on her bottle of Australian wine, she studied the cooking instructions on the sleeve of her ready meal and turned on the oven. This had long become routine now. Who had the strength to cook after work? Cooking was what you watched people do on TV while your ready meal heated up. And if you liked what you saw on telly, you looked for it – or something vaguely similar – next time you were at the supermarket. Anyway, she did cook sometimes, pasta mainly, *so there*. It wasn't that she was a useless cook; she used to cook quite a bit back in the early days, when there was someone to cook for. But hey. Supermarket's finest lamb moussaka. Her mother would finally disown her if she ever found out.

Junkies. Had they all become junkies of one form or another now, relying on their dealers to survive? A bottle of wine nearly every night was probably overdoing it too, but then sometimes she fell asleep before she had a chance to finish it. At least she didn't drink at lunchtime, like some. She had smelled cider on Sorbie more than once, but he never admitted to more than a quick half. She might one day have to breathalyse him to find out just how much he put away each time he went out for lunch.

When the timer went and she opened the oven door, the moussaka even smelled acceptable. With her first glass of wine poured and the food dished up in a fashion that bore little resemblance to the picture on the packet, she settled on the sofa in the sitting room. Balancing the plate on her lap, she reached for the TV remote, hoping to find some news item of people being pathetic in the snow. When she did, the phone rang. Typical.

'Hello?' It was a call from a mobile, and the connection was so bad she had to interrupt the man who was talking.

'Look, I can't hear a word you're saying, it's a really bad line. Hello?' The call was interrupted and she hung up. How did they always know the precise moment when you were picking up your fork? She took a sip of wine and picked up her fork. The phone rang again. She answered it. This time the connection was only marginally clearer.

'This better be good.'

'I can't promise that.'

'Who is this?'

'It's me, Kats. It's Paul. The guy you married?'

Fairfield reached for her glass and drained it.

There was never any quiet. Not real quiet. Who wanted to live in a city that never slept? Or a block of flats that never stopped reverberating with noise and anger? Mike wiped the condensation from the kitchen window, which looked directly on to the street. Snow. Perhaps that would muffle the sounds a little. More likely by tomorrow morning it would bring noisy kids on to the street. At least that would be a happy noise. Outside a van, grey or blue, hard to tell under the orange sodium lights, braked too abruptly on the settling snow and skidded to a halt opposite the house. It seemed no one was used to snow any more. He remembered his own childhood winters: there always seemed to be snow then, and everyone had wooden sleds shod with iron rails.

The day it snowed, you got your sled out and sandpapered the rust off the rails, rubbed them with bacon rinds or a stub of candle and you were ready for it. Now all most kids had were flimsy bits of plastic or just bin liners to sit on.

Was there a definite date when everything had turned cheap and tacky and flimsy, or had that all arrived gradually? Now he could see it everywhere. His counsellor had said he should avoid thinking about it. And all the other things. That they were just going to drive him back into a depressive state. That in the past he had used these thoughts as an excuse to start drinking again. As though it was that easy, that simple. Avoid the bad thoughts and stay sober. Three months in rehab hadn't done it. They had decided he needed another three months. And afterwards he was not allowed to go back to his old life, his drinking buddies and failures. So now he was here, looking for a new life, new failures. It had all started well enough; the newness had been distracting. But he was still banned from driving and still hadn't found a job. This tiny flat with its clammy walls took his breath away. It was small but cost a fortune to heat, and everything was always covered in condensation, the windows, the outside wall.

He had to get out of here for a bit; at least outside he could stretch, breathe, move. Move carefully. It felt as though they had deliberately housed him in a block of flats encircled by pubs. He knew there were off-licences and pubs everywhere; you simply couldn't avoid seeing them. What you could avoid was going inside, putting all your money on the bar and drinking until it was gone. You had to try not to think about it, stop imagining it. The warmth of it, the smells, the atmosphere, the instant feeling of relief, of coming home …

The world was floating on a sea of alcohol. He just had to make sure his little boat didn't spring a leak. Mike zipped up his jacket and pulled a woolly hat over his ears. At the kitchen table he put his ancient laptop on standby and unplugged his little camera from the charger. He hated it, ever since they had let him use a real digital camera on the photography course, but it would probably take years to save up for an SLR. And then the course had folded, of course. When the tutor suddenly quit, the community centre had cancelled the next one. Lack of funding. The cuts. He took good pictures, the tutor had said, and she hadn't just said it to humour him. She had picked them out for praise in front of the others. The others. They were all in the same boat, of course. They had all expected to see each other again, *promised* they'd see each other again when the next course started up, and then the letter came. Funding cuts ... savings ... in the current climate ... regret ... cancelled. He'd probably never see them again now. He had started saving for a real camera, in an empty honey jar, but kept having to raid it to charge the key for the electric. The camera he used came from a charity shop, but it *did take pictures*. He mustn't indulge in self-pity. Get the best you can afford, the tutor had said, and work with what you've got.

The wind was colder than he had expected. Snow was still falling, but more lightly now, whipped along the street by the icy wind. The van opposite the house hadn't moved, still standing at a shallow angle by the side of the road. The driver sat huddled, motionless. Perhaps he was too scared to continue driving in these conditions. Mike set off, stomping his feet in the snow, enjoying the crunch it produced. He'd like to find an expanse of pristine snow to photograph, without footprints or tyre marks, something that suggested calmness or purity. He thought he knew where he might find something like it, but it was quite a hike from here.

Traffic was light at this time of night. Many people had probably decided to stay at home in front of the telly. He stepped into the road to cross. Just then the van driver decided to move on. Mike slowed in the street to let him pass, but the van stopped right beside him with its side door sliding open. The man who jumped out drove his fist into Mike's windpipe, then pushed him inside.

Chapter Nine

Evidence of dealing had been discovered at Deeming's house but no significant amounts of drugs. Forensic analysis had thrown up a dizzying number of fingerprints, none of which looked promising. Some were of known drug-users, one or two of lowlifes who McLusky knew dealt small-time to finance other unsavoury habits. All of it was pond life that Deeming, who had been six foot tall and no slouch in dishing out violence, would hardly have been scared of. No matter, they still had to find them, pull them in, interview them.

In the small, drab interview room, McLusky was sitting opposite one of them now, a creature by the name of Gareth Keep. Not a junkie, but a thief with a weed and alcohol habit and, as McLusky suspected, very few brain cells to spare for the toll that it was taking on them. He was twenty-six and still only managed to grow an unconvincing line of fluff above his upper lip, making him look like a teenager trying to look older. He was clad in a blue tracksuit with double white stripes and an imitation leather jacket that was patently too large for him. The hapless punter had been scooped up in a supermarket car park after he'd been seen shoplifting CDs. He was unperturbed at having been arrested. He had been pulled in by the police and then let go by the courts so many times that now it hardly registered. In court he had a good line in contrition and promises of reforming, and he knew that the most he could expect to be handed by the magistrate was a few hours' community service, for which he rarely showed up anyway. When he did, he was usually stoned.

McLusky had teamed up with DC French for this interview. As with the last lowlife they had pulled, he was happy to let her do most of the questioning. He was really there to take a sniff at the punters and pounce should he get the slightest whiff that the specimen in front of them might be involved.

'No comment,' was how Gareth answered most questions, watched over by his brief, who appeared equally bored by the occasion. Things got more animated when McLusky sprung the news on him of Deeming's death.

'Murder? Now you're accusing me of murder? You're mad.'

'Your prints were found in Deeming's hall. His blood was on the ground and on the wall. You were there.'

'No comment.'

The solicitor instantly protested about the unexpected turn of events and demanded to speak with his client alone. McLusky was glad. He felt his energy was being drained by the necessity and futility of spending time with these drifters. Gareth might quite conceivably one day break someone's skull, stab someone in an argument or strangle his girlfriend, but McLusky found it hard to believe that he had snatched Deeming from his house, tied him up, put a bag over his head, driven him to Leigh Woods and there beaten him to death. Not unless he was taking some very strange drugs at the time.

In the corridor, he handed Gareth Keep's file to French. 'He's yours. Get all you can out of him about who else he saw at Deeming's house, how often he used to go there et cetera. Oh yes, and charge him with theft for lifting the CDs, of course.'

With a hardening heart, French watched DI McLusky walk off down the corridor. If ever she nursed doubts about being a police officer, it was at moments like this. She flicked the cover of the file with a fingernail. 'No comment.'

McLusky stuck his head in at the incident room. Dearlove sat at a computer, concentrating hard on reading the back of a crisp packet. No sign of Austin.

'He's just popped downstairs to dump some files,' Dearlove told him through a mouthful of crisps.

'When he gets back, tell him I'm in my office.'

McLusky's earlier plans had been interrupted; now he was going to set them in motion. His office was far too small to install an espresso machine, however compact. There was such a dearth of surfaces, there wouldn't even be enough space to set one down. This morning he had smuggled in a tiny electric travel kettle, which he hid in the bottom compartment of his desk, connected by an extension lead. How the mighty had fallen, he thought, as he stirred whitener into his instant coffee. He knew that according to Sod's Law, someone would knock on his door as soon as he lit a cigarette. Naturally this never worked when you wanted someone to turn up, so perhaps by wishing someone to knock on the door he could prevent it? A kind of reverse superstition. He opened the window for ventilation and reached for his pack of Extra Lights. The knock on the door was Austin's.

'I've been looking up and down the station for you,' he complained.

'Keep you fit.' McLusky lit a cigarette.

'Don't for one moment think you can't smell that outside, Liam, because you can.'

'My predecessor smoked a lot. The smell never goes away.'

'Aye, they'll believe that.'

'Did we get anything from the house-to-house around Deeming's address? Is it too much to hope that someone saw a man being led away against his will? Possibly with a bloody bag on his head?'

'I think it might be.'

'Naturally. Every day the emergency lines are jammed with idiots calling about their pizzas being late or their budgie having hiccoughs, but no one in this town takes any notice of what happens to other people.'

'People opposite saw a van, double-parked, about a month ago. It was double-parked and annoyed them, that's how they remember.'

'Did they see anyone associated with the van?'

'Nope.'

'Of course not. A van. What kind of van? Camper van, delivery van?'

'Just a van. Blue or grey.'

'Blue or grey? It'll turn out to be red, then. Great. Is that it? Well tell them an arrest will be imminent.'

There was a knock on the door and Austin opened it. DC Dearlove had added tiny specks of potato crisp to the array of cat hair on his suit jacket. 'Call from area control, sirs. Suspicious death, male body found by the river. I've got the details here.' He handed the note to Austin.

'Marvellous.' McLusky nodded to Austin and stubbed out his cigarette. 'Okay. You drive.'

Austin got stuck in traffic twice, which meant they were the last to arrive. On the Ashton to Pill cycle path, just north of the Avon Bridge, two inches of snow had accumulated, now trampled into a brown mulch by many cold feet. There were several bicycle tracks too, running close to the body. People had cycled along the river without giving the dead man under the snow blanket a second glance.

'Just a lump under the snow. It was probably the black nylon jacket,' Austin speculated. 'At least two people came past here on bicycles but probably thought it was bin liners full of rubbish dumped under the bushes. With all that snow on top of the body, it was hard to make out.'

The PC standing guard at the river's edge spoke up. 'Just recently there's been a lot of fly-tipping along here.'

McLusky whisked round. 'Yes, thank you, Constable, you can update us on the local rubbish problems later.' He turned to Coulthart, who puffed loudly through his face mask as he examined the body. 'Killed here or dumped here, Doctor?'

'Deposition site. Killed elsewhere. And brutally so. The face is … well, you can see.'

McLusky could see. The face was a bloodied, broken mess.

'I'm sure I'd be able to tell you more if you cared to join me at the post-mortem, Detective Inspector.' Coulthart tried to make it seductive, being well aware of McLusky's aversion to post-mortem examinations.

'Thanks, I'll wait.'

'You may well have to. These are busy times at the mortuary. Death rates rise rapidly in these weather conditions. How the human race ever survived the ice age is a miracle.'

'We went south for the duration, I expect.'

'And a good thing, too. That's exactly what I have planned myself. Though regrettably not until after Christmas.'

'What's his age?' From where McLusky was standing, and despite having looked closely at the man's face, he found it impossible to tell.

'Late fifties, I'd say, perhaps early sixties.'

'No ID on him, of course? Wallet? Library card?'

'I went through his clothing,' said a SOCO waiting nearby. 'No ID, no car keys or house keys. Some small change and a packet of mints.'

'Mints.' McLusky turned back to Coulthart. 'Cause of death?'

'Not mints, Inspector. I couldn't say.'

'How long?'

Coulthart stood up, signalling to the SOCOs that he had finished his examination. 'How long has he been dead, or how long has he been here?'

'Either. I mean both.'

'Difficult to say with any degree of confidence because of the frozen conditions. But he hasn't been lying here for long.'

A SOCO stopped his quiet cursing of the muddled footprints long enough to add his observations. 'He had about an inch of snow on him. There's a little bit of shelter here from the bushes, but that's about the amount that's fallen since three in the morning.'

'So to have an inch on him, he would have to have been here since the middle of the night.'

'Correct.' The SOCO, who had an encyclopaedic memory of local weather conditions, returned to the puzzle of footprints and began brushing at the snow.

Well away from the deposition site, McLusky lit a cigarette and looked around him. As a dumping ground this was pretty perfect. There was access from the A369 a few yards from where the body had been found. Austin stood next to him, sniffing nostalgically at the cigarette smoke and stomping his feet to keep them from going numb. McLusky could no longer feel his. He'd buy winter boots at the first opportunity. 'First impressions, Jane?'

'Shame about the footprints.'

'It's a SOCO nightmare. They're hoping to find some under the snow. Or in between layers. But it's pretty much buggered. The couple who found the body trod all over the site, then an ambulance crew, then a couple of constables, then the rest of us.'

'There's no CCTV here and no one about at night. Yet it's very close to the city. Couldn't be better, could it? Dumping a body is always a risky business, so this place is quite convenient.'

'Yes, but leaving a body lying about where it can easily be found is also a risky business. It's ten feet from the river. Why leave him here if you can simply tip him into the water? Even without being weighed down, he'd likely drift a bit and give us a headache.'

'Perhaps they thought someone might hear the splash. Or they meant to chuck the body in and someone came along and interrupted them. Along the path or by boat. So they dumped it and legged it.'

'Boat. Good thinking, Jane. Make sure someone does a house-to-house, or boat-to-boat rather, in the harbour and the moorings on this side, too. Establish if anyone came by here at night and saw anything.'

'There's not a great deal of boat traffic at this time of the year. Even less at night.'

'I know that.' McLusky flicked his cigarette butt towards the slow-moving water, where he instantly lost sight of it. 'I still think the river is a missed opportunity if you want to get rid of a body.'

Fairfield shoved the tiny cup under the nozzle, pressed the button and watched the evil-looking liquid dribble from the machine. Espresso was the one other vice she admitted to, and she tried to keep her daily total to fewer than five. Last night she had felt the need to open a second bottle of wine; consequently she needed all the caffeine she could get today. Why had it unsettled her so much? There were photographs of two dead people on her desk, both of whom she had also seen in the flesh, yet none of it had unsettled her as much as Paul's voice on the phone, even down a bad line. It had been her who had finished the relationship, because of his constant absences due to his job, their rows about when to have children, whether to have children, his career, her career. Why now, she had asked him, why divorce now after three years of separation? She had guessed the answer all along. Paul was thinking of getting married to his current girl-friend, also an electrical engineer. How quaint. Lots to talk about there then, she was sure. They could engineer a wonderful life together for themselves. Paul and Carrie.

She took a sip from the cup and found she had a slight tremor. Last one for today, she vowed silently. She pulled a stack of forms towards her and started reading.

Divorce. Her thoughts kept coming back to it despite her best efforts to get some paperwork done. Uncontested divorce. It was so easy now. He'd already initiated it; all he wanted now was for her to sign some papers. Or was it? She had told him to put them in the post, but he had said something about being between addresses and she had ended up

95

arranging to see him on Sunday. They were meeting at the Nova Scotia, for a drink and a quick divorce. She had agreed and now she couldn't stop thinking about it. When the phone on her desk rang, she was grateful to hear she had business out on the streets.

'Number three.' Sorbie stepped out of the way to let the photographer take pictures of the car from all angles. The dead junkie was barely visible through the windows of the clapped-out Renault. The snow had covered the windscreen and part of the rear window and there was frozen condensation on the side windows. The body had only been discovered because the car was illegally parked in a narrow residential street off Ashley Down Road, and a traffic warden had raised the alarm, saying he could not wake the person lying across the rear seats. At first it had been thought the man had simply frozen to death, but the duty doctor's suspicions had been aroused when he saw the lesions on the dead man's arms, something he had been told to watch out for.

On the other side of the car, DI Fairfield looked on stony-faced. The dead man had been young, still in his twenties. Another set of relatives to inform. Often they took it as something they had half expected; sometimes it came as a devastating shock. A good child. A normal child. A wasted child. Her mobile rang. She reluctantly took her gloves off to answer it. An icy wind was driving the snow flurries through the streets, making it feel twice as cold. 'Did he have any more visitors?' she asked the caller. 'Well, thanks for letting me know, Doctor.' She pocketed the mobile and pulled her gloves back on before correcting Sorbie. 'You were wrong, it's number four. That was the hospital. Our nameless chap didn't make it.'

'I thought they said he had a chance of recovery?'

'I know. Apparently *these things are unpredictable*. He got worse overnight. No one came to see him and we still have no ID for him. Dead loss. I'd best let the super know.'

While Fairfield made the call, she watched the coroner's van and a tow truck arrive. Soon the street would be clear again, another body on its way to the morgue, another car on its way to the vehicle pound. She folded the mobile again and nodded her head towards Sorbie's Golf. 'Drive me to my coffee machine, Jack. The super wants a word. For that I'll need all the drugs I can get.'

Outside the superintendent's office, she found that her tremor had returned. She now regretted her last coffee. She also regretted having turned up five minutes early because now she had to wait in the presence of Lynn Tiery, the superintendent's secretary. She had no idea why, but somehow she found the impassive, steel-eyed woman more intimidating than Denkhaus himself. It was more than five minutes after the appointed time when the super's 'All right, send her in' squawked from the old-fashioned intercom on her desk.

'What's this new epidemic all about?' he wanted to know even before Fairfield had managed to sit down.

'I wouldn't call it an epidemic yet, sir.'

'Well it looks like one to me: five junkies dead in one week? They're dropping at an alarming rate.'

'Four,' Fairfield corrected him.

'Not according to this,' Denkhaus said, tapping his computer monitor with a fleshy finger. 'Drug-user found dead in Totterdown.'

'That's news to me; must only just have come up.'

'Perhaps.' Denkhaus knew it had, yet he liked to keep his team on their toes. 'But I expect you to stay on top of developments.'

With difficulty Fairfield suppressed the urge to point out that she had just spent ten minutes sitting outside his door. And that she wasn't psychic. 'I'm sure Sorbie is taking care of it as we speak.'

'Anthrax, that's not something I wanted to see in our city.' He managed to make that sound like an accusation too, as though she had somehow failed to keep it out.

'The lab says it's contaminated heroin. The most likely source is Afghanistan or eastern Turkey. It may be the cutting agent that carries the contamination, but they haven't isolated it yet.'

'Not that it matters: the result is the same and we can't do a thing about it. Is that it?'

'If we go with the theory that the contamination happened over there, then no.'

'And are we? Is that the presumption?'

'If it is the cutting agent. It normally arrives in this country already cut. About ten per cent purity is normal at the moment, but it does fluctuate. It's usually cut with stuff like lactose, paracetamol or caffeine.' Fairfield felt her fingers tremble and folded her hands.

'So the contamination is accidental?'

'Almost certainly. Hygiene is appalling over there and anthrax in cattle is rife. According to the pathologist, this isn't the first case. It has cropped up before, in Europe.'

'In Europe? This is Europe.'

'Sorry, on the Continent, I should have said.'

'Quite. So no one is trying to poison drug-users?'

'They're doing a pretty good job of that themselves, sir.' The image of the dead woman, slumped forward on her bed, intruded on her mind. 'It's not impossible, but I don't think it's likely that someone has deliberately infected the heroin supply. If you wanted to kill heroin users, you'd stick something fast-acting into the batch, like, I don't know, rat poison. That would be much easier to get hold of. And less dangerous to yourself. Just inhaling this stuff can be lethal.'

'Granted. Right. We have a rogue batch of accidentally contaminated heroin in the city. How much of it is there likely to be?'

'There's no telling.'

'Then we must get a press release done immediately, tell people that this stuff is about and to avoid it at all costs.'

'Yes, sir, I'll see to it.' When Denkhaus dismissed her with a nod, Fairfield stood up, then stopped by the door. 'I doubt it'll make much difference, of course.'

'Oh?'

'You can't tell if your supply is contaminated from looking at it, and there's no test a drug-user could do.' To tell a junkie not to use heroin because it might kill him was like telling a man who was dying of thirst not to drink pond water because it might give him a tummy upset. 'They'll go on using anyway, whatever is in it, whatever the risks.'

'I expect you're right. Yet it would amount to a dereliction of duty not to warn them. At least we can tell them what the symptoms are so they can seek help before it's too late. There is a cure, isn't there?'

'For anthrax or heroin addiction? I think the prognosis is pretty bleak for both, sir.'

Chapter Ten

More snow was falling, making even Broadmead shopping centre look a little less bleak, less commercial. Suddenly the stalls selling hot soup and made-to-order doughnuts seemed like essential services. Snow mellowed many things. We are all infected with Dickensian stories, thought McLusky, for ever in the clutches of Victorian Christmas cards. Inside the shoe shop, he walked up and down along the aisle in the winter boots he had chosen, stomped his feet experimentally and decided to buy them. His mobile chimed and he dug it from the unfamiliar pockets of his new, thickly padded winter jacket.

It was Austin. 'Just thought I'd let you know, the forensics and accident report from the crashed Beemer have arrived.'

'And?'

'I've only just glanced at it, but it looks interesting. The bag we saw in the boot of the car was definitely used to transport heroin.'

'So whoever got to the wreck first probably helped himself to a large amount of the stuff and could now be tooled up with a nine-millimetre semi-automatic into the bargain.'

'Looks like it.'

'All right, I'm on my way.' He would have a quick look at the report himself, then pay the farmer another surprise visit.

At the door, a young shop assistant laid a hand on his arm. McLusky looked at her in surprise. 'S'cuse me, sir, but you haven't paid for those yet,' she said, nodding her head at his feet.

He turned around. The shoes he had come with stood forlorn at the back of the aisle. 'Oh. Sorry. I got distracted.'

The girl didn't take her eyes off him for one second while he collected his old shoes and came to the till. She had heard that excuse before. Most ran out of the shop, but some tried the casual approach, like this one. It just showed you couldn't trust anyone, however nice or normal they looked.

Five embarrassed minutes later, McLusky left the shop in his new boots, carrying his old shoes in a carrier bag. He was ninety-eight per cent certain he had paid for his new jacket.

'You wouldn't have a magnifying glass, would you?' Philippa Warren squinted at the photograph, what there was of it. 'I can't make it out at all.'

Ed, who had been at the *Herald* longer than anyone could remember, gave her a look that was probably meant to say something like 'How did you get this far in the business without owning a magnifying glass?' then went back to his own workstation to fetch one. Warren dropped the photo on her desk and picked up the note that had come with it. These days, most correspondence addressed to the *Herald* came via email. Sometimes torrents of the stuff, especially if the readership had found a contentious bone to worry. Email of course was fast and saved the price of a stamp, which meant hardly anyone sent letters these days. Ironically, this made letter-writers immediately stand out and their contributions were read before anyone found the fortitude to dive into the dreaded inbox.

The note was handwritten, too, in a neat hand and black biro. *The first instalment. But why not print it anyway? If not, keep this safe. It'll make sense later.*

'I'm glad it says *later*, because it doesn't make sense so far,' Warren said, taking the glass from Ed's hand and bending over the photo again. It consisted of only a sliver of a picture, no more than a finger's width. There was a narrow strip of golden yellow, another strip of dark grey and what could, with a bit of imagination, be the beginnings of a person. 'Okay, let me know if any more comes in. I'll hang on to this.' She swept the note into a drawer and Blu-Tacked the piece of photograph to the rim of her computer monitor. She hoped it would make a story eventually. Readers liked a bit of a mystery, and you didn't get many of those to the pound. Local newspapers had been dying on their feet for ages, and even a publication as old as the *Bristol Herald* wasn't immune to the way things had changed. If you could get the news on your phone, why buy a paper? It was the kind of news you couldn't get on your phone that local papers had to deliver, the double-yellow-line story and the supermarket protests and cuts in local services. But a mystery was good. And a murder or two never hurt the circulation figures. No one cared about dead junkies, of course. After all, that was for the authorities to deal with. Warren pulled the keyboard towards her. But what if the authorities didn't care either? Now that might get a few readers exercised.

At Albany Road station, McLusky stopped just long enough to skim the accident and forensics report. It mentioned that a motorcycle track had been found, made after the accident. So someone else had come past, apart from the farmer. He'd read it properly later. For now he dropped the report on the growing pile on his desk.

It was forty minutes later when he let the Mazda crawl slowly along the lane where the BMW had crashed. There had been several opportunities to add his own car to the RTA statistics, since these narrow lanes had been neither cleared nor gritted. Apparently no one had foreseen the arrival of winter, which meant salt was in short supply and only main routes were being kept open. At the next cross-roads he turned right, skidded sideways, caught the car before it hit the bank and drove slowly on. He could make out Gooseford Farm on the far right, beyond what had to be the field he and Austin had walked across, though it took him a moment to get his bearings. The landscape here had changed beyond recognition. Details were lost under the snow, colour had vanished, contours were eliminated, landmarks buried. There were no animals to be seen.

At the turn-off to the farm, he slowed and stopped. The track was covered in compacted snow, deeply grooved by tractor tyres. He switched off the engine. The last bit he would walk, not wanting to push his luck. Perhaps this way he'd be able to approach the farm without giving advance warning of his visit. Then he remembered what he was wearing; he'd stand out crow-black against the brilliance of the snow. Not that it mattered. Surprise was not the important thing here, but persistent nuisance was. He walked beside the tractor tracks, taking pleasure in crunching down on untouched snow. Nothing else brought back childhood memories so readily as the creaking of virgin snow underfoot. When he reached the farm gate, he briefly stopped and reminded himself that the farmer might now be in possession of a Beretta 9mm. But then most farmers had shotguns anyway. Both the Volvo estate and the Land Rover were in the yard, and he could see the back of the tractor sheltered in one of the large sheds. It proved that a tractor could easily cost as much as a Land Rover and was worth giving preferential treatment to, since much of the farm depended on it. There was no sign of the dog, but the barking started as soon as he knocked on the door of the farmhouse.

It was Mrs Murry who opened the door to him. She looked unsurprised, even unmoved. She showed no sign of recognition, so McLusky held up his warrant card. 'Is your husband in, Mrs Murry?'

'Yes, he is.'

'Could I speak to him?'

'Is it about the car crash again?'

He ignored the question. 'I won't take up much of his time.'

Mrs Murry left him standing, leaving the door half-open. He strained to hear what was being said inside, but couldn't distinguish any words.

When the farmer appeared, he stood solidly composed in the door. 'More questions?' he asked.

McLusky pretended to leaf through his notebook. 'Yes, just a couple of things that seem to be missing in my notes. Did you tell us what time you discovered the wreck?'

'A lot of questions about this accident, I must say.'

'A man died. We like to be as thorough as we can. What time was it?'

'About seven.'

McLusky paused, as though thinking about it. 'Right, seven. It would of course have been quite dark, that time in the morning.'

'That's right. I was riding the quad bike.'

'Along the lane …'

'In the lower field, I told you that. I wasn't in the actual lane.'

'Quite foggy, too, that morning, I imagine. Out here. What were you doing in the field? Sorry if I asked you this before; I can't seem to find any notes to that effect.'

'Moving the sheep. To a place where there's more shelter. I knew snow was coming.'

'O … kay.' McLusky pretended to scribble furiously in his notebook with a dried-up biro. 'I knew … snow … was … coming.' He delivered the full stop with a satisfying punch, looked up at Murry and smiled. And smiled. And smiled. The farmer broke eye contact and looked past him, squinting at the snow.

McLusky snapped his notebook shut. 'Thank you, Mr Murry. That's all I need for now.'

'You came out here for that?'

McLusky nodded as he walked away. 'Oh yes.'

Murry shut the door, and from behind a net-curtained window watched the inspector as he walked down the track, pausing every so often to look around him and take pictures on his mobile phone. 'I don't like it,' he said when his wife joined him silently by the window.

✳

105

McLusky turned the car around with difficulty. At least it had stopped snowing, and visibility was good. He was tempted to stop at the crash site, not because he thought he might find something all other investigators had missed, but because he found it easier to think out in the field, in the places where whatever he was investigating had happened; sitting in his office, he often felt as though he was working with a blindfold. But when he passed the site again, the temptation faded; it was covered so deeply in snow, he'd have found it difficult to identify the spot had it not been for the lonesome tree. Continuing on at ten and fifteen miles an hour, depending on the state of the road, he had time to take in the transformed landscape. On the left, Gooseford Farm had sunk out of sight. No more buildings were visible now, and only fences gave an indication that he was looking at a landscape inhabited by humans. Not quite, though, he now saw. Five hundred yards to his right, following the crest of gently rising fields, stood a patch of woodland, stretching for a quarter of a mile or so in the direction he was travelling. From his vantage point on the road, there was no way of telling how deep this stretch of trees ran. He saw no roofs or buildings, but he knew there was human life. From just inside the dense thicket of trees rose a pale column of smoke. It was a timeless view, if he disregarded the fact that it was framed by a car windscreen. He slowed even further and rolled down the window just as he passed a narrow track leading in the general direction of the woodland. He could smell the wood smoke on the clean winter air, and as he reached a passing place in the road he let the car come to a stop. He locked it and walked back to the track.

The snow-covered field and trees and the clearly defined smells around him had a quality that reminded McLusky of the snow-capped-mountain scenes on the walls of the Indian fast-food place by the arches; there was the same serenity and uncontaminated emptiness, except that this emptiness also had the possibility of warmth in it. He took a doubtful look back at his car, then set off along the track; wasn't it amazing what a warm jacket and winter boots could do? The going was easier than he had expected. A small tractor had come through here, judging by the tyre tracks he was walking in. The smell of wood smoke came and went as he progressed along the gentle rise. He couldn't have said what had made him stop the car, even less what made him walk up the track or what he expected to find at the end of it. A tramp trying to stay alive in the woods? Perhaps it was a charcoal-burner, though he didn't think you could get charcoal in the winter.

As he neared the edge of the wood, another smell appeared on the air. It made him stop in his tracks and sniff doubtfully. You're imagining it again, Liam. He could smell freshly brewed coffee, one of his favourite olfactory hallucinations. Soon, regretfully, he lost the smell. Then he found it again, stronger than before, which meant he probably wasn't imagining it after all. He hadn't gone far beyond the fringe along the curving track between the trees when he saw where it came from.

It looked like a well-established camp. To the left of the track stood a large blue mobile home of the type that was mobile in name only. Red curtains were drawn at the windows. From the centre of the roof, a lum-hatted stovepipe protruded – the source of the wood smoke he had seen. A precariously rhomboid shed with a tree growing through its roughly thatched roof stood beside the mobile home. There were several snow covered piles of wood nearby, not the ordered piles that one might have had delivered, but unruly branches of varying thickness. A snow-free, recently used chopping block stood close by. There was a jumble of containers and oil drums. In front of the caravan, near the door, a simply made wooden bench and table had been cleared since the last snow fall. On the opposite side of the track a small tractor and trailer, both circa 1975, were partially covered with a frayed tarpaulin to keep off the worst of the weather. A hippy camp, by the looks of it, but a well-organized one, McLusky thought.

107

Without the faintest idea of what he was going to say to the denizens of the place, he knocked on the door. Not the flat-handed policeman's knock, but a polite, knuckle-of-forefinger one. A thick red curtain moved at a window to his left, and a moment later the door was opened.

'Yeah?' The man confronting him was not quite what McLusky had expected. Neither his clothes nor his style of hair were particularly hippyish, and the expected wave of marijuana, incense and cooking aromas was not forthcoming. All he could smell was coffee. The man filling the narrow door was in his late thirties, perhaps forty, dressed in black cargo pants, tough work boots and an old blue sweater peppered with sawdust. His quick green eyes took the measure of McLusky, then looked beyond him left and right. 'Walking?' he asked.

'I am now. I smelled your coffee from three hundred yards away.'

'I was roasting some. It always travels. Knock the snow off your boots before coming in,' he said, and turned back inside.

After kicking his boots against each other, McLusky followed him in, shutting out the cold behind him. After the dazzle of the snow, his eyes needed to adjust, since all but one of the four windows had their curtains drawn against the cold. He found himself in a large, old-fashioned caravan. Immediately beyond the entrance door was the kitchen, dining area, which, apart from the expected, also contained a wooden table and chairs and a cast-iron wood-burning stove that pulsed with heat. Through an arch in a partition he could see into a small bed-sitting room. Worked wood was much in evidence.

'How do you take it?'

'As it comes.'

'That's good, because that's how it usually comes. I'm Ben, by the way, though some people call me Fish.'

'I'm Liam. Some people call me Detective Inspector.'

'I see. Here.' He passed him a mug. 'Sit down if you want.'

'Why Fish?'

'Benjamin Alexander Fishlock.'

'Blimey.' He sipped coffee. 'You've been here a while. By the looks of it.'

'This is my fifth winter.'

'Then presumably the owners don't mind you camping here.'

Fishlock relaxed back into the chair opposite him. 'You really are just out walking, then. Detective Liam.'

'McLusky. What makes you say that?'

'If you'd come in order to see me, you'd know that I own these woods. And the fields to the east of them.' He inclined his head, indicating east.

'Ah, that's different then, my apologies.'

'Oh, it never stopped them from trying to evict me from my own land. I had a small wooden house before, back there, closer to the stream. For two years no one even knew it was there. Then they dragged me into court. No planning permission. I lost. They made me take it down. If you try and leave it all behind, they'll hate you for it. They'll come after you.'

'What was it you did leave behind? This is good coffee, by the way.'

'It is. I buy the beans raw and roast them myself. The way I want them. What did I leave behind? Nothing important. An IT career. I made a lot of money quite quickly. Remember the millennium bug? Complete nonsense, but we made a fortune; that's how it started. A couple of lucky investments... But I always knew that wasn't what I wanted. Then other things happened in my life and I sold up. First I bought the woods. Later the fields adjacent.'

'What do you do with them?'

'I'm a woodsman. Coppicing, charcoal-burning. I make hazel hurdles, things like that. And I grow field mushrooms. Some of the best restaurants in Bristol take my mushrooms. And I supply some hotels.'

'So you do make a living, then?'

109

'Not a luxurious one, that's for sure.'

McLusky rose and stood by the window. He looked out into the woods, savoured the silence. 'Oh, I don't know.'

'Yes, it depends how you define luxury.' There was a long pause during which McLusky was content to sip coffee and look into the woods, where nothing stirred. Then Fishlock spoke again. 'Okay, you're welcome to warm yourself by my fire, you're welcome to drink my coffee. But I find it hard to believe that that's what you came for if you're really a policeman.'

McLusky drained his coffee and set the mug into the sink. Then he produced his warrant card. 'A man died in a car crash not far from here.'

'Yes, I know. Rolled it. No seat belts, I heard.'

'How did you hear that?'

'On the radio, Inspector.'

'So you have electricity here?' He could see no electric appliances or lights.

'I make my own. Low-voltage, just enough to run a radio and power a laptop, charge my phone.' McLusky formed a silent 'oh' with his mouth. 'I said I was a woodsman, not a backwoodsman.'

'Point taken. Did you see the car wreck?'

'No, I didn't. I did hear a noise around that time, but didn't pay much attention. Too far away.'

'Did you hear a motorbike that morning?'

Fishlock raised his eyebrows. 'What kind of motorbike?'

For the first time a false note had crept into the conversation. It was the wrong answer to a simple enough question.

'Just a motorbike.'

Fishlock shook his head. 'Occasionally I can hear engine noise, on clear mornings when the wind comes from that direction.'

'But not that morning?'

Fishlock shook his head again and buried his nose in his mug, draining it. Again, a normal reaction, McLusky thought, would have been to ask what a motorbike had to

110

do with it and why a detective inspector was interested in a car crash. No details about the drugs or ammunition had found its way into the press.

'Well, thanks for your hospitality to a complete stranger.'

'You're welcome. Any time.'

'I might just take you up on that,' McLusky said as he stepped back into the snow outside, zipping up his jacket, digging his gloves from his pockets. Before pulling them on, he gave Fishlock his card. 'In case you ever feel like a chat. You don't ride a motorbike yourself, by any chance?' He looked about him, eyeing up the shed.

'It wouldn't be much use to me, would it?'

'Then how do you get around? Not on that, surely?' He nodded towards the tractor.

'Oh, I use that a lot. But I also have a car. It's not here, it broke down. I'm having it mended.'

'A green Volvo estate?'

Fishlock looked at him unblinkingly for a few seconds. 'You're trying to make me paranoid.'

McLusky strode off in the direction of the road. 'Bye for now.' But not for long, he thought. The things you found if you just followed your nose.

The incident room was busy. With two separate killings to deal with, the mood was tense and the usual banter had all but died out. They were stretched. While on paper the personnel situation looked adequate, in reality they were constantly working below strength, due to illness, injury and people being away on courses. Contrary to gold-braided expectation, the lower the rank of the missing officer, the more impact their absence had. A missing detective constable or two left a big hole, while no one complained much about Detective Chief Inspector Gaunt's hospital stay.

McLusky quizzed Dearlove about any witness statements on the still unidentified body, then went to the quiet of his office to think things over. Denkhaus would disapprove of him spending time on the crashed drug carrier now that they had two unsolved murders on the books, but the thought of putting it on ice made him uneasy. He had an image in his mind of Farmer Murry with a kilo or two of heroin and a Beretta powerful and heavy in his hand, planning an alternative form of farm subsidy. How likely was it?

He brewed tea with the aid of his illicit kettle and finished reading the forensic report. Apart from the confirmed presence of drugs, only one item attracted his attention. On the twisted metal of the rear door frame, tiny specks of twenty-four-carat gold were found. The report suggested that they had been transferred there from a heavy gold-plated item that hit the door frame during the accident. No such item had been found at the scene. McLusky was about to open the accident report when Austin knocked on his door, bringing the first witness reports of the cycle-path murder. McLusky dropped the accident report on a small pile of other papers already on the floor behind his desk.

'I had another chat with Farmer Murry,' he told Austin. 'He of the excellent night vision. Says he was moving sheep that morning. I wonder, do sheep have good night vision too? He didn't look happy when I left, so my journey wasn't wasted.'

'Should we search the farm for the drugs and gun?'

'You've seen the place. How are you going to find a kilo of smack and a gun somewhere that size? You might find the drugs with a dog, if you can get the dog near it, but a handgun? Hardly. Even so, we'd never get a warrant to search the place. And right now, with two bodies on the slab, we haven't even got the time. I just wanted to make sure he stayed nervous.' He shrugged in his roll-neck jumper and laid a hand on the nearest radiator. It was no more than lukewarm. 'I think the cutbacks have started. Oh yes, and on the way back I found another character I want to keep an eye on. A Mr Fishlock. Lives in a caravan in the woods nearby. Something about him doesn't smell right. Though his coffee does. Anyway ...'

'The post-mortem for the cycle-path body is later this afternoon. I suppose you want me to attend?' Austin said, with due emphasis on the *me*. McLusky stubbornly refused to go, even to accompany him. Austin had come to dread post-mortems and often had bleak dreams about them, before and after the event.

'Naturally. We have no ID for him yet; let's hope it won't come to dental records.' The Police National Computer had thrown up several vague matches for missing males in the age range, but any PNC check did that. There were always candidates for males of middle age, an age group that did more than its fair share of walkabouts, due to marital break-up, stress at work, unemployment, alcoholism or mental health problems.

'None of the names were from around here; most were London, Manchester, Glasgow.'

'DS Austin, I hate nameless bodies,' McLusky said accusingly.

'Yes, sir. Let's call him Bob.'

The phone on his desk rang. 'Let's not, Jane,' he said and picked up the receiver. It was Lynn Tiery. DSI Denkhaus wanted to see him in his office. 'Now?' he asked.

'This minute,' came the curt answer.

The superintendent's secretary barely acknowledged him. Some people said you could gauge the amount of trouble waiting for you by the arch of her eyebrows, but today they gave nothing away. 'Any idea why the super needs to see me?'

Her finger hovered over the intercom button. 'You haven't seen today's *Herald*?'

'I haven't had the pleasure yet.'

'I doubt you'll get much pleasure out of it.' She depressed the button. 'DI McLusky is here.'

Denkhaus was standing by the window, looking out over the mosaic of snow-covered roofs. He ignored McLusky's entrance. Since only two seconds earlier he had to have stood at his desk to press the intercom button, McLusky knew this to be a pose struck for his benefit. On the desk lay a copy of the *Bristol Herald*. He had no time to practise his upside-down reading skills on the headlines, because Denkhaus turned around and slammed a fleshy hand across the paper, then swivelled it around as though it was heavy as lead. *Police Unconcerned About Drug Deaths* ran the headline. When McLusky skimmed the long article and his name jumped out at him several times, he knew he was in trouble. 'After the last debacle when you shot your mouth off to a reporter, had I not made it absolutely clear that you were not to speak to the press again? No officer on my force is allowed to make statements to the press without prior authorization, and you'd be the last person I'd get to do it! Here …' Denkhaus sat down and picked up the paper. ' "I am not concerned about dead junkies," said DI Liam McLusky.' Did you say that?'

'Yes. No. No, I probably said something like "dead junkies aren't my department"; I never said I didn't *care* about junkies dying.'

'What you should have said was *no comment*! That's all you'll ever say to any reporter from now on.'

'I was giving Phil Warren a lift. It was a casual conversation …'

'Reporters don't have casual conversations.'

'I'm beginning to see that.' McLusky, who had not been invited to sit down, stuck his hands in his pockets and hunched his shoulders. It suddenly felt cold in this office.

'This article makes out that we, the police, are happy about junkies dying because each dead junkie means fewer muggings and burglaries. It is trying to suggest that we are dragging our feet about finding the source of the contaminated heroin because it helps clear the city of drug addicts. And you added weight to it by giving Warren a quotable sentence, however distorted. This on the day when we released a statement to warn drug-users about the anthrax contamination. The *Herald* barely gives that two lines! I will now have to arrange a personal appearance on the evening news to repeat that message.'

'Junkies don't watch telly; it's the first thing they flog.'

'It's not about the bloody addicts, it's about the public's perception that we as a force don't care about junkies dying.'

'And do we?'

Denkhaus took a deep breath. 'No one likes a smartass, DI McLusky.' McLusky was a good officer, but he spoke his mind rather too freely for a detective inspector. He was quite a successful detective, too, but his sense of commitment to the wider concerns of the force was woefully underdeveloped. He needed to learn that solving crime was just one of many responsibilities the police force was charged with. Denkhaus continued in a low, threatening rumble: 'You know as well as I do that our job is to serve the entire community, whatever we think of them. You should also have learnt by now that these days half of a superintendent's job is political. If you don't understand that, then personally I don't give tuppence for your chances of promotion.' There was a pause in which Denkhaus folded the newspaper and laid it aside. 'Admittedly you've run some successful investigations since coming here, but trouble seems to follow you around somehow.'

'It looks like Warren is deliberately trying to cause trouble, sir.'

'Trouble sells papers. But thankfully there's an easy solution for this kind of trouble. Under no circumstances are you *ever* to speak to Phil Warren again. Not once. You will give her a wide berth, and if she approaches you, all you will say to her is *no comment*. That is if you want to avoid disciplinary action. Understood?'

'Yes, sir.'

'Good. Go and find DS Austin and send him to me immediately. I think I'll need to have an urgent talk with him as well.'

McLusky checked his watch. 'He's due to attend the post-mortem of the cycle-path victim in a short while.'

'Too bad. Send someone else. That's all, DI McLusky.'

Chapter Eleven

'So now we got a double whammy,' said Sorbie as he followed DI Fairfield into the mortuary car park. The car park hadn't been cleared, and it was snowing again.

'Yes, we'll need to get out another press statement to warn them about this one,' said Fairfield, turning up the collar on her coat. 'For what it's worth. Oh, look who's paying a rare visit. That's McLusky's car, isn't it?'

'Hard to tell under all that snow. And it's got ice blooms on the windows. Doesn't that heap have any heating?'

McLusky turned the Mazda off the road but didn't fancy his chances of ever getting out again if he continued to the car park proper. He left the car by the entrance and was crunching through the snow towards the buildings when he spotted the reception committee. Eight months at Albany Road and he was only just on first-name terms with Fairfield. But not with her DS. McLusky suspected that even his mother called him Sorbie.

'Stop press. DI Liam McLusky at the mortuary,' Fairfield greeted him. 'Can't get the staff, is that it?'

'Hi, Kat.' McLusky checked his watch, then patted his jacket for cigarettes. 'More drugs deaths?'

She nodded. 'The seventh.'

He lit a cigarette and released a large cloud of smoke. 'No sign of the anthrax source?'

'None. But only four of them died of anthrax. Three were overdoses. There's another batch around, not the usual

117

brown stuff, it's white as the driven. And we've just been told,' she paused for effect, 'it's over eighty per cent pure.'

McLusky coughed with surprise. 'Marvellous.'

'I don't know why I'm telling you this. You don't care, by all accounts.' Fairfield semaphored with her eyebrows while Sorbie turned away to hide his grin.

'You read the article.'

'Did you actually say that?'

'Of course not.'

'Didn't sound like you. That's the second time Warren's dropped you in it. Whatever did you do to her?'

'I'll be sure to ask her next time I see her.' He flicked his half-smoked cigarette into the snow, where it fizzled out. 'Got to go.'

Fairfield watched him walk to the entrance. 'Perhaps it's what you didn't do to her,' she said quietly.

'What?' asked Sorbie, who had made a snowball and pretended to lob it after McLusky.

'Nothing, Jack. Give me the keys, I'll drive.'

He shrugged out of his coat. On Coulthart's side of the screen the temperature was kept relatively low, but the viewing suite was well heated and McLusky was grateful for it.

Coulthart beamed at him. 'What an unexpected pleasure, Detective Inspector McLusky. I had expected your faithful sergeant. He hasn't been taken ill, I trust?'

'Just unavoidably detained, that's all.'

'Is it still snowing outside?' Apart from the one giving on to the viewing suite, the autopsy room was windowless.

'Yes, but it's just flurries now.'

'Good, I don't relish the thought of getting snowed in and having to spend the night here.'

'Not scared of ghosts, are you, Doctor?'

Coulthart peered at him over the top of his glasses. 'Hardly. I'm afraid I'm not a believer in the survival of the soul.' He turned to the body on the table in front of him and without further ado made the first incision.

118

McLusky's eyes drifted elsewhere. 'Not the survival of the soul. But you do believe in a soul, then? A mortal one? What would be the point of having one of those?'

'Oh, plenty of use for a mortal soul, Inspector. Love, art, music ... good food, fine wines.' Coulthart prodded the dead man's liver with a gloved finger. 'You need a soul to appreciate them. Which is why I would like to get home tonight where I can sample some of these soulful delights. So let us get on.'

'Yes, let's.' McLusky knew nothing of Coulthart's personal life, but presumed that as a Home Office pathologist, fine wine, art and music would all be well within his price range. Love had been first on his list, so perhaps that too was waiting for him at home. Coulthart's commentary on the proceedings of the post-mortem saved McLusky from examining too closely what was waiting for *him* at home.

'Mm. Okay, we have an IC1 male, late fifties, perhaps older. Multiple traumas all over his body, concentrated on his face, the kidney area, genital area and abdomen. He was severely beaten. One of his knees was shattered, probably to keep him from running. Then someone laid into him. Ruptured spleen ...'

'Were his hands tied?'

'No.' He lifted both of them in turn and examined them closely. 'They show signs of defensive wounds where he tried to protect himself.' He gestured towards the row of X-rays on the wall-mounted computer screen. 'Several bones broken there, too. There was a faint footprint on his left hand, from a training shoe. It's now all but disappeared, but forensics have close-up images.'

'Good. We have a database of training-shoe tread patterns now.'

Coulthart sounded sceptical. 'But have you managed to convict anyone with it yet?'

'Yes, we have. The general pattern narrows it down to the brand, and once you have sufficient wear on the sole, it's as conclusive as tyre tracks.'

'Well I can tell you that our man here may of course have owned training shoes, but he didn't use them to do any training. He was in quite bad shape even before he was set upon. His liver is in a shocking state, and I am quite certain that when we get to his kidneys, the picture will be just as bleak.'

'Heavy drinker?'

'Well it wasn't his love of rich foods that got his liver into that state. His last meal was probably some sort of cereal. I believe he threw most of it up. Probably during the beating he received.'

'And the beating killed him?'

'Yes. Internal bleeding.'

'Was he drunk when he was killed?'

'On the contrary. He had no alcohol in his system at all.'

The next morning McLusky repeated a digest of the post-mortem findings to the detectives in the incident room. Photographs of the victim's face were pinned behind him on the board. Some displayed his injuries; one was a reconstruction effort by the technical department, an approximation of what the victim had looked like before his death. Copies of these had been handed out to detectives and uniform alike and circulated to all stations.

'His face was not a stranger to the pub, by all accounts. He was a heavy drinker, possibly a binge drinker. Somewhere a barman must miss him.'

'Not if he drank at home,' DC French objected. 'A lot of people can no longer afford to go to the pub.'

'Very true. Is it just me, or is it freezing in here?'

A chorus of officers confirmed that it was freezing. Someone suggested *bloody freezing*. 'The radiators are just lukewarm,' said Dearlove, who was sitting next to one in a vain effort to keep warm in his polyester suit.

'Maybe it's an airlock. They might need to be bled,' McLusky said. He tapped the photograph with the back of his hand. 'No wallet, no ID, no mobile, no jewellery. M&S trousers and a cheap black jacket. Man-made fibres. M&S

120

socks and underwear. No tattoos. One ancient scar on his thigh, three inches long. Right thigh. His hands were quite soft, so probably not a manual labourer. Apart from his enlarged liver, he looks like Mr Average.'

'Perhaps he was long-term unemployed,' French said.

'I'll leave the DSS enquiries to you, then. Anyone fitting our man's profile who has missed signing on or any other appointments, training courses, et cetera. Of course, if he was unemployed he may have signed on in the past few days. So no one will miss him there for a couple of weeks. Right, let's get to it.' McLusky dismissed his troops but waved DC French over. 'Claire, the shoplifter ...'

'Gareth Keep,' she reminded him. 'Report's on your desk.'

'Anything?'

'He did say one thing; it's in the transcript, about foreigners coming to Deeming's flat.'

'Foreigners. What nationality?'

'He wouldn't elaborate. Probably had no idea where they were from or he would have used the appropriate racist term. It was just a throwaway remark, but I got the feeling that he resented it, that he was made to leave when they arrived. But mainly it was *no comment* all the way, as you'll see.'

'Did he give a description?'

'Gareth only knows two adjectives. He couldn't describe a bowling ball if you dropped one on his foot.'

'We're not allowed to use bowling balls any more. Okay, ta.'

In his office, he picked up the interview transcript and began reading it, but soon got distracted by how cold he felt. The radiator behind him was barely even warm. He put on his new jacket and hunched his shoulders, hands in his pockets. He sat like that, staring at the papers without reading, eyes unfocused, for several minutes. Then he turned off his desk lamp and left his office.

The news was full of headline stories about the unusually early cold snap, pushing even murder from the top spot it usually enjoyed. Words like *arctic, blizzard* and *whiteout* were liberally sprinkled through reports by journalists who McLusky suspected had never seen snow before. Certainly a whole generation of southern English drivers who had seemingly never experienced it were advertising the fact by skidding into ditches or each other.

The main routes through the city were cleared now, with long piles of dirty slush refreezing in the gutters and the margins of the pavements. He found a parking space within sight of Wayne Deeming's house and sat for a moment, watching the quiet residential street. It looked a depressed, unloved neighbourhood. Snow-capped nests of uncollected rubbish bags sat outside nearly every house. Some of them had split or been ripped apart by scavengers, spilling their contents on to the pavement, where it got trodden into the snow.

Despite scene-of-crime having long finished with the house, the front door had a police notice stuck to it, warning unauthorized persons to keep out. The blue curtains were still drawn. McLusky let himself into the cramped hall. When he had first entered the house days ago, the interior had been warm; now the place was as cold and lifeless as its last occupant. It already had an unlived-in, empty smell, though the furniture and some of Deeming's personal effects were still here. He lit a cigarette, strictly against protocol, and went upstairs, where he pushed with his elbow at the half-open door of the main bedroom. There was mess every-where, much of it created by the SOCO team. The decor was strictly masculine; there were no ornaments at all, and the only adornment on the walls consisted of two posters for the same violent fantasy movie. Deeming's mother, who lived in Derby, where Deeming had been born, had been informed. She worked in a high-street baker's shop where she made steak and kidney pies and sandwiches for the lunchtime trade. She had entertained different hopes for her son, McLusky had little doubt. While the causes of crime were complex, drug addiction was naturally the simplest

122

route in. He took a last look around the room, and his eyes rested briefly on the gothic film posters. Wayne had not been an addict. In his case crime could easily have been a simple lack of imagination.

He couldn't have said what he was looking for in this house apart from some sort of handle on the man's death. A few drops of blood on carpet and wall, turned nearly black now and easily dismissed as dirt, were the only indicators that the occupant had left the house to face a cruel and violent death.

'Who did you mess with, Wayne?' he said quietly as he opened the front door to flick his spent cigarette into the snow. On the other side of the thigh-high wall that divided the tiny front gardens from each other, a young man looked up, startled. He had just produced a key to let himself into the neighbouring house. 'Hello,' McLusky said. 'You live there, yeah?'

The man looked to be in his early twenties, with a Mediterranean complexion. He wore a bobble hat, scarf, jacket and gloves and appeared to be suffering from a cold. His nasal answer confirmed it. 'Yes. Are you the police?'

McLusky recognized the accent as Spanish. He nodded and showed his ID.

The man looked at it without interest. 'We already had the police here. Nobody saw anything.' He inserted the key and unlocked the door.

McLusky swung his legs over the wall. 'So you made a statement? What's your name?'

Inside the house, a phone began to ring. 'Michael. Miguel. I was not here when the police came but I did not see anything also. I'll go and answer the phone now, sorry.'

McLusky reached over the man's head and pushed the door wider. 'Would you mind if I came in for a moment? Just one or two questions.' He could see the man was torn between arguing and wanting to answer the phone. The phone won and McLusky followed him inside. Miguel rushed to pick up the receiver on the wall in the hall. He talked earnestly in Spanish to the caller while keeping an eye on McLusky.

A student house. It looked neglected, the paint work faded, the floorboards worn. Years of wheeling bicycles through it had left its mark. McLusky sniffed. He recognized the smell instantly from his own student days; it smelled of overcrowding, two-in-one oil, bad cooking and, in this case, cannabis. The door to the front room was ajar. He slowly pushed it open and nodded his head towards it for Miguel's benefit. The Spaniard became more animated, as he had expected, so he quickly walked in. The cannabis smell was stronger here. Two short sofas and one armchair, none matching, were grouped around a coffee table buried under 'what's on?' magazines, crockery and ashtrays. Torn Rizla packets, roaches and spent joints identified it as the smoking room. He picked up an open packet of cigarette papers and fanned the air with it as Miguel came through the door.

'It has nothing to do with me. I don't smoke it. I swear it.'

'I'm not interested in dope smoking. I don't approve but I'm not interested. Mind you ...' He dropped the cigarette papers back on the table. 'I could always develop an interest if I felt people were being less than helpful. So ... You naturally don't smoke, but someone around here does. Would they have bought their weed from the chap next door, I wonder?'

'Maybe.' Miguel folded his arms across his chest and tried to look at ease, leaning against the door frame.

'But not for a while. Because Mr Weed next door hasn't been around for a few weeks now. So these other people who smoke the stuff must have a new supplier.'

'Probably.'

'And that man has a name?'

'No.'

'I can send someone round to ask you that again. Someone with a lot of time to spare.'

'It's just another student, I think. At college,' Miguel added.

'And does that student offer other drugs besides cannabis?'

'I don't think so.'

'Well, that's something. Did you notice a van in the street a few weeks back? A van that doesn't belong to anyone around here? Double-parked, maybe?'

He shrugged, widened his eyes. 'A few *weeks* back?'

'What do you study, Miguel?'

'Tourism.'

'Nice job if you can get it.' The next question proved more difficult, considering Miguel's nationality. Had he seen any foreigners coming and going next door? 'Non-British people, I mean.'

'What, people like me?'

'If you like.'

'You suspect non-British people have killed Wayne Deeming?'

'You remember his name.'

'It's in the news.'

McLusky nodded. 'Of course. What's your name, by the way?'

'*Mine?* Delrio.'

'Okay, Mr Delrio. Thanks for your valuable time. Bye for now.'

Outside, he checked his watch; there was still an hour of daylight left, albeit a thin, grey variety that promised more snow. After wiping the condensation from the inside of windscreen and side window, he inserted the key in the ignition. On the other side of the street, two teenagers were trying to start a clapped-out hatchback, draining the battery until the starter motor stopped turning over. He watched the driver thump the steering wheel in frustration. It reminded him that he still had no breakdown recovery for his own car. He turned the key and the engine sprang obediently to life.

Traffic was building up. It took him longer than expected to drive north to Leigh Woods. He left the Mazda on the road, took his torch from the glove box, tested its strength and set off down the by now familiar track on foot. The dark imprints of many feet ran over and alongside it, some human, some canine. Other tracks, too, were evident, from kids' sleds to what McLusky assumed were rabbits, birds and deer, meandering and crossing each other. The snow kept a jumbled record of all the visitors, ever more difficult to untangle. The light was failing fast. By the time he found himself surrounded by trees, snow had begun to fall again.

This was it. He flicked on the torch. One tree still sported a collar of twisted police tape, yet even without it McLusky believed he would have found the place where Deeming had been murdered. The ground was covered in snow now, uneven after so much excavation. He stood where he judged Deeming had stood, knowing he was about to die. He was gagged and unable to plead. He must have known he was in the woods but did not get a last glimpse of the world because it was night and he had a jute bag over his head. McLusky closed his eyes and stood still, facing the woods. Had Deeming been able to smell anything apart from his own blood pounding sharp as metal in his already broken nose? He kept his eyes closed and breathed in deeply, felt snow-flakes land on his face, felt his heart beating.

A small crackling noise made him open his eyes wide into the darkness. He turned to where he thought the noise had come from, waited a few seconds to listen. Another furtive noise, further to his left, closer now. He clicked on his torch and with its feeble beam probed the looming dark between the darker boles of trees; it illuminated nothing. He waited. The snuffling of falling snow was all he heard. With gloved hands he fumbled a cigarette from a pack and lit it with his small silver lighter. Its flame close to his face left him half blind for a moment during which he stood and smoked greedily. He felt precariously alive in a dead man's place.

When his eyes returned to normal, he walked back to his car. Someone had scraped half the snow from its roof, perhaps to fashion snowballs with. At the end of the road the brake lights of a dark van briefly flared, then disappeared. There was no one else to be seen. McLusky started the engine and revved it a few times, just for the noise of it.

Chapter Twelve

'He's sent us another one. Did you keep the first one, Phil?'

'Let's see it.' Warren unstuck the first sliver of photograph from where she had Blu-Tacked it to her monitor. 'And how do you know it's a *he* who's sending them? Scissor-work is quite a female thing.'

'What, like poisoning is a female method of murder, Miss Marple?' Ed handed over the narrow strip of photograph paper. 'Anyway, look at the handwriting. Definitely written by a bloke, that.'

'Is there another note, then?'

'No, it just says "Number two" on the back.'

'Ah.' Warren held the two pieces against each other, first on one side, then the other. 'They don't match up. They're not adjacent pieces. That's no use.' She squinted at the new piece. 'You haven't got your ...' When Ed produced his magnifying glass from a back pocket, she took it from him without comment. 'Have you had a look at it already? That's definitely a car wheel, isn't it? A posh one, by the looks of it. And that's the edge of another person. But where is that?'

'There's another edge of a tree. And I think the car's a Mercedes. From the look of the wheel. It's very grainy; I could be completely wrong.'

'It's possible. So why send us this?'

'It'll make sense later, that's what the man says.'

129

'Perhaps we should print it,' Warren mused. 'We could make it into a competition: first one to tell us what's in the picture gets a prize.'

'Not such a daft idea.'

'Maybe. Unless he loses interest and doesn't send the rest, then we'll look stupid. Let's wait until we have more of it.' Warren Blu-Tacked the pieces side-by-side to the edge of her monitor. 'Would you mind if I hung on to the magnifying glass for a bit?'

Ed crooked a forefinger at her. 'I certainly would. Go and get your own.'

'I need a refill, mind if I use your kettle again?'

'Go ahead, squeeze round.' He shuffled his chair forward to allow Austin and his mug access to the secret kettle in the bottom of his desk compartment. It was difficult, because the DS was wearing his overcoat. McLusky himself was clad in his new winter jacket, with his bright multicoloured scarf wound twice around his neck. The heating had failed completely the previous day, and since then the last residual heat had been sucked from the building by the night. McLusky thought he could hear the walls around him creak as the frost penetrated the fabric of the station. 'How's everyone coping out there?'

Austin snorted. 'Everyone isn't. Half the station have found urgent business elsewhere. Those who can't afford to run away spend most of their time in the canteen. It's the only place in here that doesn't feel sub-zero. Look.' He rounded his lips and blew. 'I can see my breath.'

'What are they doing about it?'

'The heating engineers have been down there for a couple of hours. I don't think they know what's wrong.'

'Marvellous.'

'Custody are busy evacuating prisoners to warmer climes, like Trinity Road. They're threatening to sue over the conditions they were held in.'

'I might join them. I tried typing with my gloves on, but it can't be done. Have the posters gone out?'

'First thing. And it'll be on all the local news, the BBC Bristol website, the *Herald* is printing the picture and it's on our own website as well. Someone must recognize him.'

'That's if the techies got the face right.' The face of the cycle-path body had been too savagely beaten to be photographed. The photographs that technical support produced in cases like this were based on autopsy pictures, experience and guesswork. Sometimes they got close; sometimes they got nowhere near.

'We've had a couple of responses already; both were duds.'

Appeals to the public invariably produced a flurry of responses, some from cranks but many from well-meaning citizens. Most turned out to be false leads, but all had to be followed up. It was frustrating and time-consuming, yet sometimes it yielded results, often weeks or months after the appeal had gone out. Weeks or months, however, was not what DSI Denkhaus expected.

'It's early days. You have to live a very sad life if no one misses you at all, even if it's only your ... I don't know, chiropodist or someone like that.'

'We used to rely on people spotting the milk not being taken inside, but who gets his milk delivered now?'

McLusky spent another hour fighting the urge to set fire to his desk in a bid to keep warm, before he went downstairs to the canteen for a hot meal. The place was busy with refugees from the frozen offices above. As he contemplated his steam ing plate of wrinkly sausage, beans and mash, he idly wondered whether the wrinkliness was inherent in the sausage or a special cooking method passed down through generations of dinner ladies. He was distracted from this train of thought when he spotted the superintendent on the wrong side of the food counter. The heat lamps obscured the view, but he distinctly saw Denkhaus handing over a briefcase to one of the female staff before disappearing again. McLusky had no time to spin a delicious story of stewed steak and blackmail, because DC Dearlove appeared by his side.

'Sir? Sorry to interrupt your meal. DS Austin thinks we have something solid on the ID of the cycle-path body.'

McLusky didn't feel like having Dearlove as an audience to a display of speed-eating so he sent him on his way. 'I'll be up in a minute.'

The sausages were curiously unresisting to his fork as he hacked them into pieces and mixed them with his mash and beans. Then he spent a concentrated two minutes shovelling the resultant mess into his mouth. When he pushed his plate away from him, he realized that a few tables away PC Ellen Purkis was watching him with fascinated disgust. She looked away now and returned to a conversation with her colleagues.

Upstairs he found Austin on the phone in the incident room. The DS wound up the phone call and hung up. 'Result, I think.' He consulted a sheet of handwritten notes. 'Our cycle-path bod could be a Mike Oatley. His social worker called in, thinks something might have happened to him. No answer at his flat; they had arranged to meet. And he fits the description.'

'Where?'

'Block of council flats in St Pauls.'

'Okay, get on to the council.' McLusky paused to burp delicately behind a hand. 'Tell them to send someone there with a key for the flat, and when you know what time they can make it, ask the social worker to meet us there as well. Tell them not to enter the premises until we get there.'

An hour later, a dull stomach ache kept McLusky internally occupied while he and Austin waited outside the address for the social worker and key-holder. Both arrived simultaneously in separate cars. Hedges, the social worker, a neat individual with a sensible haircut, repeated his story for them as they climbed the echoing stairs to the first-floor flat. 'His name is Mike Oatley. He's an alcoholic, recovering alcoholic, I should say, of course. He's recently come out of a double helping of residential rehab and was housed here. He's from Gloucester really, but it would have been a bad idea for him to go back there. His only friends, if you could call them that, were in a similar situation, you might say, heavy drinkers. So they housed him here. Not an ideal area, but there you go.'

They had arrived at the door to the flat; its colour matched the pale-green PVC handrail of the banister. The man from the council found the right key from a collection of others in a bag. McLusky took it from him, rang the bell below the spyhole, then rapped a flat-handed tattoo for good measure. Only then did he slip on latex gloves and unlock the door. The council man left and Hedges waited outside as instructed while McLusky and Austin entered. The lights were on in the hall and the next room.

Hedges stood in the doorway, twiddled the buttons of his overcoat and kept talking. 'It was the lights, you see. He was very careful about electricity, always complained about the price and how he kept running out of credits on the key meter. So when I saw the light on and got no answer, I thought, wait a minute, something's wrong here.'

The flat was empty. It was also small, the rooms narrow and ill-proportioned. The two detectives constantly needed to squeeze past each other. 'Whoever designed this building must have practised on multi-storey car parks,' McLusky grumbled. To Hedges he called: 'Okay, you can come in, but don't touch anything; keep your hands in your pockets. You're sure from the picture in the news that the dead man is Mike Oatley?'

'Pretty sure, yes. And the clothes, too. The description matched the way he dressed, the black jacket.'

'Good. I'd like you to come and identify the body. Would you mind?'

Hedges swallowed hard. 'If it's necessary.'

'It would be a great help. Are there any relatives?'

'A sister, in London. But they weren't speaking.'

'Close friends? *Any* friends?'

'He never mentioned any. He only moved here three months ago.'

'In that case we definitely need you to view the body. In the meantime, have a look around you. Does anything look different from the last time you were here?'

Hedges turned a hundred and eighty degrees in the sitting room. He pointed to a scatter of papers in front of a rickety shelf unit. 'It's definitely messier. He never had things lying on the floor like that when I was here. It all looks a bit … don't know.' He searched for the right expression. 'Out of kilter,' he decided with a nod.

'Perhaps he used to clear up for you,' McLusky suggested. 'Anything obviously missing?'

'Nothing jumps out.'

'Computer? Did he have one?'

'I don't remember a computer.'

'What about a telly? Hi-fi, radio?'

'Oh yeah, the radio isn't here. He had a digital one by the window, only place he could get reception. We got that for him through a charity, refurbished. I don't think he had a telly.'

'Kettle? Would he have had an electric kettle? Because there isn't one here. Or a toaster?'

Hedges came to the kitchen door. 'Definitely a kettle. Not sure about toaster.'

McLusky opened cupboards at random. They all looked understocked to him: a tin of tomatoes, a half-empty pack of spaghetti, a crumpled pack of sugar. It reminded him of his own kitchen. 'Well, neither are here now. Could he have sold them to buy drink?'

'A plastic kettle? Anyway, he wasn't drinking.'

'As far as you know. Okay, thanks. DS Austin will drive you to view the body, or you can follow him in your own car. Best do it now.' He followed them to the door. 'One other thing: did he drive?'

'Lost his licence. That's how he lost his job, too. He used to work for an interior designer, decorating and such. He was about to get fired anyway because he drank, but without a licence he was unemployable.'

134

'He could have been driving without a licence, of course.'

'Could have done, but he wasn't like that. Okay, *as far as I know*, you're about to say. Anyway, you can't run a car on Jobseeker's Allowance. I can barely afford it on my pay.'

As Austin and Hedges walked down the stairs, talking, McLusky closed the door behind them. Their echoing footsteps and voices came clearly through the flimsy door. In the bathroom, he pulled the grimy cord that hung from the light switch in the ceiling. The claustrophobic shower smelled mouldy; the basin and toilet looked unnaturally small. One splayed toothbrush, supermarket basics toothpaste, a cracked sliver of soap. He took a last look around the rest of the flat. Through the ceiling came the thump of running feet, the muffled shouts of argument; from downstairs the slamming of a door, a child's whine. It was as though the place had been designed to drive a man to drink.

When he locked the door of the flat from the outside a black girl in her teens was bumping an empty pushchair up the stairs. He made no attempt to speak to her. She in turn watched him without expression as she disappeared through the door of the flat opposite Oatley's. It could wait. As soon as there was positive ID, he'd give the word and the police circus would descend on the building, from officers doing door-to-door enquiries to SOCO and forensics.

His stomach ache had disappeared without him noticing. There would be ample time to warm up at a café before Austin came back with the result. His own flat in Northampton Street wasn't too far away, but the Bristolian café in Picton Street was even closer. In summer, its cobbled forecourt was full of tables and benches, but now it was covered in snow. The windows in their bright green frames were steamed up, promising warmth, or at the least, steam. He left the car directly outside on double yellow lines, knowing he could keep an eye on it in case a traffic warden took an interest. He ordered a mug of coffee at the counter and compensated for the enforced tobacco abstinence with a doorstep slice of chocolate cake. The place was busy; he would have to share a table. He approached a couple sitting at a round table next to the window. By the time he realized that the woman was Laura, it was too late to back away unnoticed. The man by her side, he saw with dismay, was the same mop-haired twenty-something he had seen her with the other day.

Laura's smile came slowly, from somewhere far away. 'Hi, Liam. I was wondering if you ever came in here, since you practically live round the corner.' She leant back in her chair to clear a line of sight between the two men. 'Liam, Damian, Damian, Liam.'

Damian lifted a hand in greeting. 'Pleased to meet you.'

McLusky nodded at him. 'Mind if I join you?'

Laura gestured to an empty chair and picked up her shoulder bag from the floor. 'Sit down. Actually we were just leaving.'

Damian looked into his mug of frothy coffee; it was half full. '*Okay.* I'll just go and use the little boys' room.'

McLusky shuffled through to the free chair, dribbling coffee from his mug on to the absurdly cheerful tablecloth. '*The little boys' room?* Who's the kid?' he asked when Damian was nearly out of earshot.

'And it's good to see you too, Liam. I'm well, thank you. The course is great, I'm really enjoying it, thank you for asking.'

'That's good.' McLusky skewered a piece of chocolate cake. 'So who's the kid?'

'The kid, as you heard, is Damian. He's in my year at college, but we met before that, when I volunteered on a dig in the summer.'

'You *met*.'

'We did. And now we sometimes have coffee together.'

'Marvellous.'

'They're keeping you busy, I see. And you got into the *Herald*. Uncaring inspector says let junkies rot, or something to that effect. Is that what you think now?'

'Does it sound like me?'

'People change.'

'Do they? Not much, they don't.'

'Oh, you'd be surprised. But I get the feeling you haven't.'

'You talk as though we hadn't seen each other in years.'

'Seems like it, so much has happened since.'

'We must catch up.'

'Yes, we must. Here comes Damian, time we went back. I've got a tutorial later.'

'I've no idea where you live.'

'No.'

'Are you going to tell me?'

Damian arrived at the table and drained his mug of coffee standing up.

'I'll give you my mobile number,' Laura said, spooling through the display on her phone. 'If I can find it. Oh yeah ...' She waited while he added the number to the list on his phone.

'Hang on, let me try it, see if I got it right.' He dialled, while Laura sighed and smiled apologetically at her companion. Her phone chimed the beginning of a pop song McLusky didn't recognize. Kids' stuff.

'I'll call you sometime, then.'

'Sure.'

He cleared a patch of condensation on the window and watched them walk away, looking for any signs that might point beyond coffee drinking. They turned the corner, Laura talking. Thin, washing-powder snow had started to fall. The traffic warden had finished the paperwork and snapped the plastic-sheathed parking fine under the Mazda's windscreen wiper.

The social worker had made a positive ID. 'Michael Oatley, age fifty-six, born in Gloucester, murdered in Bristol,' Austin recited as they stood outside the St Pauls flat, letting SOCOs and their equipment pass.

McLusky listened to uniformed officers talking to the few residents who had opened their doors. Most needed very persistent knocking and the promise that the enquiry was about a neighbour before they decided it was safe to answer. For many people the St Pauls riots had moved from memory into folklore, but the relationship between residents and the police had never recovered.

'According to the social worker, he was lucky to get this place. He said, with his addiction and without any friends, he was one drink away from a cardboard box,' said one resident. 'The state his liver was in, he was a couple of drinks away from a wooden one. Now it looks like he won't even get that.'

'How do you mean?' Austin asked.

'A pauper's funeral for Mr Oatley, unless the sister he's not on speaking terms with feels like shelling out.'

'Then perhaps it's a cardboard box after all.'

They followed a SOCO into the flat but stayed in the hall. McLusky went rhetorical, as Austin called it. 'Okay, what have we got? A recovering alcoholic, friendless, new in town, in a soulless council place. He's got nothing to do except listen to the radio all day. He's on the dole. He's piss-poor. And it certainly wasn't a mugging. What they did to him was systematic, it took time. They didn't do it on the cycle path; they just found it convenient to dump him there. And they didn't do it here either, unless they did a blinding clean-up job.'

'Inspector?' A paper-suited SOCO appeared at the kitchen door. From his extended forefinger dangled a set of house keys. 'In the pedal bin with the rubbish.'

'On the top, in the middle, where?' McLusky wanted to know.

'Right on top, first thing I saw,' he said triumphantly. 'Two Yale keys. Could be front door and flat key.'

'Okay, eagle-eyes. Do you think you can try them on the door without damaging any fingerprints on it?'

'I think I can manage that. Excuse me.' He squeezed past them. The first key he tried fitted. He dropped them into an evidence bag.

'So, he didn't have any keys on him when he was found. They could of course be his spare set, but I doubt it. Because why throw them away?'

'Whoever killed him used the keys to let himself in here.' Austin continued the thought. 'In order to do what?'

'To steal a second-hand radio and a plastic kettle. People get murdered for less, but it's not really worth the bus fare from Ashton to St Pauls, is it? His social worker thought the place looked "out of kilter". Perhaps someone did search the place.'

'But what's an unemployed recovering alkie got? That he needs killing for? And they didn't exactly turn the place over, did they?' Austin objected.

McLusky shrugged. 'Because they found what they were looking for straight away.' He stepped outside on to the landing and shook a cigarette from a pack of twenty. The place was so cold, he keenly felt the heat from the lighter's flame as he touched it to the end of his cigarette. The last time he'd felt warm was at the Bristolian, and he sincerely hoped they had managed to restore heat to Albany Road by now, since his own flat was not exactly tropical either.

First the legs, then the rest of DC Dearlove appeared on the stairs from above. He checked back over his shoulder before speaking in a low voice. 'I've just been in the flat upstairs, the one right above Oatley's. Young couple, but only the chap is in. She's at her mother's. Place is a tip. Anyway, he says he didn't hear or see anything. Only, did you mention a digital radio missing?'

'Yes, but we don't know which make. He's got one, has he? Did you ask him about it?'

'No. Lots of people have digital radios these days, but I got a feeling. I don't know why, but he just didn't seem the type.'

'Not the digital type, eh? We'd best have a casual word with him, then.' McLusky took a last drag from his cigarette, thumbed the glow off the end and put the filter stub in his pocket. In answer to Austin's raised eyebrows, he hooked a

139

thumb at the forensics technicians in the flat. 'Never leave your DNA around when that lot are about. You can't trust 'em.'

Upstairs, he rapped on the door. After a long pause it reluctantly opened on the face of a black man in his mid-twenties, with close-cropped hair. He wore black jeans, black trainers and a shapeless blue and grey top. Behind him rushed the sound of a cistern refilling. Warm air streamed through the gap in the door. 'Yeah, what is it now?'

McLusky held up his ID. 'Can we come in a minute?'

'Look, man, I just chatted with the other guy. I told him I didn't see a thing, didn't hear a thing.'

'I won't take up much of your time,' McLusky insisted.

'Oh, man, I was on my way out, innit. I have stuff to do, I can't stop here all day chattin', you know what I'm sayin'?' Even while he was speaking he retreated back inside, leaving the door undefended. They followed him in.

'We'll be quick. What's your name?'

'Milton.'

'That's your first name?'

'Yeah. Milton Christiani.'

The flat was an exact copy of Oatley's below, though only as far as the layout went. Unlike Oatley's, it was crammed with furniture, all of which looked too large to have made it through the narrow doors. It was messy and smelled aggressively of cooking-spice and deodorant. The sitting room was dominated by a large hi-fi system on a set of shelves crammed with CDs.

'So,' McLusky started, 'were you friendly with Mr Oatley?'

'I just said all that to the other copper; what's the matter with you? I didn't even know his name was Oatley.'

'You're into rap, then? Hip-hop …' He slid a few CDs off the shelf, pretended to read the backs of them, wasted some time.

'Yeah, what, it's not a crime, is it? What do you want from me?'

140

'So you wouldn't have any reason to have visited his flat, then?'

'No.'

'And you never have.'

'No again.'

'And he wouldn't come upstairs to this place?'

'Look, how many times, I didn't know that man. I mean, I'm sorry he's dead and all that, but that's it.'

'Your girlfriend, perhaps?'

'What is it you is sayin'? Look, he was an ancient white man and we had nothin' to do with him.'

The chunky digital radio Dearlove had mentioned stood between two piles of CDs on a shelf above the CD player. 'Listen to the radio much?'

'Some.'

McLusky pressed the on button. Radio Bristol blared into the room. He turned it down. Then he pressed the first of the pre-set buttons. The Radio 3 lunchtime concert had just started. 'Shostakovich, I think. Or is it Prokofiev? I'm never quite certain.' He tapped a fingernail against the speaker grille. 'I bought one of these but I've never worked out how to programme these pre-set buttons.' He tried the next pre-set; it was Classic FM. 'Ah, I'm sure we all recognize this one,' said McLusky, who had no idea what he was hearing. He tried for an angelic smile and pressed the next button, which conjured up Radio 4. '... talks to the author Simon Brett about his ubiquitous ...' He flicked off the radio and turned to Austin. 'Mr Christiani here has catholic tastes.'

'So what? You sayin' I shouldn't be listenin' to that stuff?' Christiani crossed his arms. His eyes strayed to the window, as though looking for escape.

'Had the radio long?'

'I don't remember.'

'Do you think we could borrow it?' Christiani opened his mouth to protest, but McLusky carried on. 'Because if you never visited him, and Mr Oatley didn't visit you up here, then naturally there wouldn't be any of his fingerprints on

141

this radio, would there?' He could see Christiani's mind racing and his body stiffen. He nodded to Austin, who put on gloves and freed the radio from a spaghetti junction of cables. 'And of course there wouldn't be any of your finger-prints in the flat downstairs, either. So I'll also send someone up to take your prints, just for elimination purposes. When do you expect your girlfriend back?'

Christiani held up his hands. 'Okay. *All right*. I took the damn radio. It's hardly the crime of the century.'

'The century is still young. We can discuss it down the station.'

'And he's known to us?' DSI Denkhaus swivelled in his chair to move his feet closer to the halogen heater by his desk. The heating engineers were still no closer to finding the cause of the problem. Denkhaus had bought the heater from an electrical shop across the road and smuggled it in discreetly. He had called headquarters about the heating problem at the station and been told categorically that bring-ing in electric heaters for everyone would be out of the question; the forty-year-old wiring simply would not stand it. And after all, how long could the repairs take? With the heater tuned to its highest setting, the temperature in the spacious office was only just tolerable.

Little enough of it percolated as far as McLusky's chair. 'Only petty stuff. Traffic picked him up a while back, no MOT, and a roadside cannabis warning. He's on the dole but had a job in a nightclub until recently.'

'So how did he get hold of the dead man's radio?'

'It seems Mr Christiani is an opportunist thief. According to him, he saw the door to Oatley's flat ajar when he went out to the shops in Ashley Road. This was yesterday. But he met someone so didn't get back until over an hour later. Then he found the door open even further and got curious. He went in – out of concern for Mr Oatley's welfare, accord-ing to his solicitor – and couldn't resist stealing the radio, he says. But he didn't take anything else. He didn't steal the

142

kettle or the toaster. It looks like he wasn't the only one going through Oatley's flat.'

'Presumably we're looking for a DNA match to link him to Oatley's death?'

'Of course, though I wouldn't hold my breath. We're taking DNA samples from all his neighbours. No sign of anyone having a surplus kettle, but they may of course have chucked their old one, so that's a dead end, I think. I don't see any connections yet. We know Oatley wasn't killed at his flat, and I suspect more than one person was involved. He wasn't killed for his kettle and his radio.'

'So you're letting this chap go? Seems a shame.'

'Already have done, sir. We've charged him with the theft, but he's co-operating and we've nothing else on him.'

'Yes. But having someone in custody would have given us a breathing space with the press, even if we have to let him go eventually. After your disastrous gaffe with the *Herald* reporter, it would have been something, at least. So what kind of person *are* we looking for?' Denkhaus demanded to know.

Outside, snow was falling again and so was the temperature. Back in his frozen office, McLusky contemplated that same question with his hands cradling his umpteenth mug of tea, made purely for the warmth it provided. The problem was that Oatley's existence appeared to have no real substance. There was no computer and no internet service provider. He also had no mobile phone or landline. There were no phone records to check, no emails to read or browsing history to examine. They had found no personal letters, nothing that didn't come from the benefits agency or the council. None of his neighbours owned up to knowing him, no friends had come forward. Oatley had made himself small, simply surviving. In the end he hadn't managed even that.

He knew it couldn't be a mugging. He had seen the photographs, read the autopsy report, and the conclusion was

143

obvious: someone had taken his time murdering Mike Oatley. Someone who enjoyed his work, too.

Austin came in, looking glum.

'I saw the super,' McLusky told him. 'He'd rather we could have held on to Christiani to get the press off his back, but there you go. Oh yes, and about the heating, not to worry, everything is fine. He found himself an electric heater to sit next to, one of those bright orange swivelling ones. It makes him look quite demonic. And you look constipated. What is it?'

Austin nodded towards the side of the desk. 'Do you still have some of that single malt left?'

A few months ago, a flustered suspect had left behind a litre bottle of Glenmorangie. McLusky kept it in the bottom of his desk along with a couple of glasses on permanent loan from the canteen.

'A bit early for that, Jane?'

'It's not for me. It's for you. You'll need it.'

'Let me be the judge of that. Out with it.'

'The partial hand that led us to Deeming's body.'

'What about it?'

'It's not his hand. It's someone else's.'

'What? Whose?'

'No one knows.'

McLusky blinked a couple of times, then reached for the Glenmorangie.

Chapter Thirteen

He slammed the door of his car with greater force than necessary. The sound of it was followed by a weaker echo of Austin closing the door on his Nissan. Snow was falling lightly but steadily and had done so in Leigh Woods for hours.

Austin called across. 'Did you hear on the news this morning? It's the coldest weather and earliest snowfall this far south since—'

McLusky cut him off. 'Three out of ten, seven out of six, spare me statistics, Jane, whenever possible. I can't wrap my head round it and I always get the feeling I'm being lied to somehow. No offence. Let's just call it *bloody freezing*.'

'It's four below up here.'

'How do you know?'

'My car tells me.'

McLusky looked peevishly at the other vehicles already assembled in the winter landscape. Two police transport vans, patrol cars and several others. 'Your car? Perhaps your clever car can tell us how we're going to find a body up here under five inches of snow?'

'I know, it's mad.'

Yes, it was mad. McLusky had discussed it with DSI Denkhaus earlier. It was bad enough trying to find a live avalanche victim under fresh snow; there, you had something to work with. Resistance under the snow could be detected with rods, and new technologies were being developed all the time. But a frozen body in frozen ground would

145

feel to the prodding stick of a police officer much like the surrounding area. Hard. All depended on how much of it had been disturbed by animal activity. Naturally, not 'mad' but 'challenging' was the official line.

'We'll have to try, at least,' McLusky added. 'Or as Denkhaus put it more precisely, *be seen to try.*'

Ahead of them a sergeant was giving instructions and a pep talk to sixteen officers who would attempt a frozen fingertip search of the area most likely to contain the handless body. 'It's pure guesswork, of course,' the sergeant said, 'but it makes sense to start around the area where the hand was found. Then again, a fox could have carried his prize several hundred yards at a gallop, especially if he was being chased by a bloody dog.' The officers formed into one long line, starkly black and yellow against the snow. At a quiet command from the sergeant, they set off. Each carried a rod with which to probe the ground for anything unusual. To McLusky they looked like a platoon of blind men.

'At least it's not foggy any more,' he conceded.

'I do wish they'd twigged that the hand had a different owner earlier, before all this stuff came down.' Austin kicked with his heavy police boots at the snow. 'Much as I like the look of it. I've missed snow, you know, living down here in the south.'

'I'm happy for you. Pity we can't just wait until the stuff melts and the ground's no longer frozen. Makes no difference to Mr Hands, I'm sure.' But it couldn't be done. Especially not with part of a body found, foul play almost certain and without a suspect in custody. Every day they lost put more distance between the murder and its perpetrator, perhaps even literally.

Soon a flock of press photographers and reporters descended. 'Like carrion birds,' McLusky observed when the search team stopped for a rest. Everyone had long run out of hand jokes, especially after the sergeant warned them that DSI Denkhaus would personally slaughter anyone who let himself be photographed laughing while looking for a dead body. Officers were drinking tea and hot soup from flasks, eating sandwiches, or discreetly smoking behind trees, out of sight of the camera lenses trained on them. McLusky didn't join them, knowing that the presence of a CID officer would probably ruin their break, cramp their style. Instead he walked for a bit down the track until he could no longer hear any voices and there smoked a solitary cigarette, cupping the glowing end of it with his hands for the illusion of warmth it offered. The search had been postponed from yesterday until this morning, and they had been here for two hours now. His feet were numb, his ears so cold it hurt to touch them. The search team had managed to cover a large area already, now trampled by their heavy boots, a shambles compared with the untouched, snow-blanketed surroundings. Murder somehow managed to turn everything ugly, though to McLusky the scene before him also had its own special aesthetic: police officers, their liveried cars and uniforms, the purposefulness of it, the exclusivity of it, set apart from civilian life.

With the break over, the line was re-forming just as the dog handler arrived in his van. 'How do you expect the dog to find anything if you systematically trample all over the search area?' he asked the sergeant.

McLusky answered for him. 'You're right, and I raised it with our super. I was told there was no dog available and to start the search anyway in case we got a heavy snowfall. That could have been the end of searching for a while.'

'Well can you at least call them back now? There's no point me letting him out while there's a crowd of people staggering about.'

The sergeant took a deep belligerent breath. He did not appreciate having his line of officers described as a crowd of staggering people.

McLusky forestalled any exchange. 'Sergeant? Rest your men, let them run the engines, warm up in the vans.' When the sergeant had stomped off, he turned to the dog handler. 'Are we hoping for a miracle?'

147

'If the body is under that mess, then you are. But the dog'll love it. Harry hasn't seen snow before. He thinks it's great stuff.'

'Yeah? DS Austin thinks so too.'

Harry turned out to be a young German shepherd who was visibly excited at being out in the snow. McLusky watched with Austin from inside the Nissan as the handler let him run in what looked like confused patterns all over the area, holding him on a long retractable lead and calling out short commands from time to time.

McLusky squeaked his finger through the condensation on the passenger window. 'I'm not sure this is best use of manpower. Nineteen police officers sitting in cars watching one man and his dog.'

'And I'm not even sure I want him to find anything … oh, there we go.' The dog was indicating and its handler squatted down, scraping at the snow. He waved, and McLusky and Austin quit the shelter of the car and crunched across.

'Training shoe.' The handler pointed at part of a black and white trainer he had exposed.

'Anyone in it?' McLusky asked.

The handler gave him a look under raised eyebrows, then squeezed the shoe. 'No one at home.'

When it had been freed from the snow, it turned out to be one of a pair, tied together by the laces. Size four. 'A kid lost it. Nothing to do with Mr Hands,' McLusky decided. 'Carry on.'

Once more they closed the car doors against the cold. The two vans containing the dozen or so uniformed officers were steaming up with condensation and boredom and McLusky was wondering about how much daylight was left when the dog indicated again by digging excitedly, just to the right of the previously searched area. This time the handler moved the dog away and waited for them a few yards from the indicated site. 'I'd say that was your missing body. Or part of it. Arm, I think, clothed.'

'You stay here,' McLusky said, and keeping to the existing footprints approached the patch that the dog handler had cleared. Among the dirtied snow and earth he could make out a pale checked shirt with the bony outline of an elbow underneath, frozen solid. He brushed lightly at the surrounding snow, but uncovered nothing but mouldering leaves. 'Good work, Harry.' To Austin he said: 'You know what to do.' Then he turned and walked back in his own footprints.

'Another body, DI McLusky?' Warren popped up from behind a tree into his path.

He trudged around her and on towards the cluster of police vehicles. 'Get out of here, Warren, back into your pen with the rest of your lot.'

Warren was keeping pace with him. 'The morgue is filling up nicely this week. What with you coming up here to dig up bodies every so often, pensioners dying of hypothermia and junkies popping their clogs all over town.'

He walked on, ignoring her. *No comment* was what Denkhaus wanted him to say. He could think of a few sentences he would like to add to that, but swallowed them down.

He stopped by his car. 'Keep walking, Warren.'

She did. 'It's Phil,' she called back without turning around. 'How many *times*?'

'Can you tell yet whether he was killed at the same time as the first victim?' McLusky, standing under the tent next to the pathologist, stuck his hands deep into his pockets to keep them warm. He'd had to take his leather gloves off to put the latex ones on, and they did nothing to stop his fingers from going numb. An icy wind was blowing up here and the tent flapped and snapped. They watched two crime-scene technicians uncover the body with infinite care and patience. Time spent now would save time later. Or so they were constantly told.

'After such a cursory examination of the body, I'm inclined not to comment.' Coulthart looked up to see if the inspector felt like protesting, but McLusky seemed unmoved. 'It looks to me like he was killed more recently,' he conceded. 'Taking into account that the the ground hasn't frozen all that deep down yet, and this one was lying a good eight inches below the surface, I'd say he died around two weeks ago. Not someone you recognize?'

This time McLusky did react. 'His own mother wouldn't recognize him, and you know it, Doc.'

'At least this time his face hasn't been eaten away. But it took a hammering.' Half of the body had now been freed. It was clothed in a pale blue checked shirt and pale blue jeans; both were darkly stained with dirt and blood in many places. The wrists were again tied with thick wire in front of the body, and most of the hands, which had been closest to the surface, had been gnawed away. The face was almost black and the features distorted. The nose was flattened and burst. The eyes had disappeared under broken tissue. The mouth was half open, the shredded lips shrunken back from the gum tissue. All front teeth were either chipped or broken off completely.

'Okay then … After your *cursory* examination of the body, would you agree we might be looking for the same perpetrators?'

This brought forth a rare smile from Coulthart. 'I'd put money on it. Probably not my own money, but yes, I'd have to agree. It looks like the same type of wire was used, too. However, one or two immediate differences between this killing and the previous one I can point out right now. This man is obviously much older. In his fifties, I'd say. And this chap wasn't gagged.'

'He wasn't?' McLusky took a step to the door flap of the tent and lifted it. Snow was falling thinly but steadily. 'Not that you can see it now, but we're closer to the road and houses here than the other site was. If he was killed here and these injuries were inflicted without him being gagged, then someone would have heard him scream.'

'One would assume so,' Coulthart agreed. 'I didn't say he was killed here, of course.'

150

McLusky turned to the SOCOs, who were still gradually uncovering the body. 'Have a go at the other end. Show me his legs.'

The technicians shifted their attention without comment to the lower part of the body, uncovering the legs, which were not twisted, like those of the previous victim. McLusky squatted down to get a closer look. One foot was shod in a good-quality brown shoe; the other was shoeless, covered in a grey sock. The ankles were wound tightly with the same type of thick wire that secured the wrists.

'This one wasn't standing in a hole,' one of the technicians said.

McLusky looked at the SOCO, but didn't recognize him under all that protective gear. 'No. At least not here he wasn't. Okay, gentlemen,' he said, straightening up. 'I look forward to reading your reports. Preferably somewhere warm and cosy.'

Coulthart stood up too. 'Yes, I heard rumours that the heating at Albany Road station was less than adequate for this type of weather.'

'I couldn't have put it better myself. If you run out of space at the morgue, you can send the bodies straight to us. Albany Road is the biggest refrigerator in town. When's the autopsy?'

'Can't say yet, we're very busy. I shall send you my usual invitation.'

Outside, it looked as though a film director had decided to reshoot the body-discovered-in-the-woods scene, only this time with snow, which was coming down more heavily now. Generators were powering arc lights, set up against the approaching dark. Crows had appeared on a nearby tree, from where they watched the comings and goings. The officers of the original search team had nearly all been replaced by a fresh lot, and SOCOs and a forensics team had swelled the numbers at the locus. A photographer documented every move inside the tent, and as usual, a force cameraman with a shoulder-held HD camera filmed the entire operation.

A tea urn had made a welcome appearance, dispensing a virtually tasteless but nearly hot liquid from the back of a van. Austin stirred sugar and whitener into his polystyrene cup, then held it away from his body while he sneezed loud enough to startle a few crows into flight. He caught up with McLusky, who was standing near his car, a burning cigarette in his mouth, his hands buried deep in his jacket pockets. 'Are you thinking what I'm thinking?' Austin asked.

McLusky watched the crows return and settle on the same tree. 'I hope not, for your sake, Jane.'

Austin turned away to sneeze again, then went back to sipping his tea.

'Please don't tell me you're getting a cold. Go on, don't be mysterious, what *are* you thinking?'

'I was thinking, perhaps we shouldn't have sent the dog handler away so soon.'

McLusky held up his hands, catching thick snowflakes on his palms. 'I know. But another few hours of this and it all becomes academic. I'm with you. I'm glad it's snowing again. We've got all the bodies we can cope with.'

Right away it had felt like a mistake. A mistake to meet at the Nova Scotia for a start. Yet it had seemed natural when they had arranged the meeting. They'd often had a drink here when they'd first gone out together, and even after they got married, even though there were far more interesting pubs in town. In summer they'd take their drinks outside and sit by the moorings, look at the boats. Paul had entertained dreams of buying a boat one day, of going sailing on a grand journey, though taking a rented dinghy out on Chew Valley Lake was as far as he had got with it. She'd told him she got seasick, but it had made no difference to his dreams. That should probably have rung a warning bell straight away, but of course you don't start analysing until much later.

She watched him now as he queued at the bar to get another round of drinks. His clothes were suspiciously neat.

He'd never dressed like that after they got married; it was strictly courtship behaviour with him. Once he felt safely married, it had been jeans and favourite sweaters that looked like he'd already sailed around the world in them, and she'd soon given up nagging him about it. So this was courtship again. Not that she had learnt much about his new girlfriend yet; she was *great* and they *got on really well*, which was hardly an in-depth profile of someone you intended to spend the rest of your natural with. So far all Paul had done was reminisce about their own shared past, and like an idiot she had fallen right in with it.

'Cheers, Kats.' He put a fresh pint of lager in front of her and immediately launched into another episode of their life together. 'Do you remember when we took Ian down here and he met that drunk Canadian girl outside ...' It was difficult to recall their rows clearly now, with him so close in front of her, radiating goodwill and aftershave and looking no older at all, as fresh as the day she threw him out, in fact. His eyes were as green, his teeth as regular and white, his hair as thick and wavy as she had tried to forget. And he still made her laugh; it was one of his best features, the ability to be effortlessly funny, whether he was drunk or sober. She couldn't help giggling about his story now, even while the grown-up part of her, the one that didn't answer to Kats, chided her to *get it over with*. They stopped laughing and lifted their pints together. Paul's eyes sparkled with good humour and alcohol. He put down his glass, moved forward a little and let his hand rest close to hers on the table.

She withdrew her hand and leant back on her chair. 'So are you *engaged* to Carrie now?'

'Well, no, not officially. Not at all, really. After all, we're still married, Kats.'

'I'm aware of it. But you've set a date?'

The pub seemed unnaturally quiet, as though Paul had ordered silence for his next sentence to hit home. 'We don't have to go through with it, you know. We could give it another try, Kats. No, no, wait, I don't mean moving back

153

together. Not straight away, obviously, but we could try …
seeing each other? We could give it another go, couldn't
we?'

She picked up her pint and slowly drained it, her preferred way of counting to ten.

'Let me get you another one,' Paul offered.

'No. It's my round.'

She had to wait her turn at the bar, giving her time to calm
herself. It wasn't often you were offered the choice between
married life and divorce in between pints. Married life,
perhaps even children … The end of microwaved moussaka
for sure. 'Same again,' she said to the barman, relying on the
man's memory, since she had no idea what kind of beer
Paul was drinking at the moment. Did she really want to
find out? Was it possible to go back? How much future was
there in travelling backwards?

When she set the drinks down, Paul looked at her with a
soft, sincere smile, then opened his mouth to speak, but she
cut him off. 'Did you get me here under false pretences? All
that marrying Candy stuff?'

'Carrie. No. No, of course not. We did talk about getting
married.'

'On the phone you made it sound like it was imminent. I
thought perhaps you'd got her pregnant or something.'

'No. No, it's not like that.'

'What *is* it like? I'm mystified.' She also felt nervy and raw
and poured more drink on it.

'I simply had more time to think about us since I called
you. And seeing you again just made me realize how much
I miss being with you.'

'So you came here bearing divorce papers but after a
couple of pints and a chat decided it isn't Cathy you want,
it's me.'

'You make it sound like it's something that's just occurred
to me, but it isn't. I thought about it a lot.'

'Between girlfriends?'

Paul looked hurt. 'There's only been Carrie.'

154

'And you're prepared to dump her to give us a second chance?'

'I am. Yes, I would,' he said sincerely.

'And if I turn you down now, you're going to carry on as normal. It's always good to have a spare, I suppose. Give me those papers.'

Reluctantly he pulled the thick envelope from an inside pocket of his jacket and laid it in front of her.

She slid the papers out and flicked through. 'Sign at the bottom and initial the rest, right? I'm glad I thought of bringing my favourite pen.' She signed and with a flourish handed back the papers in their envelope. As she stood up and swung her jacket from the back of her chair, Paul got up too. 'No, you stay and finish your drink. Carrie is a lucky girl. Tell her I said so.'

Outside she zipped her jacket up and pulled tight her scarf. She took a deep sniff of the clean wintry air. Snow was falling thickly and audibly around her. The city sounds from across the water were muffled by it. Ice was beginning to form between the boats and snow was settling on it. The boats themselves sat motionless under thick white blankets, making her dream of spring. She needed to find a new pub. It was too early to go home. Far too early.

Chapter Fourteen

'No, it certainly is not *man flu*, Inspector. It's not any kind of
flu.'

McLusky had not yet met Eve, DS Austin's fiancée, so
could not match her firm telephone voice to anything but a
vague picture he had concocted in his mind, and which, for
Austin's sake, he hoped bore no resemblance to reality. Eve
worked at a primary school, and he decided she'd be a terrifying teacher. 'Well, if it's just a cold ...'

'Just a cold, Inspector? It's a *severe* cold and he's staying in
bed where he belongs. He'd only pass it on to you and other
colleagues, and you certainly wouldn't want that. Besides,
standing in the snow for hours on end and working in an
office without heating could soon turn a severe cold into
something much worse.'

'Okay, okay. Tell him to *get well soon*.' He returned the icy
receiver to its cradle and morosely worked his hands into
his jacket pockets. He had counted five 'certain lies' in their
short conversation and wished he could be that certain
about anything. The woman had a point, of course. The
third day without heating in the building had taken its toll.
Austin was not the only one to have called in sick; a lot of
the civilian staff had suddenly developed colds and flu, and
in CID the ranks had thinned too. How many of these were
genuine and how many had simply had enough of the
working conditions, he'd never know. It was rumoured that
the superintendent himself had made the journey into the

bowels of the station to offer an opinion about the lack of progress being made with the heating system. According to those working nearby, he had not minced his words, which could be heard as far as the front desk. As a result, there were now not one but two vans of heating engineers in the car park and the noise coming from below had doubled as a result.

Other mills were grinding just as slowly. The autopsy for the second Leigh Woods body still hadn't been done, and forensics took their time over everything, from examining DNA collected at Wayne Deeming's house and from the sites in Leigh Woods, to the new samples taken from Mike Oatley's flat in St Pauls. The recent snowfall was offered as an excuse for almost everything now, from delayed lab results to the dearth of hot chocolate in the vending machines.

The canteen was doing a roaring trade in soup, and McLusky went to stand in line for a polystyrene cupful for the second time this morning. Huge vats of it had been prepared and selections of mushroom, tomato or chicken were being doled out to shivering officers all day. As he made his selection, his eyes drifted to a female canteen worker standing at a table at the back of the kitchen. She closed a briefcase, then walked out of sight with it towards the door to the corridor. Being suspicious by nature, he quickly snapped a plastic lid on his mushroom soup and made for the exit. Taking the stairs two at a time, he caught up with the kitchen worker carrying the case.

'Is that for the superintendent? I'm just going to see him, I'll take care of it.' He held out his hand, and the girl, after a moment's hesitation, handed it over with an 'Oh, okay then, thanks.'

McLusky waited until she had disappeared towards the canteen before lifting the briefcase to his face as if listening for a ticking bomb. The case radiated gentle warmth against his cheek. Making sure first that no one else was near, he snapped it open. It contained a hot-water bottle with a Peter

Rabbit cover. He delivered it to the superintendent's secretary as casually as though the delivery of hot briefcases was an everyday police matter: 'The super's briefcase from the canteen.' Lynn Tiery, gently irradiated by a slightly smaller halogen heater than the one her boss enjoyed, accepted it in the same spirit.

Noisily slurping at the vaguely mushroomy gloop, sending unheeded drips of it into his keyboard, McLusky sifted through papers and clicked ill-temperedly through the items flagged up on his computer screen. The BMW in the hedge had once been a BMW on a drive, it said, not far away in Cheltenham, from where it had been stolen six months ago. It had been cloned with an identical model in London. Traffic police had long been looking for it, since the owner of the properly licensed car could prove she had not been driving recklessly around the West Country clocking up speeding fines and parking tickets. So Mr Whoever-he-was with his Beretta, heroin and strange traces of gold plate on the window frame really was as stupid as Austin had classified him. No doubt the man had thought of himself as a successful criminal, with his gun and his flash ripped-off motor. But clocking up speeding tickets and parking fines was as good a method as any for getting your car pulled over, whether cloned or not. It never failed to amaze McLusky how many career criminals got caught because they flagged up their criminality by not getting an MOT, or some other trivial driving offence. Sooner or later the BMW driver would have been stopped by the police. The question was: would he have pulled his Beretta on the officers doing it? And where was the damn thing now?

McLusky balanced the empty soup cup on the teetering mound of rubbish rising above the rim of his bin, then dived for a pile of files on the floor. Everything else was being held up by snow and sniffles, and he never had finished reading the accident investigator's report on the crash or the PM report on the driver. He dug them out from the

159

ever-growing heap behind his desk. After a moment's hesitation, he slid the file under his jacket, clicked the computer off and left the office.

Upstairs at the Revival Café, armed with a large cappuccino and a doorstep slice of coffee cake, he took possession of a table and let himself sink on to the chair. For a while he just sat and enjoyed the warmth and sanity of it. The café was busy, but the place was big enough to absorb the bustle. He opened the file, sipped frothy coffee, speared some cake. Who said all police work had to be done in neon-lit offices with a view of the bins?

Reading accident reports was tedious work at the best of times. Estimates on time and speed, braking distances, the road and light conditions at the time, the roadworthiness or otherwise of the vehicle, all was there in detail. Probable cause of the accident was an excess of speed and a puddle of red diesel on the road. Tax-reduced red diesel was used by farmers for farm machinery and vehicles not operated on public roads, and one little puddle of the stuff had done for Mr BMW as he took the bend too fast, without wearing his seat belt. McLusky remembered well what the result had looked like. Bringing back to mind the hand of the dead man, stretched up towards the window, he wondered how long after the crash he had still been alive, broken into pieces, twisted, shattered. It made him reach for more cake and turn the page. The next paragraph arrested his own hand in mid-air, coffee cake balanced precariously on his pastry fork.

The rolling car had scored the road surface and deposited mud on the tarmac as it travelled out of control towards its eventual resting place in the hedge. Those deposits contained tyre marks made by a motorcycle travelling in the same direction some time after the accident.

McLusky clamped his lips around the cake and savoured the gooey layer of coffee-flavoured cream. There was another witness after all. And therefore another candidate for Beretta- and drug-ownership. A biker ... The report

160

went on to suggest that the tyre size indicated a motorcycle of 350cc or more, belonging to a large trail bike. The tread pattern was so common, it failed to narrow down the possible make.

It was something, albeit a pretty hopeless something. Taking that as a basis for a search was like looking for *a car with a medium-sized engine, possibly a hatchback*. McLusky's eyes lifted off the page and focused on the desultory snowflakes dancing above Corn Street outside the windows. The weather had magicked motorcycles off the roads. Even before the snow, the exceptional cold had forced all but the most determined motorcyclists to switch to alternative transport. Who was left? A few fanatics, and those who had no choice. The accident had happened early in the morning, in mist and darkness. The biker could be a commuter. Someone who didn't have a car or a car licence and who had little choice but to use his bike because bus services in the country were few and far between. Where was he now that the roads had disappeared under five inches of snow? Standing at a bus stop with a Beretta and a kilo or two of smack? Probably not for long.

His mobile chimed; the display told him it was Albany Road. 'I think your radio is turned off, guv,' said DC Dearlove at the other end.

'Oh? Oh yeah, so it is; now how did that happen?' Airwave radios had built-in GPS, allowing control to establish the whereabouts of the officer. Or at least the radio. Which was why radios tended to mysteriously go off air from time to time, apparently all by themselves.

'Just calling to say, the mortuary sent word earlier; the PM of the second Leigh Woods victim is scheduled for one hour from now. And with DS Austin off sick ...'

With a moistened finger McLusky dabbed at the last crumbs of cake on his plate. 'Thanks, I'll attend.'

Fragile. That was how she would have described herself. Feeling a bit fragile today. To another woman, anyway. To a

161

woman friend, she further qualified the thought. She wouldn't have told a colleague, female or otherwise. You kept your private life out, almost secret, especially if you were hoping to one day be elevated above their rank. If you got too chummy with them, you'd only store up problems for later. Rumours could chip away at reputations. And *fragile* was not a good word to be mentioned in the same breath as detective inspector, not unless you were happy to stay a DI for all eternity.

Fairfield was thrown forward into the tightening grip of her seat belt as Sorbie braked sharply, having driven too close to the back of a delivery van. 'Jesus, Jack, watch what you're doing. That's no way to drive a woman with a hangover.'

'That bastard has no bloody brake lights on his heap. Am I pulling him over?'

'Not unless you want to go back into uniform. Permanently. Just drive.' *Hangover*, now that was fine with colleagues, though certainly not superiors. You could come in, grunt, make a show of taking Alka-Seltzer and say *Bit of a sesh last night*, and then get on with things. That was the accepted way of drinking too much and being one of the lads. But not *fragile*, not on the verge of throwing up all day or feeling faint because the thought of food made you want to retch.

Sorbie grudgingly adjusted his driving style; there were no more sudden jerks or stops. The call about the drug death had been anonymous, from a mobile. One that had been reported stolen, naturally. He pulled up in front of the address as smoothly as a limousine chauffeur. 'How's that?' he asked.

'Hideous.' Fairfield got out and took in the side street with as little head movement as possible. These were tiny, blunt-faced houses stubbing their noses on the litter-strewn pavements. Besides the one they had stopped in front of, she could see two more that were boarded up. Everything in sight had been covered in graffiti and tags, walls, doors and cars, in red, blue or black. Uncollected rubbish had been piled into two great heaps, someone's valiant effort at making this stretch of pavement walkable. The small car in front of number eleven had no rear window and was full of snow. The one next to it had a flat offside front tyre. Most of the cars parked in the street were so old that they made the brightly liveried police car, the doctor's Audi and even Sorbie's Golf look futuristic; gaily coloured visitors from an unlikely future. An unhappy-looking constable outside number eleven straightened up as Sorbie pointed to him.

'I'm glad he's there to keep an eye on my motor. Jesus. If I woke up one morning and found I was living in Easton, I'd just walk out of the house and keep walking until I found people who'd never heard of the place.'

'If only it were that easy.'

'It is that easy.'

'And what if you had children, Mr Sorbie?'

'Why would I have children?'

'People do have them, you know.'

'Yes, of course. I would look out of the window, see this shit and think, hey, let's have children, *they'll love it here.*'

'Yeah, well, stop being a smartass for a bit, I'm not in the mood.' She walked past the officer guarding the house as though he were invisible, followed by Sorbie, who merely noted that the man had a shaving rash.

Okay, find out like I did, the PC thought, and sniffed at the cold city air.

The house was a shell. It had been condemned, boarded up, then broken into and squatted. In the hall, the temperature was the same as outside. There were only two doors off. The one at the back gave on to a gutted kitchen. The nearer one was closed. The smell of damp decay was strong. Sorbie pushed open the door. It opened reluctantly. 'Jesus.'

The stench streaming from the room caught in Fairfield's throat. She swallowed hard and ducked her head to bury her nose in her scarf. The small front room was knee high in garbage, raw, festering, giving off a penetrating sweet odour, laced with urine. There were whole cellophane-packed loaves of bread turned blue with mould, countless

163

packs of pizzas and ready meals, layers of rotting fruit. 'Looks like they've been skip-diving,' Fairfield said from behind her silk scarf. 'It's all the stuff supermarkets chuck out. And they used it as a toilet as well. Someone will have to go through all that lot.'

'I can see needles from here.'

'Close the door, Jack, or you'll see puke from there.' Over her shoulder she said: 'You could have warned us, Constable.'

At the bottom of the stairs, she passed a jumble of electric cables hanging from the wall where the electricity meter had been bypassed. The cables snaked up the stairs. There were two bedrooms and a bathroom upstairs. The bathroom door was closed. The smell coming through the door explained why some had preferred to piss in the front room. The duty doctor had long finished with the corpse. He was merely here to pronounce the man dead. 'Heroin overdose is what it looks like to me. That's the third in two weeks I have attended personally. When will they get the message?'

'This *is* the message. And he got it.' Sorbie looked beyond the doctor to where the slumped body of the dead man lay half on, half off a much-stained mattress. 'The happy dead.'

'Do you think so?'

'Heroin kills. Sooner or later. Everyone knows it. If you do heroin, then that's what you're looking for, death on a stained mattress.'

The doctor frowned at Sorbie, wondering whether it was worth continuing the conversation. 'That's not the message I meant. It's probably the pure heroin batch that killed him. They must have heard about it by now. Why they can't go easy on the stuff until they know what they bought is beyond me.'

Fairfield put a hand between Sorbie's shoulder blades and pushed him into the room, then leant against the door frame. She thought she'd give a month's wages not to have to look at another dead junkie. 'Once you've started using heroin, you've crossed a threshold somehow. You're no longer rational; the drug makes the decisions,' she said. 'How old was he?'

'Young.'

'Forever young, Doctor.'

'It's what I said,' Sorbie said from inside. 'The happy dead. Hey, there's someone in the back yard.'

Below the window, beyond the snow-covered roof of the kitchen extension, lay a small, lifeless yard, half choked with broken furniture and more garbage. Sorbie watched as a man in his thirties appeared through the jumble of vegetation that grew over the tattered fence. With difficulty he got the sash window to open. 'Hey, you, stay right where you are! Police!'

The man stopped in his tracks and looked up. Above the upturned collar of his leather jacket and his scarf, only the eyes and forehead were visible. He wore a leather cap over what had to be very short hair. Their eyes met only briefly before the man turned and ran back the way he had come.

'Stop, police!' Sorbie hesitated only a fraction. 'Bugger.' Then he squeezed through the window and lowered himself on to the roof of the extension below. His quarry had fought his way back through the fence; he could see glimpses of him as he ran along the narrow passage that divided the backs of the houses from those in the next street.

Fairfield pushed herself off the wall and had launched herself towards the stairs when she heard a crash and a sound of dismay from Sorbie. The doctor got to the window before her. 'Are you okay?' he called down.

'Just dandy. Someone get me out of here.'

It took the PC and the doctor five minutes of pushing and pulling to free Sorbie from where one of his legs had gone through what turned out to be a tarpaper-covered roof of woodwormed boards. His trousers were torn, revealing a raw, bleeding gash in his leg.

'Why did you go after him?' Fairfield wanted to know. 'You haven't seen enough of junkies?'

'He didn't look like a junkie. Yeah, ouch, thank you, Doc,' he added as the duty doctor dabbed at his bloodied leg.

165

'What did he look like?'

'He looked too sorted for a junkie. Didn't move like one. About thirty. Broad shoulders, fourteen stone, five eight. Blue eyes, I think, light eyebrows. Heavy biker jacket, not cheap. Black scarf, leather gloves and a leather cap on his head. Probably shaven head, or very short, anyway. Couldn't see much of his face because of the scarf.'

A few SOCOs had arrived, purely routine where drug deaths were concerned, but with the search on for the suppliers of two types of lethal heroin, they showed more animation than usual. One of them held up a half-empty heroin wrap inside an evidence bag. 'It looks like the same type of wrap, very small resealable polythene. One day we're going to get lucky and get the guy's DNA and fingerprints.'

'One day. Unless he wears gloves, because it's bloody freezing. I got to go and get into a new pair of trousers,' said Sorbie.

'Okay. Thanks, Doctor. Let's go, Jack.'

In the hall, they squeezed past two crime-scene officers, in full protective gear and dust masks, contemplating the immensity of the garbage heap in the front room through the narrowly opened door. Fairfield ducked back behind her scarf.

'CSI Bristol,' Sorbie offered. 'The glamour of it.'

McLusky always thought he could smell it. He knew that no odours penetrated the viewing screen of the autopsy room, but ever since he had caught the stench of his very first decomposing corpse, even a photograph could trigger the memory. A brief delusion of smell, like an echo, triggered somewhere in his brain. The same way it sometimes happened with coffee, he could smell it when it wasn't there. Once it had happened with roses when the word had been mentioned.

'So you haven't suddenly developed a taste for it, then?'

'DS Austin has taken to his bed with a cold. So have scores of others.'

'Has your heating been restored at the station?'

'Not yet, but I'm told that if it hasn't by tomorrow, we'll shut up shop until it is.'

'I hope the temperature on your side of the screen is adequate?'

'Tropical.'

'Then we'll proceed, shall we?'

Roses. McLusky tried to conjure up the smell of roses as Dr Coulthart started his examination of the mutilated body.

'I usually shy away from any conclusions until after the examination is complete, but I can tell you right now that you have a murderous sadist to catch.'

'I have already come to a similar conclusion.'

'These wounds, we'll count them later, are, how shall I say ... *gratuitous.* His teeth have all been shattered. So have both testicles. He would also probably have lost sight in both eyes had he lived. The X-rays' – Coulthart indicated a quartet of them on the computer screen behind him – 'show broken feet, elbow, collarbone, ribs ...'

'Could he have been tortured to extract information?'

Coulthart considered it briefly. 'Anything is possible. But if you wanted to inflict pain as part of an interrogation, you wouldn't do this. A torturer who interrogates assumes a role that allows him to inflict pain and then take pain away again. Tell me everything and the pain will stop. Can't do that once you've broken the chap's teeth and testes, Inspector.'

'Could torture have been its own motive?'

'I doubt that, too. Both this victim and Wayne Deeming were eventually killed by having their heads bashed in. I think you are looking for a killer or killers who *also* enjoy inflicting pain. But killing was the objective. The injuries weren't inflicted over any great period of time.'

'So who is he?'

'I'm afraid we got no useful prints off his severed hand, and there are no lab results yet; everything has slowed down because of the weather.'

167

'Not everything. People are still happily mugging and murdering each other. Exhibitionists prefer not to 'exhibit' in bad weather, but, I'm happy to say, that's not my department.'

'I can tell you he lived pretty well; he was relatively fit, for his age, which was mid-fifties. His skin … mainly his arms and what remains of his face were once tanned quite deeply. The skin there, though relatively pale, still remains several shades darker than anywhere else.'

'Just face and arms. Not due to sunbathing, then. Worked outside, perhaps. But we just had a lousy summer; he wouldn't have got much of a tan here. Probably got it abroad then.'

'Quite possibly.'

'Deeming was a small-time drug-dealer. And user. Any sign of drug use here?'

'None at all. He carried a bit too much weight round the middle, so probably liked a drink.'

'All his teeth were bashed in; is it possible that they did that to make identification more difficult? From dental records?'

'I doubt it. He swallowed half of them. And he was buried with his hands, remember? They wouldn't have left those if they were trying to conceal his identity. If they were, they've been very incompetent.'

'Perhaps they are. The burials weren't very good. Not deep enough for a start, especially the first one. A bit sloppy, if you ask me. You go through all the trouble of grabbing someone, taking him to a dark spot and murdering him, and then you can't be bothered to dig a decent grave.'

It was getting dark fast when McLusky drove away from the mortuary. He hadn't learnt much about the victim, but he had come away with that one new thought: taking Deeming from his house to Leigh Woods and killing him had been an effort. So presumably had been the murder of the second victim. But the graves had been shoddily dug.

There was more than one person involved, that was almost certain.

And the one with the shovel was a lazy sod.

The concrete jungle thing, there was some truth to it. The thing about the jungle was that it was full of stuff. One thing growing through another and on top of the next. The city streets were like snakes or vines: too many houses meant you couldn't see very far; people crawled all over the place like ants. You had to decide what kind of jungle animal you wanted to be. In the jungle it was eat or be eaten. Well, come to think of it, it was really eat *and* be eaten. Eventually. And the *eventually* made all the difference.

The important thing was a safe burrow. If you were rich, you made yourself one your enemies couldn't get into. If you were poor, you made one they couldn't find. He had slimmed down his possessions, had made himself light on his feet; he had moved to this obscure place, a bedsit next to a hardware store on a non descript road. It was noisy and the stairwell smelled damp, but he was allowed to park his van out of sight behind the hardware store, and when the big man paid up, as he would have to, he'd soon find himself more salubrious digs. It would have to be far away, of course. Might even have to be Spain. The big man wouldn't pay up and forget about it; he'd hunt him for ever. He would have to disappear; he'd be an obvious suspect, even though he was in hospital when the photograph was taken. He had found the date on the file information. But alibis would not cut any ice. The big man would send Ilkin to strike first and ask questions later. And Ilkin's kind of methods often meant that questions were left unanswered.

He had sent narrow strips of the picture to the big man's house. He had added a printed note, telling him that identical strips would go to the *Bristol Herald*. He had made no demands yet. Let him wonder about it, let him worry about it. Let him have sleepless nights about it. He could take his time. Safe in his new burrow, he could let his plan ripen.

169

The dangerous bit, the part that gave him the biggest headache, was the handover. That was where they would try to get at him. He had made a list of possibilities and scenarios, and every day he thought about it for hours. There was no point in making a move until he had sorted it out, found a foolproof one. Yet one by one they revealed their flaws. He couldn't afford any flaws. Even the tiniest would prove fatal.

Chapter Fifteen

'They think they've done it,' was how Sergeant Hayes greeted him as McLusky carried his custard Danish past the front desk. Hayes, whose double layer of thermal underwear was straining his uniform buttons, tried to look convinced, but McLusky knew bad acting when he saw it.

'Then why can I see my breath in the lobby? We're staying open for business, then?'

'Looks like we got a reprieve.' It hadn't taken long for the rumour to spring up that the latest round of cuts in police funding meant that Albany Road station, which was crumbling and in need of constant repair, would not reopen once they had closed it down because of the broken heating. It sounded far-fetched to McLusky, but there was no doubt that many police stations around the country would close and not reopen.

Coats, scarves, gloves and an assortment of hats were worn by everyone in the building not in direct contact with the public. The hot-drinks machines at the ends of the corridors had run dry and not been refilled. The kettles, deemed by health and safety to be too dangerous for police officers not trained in their use, had made a comeback everywhere and were being kept busy. The temperature on McLusky's floor still appeared the same, but he noticed that the mere promise of warmth and the reappearance of the kettles had lifted the mood. He had planned to breakfast on coffee and Danish in his office before tackling anything else, but a bellowing sneeze as he passed the CID room made him stop in the doorway. Austin was at his desk, wiping the sneeze off his monitor with a crumpled tissue.

'I thought you were bedridden,' McLusky said by way of greeting.

Austin's nose was red and flaking from constant tissue use. He looked like the 'before' shot of a flu remedy commercial. 'Much better, thanks,' he said snottily. 'Couldn't face another day in bed.'

'Sneeze in my direction next,' called French. 'I could do with a day off.'

'You don't want what I got,' Austin complained.

McLusky walked out. 'I certainly don't. I'll be in my office. Hiding from all your germs.'

He spent the morning making phone calls and working at the computer while Albany Road's central heating tuned up. The frequent metallic clanging that for days had echoed through the building had ceased. It had given way to a deeper, infrequent rumbling and foghorning. From time to time the radiator at his back emitted additional sharp popping noises that made him jump and curse. Each time, he stretched out a hopeful hand to feel for heat, and eventually *there it was*. Not warm, exactly, but no longer icy. McLusky sighed with anticipation. The banging was replaced by a metallic groaning that reminded him of submarine movies. Any moment now Albany Road would start popping its rivets.

At midday a heating engineer in a suspiciously clean boiler suit knocked on his door. 'Are we sinking?' McLusky asked him.

'Come to bleed your radiator. Cor, this is small. I think it's the smallest office I've seen so far. You'll have to come out, sir, so I can get at it.'

McLusky flicked off the monitor and closed any open files. As he squeezed out into the corridor, Austin came walking up, carrying his notepad. Before he reached McLusky, he turned around again to let off a sneeze in the direction of the CID room, then carried on as before. 'We got a DNA match for the second Leigh Woods body.'

'The whole corridor's got *your* DNA now.' McLusky looked over his shoulder at the engineer, squatting by the radiator. He closed the door. 'We know him, then?'

'Donald Bice.' Austin saw McLusky frown, and elaborated. 'He was the skipper of Fenton's multimillion-quid yacht.'

'So he was. The one that slipped away.'

Behind him, the door opened and the engineer emerged. 'Should warm up a treat for you soon, sirs.' He walked off along the corridor, looking for more bleeding work.

In his office, McLusky felt the radiator. It was getting warm. 'The patient is recovering. Close that door, I'm keeping this heat for myself. Every therm of it. Bice was acquitted, wasn't he?'

'We got him for obstruction and petty stuff. Cleared of all the major charges. By then, he'd spent so much time in remand, he was out again in days.'

'In time to get himself murdered.'

'I wonder why. He convinced the jury he had no idea how Fenton made his money and that all he was responsible for was captaining the boat and hiring the rest of the crew.'

McLusky, who hadn't transferred to Bristol when the arrests were made, narrowed his eyes. 'Rest of the crew? Just how big was Fenton's bloody boat?'

'Huge.'

'What happened to them?'

'There was only a cook at the time of the arrest, and he wasn't involved.'

'Do we have an address for Captain Bice?'

'He owned a flat in Portishead. I seem to remember it was in his son's name, though.'

'In case Assets Recovery tried to take it off him. What's the son do, fly seaplanes for drug-runners?'

'No, apparently he's totally straight and a landlubber.'

'Oh yeah?'

173

'He owns a cake shop in Keynsham.'

'That's quite straight,' McLusky admitted. 'And where's the yacht now?'

'It's still in Portishead marina, where it was moored when Fenton had her. Impounded, of course, proceeds of crime, but hasn't sold yet.'

'Who's handling the sale?'

'London company. But they have an agent in Portishead.'

'Get someone to go break the evil news to Bice's son. Find out if he has a key to his father's flat so we don't have to get the locksmith out. Then tell the brokers handling the yacht sale that we need to look over the boat again.'

'We do? What are we hoping to find?'

'Oh, erm, barnacles.' McLusky couldn't have said what he hoped to find. He had stood in the dark place where Donald Bice had been murdered; now he wanted to stand in the bright place that had given him the suntan the pathologist had mentioned. 'Nothing at all, I expect.'

After the arrest of his father, James Bice had changed his name by deed poll to Boyce. James Boyce handed over the keys in the car park of the building where his father had lived in a third-floor flat. He had been told not to enter it. If he had spent the night grieving, then it had left no visible marks. He was a soft-fleshed man of about thirty. His eyes were a clear pale blue, his hair a dusty blond and his skin made McLusky think of marzipan. He gave the impression he had never been exposed to sunlight. He looked uncomfortable standing in the slushy snow by his car, in a grey overcoat, squinting up at the building. It was a fairly new development, not all that far from the marina, but its nearest neighbour was a business park with a jumble of warehouses. McLusky had come with Austin in the Mazda. He asked Boyce to take a seat in the back of the car for a few routine questions.

The man obliged, looking bemused, as though unsure of what to say, or perhaps what to feel. 'His death came as a

174

surprise, though it wasn't that great a shock,' he explained. 'The kind of people he chose to work for … criminals, drug-dealers … I often thought he'd simply disappear at sea one day. How was he killed? The officers who brought us the news didn't seem to know. Or pretended not to know.'

'He … died from a head trauma,' McLusky said. Boyce would eventually get to know all the grisly details of his father's demise, but no matter how unshocked the man professed to be, McLusky didn't feel like telling him in the back of his car.

'What will you be looking for?' Boyce asked, nodding towards the balcony of the flat above.

'We don't know; it could be a crime scene, but it's actually routine. A forensics team will enter the flat soon and make a thorough search. You didn't go up, as we asked you?' The man shook his head. 'When did you last see your father?'

'About a year ago.'

'You didn't go to the trial?'

'No.'

McLusky glanced at Austin, who was in the passenger seat, looking straight ahead. Austin pushed his lower lip out and nodded imperceptibly, meaning he hadn't seen Boyce at the trial. 'Why not?' McLusky asked. 'He was your father, after all. Did you not care what would happen to him?'

'Not particularly. We didn't get on very well. My parents split up. My father left on my fourteenth birthday. I stayed with my mother. We live quite a different life from the one my father chose.'

'A cake shop?'

'Yes. Cake craft.'

McLusky wasn't quite sure what that meant, but he let it pass. 'Yet this flat. It's in your name. Why?'

Boyce hesitated and looked out of the side window, as though asking himself the same question. He sighed. 'Because he asked me to. He said it would help him, something to do with tax. And it would also mean I'd definitely inherit something.'

175

'In case his assets were seized?'

'In case it all just … disappeared. Like he always did.'

'When were you last here?'

'Not since he signed the place over to me, nearly two years ago.'

'Had he always been a skipper for large yachts?'

'God, no. He'd done all sorts, though mostly to do with boats in one way or another. He did have all the licences and certificates. But not million-pound yachts. How he landed that job, I don't know. I suppose only a drug-dealer would have looked at his work record and given him the keys to his pride and joy.'

There was a pause, and Austin asked: 'How often would you say you saw your father in the last few years?'

Boyce snorted joylessly and stared out of the window at nothing. 'Once every couple of years. It would usually be him, calling us, on the phone, quite drunk, you could tell. Gone sentimental. Wanting to meet. To see me, not my mother. We'd agree to meet and half of the time he wouldn't even show. Something would *come up*. Something always *came up*,' he added sharply.

McLusky felt Boyce was probably talking about his child-hood now. He had no idea where his own father was. He'd already left school when his parents finally went their separate ways. When his mother died, his father didn't make it to the funeral. No explanation was offered. The next time he tried first his father's number, then his address, he had drawn a blank. And he'd let it slide, not looked further. Things had come up then too, like university exams, like entering police college, which took him away from Devon to Hampshire.

Through the rear window he saw the van of the forensics team, the driver going slowly, looking for a police presence to confirm his sat nav had taken him to the right location. McLusky wound his window down and waved, and the van pulled into the car park. 'Thanks for coming all the way out here,' he said to Boyce. 'We should have told the officers who spoke to you at your home to get a key from you, but it was good to be able to talk to you in person. Thanks again,' he said as Boyce quit the car. He had wanted the man to be there when they entered the flat, but if what he said was true and he hadn't seen his father for that long, he'd be of little help. And if he was lying, then he would be worse than useless. When Boyce reversed his Vauxhall out of the parking space, McLusky gave him a wave, which Boyce either didn't see or chose to ignore.

Forensics, a team of four, followed them into the building, carrying their gear. McLusky and Austin left them to take the lift, which they would fill to capacity, and walked up. 'Did you believe him?' McLusky asked.

'Seemed genuine. You didn't want him coming up to the flat, then?'

'No point. Strange character. I can see him in a cake shop. Can't see him on a boat at all.'

'He didn't murder his dad for the flat, then?'

'It's a good enough motive.'

'Yes, it's paid for.'

'Not by Boycey's father, I'm sure.' McLusky took a five-second pause, then carried on climbing. He thought he was doing far too much exercise lately, and wished he'd waited for the lift to come down again.

'Not by him, why?'

'I'm sure it was one of Fenton's many money-laundering schemes. Putting it in his son's name was shrewd of Bice. I'm sure Fenton would have tried to reclaim it once he got out. Not so easy now, I should think.' McLusky stopped again, out of breath.

Austin didn't seem at all affected by their climb. 'Perhaps Bice expected Fenton to be arrested. I wonder if the drug squad got any anonymous tip-offs ...'

'Oh, I see your scenario. Boycey knows his father's boss is a big drug-dealer, talks his father into signing the flat over to him, then makes sure Fenton and his dad get arrested, and when he sees his dad get off scot free, he kills him.'

177

'And changes his name.'

'You know, I'd have bought that as a million-to-one chance if only we'd found Bice with his head in the gas oven or drowned in cake mix. But not the way he was killed. Not unless cake man is one hell of a psycho and his mom helped him do it.'

They arrived at the right floor. The forensics team were squatting and leaning around Bice's door like moody teenagers, posing as though they'd been waiting there for hours. McLusky unlocked the door for them and they entered the flat while he and Austin suited up. Not that either of them expected the place to be the scene of Donald Bice's murder. With his injuries he'd have screamed the entire house down. But he might have been snatched from here, and there could be evidence of a struggle.

The two-bedroom flat was one of two on the floor. It was what estate agents would call well appointed, but it lacked anything McLusky would call soul. There was CCTV for the lobby entrance door, laminated wood floors, a plasma screen, a wood and brushed-steel kitchen. There were quite a few pictures, all nautical, nearly all showing Donald Bice himself, on boats, in front of boats, climbing from a glittering sea on board a boat. Beds in both master and second bedroom were made.

McLusky opened the wardrobe in the main bedroom, searched through clothing hanging up – two suits, one sporting an anchor motif on its silver buttons. He searched the pockets, found nothing. 'Not even fluff! I want the name of his dry cleaner's; they check for fluff.' The rest of the wardrobe was unremarkable apart from a whole pile of knitted sweaters, most of them cream or blue. He pushed the door shut.

While the place had certainly been lived in, it was obvious that Bice had not cared much for lubbing on land. Even in the bedroom McLusky found a picture frame containing four small colour photographs, three of which showed Bice in front of a wooden sailing boat called *Beatrice*. The third just showed the vessel, in some kind of boatyard. There were no pictures of his family. McLusky set the frame back on the substantial bedside cabinet and searched through the drawer. Painkillers, antacid tablets, nail clippers, sweet wrappers. He slammed the drawer shut. Coffee-table books on nautical subjects in the space below the drawer, *Ultimate Yachting, Classic Motor Yachts*, glossy yachting yearbooks. 'Marvellous.'

Austin was standing on the balcony. The view, if you ignored the nearby industrial estate, at least hinted at the ocean; you could just make out some masts where the marina lay, and beyond it the sea, or the Severn Estuary at any rate. Covered in snow, Portishead looked all right to Austin.

'Come in and close that door,' McLusky called from inside. The temperature in the place was dropping fast. Austin obliged reluctantly.

One of the forensics team was waving a hand-held machine over surfaces in every room while keeping an eye on a laptop nearby. The team leader came from the bathroom, shaking his head. He had sprayed reagent over every surface in the bath and come up negative for blood traces. 'When did you say the owner of this flat died?'

'The owner of this flat is very much alive, at least he was half an hour ago. The chap who lived here got himself murdered about two weeks ago.'

'Well he's done a lot of cleaning since then.'

'Has he?'

'Yes,' said the man, running his finger over the top edge of the plasma screen on the wall. 'And I don't mean someone *cleaned up*, did a clean-up job. I consider myself a bit of an expert on house dust, and this place has never been filthy. But it has been cleaned no more than two days ago. Probably yesterday. In fact, it's so dust-free I thought the Hoover must still be warm.'

'Did you check?' McLusky asked.

'I did, actually,' he said, smiling. 'It wasn't, but it was itself very clean. And empty.'

In the kitchen, McLusky opened the fridge compartment of the tall fridge-freezer. Apart from a tub of cholesterol-lowering margarine, there were no perishable foods in there, no charcuterie, cheese or milk, no meat, no leftovers. The top shelf was empty apart from two bottles of non-vintage champagne; the door held two rows of condiments and salad dressings. The freezer below was better stocked: some ready meals but also cuts of lamb and bags of sea fish. He opened the fridge door again for a last look. 'Either he mainly ate out, or someone cleaned this up, too. Something should have been festering in there by now.' He turned his attention to the adjacent work surface. Next to a stylish electric kettle sat a stainless-steel breadbin. He flipped it up. 'That does it. There's not a crumb in there. Someone blitzed the kitchen.'

McLusky and Austin spent the next few minutes on their phones, ordering up a storm of routine checks on Donald Bice's life. Door-to-door enquiries would get under way soon. The entire infrastructure of the man's life would come under scrutiny: bank accounts, tax, credit-card use, internet history and phone records, DVLA and every other recorded contact with society, down to the smallest parking fine. McLusky looked up at the large framed print on the wall above the sofa, a painting of a tea clipper under full sail. He wondered what detective work must have been like when that was the fastest way to outrun the pirates. Back then you could step on and off a boat and you had disappeared. Got away. Not now. Most people left traces, most of them electronic, long after their death. There were dead people with functioning Facebook accounts. He watched one of the SOCOs close a large clear polythene bag around the computer on the little writing desk in the dining room. The contrast to Mike Oatley's mouldy little flat in St Pauls was striking. Little lives left little trace. His own life probably still fitted in the back of a hatchback. 'Right, what time are we meeting the yacht agent?' he asked.

Austin checked his watch. 'A Mr Hobbs will meet us exactly one hour from now. Want me to see if we can bring it forward?'

'Forward? Why? They got pubs in this town, haven't they?'

He knew they did. Portishead was home to Avon & Somerset HQ, and he usually felt the need for some fortification whenever he was required to visit it, which thankfully wasn't often. To McLusky, Portishead had an air of being on the edge of things, which of course it was, being situated on the estuary. It looked reasonably affluent and pleasant enough, but it had grown too fast and was in danger of becoming a mere dormer town for commuters to Bristol.

The solid nineteenth-century Royal Hotel at the end of Pier Road also seemed to have had its soul refurbished away, though in summer it would naturally do impressive trade in its large beer garden. Still, it wasn't far from the marina, there was a fire and it served Guinness, so McLusky was quite happy to kill half an hour there. Despite the weather, he could glimpse Avonmouth across the water, with its wind farm and loading cranes. They found a table, where McLusky split open a bag of crisps.

Austin blew his nose into a minute hanky and shook his head. 'No point, can't taste a thing.'

'Oh, all right, you won't want that beer I bought you, then.'

It was difficult not to talk shop. 'Fenton is inside, and six months later the skipper of his yacht gets himself killed. In a similar manner and obviously by the same people as our local small-time but up and-coming drug-pusher, Mr Deeming. Suggests to me that Bice did more than just drive a pleasure boat.'

'I don't suppose anyone kept tabs on what he did when he got out?'

Austin looked pessimistic. 'Why should we have done? He was acquitted; the big fish had been landed. Bice had a job, his paperwork was okay. He got paid a small fortune for skippering that boat. There was no real evidence that he was anything but a minor employee. There was an outside chance he didn't know anything about Fenton's real business.'

'The way he got himself killed suggests otherwise,' McLusky said into his beer, then drained it. 'Time to meet Mr Hobbs, I think, and see what he has to offer.'

Mr Hobbs offered house shoes. 'There is a selection; I'm sure you'll find something in the right size,' he said. McLusky would have offered to take his shoes off even had he not been asked to. Despite himself, he had been impressed by the sheer size of the boat even before they had stepped aboard. At just under ninety-five feet in length, it was about twice the size he had imagined it to be. But even that hadn't prepared him for what waited for them on board. He was not sure he had ever been in more luxurious surroundings. Every item, every surface, every fitting had been designed to scream 'expense'. If it wasn't expensive enough to begin with, someone had gone and gold-plated it. Hobbs, a bland man of about thirty with a confident, educated voice, read from the glossy catalogue produced for the sale of the boat. He was enjoying himself. These weren't real clients and they seemed easily impressed. He tried to impress them some more. 'Four cabins, one master, one double, two twin. All with en suite. Berths for the crew forward. Bose hi-fi, flat-screen TV, DVD, PS3, satellite TV in each cabin. Cherry wood cabinetry, zoned air-conditioning …'

'What's this boat called?' Austin asked.

'Ah, it's nameless for the moment. It was felt that since it had belonged to a criminal, it would be unwise to sell it on with the original name. It was *Moondance* before.'

'It's bad luck, changing the name of a boat, isn't it?'

'Even more bad luck turning up in Tangiers or Miami and being pounced on by old associates of the previous owner.'

'Good point. How much?'

'One point six. She's worth twice that.'

'I don't think my pension would stretch that far,' said McLusky, 'not even if they made me Chief Constable.'

The steel and glass galley could have served a restaurant. Every single item on the boat appeared to be controlled by touch screens or built-in sensors, from lights to toilet flush. Austin was disappointed to find there was no wheel for the helm, only an insignificant-looking joystick.

'What exactly is it you're after?' Hobbs asked when they were back on the bridge where the tour had started. 'Customs and Excise and the drugs people practically ripped her to shreds after the owner's arrest. They had her in dry dock and caused a hundred thousand pounds' worth of damage searching her.'

McLusky shrugged. 'I know. Nothing was found.' Not even the tiniest trace of drugs had turned up, no weapons, nothing incriminating apart from a few fingerprints of known villains. 'The skipper of this boat was found dead. I wanted to get a feeling of where he used to work.'

'Nice work if you can get it.'

McLusky wasn't sure if Hobbs was referring to him or the skipper. If he meant the skipper, he'd have to disagree. Not such nice work if the people on board were criminals of Fenton's calibre. It was easy to disappear overboard. The *Moondance* was large; his own flat would fit several times on this boat, he judged. And yet … He tried to imagine the yacht with its full complement of guests and crew, up to eleven people. Suddenly it seemed a crowded place to him. It would be difficult to keep secrets from the man who skippered the thing. Did Donald Bice learn things here that got him killed six months later?

Back on dry land, after Hobbs had left, they looked back at the *Moondance*. 'It's the arrogance of it that amazes me most. To draw *that* much attention to yourself, how safe must he have felt?'

'It's also not a bad getaway vehicle, I should think,' Austin added. Hobbs had told them that the twin two-thousand-horsepower engines could propel the yacht to twenty-eight knots. He had also said that at full speed they would burn a thousand pounds' worth of fuel an hour.

'Whoever took over from Fenton might be just as ostentatious.'

'Yes. Fenton was highly visible but had so many legit businesses that explained his wealth, it took us forever to nail him.'

'Perhaps we should keep an eye out for whoever shells out one point six million for Fenton's old tub. In the meantime, I think they should use it to house a family on the waiting list for a council place. Give them a break from living in bed and breakfast.'

They did not go back to the flat, and once they had returned to Albany Road, McLusky sent Austin home. The constant changes in temperature as they entered and left heated places had played havoc with his throat, and his voice sounded increasingly croaky.

'If you're sure ...'

'Sure I'm sure. I don't want to catch your sniffles anyway.'

Three hours of desk work later, discharged in his once more well-heated office, McLusky logged off, feeling his own throat getting a little raw. I'm probably imagining it, he thought. 'You're imagining it,' he croaked experimentally, and went home.

The temperature in his flat came as a shock even after the frigidity of the Mazda. He turned on every available heat source, including the three gas rings on the stove, then, still wearing jacket and gloves, contemplated the chilly wastes of the fridge's interior. He ought to go shopping more often. At intervals he stuffed his fridge to bursting with food, then ended up throwing half of it away because it had gone off. Little and often was the solution, he decided. Rossi's, the Italian grocer's downstairs, where much of his shopping was done, had shut up shop for today. He opened the freezer department and discovered an Indian ready meal for two, which he shoved in the oven. He hunted without success for some rice to go with it. Fifty minutes later, with the kitchen nicely warmed up, he poured his curry-for-two over a

184

steaming bowl of spaghetti and cracked open a first can of Murphy's. When the phone in the sitting room rang, his years of experience of life on the force made him take a long draught from the can and twirl more spaghetti into his mouth. Too many phone calls had curtailed too many meals in the past. He found the handset on the sofa and brought it back into the warmth of the kitchen. He didn't recognize the caller number, which to McLusky was a good sign.

'Yup?'

'Hello, Yup.' The caller at least seemed to know who she was talking to. McLusky needed further prodding. 'Your friendly neighbourhood chemist.'

'Louise.' Louise Rennie, senior lecturer in chemistry at Bristol University, had helped McLusky on his first case in Bristol, a few months ago. Their subsequent relationship had progressed as far as the sofa next door but had been cut short by an unexpected caller. He hadn't been in contact since.

'Louise what?'

'Louise, erm, nice to hear from you?'

'Is it, Liam? I saw you yesterday outside the newsagent's off Albany Road. I waved and you looked straight through me.'

'Did you? Did I? I didn't see you.'

'Really? I was sure you had. Not ignoring me, then?'

'Not at all.'

'Thought I'd better check. But you've not been pining, either.'

He had of course thought about her on and off, only after their last encounter he hadn't imagined she'd be too happy to hear from him. Wrong again, perhaps. But she was right. Not pining. McLusky chose his words carefully. 'I, eh, have of course thought of you. And of our last encounter, erm, with regret.'

'Good. So ... how would tomorrow night at eight at the Myristica sound to you?'

'The Myristica again, isn't that tempting fate? That's where we went the last time.'

'I like it there. And I could do with a good curry.'

McLusky looked down on his cooling plate of spaghetti vindaloo. 'Yes,' he agreed. 'So could I.'

Chapter Sixteen

Fifty thousand. A hundred thousand. Two hundred thousand. He had agonized about it. How much was enough, how much too much? If he asked for too much, the big man would never pay up. Of course he couldn't simply afford to refuse – the picture was too clear for that – so he would pretend to pay up. And then kill him. If he asked for too little, it would hardly be worth risking his life for it. In the end he had settled for a hundred and fifty thousand. Chicken feed for the big man, surely. Not that he had asked for money yet. Let him sweat. With every piece of the photo, he must feel more threatened. *A copy of this piece goes to the Herald. And of the next pieces.* He'd be wanting to pay up. He'd be glad of the opportunity to pay up, to stop any more bits arriving. A hundred and fifty. It didn't feel right, it didn't feel enough. The price of half his eyesight, half his manhood. Not enough for what he'd had done to him, not enough for what he was. Perhaps not Spain. Too close to England? Or India. You could live like a prince out there. Too hot, perhaps. A hundred and fifty.

Now he worried about the size of it. What did a hundred and fifty in used notes look like? Tens and twenties. How big a bag would it be? How heavy? Yesterday he had taken a carrier bag of newspapers from a recycling bin up the road and brought it back here. He'd taken a pair of scissors to them and started cutting them into banknote-sized pieces. Until his thumb ached from closing the scissors. It seemed

187

to take for ever. Eight thousand pieces of paper. They fitted into quite a small space. Nothing to worry about there. Now he worried about the bits of paper. How would he explain these? They were banknote-size, after all. Then he realized with relief that he didn't have to explain them; no crime had been committed. He flung the wads into a bin liner with the content of his kitchen bin.

The next question, the big question, the all-important question, was: *how*. A question of life and death if ever there was one.

'I still find it hard to get over this déjà vu date,' McLusky said, sipping his coffee and wishing he could smoke. It was as if they had tried to re-create their last evening in the spring. Her fine blonde hair was still cut short, both wore the same clothes, though in McLusky's case out of necessity rather than design, and both had chosen the same dishes.

Louise narrowed her eyes. 'Here's hoping it wasn't tempting fate.' They gently clinked coffee cups.

When the bill arrived, she made a grab for it. '*I'll* pay.'

'It should be me really. To make up for the debacle we had last time.'

Her eyebrows rose. 'You think buying me a curry will make up for that? Think again.'

'Well … I thought it could be a start.'

'Start somewhere else. Anyway, I checked what freshly promoted detective inspectors earn, so I insist. You can buy me a drink down the road.'

'Where?'

'I fancy a snowy harbour scene.'

The Boat House was one of the new, busy and antiseptic bars that McLusky, had he been looking for a place to drink by himself, would have given a wide berth. He'd have preferred almost any old pub to this blond-wood and brushed-steel bar with its overlit reflective surfaces and carefully dressed clientele, despite the beautiful harbour-side setting. And he generally avoided bars that felt it necessary to employ bouncers at the door. Even though most of the drinkers were around his own age, he felt the absence of anyone over forty unnerving. It had been Louise's choice of venue and she obviously felt comfortable here, even nodded at one or two people she recognized. They found seats, and McLusky forgave the place some of its glitz when he discovered Murphy's on tap at the bar. Louise had decided to stick with white wine. The barman who served him looked so well-pressed and fresh-faced, McLusky felt tempted to ask if he was old enough to work there.

Louise, he now knew, was a couple of years older than him, and at work she was Dr Rennie. 'So what are your own prospects, Doc?' he asked, when he sat opposite her, sipping his drink too quickly. 'If a detective inspector seems such a lowly occupation to you?'

'I never said it was lowly, I merely remarked that it was not well paid, considering how unpleasant a job it is.'

So she had checked up on his spending power. It wasn't something he would have thought of doing with her. He'd have simply asked. If he was interested. 'I get by. And I never think of it as unpleasant.'

Rennie didn't look convinced. 'What about all those thoroughly nasty people you meet doing your job? That would put me off for a start.'

McLusky nodded as though agreeing. 'I met you while doing my job, of course.'

'A good point, Inspector.'

They bickered happily on until their drinks were finished 'Another?' he asked, knowing what the answer would be.

'Take me home, please. Let's go find a taxi.'

'We could walk to mine.'

'Not unless you've had central heating installed.'

They passed the bar on the way out. Behind it, one of the barmen, the one who had served McLusky earlier, was being pushed roughly against the optics by a large man with a crew cut and a shiny leather jacket. He had grabbed the barman by the tie. It was difficult to hear what he was shouting at him,

189

but he punctuated his argument by repeatedly slapping the barman's face. The barman made no attempt to pull away, nor did the other two employees try to help him; they just glanced nervously over their shoulders while continuing to serve customers, who seemed not to notice.

McLusky squeezed Louise's arm. 'One minute?' In ten seconds, he was behind the bar, stiff-arming leather jacket away from the barman.

The red-faced man turned on him. 'What the fuck do you want here? Get the fuck out from behind the bar, pal.'

The man had a light Mediterranean accent; McLusky couldn't place it. He showed him his ID. 'Do you work here?'

'I am part of management.'

'I'm not impressed by your management skills.' He turned to the barman, who looked pale, apart from his right cheek, which had lit up scarlet. 'Are you okay? Do you want to make a complaint?'

The boy, still terrified, shook his head and withdrew. The part of management in the leather jacket squared up to McLusky. 'Nobody called you, nobody complains. And I can smell you have been drinking. So perhaps you are off duty. You have no business here.'

Although he was far from being drunk, McLusky nevertheless knew that alcohol would come into it if this went official, so he decided to bluff. 'Makes no difference. I don't like the way you manage your staff. And I could easily make this my business. I could start by checking their work permits, and your own, working hours, the provenance of your vodka ... It could get very tedious. Not for me, of course. I'll just make one phone call.'

The man visibly deflated a little. Whether there was anything to hide or not, he probably understood the nuisance value of a narked police force. He shrugged, adjusted his leather jacket. 'No problems. All over. You and your lady were leaving.'

They did. Rennie's mood had changed. 'You were doing so well until then. No police radio, your mobile didn't go off once. It was almost like a normal date. But you couldn't walk past that.'

It hadn't been a question. He answered it anyway. 'No, I couldn't.'

'So that's what it's going to be like?'

'Of course not. Sometimes I get through a whole evening without arresting anyone.'

They were lucky with a taxi from St Augustine's Parade. McLusky was glad. Rennie's mood seemed to have nose-dived after what she called his 'performance' at the bar, and he had never been good at placating women, despite having considerable practice at it.

The streets in the centre were well gritted, and no new snow had fallen for a while. A good-natured snowball fight was in progress in Park Street, where two groups of revellers exchanged missiles from one side of the road to the other, scraping snow off the roofs of cars and sniping from behind them. A snowball splattered against the driver's window of their taxi; the driver grumbled to himself, not amused. It was a short ride to Clifton Village. A tourist guide would have described the area as affluent, upmarket, even exclusive. Its mainly Georgian architecture certainly made it stand out from all other districts, but it had other reasons, too, for feeling superior to the rest of Bristol: Clifton was older than the city itself. McLusky paid off the cab outside the large Georgian townhouse where Louise owned a first-floor flat.

It was immaculate. The sitting room had high windows, shuttered now against the night. She started the music system with one remote control, the coal-effect gas fire in the grate with another. A pair of cream two-seater sofas faced each other across an oriental coffee table. The wall opposite the windows was lined with books. The place suited its owner; McLusky told her he thought so.

'I fell in love with it. It doesn't have any famous views, or even decent views, but I wouldn't have been able to afford it if it did. And the Primrose Café is practically around the corner.'

McLusky didn't have time to wonder if they were going to have to talk house prices. She swiftly changed the subject and concentrated instead on showing him some ways in which he could make up for last time. They spent hours in front of the fire before shifting camp to the bedroom.

When McLusky woke in the morning, he didn't need any time to remember where he was; he hadn't been asleep that long. He shot a quick glance at the clock on the bedside table – it was seven exactly – and relaxed again. What had woken him was the clattering of crockery on the tray Louise had set down on the bed next to him. A cafetière of coffee, glasses of orange juice, and blueberry pancakes with snowy dollops of crème fraiche, dusted with cinnamon. Louise in her black dressing gown was fresh from the shower, her hair still damp. He reached up and kissed her, but she soon pulled away and poured coffee. 'I hate cold pancakes.'

He sat up, examined the array on the tray. 'Pancakes and freshly squeezed orange juice for breakfast. I could get used to that.'

'Well don't. I usually do the domestic-goddess thing just once. After that, it's a bowl of Special K and juice from the carton in the fridge.'

'Well that's definitely another person,' Warren said, peering through Ed's magnifying glass. 'But the face and the back of the head are missing. Crafty bugger. Look, the slice is even narrower than the other two.'

Ed grunted agreement. 'And it doesn't match up against the others. Mind you, sooner or later they'll start knitting together. From the dimensions, I'd say there's five more bits to it. Unless they get smaller and smaller.'

'But why send it in bits in the first place?'

'He said "why not print it anyway". Are you going to wait until they're all here? Why don't we print them, slice by slice? Someone must recognize it.'

Warren was thoughtful. 'Look at the way this is cut. The face is missing deliberately. So whoever is sending these must assume we'll recognize the person. I don't know, Ed. Something about these bits gives me the creeps. It's the lighting, maybe. Or the graininess. And whoever is sending them has some sort of agenda of their own. I don't like being used. There's no way we can print it without seeing the whole picture, to coin a phrase.'

'Shame. I fancied it as a puzzle. With a prize for the first one to get it.'

'Yeah, I know the type of thing you mean. But we don't need to use a creepy pic like this one.' She stuck the three pieces on to the frame of her monitor. A moment later she unstuck them, laid them on the glass of the scanner and saved the image to her computer.

'It's *bloody* freezing.' Despite wearing gloves, Sorbie's fingers felt icy. He huddled deeper into the driver's seat like a truculent teenager, barely able to see above the steering wheel. He wasn't sure he wanted to. There wasn't much to see anyway, only cramped little houses, uncollected rubbish and slush. It looked like home.

Fairfield didn't bother acknowledging the sentiment, since Sorbie had said something to that effect a dozen times already since the beginning of their shift. She wasn't exactly happy either. Just when the heating at Albany Road had been restored, they had business out here. And this was really a job for uniform. But the number of drug deaths continued to rise, albeit more slowly, which was why they found themselves sitting in Sorbie's Golf, parked up in a drab street in Whitehall, watching a public phone box. Fairfield knew street dealers were operating around here. The phone box was often used to order up a drop of drugs. The area hadn't recently been targeted by the drug squad, meaning things would hopefully be nice and relaxed. The idea was to catch some small-fry dealer and scare him enough with a manslaughter charge for supplying contaminated heroin to make him reveal the source of the stuff. In a city this size, they'd be extremely lucky to catch the contaminated heroin being dealt, but one addict had died in Whitehall, one in neighbouring St George in the last week. This was the right area.

They'd been to a pub at lunchtime, to get something warm to eat and to fortify themselves, Fairfield with a large glass of acidic red wine, Sorbie with a pint of industrial cider. The cheering effect of both had now worn off, making them irritable. Sorbie wished he had used the toilet before leaving the pub.

Since even a rattling drug addict would notice the clouds of hot exhaust from a car with its engine running, they sat in the unheated Golf. The temperature was near zero. After two hours, they had eventually pounced on one lot of likely candidates but had found nothing more than half an ounce of herbal on the supplier. Fairfield was so disgusted, she told Sorbie to let the lot of them go. They ran the engine of the car for fifteen minutes, shouting at the heater to hurry up, then waited once more. Another hour had passed since then. They had long run out of casual conversation. There were things Fairfield might want to talk about, but she wasn't sure Sorbie was the right person, even though it was he who had made her think about it. A few days earlier, after the DS had gashed his leg trying to take a short cut through the window in Easton, they had driven to his house in Windmill Hill so he could clean up and change from his torn trousers. Sorbie lived in a narrow Victorian terrace not unlike the ones around here. She had never been there before. By the looks of it, he hadn't got around to changing a thing since he moved in, apart from adding awkwardly parked IKEA furniture and a large TV. It looked like every-thing in the house had come flat-packed. While Sorbie got changed, Fairfield had taken a good look around down-stairs. 'You're snooping in my cupboards,' Sorbie had shouted from upstairs. 'I can hear it!' He hadn't, but he knew Fairfield would be unable to resist. He was still

194

convinced women only joined the force because they were basically nosy. It had been the freezer door Fairfield had opened first. She had counted three bags of frozen chips. The rest were burgers and sausages. The greasy chip pan on the electric stove showed every sign of being well used, as did the blackened non-stick frying pan in the sink. Next to the cooker on the pretend marble counter stood the largest bottle of ketchup she had ever seen; a squeezy bottle of American mustard was keeping it company. The kitchen window over the sink allowed a view of a narrow, empty garden. The recycling bins near the back door were overflowing with plastic cider bottles and beer cans, the only evidence that Sorbie had been here more than a week. Even the sitting room looked like he had only just moved in and hadn't had time to create any kind of atmosphere, yet she knew he'd bought the house four years ago. Sorbie had never mentioned girlfriends, and by the looks of it, no woman had spent more than five minutes in this room. Or would have wanted to, unless her sole purpose was to sit on a sofa and look at a plasma screen.

Fairfield had heard through the station grapevine that DI McLusky lived in even less salubrious accommodation, over a shop, with second-hand furniture and no proper heating. She had been wondering since why so many officers seemed to lead marginal lives. And what they expected to get out of those lives. Of course there were plenty of happily married or hopefully engaged colleagues she could cite, but she suspected at least half of the team had put their social lives practically on hold, simply living from day to day, just treading water, as though waiting for something to happen, for something to enter their lives from the outside that would decide things for them. One day, when they weren't working, she would ask Sorbie what he wanted out of life. Apart from getting promotion. And when he got it, would it make any difference to what he kept in his freezer? Or to anything else in his life outside of work, apart perhaps from his pension prospects?

195

Sitting in a freezing car, staring at a barely functional phone box, waiting to scoop up small-fry drug-dealers and their pathetic clientele was not what she should be doing at this stage in her career. Even the thought of returning to her warm office and her cappuccino maker failed to cheer her. It wasn't really the cold that affected her; it was the endless hours of darkness that got her down. It made everything else weigh heavier, look dingier, feel harsher than necessary. How did people up in the north of Scotland cope, or the Orkneys even? But then, of course, they'd have the compensation of all that extra daylight in the summer.

Summer. She wanted to be teleported back to long, light, balmy evenings, spent at home in the communal gardens behind her house with a book and a glass of wine. How many of those evenings had she managed to enjoy this year? She couldn't remember more than two. Not much to show for a whole year of work if that was your idea of reward.

Her radio came to life and she answered it.

'We have a drug death reported in your area; officers attending suspect a heroin overdose. You said you wanted to know. The suspicion is that it's pure heroin again.'

Fairfield tried to summon up some enthusiasm. 'Yes, thanks.'

'There is a witness who's given a description of the person she thinks is the supplier.'

She sat up straighter. 'Are they still at the address?'

'She's been detained for the purpose of a drugs search.'

'Albany Road?' Control confirmed it. 'Thanks, control.' She elbowed Sorbie into action. 'Jack? Home!'

Snowing again, bloo-dy hell. Where did it all come from? Who needed it? Still, not quite as depressing as rain would be, but look at it: wind and ice and snow and slush. The real problem was that the few decent clothes she had were summer clothes. It had been warm enough at the pub, but she now had to stagger home for miles with no money for a taxi. All because Ali insisted she meet her halfway, so they'd ended up at the Old Fish Market. A bit too glossy for her. She'd rather have gone to a local pub and Ali could have kipped at her place, now that Gary was gone. Hurrah hurrah hurrah.

With all the layers she had on over her dress and her old clompy boots, she looked like a frump. And winter had only just started, yuck. Soon, though, she might have enough money for taxis. Well, not to take them everywhere, natch, but to get home after a night out. And she might get more nights out too, because – ta-daa – she had found a job. A shit job, Ali had called it. Ha-ha. Not because it was crap, though she hadn't started it yet; could still turn out to be crap. Laboratory technician. At the Bristol Royal Infirmary. They were paying her while she was training, how good was that. Yeah, to look at poo, Ali had said. It wouldn't *all* be poo. Yeah, some of it's going to be piss, Ali had said. Well, she'd get used to it. Otherwise she'd wear a clothes peg on her nose, there, sorted. Whoops, bloody icy here, she thought they'd gritted all that. Because that was what it was all in aid of, celebrating getting a shit job and getting rid of a shit boyfriend. A double celebration. After four months of Gary-the-dickhead cluttering up her flat, not even looking for a job, and her being jobless herself for over a year. At least she'd gone out looking, and found stuff to do outside the flat, while he had basically set up camp in front of the telly. Watching crap or playing martial arts games on his Xbox. She hated that Xbox, it was so pointless.

She crossed the street. Short cut between the houses here. She shouldn't go through little alleys like this, not alone, not at night, but it saved time and she was freezing her butt off, woolly tights or no. Anyway, her own neighbourhood. Where could you walk and feel safe? If she hadn't given Gary the push, he'd have kept sitting there and started spending her money. The money from the poo job.

Nearly home. Starting Monday. Not that it was much money while she was being trained, but hey, it was more than the dole, and training was only three months, and after that it went up a bit immediately … Bloody hell, what a way to park a van, halfway across the pavement. Whoever did that was either drunk or else had no consideration for others. Thanks a bunch.

She was too surprised to scream. The side door of the van slid open next to her; a hand shot out and dragged her inside by the hair. A punch to the stomach winded her, made her want to throw up. The door slammed shut behind her. She was on the floor; he forced sticky tape across her mouth, and then it went dark and she couldn't breathe. There was a bag over her head . The van was moving, driving away, driving her into the darkness. *And no one had seen. No one. I bet no one saw a fucking thing.*

Denkhaus promised he would keep the case conference short but not sweet. He congratulated the team on being the only one in the building where no officer was off sick with the dreaded lurgy. Austin supplied an explosive sneeze at that precise moment, drawing laughter even from the super. A couple of civilian operators still hadn't returned to work, but Denkhaus appeared not to count them in. That was all the congratulations they were going to get. No real progress had been made, no arrests, no suspects, even.

It was the MO that set the Leigh Woods murders apart from all the drugs violence dealt out in the city, before and since Fenton's conviction.

'Could it be revenge of some sort? Could Fenton be directing it from inside?' DS French wondered.

Fenton was presently doing time at Whitemoor, a Category A prison in Cambridgeshire. 'He's being closely monitored. Three of his associates are also doing time, all are in different prisons. We're not giving him the chance,' Denkhaus said. 'Donald Bice was of course an ex-associate, though we couldn't prove his direct involvement. But Deeming was just a small-time dealer. We never connected him with Fenton before. And Fenton had different methods. We may not have managed to connect him to any murders, but three Yardies disappeared, and the general opinion is that it was Fenton who disappeared them.'

'Yes,' McLusky agreed. 'And they stayed disappeared, which is usually what happens. Someone disappearing is a lot scarier for your adversaries than finding them dead. It has that added spookiness that makes you feel unsafe.'

'Indeed,' Denkhaus went on. 'The power to make you disappear without trace is more feared than any drive-by shooting.'

'The thought had struck me before. The bodies were hidden, but really not very well. The graves simply weren't deep enough. Both Deeming and Bice were killed slowly. They took their time killing them, but then hurried the burial.'

'All that means is that they prefer murdering to digging holes,' Denkhaus said. 'Shame it doesn't get us very far.' McLusky hoped it might, but having nothing more than a vague feeling about it made no comment. Denkhaus went on: 'Moving on to the cycle-path murder   ' He reached behind him to tap against Mike Oatley's reconstructed photo on the picture board. 'We're still no further. We don't even know where he was murdered, and forensics are dragging their feet in the snow.'

'House-to-house enquiries came up with nothing,' French supplied. 'We spoke to everyone we could find who uses that stretch of the river, and everyone on this side of the river. We posted incident boards at both ends of the deposition site. Plus your own appeal for info on *Points West* two days ago. Nothing useful so far.' In fact Denkhaus had done appeals on two local TV news programmes, as well as Radio Bristol. He enjoyed it and he was good at it.

'Right, we need to dig further into Oatley's background, his activities. Interview the social worker again. Anyone in his building friendly with him?'

'Only friendly enough to go through his flat when the door was left open and make off with whatever they fancied.'

*

When the meeting broke up, McLusky, instead of turning left towards his cubbyhole office, turned right along the corridor to the CID room in order to make himself some coffee with the help of the reinstated kettle. The steam of his own little kettle inside the bottom compartment of his desk had managed to warp the wood to such an extent that the door now refused to open. It had trapped his coffee mug inside and, tragically, also held the bottle of Glenmorangie hostage. There were no spare mugs to be had in the CID room, so he clattered downstairs to the canteen. He bought a clingfilm-wrapped chocolate brownie, and while he paid for it with one hand, he stole one of the canteen mugs from the counter with the other.

'Hey, I saw that,' said the girl who gave him change.

'Someone will be along later to take a statement,' he promised and made off with it.

Back in his office, he stared down glumly at a mug of instant that had brown bits of undissolved granules and white bits of undissolved whitener floating on top. 'Looks more like soup,' he told Austin. 'You'd get better coffee on a building site, I'm sure.' He suddenly felt a stab of nostalgia for the freshly roasted coffee Fishlock had served him in his caravan, out in the clean woodland air. He opened the window behind him and lit a cigarette from his pack of Extra Mild. 'How's the no-smoking going, Jane?'

'Better if I don't talk about it. Or breathe yours.'

'Did you find out what Donald Bice was living off since he stopped skippering for Fenton?'

'Yeah, he'd been claiming unemployment benefit since the trial.'

'No way. He had a freezer full of high-end ready meals and a leg of lamb and other stuff, and a couple of bottles of bubbly in the fridge. He wasn't going to toast the arrival of his dole cheque with it. What's the status of the flat?'

'Mortgaged and in the name of the son.'

'And the holy ghost. Bank accounts?'

'They haven't sent the details yet, but the man Deedee talked to told him there were no significant outgoings apart from a few credit-card transactions at petrol stations and a couple of standing orders. Credit activities ceased around the time of his death. Looks like Coulthart's estimate was spot on.'

'Bice must have had some other income. And it would have been cash.'

'The stuff in the freezer could all be left over from when he still worked for Fenton.'

'True. I didn't check the use-by date on the ready meals. Should have done. If he bought them when he was still working, then they'd be out of date now. But then again, if he lived on benefits, he'd have eaten them by now. Surely. No, it stinks,' McLusky decided. 'So no transactions apart from petrol stations ... what car did he drive?'

'VW Passat.'

'How sensible. And presumably nothing interesting turned up in there either?'

Austin shuffled a few papers in the file. 'Erm, no, since, erm, we never found the car.'

'What?'

Austin looked apologetic, though he didn't know what he was apologizing about, he was sure. It hadn't been his case and Bice had been considered a minor figure, a sideshow. 'I've no idea why his car never figured back then, I suppose they had everything they wanted and the main man was Fenton, after all. We're looking for it now, of course.'

'I should think so. Are there garages at his place?'

'No, dedicated parking spaces.'

His phone rang and he snatched it up. 'McLusky.'

It was DC Dearlove. 'Donald Bice had a regular cleaner. She does several flats in the building. She's there now.'

A small metal disc nailed to a wooden post and rammed into a narrow bed of struggling vegetation proclaimed that the parking space belonged to Flat 5, which was Bice's, or rather his son's, as McLusky reminded himself when he parked the Mazda there. He rode the lift up to Flat 3, even though it was on the first floor. There'd been quite enough walking recently,

201

for his taste. The door was answered by an attractive woman in her early thirties. She wore a grey tracksuit, a white T-shirt and white training shoes, and had her hair tied in a ponytail. Tiny studs sparkled in her ear lobes. In the background he could hear classical music, something he recognized but couldn't place. 'I'm looking for Julie Milne.'

'You found her,' she said, when he showed his ID.

'You're Julie Milne? Sorry. It's just you don't look like my idea of a cleaner.'

'Who did you expect, Mrs Mop? Come in if you must, but take your shoes off. Unless you have smelly socks like the PC who was here earlier, then I'd rather you stayed in the hall. With your shoes on. I don't want you transferring odours into the carpets.'

'You're certainly looking after your client's property.'

'They pay me a lot of money for it and I do it well.'

'I know,' said McLusky, now shoeless and relieved to see no holes in his socks. 'I've admired your work upstairs, in Mr Bice's flat.'

'Yes, I do that. It's what you've come about, is it? Shame about Donald. Shocking, really. He was okay, and I like the place.'

'Easy to clean?'

She managed a smile. 'Yeah, that too.'

Flat 3 could not have been more different to the flat of the same layout above. Floral upholstery on a traditional three-piece suite matched the rest of the dark-wood furniture and dark-red carpet. Here, combing straight the tassels on the Persian rugs and runners alone had to consume masses of time. Ornaments abounded.

Julie Milne crossed to the hi-fi and turned off the CD. 'So what can you ask me that the other officer didn't?'

'You said *shame about Donald*. How well did you know him?'

'Not well. He was pleasant, that's all I meant. Not all my clients are; some are never satisfied or want you to do the impossible but not pay for the hours. That sort of thing.'

'Yes, you get people like that in policing.'

'I've been cleaning his flat and all the time he was dead. And I had no idea.'

'You must have noticed the place wasn't being used.'

'Of course. But it still needed cleaning; dust still falls, and actually it's a good opportunity to get things done you normally have to put off to clean up the mess your clients make.'

'I thought most people cleaned up the day before the cleaner comes, out of embarrassment. It hadn't worried you that your employer didn't seem to be using the flat?'

'He wasn't my employer, he was a client. But no, not at all. He's often away; *was*, I should say. Captaining yachts. Though not so much recently.'

McLusky picked up a figurine from a group of china ornaments on a shelf and sensed Julie Milne tensing. He pretended to examine the maker's stamp, then set it back on the shelf, not quite where it had been. 'So it was you who cleaned out the fridge.'

'Yeah. Not that there was so much, but I chucked all of that last time I cleaned.'

'How long have you worked for him?'

'A couple of years.'

'Did you notice any change recently?'

She briefly considered this while lifting her eyes to a gilt-framed reproduction of *The Hay Wain* above the fireplace. 'Not really. You mean in himself?'

McLusky ran a finger over a high shelf, then inspected it as though checking for dust. 'Anything.'

'Well, he spent more time at home than he used to. And I think he had more money.'

'More money? What makes you say that?'

'I don't know. He spent more on food and drank posher wines, that sort of thing. Not really top-end wines, but mid-range, I'd say.'

'You know your wine, then?'

'You'd be surprised what you can learn from other people's kitchens.'

203

McLusky thought that, being a police officer, he probably wouldn't be, but kept that to himself. He crossed the room to the balcony door, which gave a view very similar to the one upstairs, only the sea appeared more distant today. He could see his own car parked below, the road and the nearby industrial estate, and a few buildings of the same development. 'Did he always park his car in the car park?'

'Yes, mostly.'

'Mostly.'

She joined him by the window. In her trainers she was nearly as tall as McLusky in his stockinged feet. 'Well, yeah. He's got his own space, erm … on the left somewhere.'

'I know, I'm parked in it. You said *mostly*.'

'Yes. Only I did notice that a couple of times he was here but his car wasn't. And once I saw him drive out of the parking lot and turn right instead of left. Then half an hour or so later he came back without his car. On foot.'

'Where does that lead to? When you turn right?'

'Well nowhere, that's the thing. It's just the industrial estate, but the back of it. The front entrance is on the main road on the other side. The rest is just waste ground back there; they're thinking of developing that as well. Same as this, I think.'

'Right.' He was already on his way back towards the hall, where he had parked his boots. 'Do you have any police officers as your clients?'

'No, why?'

'I was just wondering if I could afford your services.'

While he struggled into his boots, she bent over a handbag on the hall table and produced a card. *Prestige Domestic Services*. Daily, weekly, monthly, one-off cleaning. She handed it over once he was booted. 'Where is your home?'

'Montpelier.'

'That's quite far. Not really worth my while travelling all the way there unless it's a big job. It's the petrol cost.'

'Thanks, anyway.' With any luck, Julie Milne had already made it worth his while travelling all the way here.

The lift was busy; he took the stairs. Fine snow was dancing in the air outside as he pulled out of the car park and turned right.

Chapter Seventeen

What had been dancing flurries only minutes ago had now thickened into dense snowfall, driven westward by a squall from the estuary. Within moments the road, which had only had a single lane cleared, was covered with a fresh blanket of white in which McLusky's Mazda left the only tyre marks visible. On his right, the housing development had fallen behind, giving way to waste ground and scrubland, prettified by the snow. On his left, the industrial park could never be prettified. The wall that surrounded it occasionally gave way to chain-link fence or the backs of solid sheds and low buildings, only to pick up again further along. The day was darkening and the snowfall was so dense that it wasn't until he was right in front of it that he spotted the iron gate in the wall. A few yards further on, the road simply ended, a fact advertised by three snow-hooded concrete bollards big enough to stop a truck. Street lamps had abandoned this dead end a while back, but there was lighting in the yard beyond the gate, and he could hear a heavy engine revving somewhere nearby.

Leaving his car running, he got out and approached the gate. It was made from welded box section, wide enough to let through heavy goods vehicles, and topped with barbed wire. It was locked. Set into the wall beside it was a rusting box with a speaker grille and a button below. It looked as though someone had once tried to set fire to it. He pressed the button for a few seconds with little confidence that it was still attached to anything meaningful. A full minute passed before it crackled. 'Hello?' The voice sounded far away and doubtful.

'Police. Would you open the gate, please?'

'Police? Yeah, okay. It'll take a minute, mind.' The loud-speaker emitted a hollow crackle before returning to silence.

It took several minutes, during which the snowfall had time to diminish, before a middle-aged man in a donkey jacket, scarf and baseball cap appeared at the gate and swung it back. McLusky drove in, stopped level with the man and showed his ID. He was waved on. 'Park over there if you want.' He pointed to the lee of the nearest unlit building. McLusky did as suggested. As he got out of the car, the snow abruptly stopped falling, apart from a tardy flake here and there.

The man had caught up with him. 'We don't normally let people in by that gate.'

'Then why do you have an intercom out there?'

For idiots like you, the man's look seemed to say. 'That used to be the main entrance but they made them change it to the other side since they built those houses, to stop all the traffic going past there. Is anything the matter?'

'No, I just have a few questions, routine enquiries. Does no one use that gate, then?'

'Erm, can we walk while we talk? I need to get back across. It's easiest if you leave that way too when you're done.'

'Sure.' They fell into step. 'You're the caretaker here?'

'That's me. Though I only just started the job, so go easy on me.'

'Okay. Tell me, does anyone use that back gate?'

'Well, apparently most people know to use the other side now. That's been the main entrance for years. Of course people can if they want to, but no one has buzzed that gate since I started here last week. The sat nav takes you to the other side, anyhow. And the big artics must have hated that entrance; it's just not built for it.'

'Okay, that's most people. But people do still use it.'

'Some people have a key, I know that much, and if they want to they can.'

'What about Donald Bice? Does he have a key?'

'I'm not familiar with the name, but we'll soon find out for you.'

The industrial park consisted of several units that looked like warehouses, with rows of delivery vans parked in lines outside, and a few older, smaller units with corrugated roofs, that seemed to have grown up more haphazardly over many years. Between them lived mountains of palettes, tyres or plastic barrels, now disappearing under snow. For all that apparent industry, the place felt quiet, apart from the occasional engine noise of vans coming and going.

The generously heated Portakabin that served as a gate-house looked like it had been installed in the seventies, along with its fittings. A row of three black-and-white six-inch monitors served the CCTV. Filing cabinets were covered in papers, tea stains and empty takeaway containers. Prestige Domestic Services would throw a fit in here. The large ashtray on the desk was full. The place smelled strongly of cigarettes and faintly of pizza. The caretaker keyed the name into his old-fashioned desktop PC on a much-abused keyboard.

'Yes, we got him.'

'Donald?'

'Says D., seems likely. What's he done?'

'It's just part of a larger inquiry. But I do need to take a look at the place. What kind of unit is it?'

'It's in one of the old buildings at the back; they're divided into lockups inside.' He pointed to a yellowing site plan on the wall. 'It's in A3. You can't miss it; it's the oldest building and your car's parked next to it. I'll get you the keys. But won't you need a search warrant?'

'Donald Bice is dead. He was murdered.'

'Oh, was he one of the dead people found in the woods in Bristol?'

'I think it may turn out to be that D. Bice. I'm here to find out.'

'Blimey.' After some rummaging in the bottom drawer of a metal filing cabinet, the caretaker handed over three large keys tied to a wooden block. *A3* and the Roman numeral *II* had been burnt into the wood.

McLusky thanked him. 'Is this *a* set of keys or *the* set of keys?'

'Oh, that's just our set. They have keys themselves, of course.'

'I'll lock up again, but I want to hang on to this key to make sure any evidence remains secure in there.'

'Fine with me. But you might want to borrow this or you won't see much.' He produced a long rubberized torch from a desk drawer. 'Make sure you bring that back, though. I'm buggered without it.'

'No lights?'

'In the entrance bit. But not in the lockups themselves. Leccy not included.'

Outside in the yard, the lighting was just about adequate, McLusky thought, at least if you knew your way around. He did see several lamps that weren't lit on his way to unit A3, either from economy or neglect. He spotted his car and found the building. It was weathered red brick and had once had a tiled roof that had long been replaced with what looked to him like well-worn corrugated asbestos. The high windows were covered in wire mesh. The entrance was a large wooden double door painted wine red, high and wide enough to let in a lorry. Inset on the right-hand leaf was a smaller door for foot traffic. It reminded McLusky of a prison gate. Very unlike a prison gate, the door was ajar and light showed in the gap. He stepped inside and called: 'Anybody home?'

It took him a moment to make out what he was looking at. The entrance hall was feebly lit by a single naked energy-saving bulb that would have struggled to illuminate a broom cupboard. This space was perhaps twenty-five feet deep and twenty high and had a perished concrete floor. He could just see the two further wooden doors either side of the central partition through all the clutter piled high in front. Palettes loaded with boxes and cellophane-wrapped bundles of what looked like piping or metal rods had been dumped haphazardly and stacked high, right in the centre, as though whoever delivered it hadn't been sure which lockup they were destined for. McLusky squeezed between piles of boxes into the space in front of lockup II. The Roman numerals had been rendered in black paint on the red doors. It was dark enough in this canyon for him to switch on the torch. All three keys were of similar size. He chose one at random and stopped dead.

It was a kind of snuffling sound, like a suppressed cough or laugh, and so close that he could not tell which direction it had come from. He swung the torch left and right. Then he turned it off and closed his eyes. He thought of Leigh Woods in the dark. He thought he could smell something that did not belong here. 'Police, show yourself,' he called loudly.

It was as if the echoing call itself brought the place crashing down on top of him. It was the tilting shadows and movement of air that warned him, only too late. Even as he turned to ward off the avalanche of boxes, the first one knocked him off his feet. Bundles of piping, each weighing five stone or more, cascaded after it, pinning him to the concrete floor, burying him, crushing down. He cried out first in dismay, then in pain as the last bundle of metal rods dealt his left ankle a hammer blow in the dark. The light had been turned off. He heard the door he had entered by being gently closed, making the darkness complete.

'It's not much of a lead, but it's the first bit of good news we've had since the deaths started,' Denkhaus said.

'It feels like it. Sugar?'

Denkhaus made a show of patting the pockets of his suit. 'Yes, I don't seem to have brought my sweetener.'

It was one of the superintendent's favourite delusions that he carried his little box of sweeteners everywhere to shave a few calories off his daily intake. Fairfield had never even seen the thing. She stirred both sugar and cream into his cup before putting it down in front of him and sliding back into the seat behind her desk. She always made sure that the superintendent's chair was placed slightly to the left, making it less formal. She disliked Denkhaus and found him hard going. She had treated the discovery that his super-efficient secretary was mysteriously incapable of making decent coffee as an opportunity to fit another string to her bow. It wasn't much, perhaps, but whenever he deigned to come to her office and drink her coffee, he seemed better disposed to listen to whatever she had to say.

'I knew persistency would pay off eventually. We got lucky, doubly lucky. It was the sisterof the dead junkie who decided to talk. She's not an addict. She does use drugs, of course, E and blow, but she's against hard drugs. And perhaps she's not yet quite clear about what dangers squealing can bring. But she's given us a good description of the man she says was her brother's dealer.'

'Shame it's not the anthrax we're talking about.' Denkhaus frowned, took a sip of coffee. His frown disappeared. 'Still. Doubly lucky, you said?'

'Yes. The description fits the man both Sorbie and I saw making off from a squat in Easton where a dead junkie had been discovered. He had his face obscured then, but together with the description, I'm confident we'll recognize him.'

'Well, that sounds like at last—' A knock on the door, fast, urgent, interrupted him.

'Come,' Fairfield called.

It was DC Dearlove. 'Sorry, sir, ma'm, from control: DI McLusky has been injured. They've taken him to the Royal Infirmary.'

'Right. We were finished here anyway, weren't we?' Denkhaus said. He left his barely touched coffee behind as he followed Dearlove into the corridor. 'What happened and how bad is he ...?' Fairfield heard him say before Denkhaus closed the door.

For a full minute Fairfield stood by her desk, staring down at it. Then she cleared away the coffee cups. As she did so, she noticed that her tremor had returned.

'Have you come to spread your germs through the entire hospital?' McLusky complained. He was sitting on an easy-wipe chair in the A&E cubicle. His left foot was heavily bandaged.

Austin thought the DI looked pale. 'I don't think my germs can survive their germs. Are you ready to leave, then?'

'I am, but you can put the wheelchair back where you found it. I hurt my foot, not snapped my spine.'

'They said you broke your toes, too. Cracked your ribs ...'

'I did, I did. But it's hardly tragic. They don't even put you in plaster. *And* ...' He reached beside him. 'I have been furnished with these excellent NHS crutches and shall walk out under my own steam.'

'You know how to use those?'

'You forget, they ran me over in Southampton. Got plenty of practice then.' He pushed himself up and tried not to wince. It was his two cracked ribs that hurt most whenever he moved. 'Do me one favour, though.'

'Sure.'

'Carry my boot.'

Austin did, feeling slightly foolish without quite knowing why. 'Was it deliberate?'

'Oh yes, someone put his weight behind the stuff and pushed hard.'

'Who, do you think?'

'Not sure what I think.' He propelled himself expertly along the ground-floor corridor on his right foot and the crutches.

'You're a natural,' Austin said. 'Were they waiting for you there?'

'No, I don't think so. They could have seen me coming, but as a method of attacking someone, it's rubbish. I think

213

they were there, heard me stupidly announce myself as police and panicked. I'd clocked someone was in there and said so. Not so clever in retrospect.' They had reached the exit and the doors opened in front of them. 'Oh, crap. I'd forgotten all about the snow.'

'Thought you had. Don't worry, I'll try and catch you if you slip. Car's over there.'

With some groaning and much complaining about the smallness of Austin's car, McLusky managed to get into the passenger seat.

'Where to now?'

McLusky checked his watch. 'Might as well just drive me home. Or better still, drop me at the pub.'

'What about the lockup?'

'I got the local nick to secure the doors for us. We'll pick up the keys tomorrow, bright and early.' Just now he was ready for a bit of self-medication. 'Not sure how bright I'll be, but I'll be early.'

Not very, the answer would have been had McLusky remembered the question when he poured himself his first coffee in the morning. It was still dark outside, and even the Rossis, who ran the Italian grocer's downstairs, hadn't yet started setting out their vegetable stalls on the pavement. McLusky moved convincingly on one crutch around his kitchen, putting the pot back on the heat diffuser on the stove and catching toast from the toaster one-handed.

He had stayed at the pub until closing time and hobbled home across the street in optimistic mood. Yet by two in the morning the self-medication had worn off. He had woken up feeling cold, with his foot throbbing and his ribcage sending out jabs of pain with every careless breath he took. After washing down a good dose of painkillers with some water – strictly a night-time drink – he had slept fitfully for another few hours until finally giving up altogether around five. Three times he had woken from dreams that involved things falling on him, knocking him

214

down, burying him alive. The dream felt worse than his memories of the real event. In reality, it hadn't taken him long to fish out his mobile and call for help. By the time a PC together with the caretaker arrived to fuss over him, he had managed to extricate himself from the boxes and even found the torch he had dropped. The trip to the hospital hadn't been his idea, but the ambulance crew were adamant that he needed X-rays; his protestations that he was 'just fine' were soundly contradicted by his obvious inability to walk unaided.

Now all he needed, apparently, was time to let it heal; keep it propped up; not move about too much. And the cracked ribs? Avoid exercise and, of course, coughing. He lit another cigarette, and the thought of not coughing made him cough.

Austin called for him at eight. He had DC French with him, already sitting sideways on the back seat to allow the passenger seat to be pushed right back for the DI. French thought McLusky was mad not to stay at home, but she was in a good mood and glad to be out of the office. The last three days she had spent stuck in interview rooms with dickhead druggies or in front of the computer doing back-ground checks. Not that they wanted her along for her expertise. She was only going to Portishead to drive the DI's car back.

Coffee sloshed around in McLusky's stomach. He imag-ined it there, darkly bubbling and acidic, with bits of toast and paracetamol floating around on top. His foot throbbed and was cold, despite the fact that he had managed to pull a thick sock over the bandages. That in itself had been a painful procedure; so had dressing and undressing, because it made his ribs sing out. This morning he felt too groggy even to wind up Austin about his car.

Austin noticed it. He didn't admire machismo when it came to working despite illness and injury, but thought McLusky had other reasons for not taking a day off. He probably wanted to see if it had been worthwhile. He

215

wanted to see what was in the lockup. Austin hoped for all their sakes they'd find more than yacht varnish and *Sailing Monthly* magazines.

A PC from the local nick was already there, supervising the removal of the messy delivery that had done for McLusky's foot. It belonged to the lockup on the left, where a small heating-engineering firm stored its supplies. The PC had opened the lockup for the owner, Roddy Gow, and when McLusky heaved himself through the door, most of the delivery had disappeared to where it belonged.

'You weren't here yesterday afternoon by any chance?' he asked.

Gow, who was working in nothing but a rugby shirt despite the cold, let the box he had begun to lift slip back to the ground and straightened up. 'Are you going to ask me this question many more times? Because if you do, I'll have a card printed: *No I wasn't. He*'s asked me twice,' he nodded towards the constable, 'the caretaker did, and I had phone calls from you lot about it last night. I wasn't here; I was in Cardiff, with the missus. This stuff,' he picked up the box again, 'should have arrived today, not yesterday. It's called a clerical error.'

The outside door had been secured by police; the double door to Donald Bice's lockup had been sealed with police tape. Like a conjuror, McLusky produced the keys attached to the block of wood from his black jacket and handed it to French. 'In we go, then.'

French chose the right key first time. She pulled back the first leaf of the large door. McLusky only noticed that he had been holding his breath when he audibly expelled it. 'Right, get SOCO down here pronto. I'm not going in there, there's no room to swing my crutches. But you two have a careful look round.'

The lockup was three times as long as it was wide. Right at the front stood the missing VW Passat, driven in nose first and parked close to the partition wall on the left. Behind it, in the gloom created by the snow-covered skylight, he could make out the shape of a sailing dinghy, covered in faded tarpaulin. A narrow corridor allowed access to the back, while the right-hand side was taken up by a workbench, storage lockers, and shelf units crammed with sailing paraphernalia, tools, paint cans, sagging cardboard boxes and generally the kind of clutter that accumulated when people had a lot of space to leave it in.

French pulled on her gloves and clicked on a penlight. 'Are we looking for anything in particular?'

'Yes. We're looking for anything that might have got Bice killed.'

Austin opened the boot of the Passat. 'I wonder if our dust expert SOCO can tell us how long the car's been in here undisturbed. Boot's empty.'

French, meanwhile, had gingerly opened the driver's door. 'Forensics can probably tell us. Nothing interesting in the car that I can see without crawling all over it. Mind you, the keys are in the ignition.'

'Perhaps they attacked him here, or got to him in his car and parked it here.' McLusky remained leaning in the door frame. 'Right, leave it, keep SOCO happy; tell me what else you see.'

'Dinghy on a trailer.' French lifted the tarpaulin, shone her torch underneath. 'Sailing stuff inside.'

'*Sailing stuff?*' McLusky managed the first smile of the day.

'Oars or paddles or whatever.'

'You come from a long line of seafaring folk, DC French?'

'Normandy peasant stock, sir.'

'Sailing stuff it is, then. I think I'll go next door.' Bice's lockup neighbour Gow was getting ready to leave. 'How well did you know Donald Bice?'

'I didn't. To say hello to, but when I'm down here, I'm usually in a hurry to load stuff or drop things off and have no time to chat. Not that they were chatty themselves.'

'They?'

'Did I say "they"?'

217

'He brought people with him?'

Roddy Gow thought for second. 'Erm, no, but it wasn't always him. Once or twice I saw a younger bloke.'

'Could you describe him?'

He could. 'Yeah, quite a contrast to the older guy. *He* always had a tan. The younger one, he was blond, blue eyes, and quite pale.'

McLusky thought he could smell marzipan. 'When did you last see him here?'

Gow shrugged and secured the door to his lockup, tested the lock. 'Not sure. Last week, I think.'

'There it is, page three.' Ed folded the page over to give Phil Warren an opportunity to admire the item. In the top right corner, set into a box, ran the fat headline CAN YOU HELP SOLVE THIS MYSTERY? Underneath, a few lines set out the information that the 'mysterious fragments' had been received anonymously. The lucky puzzle solver would win a meal for two at a well-known pizza chain. The text surrounded the reproduction of the first piece of the photograph that had landed in the *Herald*'s post room. Warren glanced at it without comment and went back to clacking away at her keyboard, though slower than before. Ed picked up the paper and looked at it again. 'Well, *I'm* glad we're running it. We haven't had anything like it for ages. We used to run stuff like that all the time.'

Warren snorted. 'Spot the ball.'

'I know it seems naive now, but people really loved it. I remember blokes arguing over the pictures in the pub. And we used to stick close-ups of architectural detail on page three and give cash prizes to the eagle-eyed readers who could tell where they were taken.'

'This is different. *We* don't know where it was taken, or who the people are.' She couldn't believe the editor had gone for it. She wished Ed had never mentioned it to him. But circulation figures had dropped again, and even hits on the online edition had fallen. People were becoming news-weary. By the time they got home, they were convinced they had seen it all on their mobiles.

This was different in other ways, too. Another slice of photograph had arrived, even narrower than the others. You could now see there were at least three people in the picture, though one was a little blurred. It was a night-time scene. Trees, a silver car, possibly a Mercedes. The tableau was illuminated by the headlights of the car, or another car. It was grainy, and it gave her the creeps.

'That's why we're asking for "help to solve this mystery".'

She had argued against it with the editor. Whoever had taken the picture wanted something. It hadn't been taken by a professional photographer, at least not a press photographer, or they wouldn't be playing games with a local paper. To publish the picture slices meant doing the photographer's bidding without knowing what his purpose was.

The editor had asked her if she was feeling all right.

The item would not appear in the online edition, only in hard copy. 'It's even grainier in print,' Warren said. 'With any luck, no one's going to recognize it.'

Ed shrugged and walked off. 'The people in the photograph will, surely.'

'You won't even try and guess?' Dearlove asked French, flicking the copy of the *Bristol Herald* on his desk.

French shook her head and went back to work, logging on to the network. 'Deedee, that could be anything. Could be the bottom of my garden. In fact I'm sure it must be.'

'I'm going to keep this; they'll print the next piece tomorrow.' Not that he had any idea who he might invite out for a meal-for-two should he win. He definitely couldn't ask French; she'd just laugh at him. He tore inexpertly around the mystery picture and stuck the piece of paper under a tin mug full of chewed and leaky biros. As he did so, one of several empty crisp packets from his desk sailed to the floor.

McLusky, holding a full mug of instant in his right and wielding a crutch with his left, eyed Dearlove's desk with distaste as he hobbled past it. It was even messier than his own, and that suit definitely needed dry-cleaning. He'd talk to him about it in a quiet moment. Of course when he did, he would first have to make sure his own desk wasn't strewn with pastry crumbs.

In his office, he checked his watch. Twenty minutes or so. They'd call his mobile. He sat the mug on his desk and began straightening piles of papers, and the tottering hill of files on the floor beside his desk. The bin was heaped high with rubbish. He tried compressing it down, but he had done it several times before and it appeared the rubbish could only be compressed so far and no further. Still, the place didn't look so bad now. Not as bad as Deedee's, surely. His mobile chimed and he answered it. 'Be right down. Well, actually it'll take a couple of minutes.'

Since his first outing to the Portishead lockup, McLusky had slush-proofed his left foot by tying a plastic carrier bag round it and stretching a second sock over that. It now looked even bigger, but it was no longer cold and felt better protected. He grabbed his second crutch and left the office.

'That looks painful. I can see why you asked for an automatic,' said the man who handed over the keys. The hire car, a graphite-coloured Alfa Romeo MiTo, looked improbably clean and shiny, at least for a vehicle that McLusky was going to drive. It brought back memories of a short-lived police Skoda he had once driven. He signed for it, adjusted the seat, stowed his crutches in the passenger space and drove off. He didn't bring a camera; his phone took adequate pictures for what he had in mind.

He escaped south-west out of the city in playfully dancing snow, with the heating in the Alfa on high. Driving with a redundant left foot was a novelty; so was the effortlessness with which the car dialled up and down through the gears. It kept him amused until he got to the large roundabout and turned off towards Keynsham.

He spotted the cake shop only after his second pass of the high street. Back at Albany Road, he had fondly imagined that he could take a picture of James Boyce from the comfort of his hire car, but that seemed unlikely now. The window of Keynsham Cake Craft was impenetrably overstuffed with cakes: children's birthday cakes, 70 Today cakes, Happy Retirement cakes. The centre of the display was taken up by a multi-tiered nightmare of a wedding cake, slowly rotating on a glass stand. The space between cakes was taken up by the arcane paraphernalia of cake decorating. None of it made McLusky want to eat cake. A horn bleated behind him – he was holding up the traffic again. He drove on until he found a space on a single yellow in a side street, and swung on his crutches back to Keynsham Cake Craft. His plan B had always been to go and unnerve Boyce in his shop.

McLusky liked the old-fashioned shop bell set off by the door sweeping against it, but that was the last thing he enjoyed in there. The small part of the shop devoted to sales was unconvincingly old-fashioned. He had probably expected it to smell like a patisserie, darkly of chocolate, vanilla and coffee, but the place had no particular smell apart from a vague sweetness in the air. The grey-haired woman behind the counter wore a pink-and-white apron and looked up from studying papers in a ring binder. 'How can I help?'

He swung close to the counter so he could lean on it. 'Is James about?'

The woman looked at him first puzzled, then with suspicion. *I know all my son's friends, and you're not one of them*, her look seemed to say. 'May I enquire who is asking?'

'Liam. Liam McLusky. Bristol CID.' He held open his ID wallet for inspection.

'Oh, it's about his father. I'll get him for you.' The woman's complexion, as pale as her son's, didn't alter, but she looked almost relieved. 'Will you be all right there on your crutches? Do you want me to bring you a chair?'

'Very kind, but I'll manage.' While the woman disappeared through a half-glazed door, McLusky primed his mobile. He had practised covert photography with his phone, and now considered himself a dab hand at pretend-ing to make a call while actually taking pictures. He propped himself against the counter, pointed his right ear in the direction Boyce would appear from and started taking pic-tures as soon as he did. His mother followed close behind. 'Aha … aha … yes …' He spoke into the silent mobile, then mouthed *Be right with you* at James, who looked less relaxed than his mother. McLusky pretended to terminate the call, then quickly checked his display to see if it had worked. Cakes, bits of counter, the dado rail on the wall. No James. Had to be the crutches that had put him off his aim. The shop door tinkled open and a woman with two young chil-dren entered, directly followed by an elderly man. Suddenly the tiny shop was crowded and noisy.

'Is there somewhere we can have a quick chat, Mr Boyce?'

Boyce looked at his mother, but she was busy attending customers. 'I'm fairly busy right now.'

'How about in the back?' McLusky suggested, making ready to swing behind the counter.

Boyce fluttered his hands between them. 'It's a food prep-aration area, I can't let you in there.'

McLusky jerked his head. 'Okay, outside.' Once on the slushy pavement, with the door closed behind them, he brought out his mobile and turned the camera on. 'Say cheese.' He took a picture and, as arranged the day before, sent it via text message to Roddy Gow.

'Hang on, what are you doing?' Boyce coloured rapidly. 'You can't take a picture of me without my consent!'

'You're in a public place; here I can take all the pictures I want.' He pocketed his mobile, leaned close to Boyce and planted the tip of the left crutch firmly on the other man's foot, then leant all his weight on it.

'Hey, you're on my …' Boyce stopped himself, swallowed hard. His foot hurt like hell. He tried to pull it back, but the infuriating man had it pinned to the pavement.

'You were saying?' McLusky watched Boyce fumble; he looked to be in genuine pain. Good. Not so good if he had

the wrong man, of course, but he didn't think a wholly innocent one would put up with this treatment. He bounced a
couple of times on the crutch for emphasis.

'Ow! Okay, I'm sorry. I didn't know you'd get hurt. I just
panicked. I thought it would help me get away. I had no
idea it would put you on crutches. I'm really sorry. Ow!'
McLusky taking the crutch off his foot sent another jab of
pain through it. Now freed, he lifted it off the pavement and
gently shook it from side to side. 'I'm in trouble, aren't I?'
He glanced over his shoulder towards the door.

'I'd say so. Assaulting a police officer, withholding evidence, obstructing a murder investigation. Excuse me.' His
mobile chimed an alert. He checked the text from Roddy
Gow: *That's him*. Despite having been almost certain before,
McLusky felt relieved.

'How did you know?' Boyce asked.

'I didn't know. But we checked CCTV footage, and your
car showed up.'

Boyce pulled a pained face. 'The shop's not doing well;
we have debts up to here …'

'You can sell the flat your father lived in. There'll be plenty
of money to go around.'

'Perhaps not as much as you think. This place was expensive, smack in the high street.'

'You live over the shop?' A nod. 'With your mother?'

'She doesn't know anything about it, the lockup or anything. I thought I could keep it to myself. Keep the money to
myself, I mean. I thought I could get out. Set her up right
and get out into something else, something of my own.'

'Even though you knew the money had almost certainly
come from drugs? And that your father might have died for
it? You changed your name to distance yourself from your
father, but you're quite happy to walk away with his money.'

Boyce shrugged impatiently and lifted his aching foot
again, rubbed a thumb over the scuff mark on his shoe. 'It's
money. It's just money, it looks like any other. It was an
opportunity.'

223

McLusky was getting tired of standing around on crutches in the cold. 'Not so much, as it turns out. Okay, where is it now?'

'It's just in there,' Boyce said, deflated. He pointed at the shop window.

'Where "in there"?'

Boyce tapped the window. 'It's in that one.' He indicated a garish child's birthday cake covered in bright red marzipan, chased with multicoloured sweets and the piped greeting *Happy 14th Birthday* on top.

'You baked it into a cake?'

'*No*,' Boyce said impatiently. 'They're not real, are they? They're display cakes. Cardboard covered with marzipan.'

'Is it all in there?' A reluctant nod from Boyce. 'How much?'

'A hundred and ten. There was a bit more; I spent some.'

A hundred and ten thousand pounds. With the cake in a gift box inside a carrier bag dangling from his arm as he swung along the high street back to his car, McLusky thought that people, and that included police officers, had been tempted off the straight and narrow by less than that. He stuffed the bag behind the driver's seat, stowed the crutches and was reaching for the ignition when his mobile rang. It was Austin. He listened, keeping his side of the conversation short.

'What? Where? Oh shit, that's all we bloody need.'

Chapter Eighteen

All the way back up to Bristol he had driven into worsening snow. While Keynsham had received picture-book flurries, dirty grey clouds had dumped a heavy load of it on the city, bringing visibility down to a few yards and slowing traffic to a crawl. On the car radio, McLusky listened to talk of closing more schools and to announcements of cancellations of trains and buses. Bristol Airport was closed due to fog.

When eventually he crawled up the A360 to the bottom of Rownham Hill, found a gap in the traffic and crossed over on to the grass verge, he seemed to be the last to arrive. He left the Alfa at the end of a row of police vehicles. His crutches earned him curious looks from a couple of constables but no comment.

When he rounded the corner on to the familiar cycle path, he stopped and glared with a feeling akin to hatred. Here he stood again, and the victim, surrounded by SOCOs and attended to by Dr Coulthart, lay, as far as he could make out, just where the body of Mike Oatley had been found. Cables were still being run and more arc lights set up, which was just as well. It was dark now, visibility was bad and it would have been all too easy to walk straight into the black, icy river.

Austin spotted him and came towards him, but McLusky moved forward to meet the DS halfway. He didn't want to give the impression that he needed special treatment. Before each swing he jabbed the crutches hard into the snow to make sure they didn't slip. 'They really did dump her in the same place,' he said with disgust.

'Yes, pretty much. Right in the middle of the path this time, but otherwise, same place.'

'Tell me it wasn't the same damn cyclist who found her, Jane, because if it was, then I'm going to have him.'

'No, a couple of kids, ten-year-olds, came down here to smoke.'

'That's a fag they won't forget in a hurry. I suppose they trampled all over the bloody locus.'

'They did a bit. No more than anyone would have done, though.' It was obvious the DI was in a foul mood. 'Is your foot playing up?'

Throbbing was the word. 'Just a bit. Painkillers must have worn off. Hang on.' He reached into his pocket, found the bubble pack of painkillers and pressed two pills into his hand, then another one for good measure, and popped them into his mouth. He turned the crutch upside down and with the ring of the armrest scooped up a clean-looking dollop of snow, which he stuffed in his mouth to wash down the acrid pills.

'You really have done this before,' Austin said, almost impressed.

'Too right. But tell me it doesn't feel déjà-bloody-vu to you too.' He swung forward a pace and called to the group around the body: 'Okay to come closer?'

One SOCO looked back. 'Fine. Come along the corridor, gents.'

McLusky travelled along the marked-out corridor to the deposition site, where an upbeat Dr Coulthart waited for them. 'Good afternoon, Inspector. You're handling those crutches like Long John Silver. Injured in the line of duty, I hear. I wish you a speedy recovery.'

'Thanks, Doc.' He nodded at the body. 'Not killed here, then. Enlighten me: same place, same method, same killer?'

At their feet in eight inches of snow lay the body of a woman with mid-length brown hair, now caked with dried blood. Her features were unrecognizable, a puckered mess of black and blue, swollen and in places ruptured. The body was clothed in a pink and white jumper, shortish blue skirt, opaque black tights and walking boots. The tights were torn just above the boots. Her clothes were filthy and bloody.

'You don't really expect an answer to that here and now, do you? There are a couple of differences, however, that might puncture that theory straight away.'

'Oh yes?'

'The victim is female.'

'I'm glad you are here to point this stuff out.'

Coulthart ignored it. 'And she was strangled. Manual strangulation marks; you can just make them out there.' He pointed to the dark bruising on the side of her neck. 'I'm not sure that's what killed her yet, but there you go. That's two differences. We might find more.'

'By all means make our lives as difficult as you can, Doctor.' Austin had caught some of McLusky's gloom.

McLusky, however, appeared to lighten up. 'No, DS Austin. We want the good doctor to tell us categorically that this can't be the same perpetrator, because then we can simply hand it over to Trinity Road and be on our way. We couldn't possibly be asked to work on two separate murder inquiries.'

'But we already are. The Leigh Woods murders and now these two.'

'Same perpetrators.'

'We've no real evidence for that yet.' He turned towards Coulthart, looking for support.

'Don't look at me; it's forensics who are dragging their feet.'

'But surely … Both Deeming and Bice were involved in drugs. There isn't the slightest indication that Mike Oatley was. Then we have two different ways of getting rid of the bodies for starters. And both Deeming and Bice had been tied up. Not Mike Oatley.'

'Because he was already too beaten up to run.' McLusky stomped a crutch for emphasis. 'One of his knees was

227

shattered.' He had already had this argument with Denkhaus. *Same perpetrators.* He'd been as stubborn as a child about it, without any real evidence to back it up. In the end, the super had relented, probably because he didn't want it to be two separate investigations either.

'Any sign at all that this one was tied up?' Austin asked Coulthart.

'Yes, there are signs that her arms were tied with tape. I think we may find that her legs were as well. She was probably gagged with tape too.'

'Okay, I give you that,' Austin said. 'But it's a different method of tying up and gagging.'

'You're nit-picking now,' McLusky said.

'At least admit there are nits to pick.'

'Not on me. But maybe, yeah. Time of death, Doc?'

'Oh, sometime during the night, perhaps, though that's merely a guess at this stage,' Coulthart said. For once the pathologist looked genuinely uncertain rather than deliberately vague. By now McLusky had learnt to tell the two states apart. 'We've no way of knowing what the temperatures were like in whatever place she was before. And it's sub-zero out here.'

'How long do we think she's been lying here?'

'SOCO think about an hour before they got here, which makes it about four.'

'What?' McLusky looked about him as though searching for the originator of this wild theory. 'You're telling me they dumped her here in broad daylight? And no one saw a thing?'

'Hardly broad daylight. It was already quite dark then. There was a heavy snowfall, heavier than now, and look …'

McLusky did. He couldn't see far in any direction, and the opposite side of the river was completely obscured. He went rhetorical. 'Still. Look at it. This is the nearest access point, so they probably stopped out there rather than carry the body along the path. But that road must have been hellishly busy at four. And for what? I can't see anything special

228

about this place. And if it isn't special, then there's another reason for dumping them here.'

Coulthart picked up his case. 'I'll leave you to your musings, gentlemen.'

McLusky watched him go, remembering the doctor's perishable soul and briefly wondering what soulful delights he might be travelling towards tonight. Then other matters claimed his attention. He found the senior SOCO. It was the same man who had predicted the time of deposition of Mike Oatley's body. 'You think she was dumped here an hour before she was found?'

'That's our estimate, and we don't think we're out much either way.'

'No chance of footprints, I guess? Or better still, tyre marks?'

'I think we might be lucky with both. We've been digging out quite a few, last time as well. The footprint compacts the snow, then snow falls on top, but its infill has a different density. We dig around it, take away the whole thing, stick it in a box and keep it sub-zero. We won't get much of a tread pattern, but size and shape definitely. Same with tyre marks.'

'Is that what all the digging was back there?'

'Yes. We might get lucky. If I'm right, then I think it's a van rather than a car.'

'Interesting.'

'Yes, a red one, we think.'

'Very funny.' SOCO humour. McLusky could do without it today.

It was after one in the morning when he got away from the site and drove home. He liked driving in the city at night: there was space and air to move about in; you could look further than the nearest car. He could hear sirens close by as he turned into Stokes Croft. Checking his mirrors, he saw two fire engines following. He pulled over and waited for the heavy diesel engines to growl past, then followed in their wake. When it looked as though they were going his way, turning into Ashley Road, he did a quick mental check of his kitchen: yes, he had turned the gas off this morning. The fire engines carried on down Ashley Road. Just out of sight around the next bend, he could see the bright glow of a fire and black smoke billowing skywards. Instead of turning off, and purely for sightseeing purposes, he drove along until he got to the site of the fire.

When he got there, he saw Constable Pym standing in the middle of the road, signalling him to stop. Flames roared behind two first-floor windows of a 1960s three-storey building. He was in time to see the well-rehearsed routine of the firefighters connecting and rolling out hoses. A small crowd had gathered on the pavement opposite, being shouted at to move further away from the engines. McLusky got out of the car. He was instantly hit by the heat of the fire, even at this distance. He could hear its dark roar too, until the noise from the pumps drowned it out. The flames soon collapsed as jets from two hoses pumped through the shattered windows on to the flames. Pym stopped another car, which then started a laborious U-turn. McLusky swung on his crutches to the constable.

Pym brightened up. 'It's you, sir, I didn't recognize your car. Did they call you out for this?'

'I was on my way home. I live round the corner.'

'Seriously? Well I thought I was on my way home too. Then this cropped up.'

'What is that place? It's not residential, is it?'

'No, it's a local charity. A community centre sort of thing.'

'No one in the building?'

'There was no sign. It's normally closed this time of night.'

McLusky nodded, prepared to turn around on his crutches. He was tired and had lost interest.

'It could be arson, sir.'

'Could it?'

'Someone reported hearing a crash. Broken glass. Just before the fire broke out. And the centre's van was torched a few days ago.'

'Was it? Okay, Pym. Let me know what the fire officers say once they've been over it.'

He turned his car around and drove home. Once inside the flat, he flicked on the light and exhaled. He could see his breath in front of him. He thought he'd probably be more comfortable sleeping in the car.

'I wasn't a *hundred* per cent sure it was drugs money. He did get paid a lot, might have put it by over the years.'

James Boyce had handed himself in as McLusky had counselled. This advice had earned him another rocket from upstairs, and he had to admit to a certain amount of relief when Boyce actually turned up at Albany Road, on his own, without a solicitor. Now in Interview Room 2, Boyce was contrite and co-operative. McLusky let Austin conduct most of the interview so there could be no question of animosity.

'Is that what you want us to believe, or is it what you wanted to believe yourself?' Austin didn't wait for an answer. 'Did you see any drugs in the lockup?'

'No. There was nothing.'

'You didn't find some bags of yellow or brown stuff and put them aside for a rainy day?'

'No, I wouldn't deal in drugs. There was nothing. I would tell you. I'm totally against drugs.'

One of the things SOCO had found and didn't need forensics for was a note band that had once belonged to a thousand-pound bundle of twenties. 'And you found the money how? Presumably a hundred and ten grand hadn't just been left lying around?' Austin asked.

McLusky spluttered as the tea he'd been sipping went down the wrong way. 'Excuse me, back in a while,' he said when he had composed himself. 'You carry on.'

'DI McLusky leaving the room,' Austin said for the benefit of the machine recording the interview.

Once in the corridor, McLusky hurried. He had exchanged crutches for a single walking stick this morning and had also managed to fit his left foot into a shoe one size too large for

231

him, both items bought at a charity shop in St Pauls. Using the stick and walking on his heel, he hobbled along as fast as he could manage. 'Like a demented cripple,' Sorbie muttered to himself as he watched the inspector limp past the CID room.

McLusky felt in too much of a hurry to wait for the lift, and propelled himself down the stairs. His haste drew an interested glance from Sergeant Hayes at the front desk as he clattered out of the door into the car park. The MiTo bleeped and unlocked itself. Only when his hand had closed around the handles of the carrier bag did his heartbeat begin to steady. He travelled back up serenely in the lift.

'DI McLusky enters the interview room,' Austin informed the recorder.

McLusky liberated the gift box from the carrier. He commented on it for the benefit of the recorder as he opened the box and lifted out the cake, which seemed none the worse for having bounced around on the floor of the car. The money was tightly crammed into the hollow cake. He lifted it out, counting as he went. Most of it consisted of neat bundles of twenties, with only some rolls of mixed notes on top, secured by rubber bands. 'Happy fourteenth birthday. One hundred and ten grand, accounted for.'

Austin didn't comment on the fact that it hadn't arrived in an evidence bag until after the interview was wound up.

'The money totally slipped my mind. Dead bodies have that effect on me.'

'We have a preliminary from forensics on the garage, minute traces of heroin found in a storage box. You think Boyce is telling the truth? That he just found the money, not sold the drugs?'

'Can you see him dealing drugs? I don't think he'd have walked away with the money; they'd simply have taken it off him.'

'Then it was his dad. But *he* walked away with the money.'

'Yes. Donald Bice knew more than just how to drive a boat. Either he was aware of a consignment of drugs hidden

232

somewhere and laid his hands on it after Fenton was securely inside, or it was hidden in the lockup all the time. And he was no street dealer. You know what street dealers' cash looks like: bags of grubby notes. You saw the money. That came in one lump.'

'And it's about the right amount for two kilos of good-quality heroin.'

'Exactly. But if he managed to walk away with the money, why was he killed?'

'Good question,' Austin admitted. 'I've got one of my own, though: what makes you so sure the cycle-path bodies tie in? Especially the woman? She could turn out to be a rape or robbery victim. Beaten for her credit-card details, for instance.'

'Did you see what she was wearing? If she'd had credit on her card, she'd have bought some decent clothes.' McLusky saw Austin take a deep breath and held up his hands. 'I know, it's all pretty vague. In both cases the killer takes a lot of time over the killings and much less care over the disposal of the body.'

'But at least the first two *were* buried. These were just dumped.'

'That's because they were killed for a different reason, Jane. Same killers, different reason.'

Austin took another deep breath, but McLusky cut him off again. 'No point arguing about it. Listen to the oracle. When forensics dig their lazy arses out of the snow, they'll confirm it. Anyway, we've a more pressing question. Who's the second cycle-path body? Let's try and find out before a third one lands on the mat, shall we?'

Chapter Nineteen

Alison Laing jabbed the ball of tissue into her eyes and made an effort to stop sobbing. Constable Purkis, who was sitting opposite her at the kitchen table, pushed the box of tissues closer to her. The woman pulled out a fresh one and noisily blew her nose with it. She was glad they'd sent a woman; you didn't have to try and be delicate around them.

'We can't be certain yet that it is Deborah.'

'Debbie. No one calls her Deborah. But if she's not at home and she didn't start her job, then where is she?' She had tried for two days to get hold of her, even went around to her place in St Pauls and leant on her doorbell. In desperation she had called the Bristol Royal Infirmary to see if she could reach her at her new job. And eventually she'd been told that Deborah Glynn had not shown up for work. Not on the Monday, and not today.

The doorbell rang and Alison made to get up.

'No, don't worry, I'll get it,' Purkis told her. In the hall, she used the spyhole and saw a fish-eye view of DS Austin, scratching his nose. 'Come in, sir.'

'How's ... erm ...'

'Alison Laing. Tearful. Any news?'

'All bad, I'm afraid. We went to Glynn's flat. It's definitely been searched without any sign of a break-in, and the neighbours haven't seen or heard her music since Saturday. Apparently she likes to play loud music. Hip-hop. The neighbours had noted the quiet with relief; now they feel guilty about it. She used to have a boyfriend living with her until recently. I'm hoping Ms Laing knows where we can find him. McLusky is still at Glynn's place, grilling one of the neighbours.'

'How's his foot?'

'Making him short-tempered and more stubborn than ever.'

Five miles away, at a window of Deborah Glynn's second-floor flat, McLusky was struggling to subdue his stubbornness and short temper as he saw DSI Denkhaus arrive in the street below. The super's Land Rover was the only thing down there not covered in snow. Upstairs and downstairs neighbours were being questioned. SOCO and forensics still hadn't arrived, and McLusky had sent Austin to talk to the girlfriend who had alerted them. He had hoped to find a few minutes of breathing space, to get a feeling for who Deborah Glynn was and what had written a violent death into her life story, along with that of three others.

There were more possessions here than in Mike Oatley's place, more books, CDs and DVDs, only it wasn't differences he was looking for, it was similarities. If they were here, they didn't show up easily. Except that again papers were strewn all around a couple of box files on the floor, and drawers had been left open. If the intruders had found what they were looking for, then it was no longer here, and today it was beginning to get him down. He was profoundly grateful that the kettle hadn't disappeared from Glynn's kitchen as it had from Oatley's. Strange events he didn't mind; weird McLusky hated.

Playing catch-up was a police officer's lot for most of the time, with a few bright moments of 'catching them red-handed' thrown in, but he knew he was about to have his ear bent about the lack of progress and the tenuous connections between the killings, and for a brief moment he wished he'd stayed at Louise's place, as she had urged, put his injured foot up on a cushion and let someone else have a go.

He leant heavily with both hands on his stick and nodded at Denkhaus, who stepped gingerly into the little sitting room.

'No SOCOs, McLusky?'

'Imminent.'

'She wasn't killed here?'

'No way.'

'Again no sign of a break-in. Could be both knew their killer and let them in. The two could still be unconnected and the second killer simply used the same place to dump—'

McLusky cut across him. 'No. They were grabbed elsewhere, killed, dumped and their house keys used to gain entrance to their flats.'

'We've not established that yet ...'

McLusky limped into the kitchen to the waste bin and stomped his walking stick on the pedal. The plastic lid flipped back. He reached inside and with his little finger fished out a bunch of house keys. He held them up for Denkhaus, who had watched from the sitting room. 'We have now. Same place scene-of-crime found Oatley's set.'

Denkhaus still made a show of hesitating but was already nodding. 'All right. Carry on.' McLusky and his bloody conjuring tricks. He turned on his heel and walked out just as SOCOs and forensics clattered their gear on to the landing.

McLusky lifted his stick and let the bin lid drop. He raised the keys dangling from his little finger to eye level and shook his head: a McLusky hunch that actually came off; well what do you know? He left the field to the white-suited army and had just started the engine of the MiTo when his mobile rang.

'Deborah Glynn's ex-boyfriend Gary,' Austin said. 'He was not a happy camper when she threw him out. According to her friend Alison here, they had huge rows about it.'

'Yes, neighbours here said there were noisy rows.'

'Apparently he picked up a couple of ornaments and threw them at her.'

'Tut. Can't have that, can we. Have we got an address for him?'

'He went to kip on a mate's sofa when he moved. Alison thinks he might still be there. Gary is difficult to shift, she said.'

'All right, give me the address, I'll meet you there. We can deliver the news together.'

A small attic flat in St George. There was no door release. It had taken them quite a long time to get Gary Hunter to come down and open the door, then to persuade him to climb upstairs again before they told him what it was about. Made him sit down on the narrow sofa; delivered the bad news.

Gary was a runt of a man with a narrow triangular face and large eyebrows. He was alone, his friend at work. The TV was turned on, the games console plugged in. On the screen, two Japanese warriors faced each other for unarmed combat, not quite motionless, quivering. Gary stared at it, hands on his knees, similarly frozen, his life paused.

Besides the sofa, which had blankets and a sleeping bag rolled into one corner, there was only a fat blue cushion on the floor to sit on. They remained standing on either side of Gary, Austin by the window, McLusky leaning in the door to the hall. 'Can we get you anything? Glass of water?' Gary managed a tiny shake of the head. 'I appreciate how it must affect you, but I'm afraid we'd still like you to answer a few questions for us. If that's all right.'

'Sure.'

'You two recently broke up; when exactly did—'

Gary suddenly spluttered alive. 'Murdered? How, how was she murdered? Why? I mean …' He subsided, looking from McLusky to Austin and back.

'We can talk about that later, when he have more facts. At the moment, all I can tell you is that Debbie's body was found on the Pill cycle path. We need to establish some basic facts that will help us put this crime into context. I believe you used to live together until recently.'

'Yeah. At her place.'

'So that was her place. She lived there before you two met?' A nod. 'And you broke up when?'

'Ten ... ten days ago.'

'She asked you to leave.'

'Yeah.'

'Threw you out.'

'What's that got to do with it? What, you think *I* killed Debbie because she dumped me?'

Austin, who was blocking out half the light from the small dormer window, took over. 'You had a row. Several rows. The neighbours heard you.'

'So what? Everyone has rows.'

'But yours were more violent than some. You threw things.'

'She chucked stuff back. It was almost comedy, only she was really angry.'

'You must have felt resentful. At being made to leave.'

'Well I wasn't exactly chuffed. I mean, what do you expect? I'm homeless now.' There was a short pause, in which his eyes unfocused. 'But I ... I really liked her. Really. She was my *girlfriend*.'

'When were you last there?'

'I said, ten days ago.'

'You haven't been back?'

'She chucked me out; why would I go back?'

'It's only that obviously your DNA will be all over the place. How did you make the move?'

'What?'

'When you moved, did you hire a van?'

'A van? What are you talking about? No. Dan picked me up in his car. I don't have much stuff.'

'Dan?'

'Bloke who rents this place.'

Austin's mobile rang. He listened for a moment before interrupting the caller. 'Hang on, Deedee, he's here, you can tell him.' He handed his phone across.

'McLusky. What you got, Dearlove?' He listened while his eyes rested heavily on Gary, who began chewing his nails, looking from one officer to the other. 'Don't read me the

239

whole damn thing, just give me the gist of it.' McLusky listened, nodded, nodded, then said: 'Thanks, Deedee, excellent.' He handed the mobile back to Austin and turned to Gary. 'Can you account for your movements over the last weekend?'

'I was here.'

'All weekend?'

'We were playing computer games. Ask Dan.'

'We will. Okay, thank you for your time.'

'Is that it?' Gary asked. He remained sitting, wide-eyed.

'Yes. We'll see ourselves out.'

Austin followed McLusky down the stairs. They had to let pass a gaggle of students and a man carrying a BMX bike, which meant that only when they reached street level could he echo Gary's question. 'Is that it?'

'That is it.'

'What did Deedee have to say?'

'We've been wasting our time here. Forensics are backing me up for once. The two in the woods and the two on the path were most likely killed by the same person or persons.'

'How do they make that out?'

'Something to do with bricks, apparently.'

A hundred and fifty thousand. Why hadn't he asked for more? Two hundred? Two hundred and fifty? It might have to last him a lifetime. The phone call had been the scariest bit, much scarier than anything so far. Even though he had been close to him for months, knew his distinctive voice, had heard it many times on the phone too, the phone call had frightened him. He'd had a few drinks beforehand; that helped a bit. He'd written down everything he needed to say. Mouth dry, hands slippery with sweat. The voice changer he had ordered from the gadget shop really had worked: he had sounded like a woman, a distorted, electronic woman, but definitely female. He kept saying 'we want' and 'we demand', as though he wasn't alone in this. And the big man had fallen for it. He'd called him 'bitch' and said 'whoever you are'. Once he heard that, he knew

240

the disguise had worked. He was so relieved, he nearly missed the next sentence completely. But the big man had agreed. To everything. *Just say the word ... reasonable ... we can do business ... as long as the picture gets destroyed. As long as no more strips go to the* Bristol Herald. Time and place had been agreed. And if he saw anything suspicious, then the deal was off. *I'm as anxious as you are ... you have my word.*

That was when he knew they would kill him. A lousy hundred and fifty thousand and he was inviting them to kill him. *Anxious.* It wasn't in the man's vocabulary; it was an act to allay his fears. He had never heard him speak like that, not to anyone. Or could the picture puzzle really have scared him? Perhaps it had. It could definitely destroy him, force him to flee the country, have plastic surgery even. That wasn't such a bad idea either. How much did a new face cost? he wondered. He had done his best over the past few weeks to change his own appearance. He had grown a beard, shaved his head, bought unfashionable, middle-aged clothes at the charity shop down the road. He looked older now anyway, just eight months on from the beating. It had aged him inside and out. Perhaps the big man would get a few grey hairs before this was over. He certainly hoped so. But first they would try and kill him. The age of handing over photographs was over. There were no negatives now to destroy; digital pictures could get endlessly copied and disseminated. Once you had been photographed, and as long as that image lived on a computer, you were at its mercy. That was why the man hadn't argued; that was why he had agreed so quickly: they were going to kill him anyway. It was the only way the big man could ever be sure. Sweat pricked on his chest now as he prepared two more envelopes to send to the *Herald*. The big man had no intention of letting him walk away with the money? Well, two could play at that game.

McLusky's delight about forensics backing up his wild hunches was short-lived. If anything, it seemed to highlight just how little had been achieved and how much the

241

investigation was in danger of bogging down. He'd been here before. Many murder investigations that dealt with an unknown perpetrator went through a phase like this, where they all worked flat out following up witness statements, interviewing witnesses, hunting around on computers, hanging on the phone for tedious hours with nothing tangible to show for it apart from having eliminated the obvious, like the man upstairs, the irate neighbour, the ex-boyfriend, the disgruntled customer. This phase was not McLusky's forte; this was not where he excelled. He performed adequately, but it took a more organized mind to do it reliably well. He admitted it quietly to himself, tentatively to Austin, never to anyone else.

Breakthrough. It was what everyone hoped for, but no one even used the word, since it implied that until then, you'd been staring at a brick wall. What he was staring at right now was a room full of less-than-enthusiastic detectives. He was acutely conscious of the problems ahead, and opted for a mix of optimistic spin and pushiness. 'We can now say with some certainty that all four victims were killed by the same perpetrators. We are most likely looking for more than one person, since all four appear to have been snatched, probably held prisoner for a while and systematically murdered. All were severely beaten, but three also had been stoned.' He tapped the forensics report. 'In case you were wondering what *lapidation* meant. The two Leigh Woods bodies and the woman. Many of the injuries were caused not by blows, but by some bastards throwing stones at them. It is, of course, a good way of delivering injury without getting close, without getting your hands too dirty, without getting blood on your own clothes. The victims were tied up while this went on. I'm told that some of the missiles used were brick, and that these three had brick dust embedded in their skin where they were hit, not by whole bricks but probably by bits of broken bricks. Brick dust was also present in Mike Oatley's hair. It means all four were taken to the same place to be killed, then their bodies were disposed of elsewhere.'

242

A young DC raised a hand. 'But broken bricks are everywhere, sir. They could have been killed in all sorts of locations. A brick's a brick, innit?'

'No it ain't, though until a couple of hours ago I'd have said the same. I called forensics about it, who put me on to a guy at the university who convinced me otherwise. And if anyone's interested in a forty-minute lecture on the fascinating history of brick-making, I can give them his number later. The ingredients of bricks have changed, and these are early nineteenth century. That's sufficiently old to narrow down the location even in a city like Bristol.' There were optimistic murmurs. 'Bearing in mind, of course, that brick has often been recycled.' Disappointed groans. 'But we might be looking for a derelict nineteenth-century place somewhere. There aren't many left; everything is being developed now.' He patted the handle of his walking stick with the forensics file for emphasis. 'There's further evidence that the murders are connected: we have two partial footprints, of a trainer, one on Oatley's hand and one on Deeming's trousers, in the groin area, in case you were wondering.' Several male officers pulled a face. 'Both prints came from a Nike trainer, probably size ten. Questions.'

French started it off. 'The victims are so different, though. We know the Leigh Woods bods had drug-dealing in common, but the cycle-path bods hadn't. And the disposal is so different.'

'Horses for courses. The dealers ended up in Leigh Woods because they'd been "disappeared". The cycle-path bodies landed where they did because they were meant to be found. They were both left right next to the river. The obvious thing would have been to at least dump them in there, just a few feet away. With a good weight on them, they might not have been found for quite a while, if ever. So killing those two had a different purpose. Mike Oatley and Deborah Glynn have things in common; have to have. For a start, they were both unemployed.'

French piped up. 'Glynn had just got a job.'

243

'True, but that's splitting hairs. She didn't live to start it. They were both working class, piss-poor, Glynn had been unemployed for ages, both lived within a couple of miles of each other on this side of the river, and their bodies ended up on the other side of the river. There must be more things they have in common.' A civilian had quietly entered the room and handed him another forensics report. McLusky nodded his thanks while carrying on. 'They connect to each other or the killer in a similar way; perhaps to both. Find that connection. We need to work on the location, too. Find that, and we've practically nailed it. Right, go.'

McLusky stuffed both files under his arm and left, while detectives returned to their workstations, picked up phones, logged on to computers.

Dearlove opened the *Bristol Herald* on his desk and quickly turned to page three. Another grainy slice of the mystery picture. He tore it out, then laid the others he had saved next to it. They didn't add up to anything; he was sure they did that on purpose so you could only see it when you got to the very last bit. A gimmick to sell more papers, obviously, but hey, if it took his mind off file-sifting and form-filling for five minutes, then he didn't mind. Anyway, he liked pizza, and on his pay, a free pizza was a glittering prize. He slipped all three cuttings under his pencil jar.

McLusky managed to lever open the warped door on his desk with a knife purloined from the canteen, and at last regained access to his private kettle. 'Progress of sorts,' he informed his empty office. The litre bottle of Glenmorangie had also been liberated, but he ignored that, since only disaster and triumph deserved to be toasted with it. Once you told yourself that the hard, dull grind of detective work that lay at the centre of a murder investigation needed the fuel of single malt, then you might as well install an intravenous drip. He stirred whitener into his mug of instant and opened the forensics report he'd been handed in the incident room. People were beginning to get used to the snow now,

244

and more or less normal service – i.e. excruciating slowness – had resumed at forensics, though things were about to get speeded up by the government cuts. The cuts meant that far fewer tests were commissioned now, and detectives spent their time arguing with their superiors over what they were allowed to send for analysis. Murder still enjoyed a certain priority, but McLusky wasn't brimming with optimism.

He took a sip of instant, pulled a face and turned the page. After reading a single paragraph, he smiled, picked up the file and abandoned all thoughts of drinking instant coffee. This report wasn't quite Glenmorangie stuff, but a cappuccino matter, surely. Further down the corridor, he gave a cheerful knock at Fairfield's door.

'I'm just on my way out,' she told him. McLusky ignored her, closed the door behind him and let himself drop heavily on to a chair. 'By all means, Liam, make yourself comfortable.'

'Is that coffee machine hot?'

Fairfield looked over her shoulder and saw with annoyance that the red light was on, meaning it was ready for action. 'What is it you want?'

'Cappuccino, if you can manage it. Oh, this.' McLusky waved the report. 'This just arrived. We found the source of the contaminated heroin. Just a dusting of cinnamon for me, please.'

God, the man was annoying. 'You didn't find it,' Fairfield said when McLusky at last handed over the file in exchange for his cup. 'You stumbled over it when you poked around in Bice's lockup.'

'I didn't even do that; I never set foot in it. It was forensics who found traces of heroin, and when they got around to analysing it, they found it was contaminated with anthrax spores. I'm afraid it won't really help you, though. Bice is dead and the stuff is gone. Are they still dropping like flies?'

'They're not, actually. We only had one more case last week, nothing since. Perhaps the message did get through.'

'I doubt it. I have another theory altogether …'

245

Less than an hour later, he found himself explaining it to DSI Denkhaus in the super's office. 'Bice, if he wasn't actively involved in drugs when he skippered for Fenton, would have been in an excellent position to find out about Fenton's deals. He had to have known something about it anyway, Fenton wouldn't have trusted a complete outsider. I went and looked over the yacht. It's massive in terms of boats, but not so massive that you couldn't overhear any business talk if you wanted to.'

'I see. Bice knows of a couple of kilos of heroin, but before it has a chance of going anywhere, Atrium strikes and they all get scooped up. Bice is the only one who walks away without getting a lengthy custodial. He waits for the dust to settle, picks up the drugs and finds himself a buyer. Do you think he knew the stuff was lethal?'

'Hard to tell. My guess is not. You don't sell on contaminated heroin and then hang around for the complaints to arrive. That would be suicide, and Bice knew that. You might sell it and run, but there is no evidence that he had his bags packed. I think he sold the heroin to whoever is the new big noise and got bumped off when it turned out to be killing people. After all, it's not good business practice to poison your own customers. And whoever parcelled up the stuff for street distribution could well be dead and buried now too. Inhalation is lethal.'

'What about Bice's son? How is he involved?'

'Not at all, as far as I can see. He really does work in a cake-decorating shop with his mother. If he denied any knowledge, then we'd have a problem proving that he even knew the money represented proceeds of crime. I doubt the CPS would run with it.'

'Shame, though it saves us a lot of work. At least it looks like my press conferences worked and people are avoiding the stuff now,' Denkhaus said, more upbeat. 'No more deaths for a few days.'

Because whoever had bought a couple of kilos of it had stopped selling it on, McLusky thought but said nothing.

Perhaps it wasn't a good idea to question the miraculous properties of a Denkhaus press conference. 'True, not from contaminated heroin. But there was another overdose from pure heroin, saw it flagged up earlier.'

'I know. Not for you to worry. I got Fairfield on the case.'

At least, McLusky thought, there was no more snow forecast for a couple of days. After the public outcry over unpreparedness and tardy road clearing, the Highways Agency and city council were catching up. Most roads and pavements were now more or less passable, even to a cripple walking with a stick. Using it was by now second nature, so much so that, he noticed with a kind of shock, he had developed new mannerisms around it. He used it to pull things towards himself, twirled it when thinking and stomped it when impatient. If he wasn't careful, he'd end up shaking it at car drivers and children.

Broadmead traders tried to make the most of the snow by alleging that Christmas was imminent. The absence of new snowfall, however, meant that slowly the stuff turned grey and brown and lumpy where it had been shovelled into piles and ridges, leaving permanently wet and gritty pathways for the shoppers. *If you're fit enough to hobble to work, then you're fit enough to take me out*, had been the message from Louise. *Tomorrow night you can take me to the Primrose Café, then it won't be far for you to hobble me home.* Not wanting to expose himself to more ridicule by wearing the same clothes again, McLusky went shopping.

Avoiding clothes shops was the closest thing he had to a hobby. Each time he did go shopping, he did so with the firm intention to buy enough clothes to last him for several years so that the odious experience needn't be repeated too soon, but patience usually deserted him after finding a single pair of invariably black trousers. So it was today. There was nothing worse than having to spend *hours* shopping for stuff like clothes. He grabbed a likely looking dark blue shirt and a handful of black socks on his way to the till, and fled the shop. Operation Smart Casual had been completed in twelve minutes. It had felt like for ever.

Late afternoon. He had left his car at the station and started walking with his purchases towards Albany Road when he heard a shout of dismay behind him. When he turned, he saw a woman on her back in the snow and a tracksuited teenager running in his direction, pursued by a community support officer. She'd never catch up with the kid, who was barging through the shoppers, shouting, 'Get out of the fucking way, get out of the fucking way, get out of the fucking—' McLusky stepped out of the teenager's fucking way, then flung his walking stick between his legs. He crashed face first into the dirty snow with a satisfying thud. McLusky put his best foot forward and stood firmly on the fallen kid's ankle. A second later, the support officer arrived and made sure of the runner. McLusky showed his ID.

'Oh, excellent, sir. He's just robbed a couple of school kids of their mobiles.'

'Then, allow me.' He turned to the now silent street robber. 'I'm arresting you on suspicion of robbery. You don't have to say anything ...' Community support officers had no powers of arrest, which in McLusky's view made them purely decorative. Fortunately a patrol car came into view even before he had finished the caution. 'Genius. Here's the cavalry.' He retrieved his walking stick, stomped it on the ground a couple of times and walked away. A few feet further on, an old man stood smiling broadly, nodding approvingly and waving his own stick at him. The man carried a library book, and his upper jaw was devoid of teeth. McLusky nodded too, and waved back at him in a brief moment of walking-stick solidarity with his customer base.

Chapter Twenty

At last. Five times he had called the council about it. *We are receiving a large number of calls at the moment.* Well of course you are; it's because you're useless twits. *Your call is important to us.* Oh yeah? Then why don't you pick up the bloody phone? When he finally did get through, they had tried to fob him off: it would take time, it was an unusual amount of snow… What was that supposed to mean? If it was three inches you'd be out there clearing the pavements, but because it's eight you're not bothering? Eventually he'd been told that the pavements in his street had been cleared.

Yeah, right. Even without leaving the flat, he could see that the troupe of community-service trolls they'd sent had merely shovelled an undulating gangway barely wide enough for one person to shuffle along. He'd called them again. Did they even know how wide a wheelchair was? Did they have any idea how a wheelchair behaved on ice? How easily the little front wheels got bogged down in snow?

He himself had found out the hard way. This was his first snow since the accident, his first snow since the chair. He'd been naive, of course, to go out when the first inch fell. He'd even felt something akin to excitement; he'd brought his camera, taken pictures of St Pauls in the snow. Only back at his building he couldn't get up the ramp. Someone had scraped a path down the stairs, but the ramp had not been gritted. Worse, kids had tried sliding down it and compacted the snow into a shiny, slippery surface. In the end, a couple of teenagers had scraped some of the snow away with a plastic tray they'd been using as a sled, and with both of them pushing and pulling he had made it back into the house. *Independent living.* Thirty-six years old and depending on the kindness of strangers to get into his bloody flat.

He was getting better at it. He had to admit it. They had said it would get better and some of it had. But most of it never would and much of it could only get worse. He still flew into rages, especially after a few drinks. There was so much anger, so much rage inside him, especially against the bastard who had driven the car, whoever he was. The police had never caught them. There were at least two in the car. The accident had been caught on private CCTV, but it was dark and the picture grainy. The camera angle didn't show the number plates or the faces of the kids in the car – looked like kids – but it showed clearly what had happened. He had been able to watch his bicycle be hit from behind, watch how he was catapulted through the air, seen his back break across the lamp post, watch himself crumple in slow motion, over and over. In a few seconds of footage he went from whole man to half a man. They'd never even found the car. Probably not insured anyway. He was still waiting for compensation. It wouldn't be much. Even had they been caught, even had they been insured, the payout could never be enough. Nothing could make up for this prison. Nothing could pay for the way people looked at him now. The way women looked at him, the way women didn't look at him. Not that there was anything wrong with his equipment, but he wasn't bloody likely to get a chance to prove it. Women didn't exactly queue up for sex with a cripple. Only one woman had so far shown the slightest interest, the one who had chatted him up at the harbour festival. And what a nightmare she had turned out to be; she'd just needed someone to mother. She'd *wanted* someone helpless. It had made him feel even more pathetic.

Retraining. They were no longer talking about rehabilitation, they were talking about retraining now. But what was he good for? What qualifications did he have? A couple of GCSEs and a mini-digger licence. Fat lot of good that was. What were his interests? Rock-climbing and cycling. He had never actually done any rock-climbing, he had just said it to rub it in how crap everything was now, to staunch the relentless stream of positive bloody attitude they directed at him. He could add photography to his interests, since he'd gone on the course at the community centre. His social worker had got him to go. It was just down the road. Of course with the bloody cuts the next course had promptly been cancelled. Then someone had set fire to the van they'd used to go on their outings. And now some idiot had torched the offices. All the computer equipment that had been donated completely destroyed. Once, on the course, they'd gone up to Leigh Woods, the place where the dead bodies had later been found. They had gone up at sparrow's fart, in that van, just a few of them, to take pictures at dawn. They'd bumped his wheelchair into the woods. It had felt amazing to be outside again, in nature, away from the tarmac that was now his prison. He had no longer felt like a bloody Dalek. But even there some weirdo in a posh car had come out of nowhere down the track and asked what the fuck they were doing there. He would never have taken any lip from people like that before, but if you were stuck in a wheelchair, things were different. You didn't feel like a whole bloke. Because you patently weren't. Any arsehole with working legs towered over you, had the automatic advantage.

And so the anger ate at what was left of you. Actually they had all been really good, the doctors, the nurses, the physio. But none of them were stuck in a wheelchair, were they? At the end of their working day, they literally walked away from it all. When the compensation came, it should be enough to adapt a car for wheelchair use so he'd be able to drive again, not be driven, not depend on others.

But until then it was muscle power. He pulled the padded jacket on over his broad shoulders. And what a set of muscles it had become. All the bloody leg muscles he'd developed from cycling had wasted away, but his upper torso had changed beyond recognition from the relentless workout. Quite ironic, really: he was probably fitter now than he was before the accident. But if these muscles gave out, then you were on your way down. You'd stall. You'd roll to a halt. And become a target for the do-gooders. He tucked the tartan blanket around his lower body. He hated it, it made him feel even more like an invalid, but it was minus whatever out there. He slipped his mobile phone and a couple of heat pads that he could activate into the side pocket of the chair. His hand hovered over the camera on the table; he hesitated, then decided against taking it. He was only going shopping. Of course the photography tutor would have frowned at this. A real photographer, Ellen would have said, never leaves the house without his or her camera.

The ramp had been completely cleared, swept and gritted. Once at the bottom, he powered himself on to the pavement. It was a pleasure to be moving again, even at these modest speeds. He enjoyed the exertion, the forward movement, the crisp air. Even car fumes became sharp, separate smells in this cold, rather than an all-enveloping miasma. The sun was beginning to break through and the light intensified as it reflected off the snow on cars parked along Ashley Road. The going was good until a cluster of uncollected rubbish sacks forced him to slow down. A stupid van had been parked half on the pavement by some thoughtless moron. The side door slid open and a swarthy-looking idiot jumped out right into his path. Before he could shout his protest, the man landed a punch on his throat. Now all he could do was struggle for air; it was like trying to breathe through a straw. A broad sheet of MDF slid like a ramp from the van, his chair was tilted backwards, and seconds later the door slammed to behind him, shutting out the light.

Fairfield checked her purse for cash. Had to leave enough for a cab. Plenty there. Not that this pub was that expensive.

252

It just felt like it. Another pint of Butcombe, then. She always drank beer in pubs, wine at home. Though this being a posh gastropub, they probably had drinkable wine here. Not the same, though, not when you had worked up a thirst during a long, frustrating, annoying, bloody tedious day at work. What you dreamt of then was a cool pint standing on a polished bar top with many of its mates waiting in the barrel.

Not exactly her usual haunt, the Albion. Or Clifton, for that matter, though she did like Boyces Avenue in summer. She was looking for a new pub to adopt, one uncontaminated by association with her ex or her job. She'd left the car at the station, knew then already she would drink more than was good for her, and had taken a taxi. It was an ancient place tarted up tastefully and minimally, with polished wood floors and practically bare walls, just the antidote she needed tonight for the poison that had leached into her mood from interview rooms full of stupidity and frozen squats smelling of stale piss. Two men drinking at a table across the room kept looking over. Only a matter of time before *woman drinking on her own* would transform in their minds to *woman needing to be chatted up*. There were other, slower poisons, too. Being stuck at a small station with Superintendent Denkhaus was one. It was inner city but definitely not inner circle; for that you had to be at Trinity Road, not at a crumbling, make-do-and-mend nick like Albany Road.

'Anything else for you?' the barman asked.

She realized she'd been staring into space, staring right through him. She was getting drunk, no doubt about it. And why the hell not? Should have eaten something, though. Should probably eat something now, before it was too late. 'Yeah, some olives would be nice.'

The barman furnished her with a triangular dish bearing a small mount of olives, a little dish of olive oil and some pieces of crusty bread to dunk into it. *Meze*. Her mother would approve. In Greece, no one drank without some food on the table. She dunked the bread and savoured the earthy taste of the oil – it wasn't bad. For a split second Katarina Vasiliou made an appearance, remembering Corfu, smelling the dusty tracks through the olive groves. A good draught from her pint of Butcombe should have washed her away. Not this time, it seemed. Of course after the divorce she could go back to her maiden name, though she had not felt maidenly for some time. She had only toyed with the idea out of anger, had long decided that Fairfield worked for her and changing her name back would simply attract attention to her domestic arrangements and the failure of her marriage. As a police officer you could more or less do what you liked in your private life as long as it didn't attract public attention, but if you wanted to progress beyond inspector it became an issue, and beyond superintendent you could forget it. A presentable spouse and preferably a couple of kids at uni were practically a precondition.

Ah well, here it came. The one who'd been sitting with his back to her had decided to make his move. He came over carrying two empty pint glasses. 'Hi. Erm, I, that is, we couldn't help noticing you were on your own. I hope you've not been stood up?'

Fairfield took a draught from her pint before looking up at him. 'Shouldn't that be *I hope you've been stood up*? I haven't, thanks for asking.'

'I'm just off to the bar. Can I get you a drink?'

'No thanks, I'm fine.'

'You're quite welcome to join us at our table.'

'Ditto.'

'Suit yourself.' He stood there for a few seconds more, looking down at her with an expression that was meant to say *what* are *we going to do with you?*, then went on his way.

Fairfield's mood plummeted further. He'd been an okay-looking guy, nothing wrong with him, not pushy or geeky or full of himself, and she'd even liked his sweater, but somehow the mere thought of nice blokes in nice sweaters made her heart sink. Nice shoes, too, she noticed. She drained her glass, popped the last olive into her mouth and got to her feet. She wanted another drink, but it was getting late. She'd call a taxi out there, from her mobile, rather than wait for one in here, with the nice bloke and his mate throwing glances in her direction.

The narrow little street was still busy. The air didn't feel as cold as when she had come up here, or perhaps that was the alcohol. While she stood on the pavement buttoning up her coat and digging for her mobile in her bag, the door of the Primrose Café across the street opened to let out a murmur of conviviality and a couple linking arms. Fairfield looked up and froze. McLusky with what had to be his partner. She didn't know he had one. It was too late to hide; he had spotted her straight away.

'Hey, Kat!' He happily steered his companion towards her and made the introductions. 'This is Kat Fairfield. Katarina. Louise Rennie.'

'Hi, Katarina. I've heard a lot about you,' Louise said.

'I'm sure you have,' Fairfield said. 'It's all lies, you know.'

'I see. But the idiot failed to mention just how stunningly beautiful you are.' Rennie squeezed McLusky's arm to stop him protesting.

'What are you doing up here?' he said instead.

'Oh, I just came up for a quiet drink after work.' Damn, why had she said that? She could see on McLusky's face that he had no problems doing the arithmetic: four hours of quiet drinking. And Louise had also lifted one ironic eyebrow. 'I was just calling myself a cab.' She waggled her phone as evidence.

'On a Saturday night? Forget it,' Rennie said. 'You'd be waiting out here in the cold for ever. I live just around the corner. Literally. Come in for a coffee, then you can call a cab and wait for it in comfort.' Fairfield was still looking for polite words of refusal as Louise Rennie gently took the mobile out of her hand and with a smile dropped it back into her handbag. 'Good, let's go.' She abandoned McLusky's arm and linked hers with Fairfield's instead. 'You're the first of Liam's colleagues I've met. At last someone who can dish the dirt on DI McLusky.'

255

As Louise steered her away, Fairfield looked over her shoulder to see how all this was going down with him, but he seemed in an indestructibly good mood, smiling back at her. She fell into step and sighed with resignation. She was not in the mood for chat, but if the woman really lived just around the corner, then perhaps waiting for a cab there did make sense. Two minutes later, Louise disengaged her arm to unlock the front door.

'When you said literally round the corner, you meant that ... literally.'

'Yes, it's different from *practically round the corner*, which in my experience means a ten-minute walk.' Their eyes met for a second. 'For the record, you can always take me at my word. Literally.'

Once inside the flat, McLusky was dispatched to the kitchen to make the coffee. Louise flicked on the gas fire in the grate with the remote.

'Witchcraft,' Fairfield said accusingly. Despite herself, she was impressed. The size of the sitting room, of the windows, of the bookcases. The quality of the furnishings. None of this had arrived flat-packed. 'I obviously have the wrong job, I see that now.'

'How's that?'

'Well, for a start you must get a lot more leisure time than me if you have time to read all those books.' She also wouldn't have the space for them; there had to be a couple of thousand volumes.

They faced each other across the coffee table, each sitting in a corner of their own two-seater sofa while McLusky clinked and clattered in the kitchen. 'Do you have a television?' Louise asked.

'Yes, why?'

'Put it out for the binmen to collect. You'd be surprised how much time to read books you'll find once you've got rid of it.'

Fairfield looked around. 'I take it you don't have a TV set?'

'Listen, no woman lies on her deathbed thinking *I wish I'd spent more time watching telly*.' She got up. 'I can smell coffee; I'd better give the invalid a hand with the carrying.'

Fairfield watched her traverse the room and disappear through the door. There was so much space here, and air. The room seemed to breathe clarity, exhale order and purpose. You could feel freer in a room like this, uncrowded. And Louise belonged here, she saw that straight away; it was *very her*, as the cliché went.

'Right,' said Louise as she reappeared carrying the tray of coffee things and with McLusky in tow. 'No cop-shop talk allowed tonight, however tempting it must be for you two.'

McLusky dismissed it. 'Shop talk tempting? Hardly.'

'Well, detectives do moan a lot at each other,' Fairfield admitted. 'Pay and conditions, that kind of thing. It's a stressful job and it's easy to take it with you everywhere.'

McLusky sat down, then wriggled a moment until he had freed his radio from the back of his trousers. He slid it on to the coffee table.

'I rest my case,' Fairfield said.

While Louise poured the coffee, McLusky lit a cigarette. 'If you're smoking, then so will I.' She took a short, slender cigar from a box on the coffee table and lit it, releasing blue smoke towards the ceiling. She sat back and gave Fairfield an inquisitive look. 'Right, I'm starting my own investigation now. Your parents are Greek? Where in Greece are they from ...?'

Half an hour later, it was McLusky's mobile that interrupted the conversation. He answered it and limped towards the kitchen as he talked, but stopped before he even got to the door. 'Hotwells? Give me ten to fifteen, Jane.'

Louise closed her eyes and took a deep breath before self-control was restored. 'You're not, are you?'

'Yes, sorry.'

'Another body on the cycle path, perhaps?'

'Oh no, this one's different.'

Louise walked McLusky to the front door and put her arms around him. 'Will it take all night?'

'I expect so.'

'How about breakfast, then? Here, take my keys. It's your turn to wake me with something freshly squeezed. Pick up a few croissants or something.' She kissed him goodbye and gently closed the door behind him.

In the sitting room, Fairfield was standing up, mobile in hand. 'I'd better call that taxi, then.'

'Oh, nonsense, put that phone away. I think more coffee would be a bad idea, though. How about some whisky? Or better still: some brandy. There's a bottle I've been meaning to open for ages. And then I'll teach you how to smoke cigars. Brandy and cigars were meant for each other.'

He stood by his car, waved to Austin and quickly lit a cigarette to fortify himself before he had to enter the zone where face masks and protective clothing would make such luxuries impossible. The dead man had been a wheelchair user; that was as much as McLusky knew. His chair lay upturned near a concrete pillar, more than thirty feet from the body, which was lying in the snow closer to the road.

The body had ended up in the unclaimed wilderness under the Cumberland Basin flyover. Even drifts of snow and the darkness of the night could not hide the hideousness of this place. It was a non-space, a forlorn area in the concrete shadows of the roads, between fat concrete pillars. This stretch of the A4 had now been closed to traffic. Police vehicles with blue lights flashing marked each end of the area. Torchlight swept the ground; generators for the arc lights were being unloaded from a van. An ambulance stood idle.

McLusky had pulled on to the verge before the roadblock, next to a burnt-out motorbike. There was so little left of it, he found it impossible to guess what make it had been. He tried not to think of the place he had just left as he stood there and quietly cursed with smoking breath. Even the graffiti on the nearest bit of concrete looked as if the artist had been depressed by his canvas. Austin walked up. 'Give

258

me one minute,' McLusky told him, holding up his cigarette in defence.

'All right if I talk?'

'Oh, by all means, Jane. Have you caught who did it yet?'

Austin ignored him. McLusky was not the only one in a bad mood; when the call had come, Eve had been halfway through undressing him on the sofa. While he took the call, she'd slammed into the bathroom and not answered his knock on the door. 'You'll like this one. We have a witness who saw the body being dumped.'

'What? Where? How? Is he still here?' McLusky took a last greedy drag from the cigarette before flicking it towards the burnt-out bike.

'He's over in that Polo, a Mr Hicks.' Austin waved his notebook towards a red car parked close to a police vehicle under the flyover. McLusky was already limping in that direction. 'Nothing brilliantly useful, though; he only saw the vehicle.' Austin fell into step. 'According to him, the victim was pushed out of a moving van. In his wheelchair.'

'Marvellous. That really is the height of laziness.' The man in the Polo was talking on the phone, but when McLusky approached the car, he put his mobile away and got out. 'We can talk in your car if that's better,' McLusky told him.

'No, no. Been sitting there for ages. Good to move about a bit.' He was a plain-looking man in his forties; the blue flashing lights gave his pale face an unhealthy tinge. 'Will I have to stay much longer?'

'I'll just need to ask a few questions. You saw the incident?'

'Yes, it happened right in front of my eyes. I mean, I couldn't believe it; it was just like you see in a film. Totally unreal. I didn't actually see the door open, but the van was driving along and then this bloke in a wheelchair just shot out the side and hit the road. The van never slowed down. It was horrible.'

'Where were you when this happened?'

'Oh, I was driving about seventy, eighty yards behind. I stood on the brakes, I can tell you. The bloke flew out of the wheelchair and tumbled along the side of the road, turning over and over, and the wheelchair flew on even further. They must have been doing about fifty? I stopped and ran to him, but it was too late, he was dead; I mean, you could tell straight away he was dead, his head was all smashed in. And they never even slowed down. I mean, who'd do that to a man in a wheelchair? It can't have been an accident, can it? The way he shot out of there, someone must have pushed him.'

'Quite possibly. Can you describe the van for me, please?'

'It was just a van. One of those box-like ones. I don't know what make.'

'Colour?'

'I think it was blue or green. It's hard to say with the orange street lights; everything looks a bit ... grimy. Oh yeah, and I got the impression it was dirty, sprayed with mud at the back.'

'I don't suppose you noticed the index number? The number plate?' Austin asked.

'At that distance? Actually, I'm not sure there was a number plate, come to think of it.'

'And you couldn't say what make the van was.' Austin already knew the answer.

'No idea. Sorry. Can I go now? I've someone waiting for me.'

Austin glanced for guidance at McLusky, who just nodded morosely, turned on his heel and limped away towards the corpse. 'We could show him photographs of the backs of vans,' Austin suggested when he caught up with him. 'See if anything rings a bell with him.'

'We already know how that will go. He'll either confidently point at the wrong one or give us a choice of six different makes, either green, blue or red, which narrows it down to a million bloody vans.'

'We know it has a side door ...'

'Half a million bloody vans.'

260

Keeping the A4 closed, even at this time of night, was giving traffic division a headache, but McLusky didn't care. *It'll take as long as it takes*, he had told them helpfully. He spent nearly an hour waiting in his car, sheltering from the icy wind that blew out of the Avon Gorge, snatching and whistling around the flyover. Eventually Austin joined him, having organized a fingertip search of the road. He instantly regretted having got into the inspector's Mazda. It was barely warmer than outside, and thick with cigarette smoke. A large car arrived behind them, flashing its headlights. 'Is that Coulthart's Jag coming up?'

McLusky grabbed his stick and got out. 'He took his time changing out of his jim-jams.'

Coulthart did not have the air of someone who had recently struggled out of his pyjamas; as he suited up beside his night-blue Jaguar, he looked exactly like someone who could hardly wait to look at another corpse in the snow. 'The other side of the river this time,' was how he greeted McLusky, who had put on protective gear himself.

'Yes, the windy side. Have a look at him, tell me if he's one of mine.'

'A wheelchair user,' Coulthart remarked during his examination. 'It's a cruel world.'

'An impatient one, too. He was pushed from a moving vehicle.'

'At what time was that?'

McLusky checked his watch. 'Four hours ago exactly. And you took your time getting here, if you don't mind me saying, Doctor.'

'I do mind you saying, Inspector. I did not take my time. When the call eventually found me, I was asleep in my room at the Royal Crescent Hotel in Bath and I did not delay coming here. As I was travelling without the benefit of blue flashing lights, I'd like to think I made good time. Now, this chap here could well be one of yours. Hard to tell at first glance which injuries were inflicted before and which during the accident, but I'd say he'd got the same treatment as all the others before they pushed him out.'

'It was no bloody accident.'

'Incident, I should have said. But it's certainly also different from the others.'

'Yes, there's all that blood, for a start.' The dirty roadside snow had soaked up a great amount of it, pink in the arc light, reminding McLusky of an ice lolly dropped into the gutter.

'Precisely. And what does that tell us, Inspector?'

'Bugger me. He was alive when they pushed him out?'

'Quite possibly. They may not have *known* he was still alive. Or he may have been killed in the vehicle and pushed out immediately afterwards. But this amount of bleeding suggests to me that he was alive when he hit the tarmac and that he died right here in the snow. What conclusions might be drawn from that, I gladly leave for you to ponder, Inspector.'

'Thank you so much, Doctor. Well, the first thing that comes to mind is that our killer is in a bloody hurry. And my guess is: he's hurrying towards his next victim.'

Fairfield couldn't tell what had woken her. It was still dark, but the shaded lamp on the far side of the bed was on, bathing the room in a soft, warm glow. She didn't dare move for fear of waking Louise, who was lying with her face buried into Fairfield's side, as if she had fallen asleep in the middle of the last kiss. She needed this quiet moment, savoured it; the replay of their lovemaking in her mind and the realization that something had at last happened to her life. Things were definitely not the same this morning. Whatever happened next, and whether it continued with or without Louise in it, her life would change. How and in what way was uncertain, and perhaps that was part of the excitement she felt. Just for now she was happy to lie here, hold Louise close and breathe in the unfamiliar: their combined body odours, the smell of Louise's shampoo, the perfume of the bed linen, the faint smell of coffee, a hint of cigar smoke.

By the time Fairfield realized that the smell of coffee was not an echo from last night, it was too late; the time between the sound of clinking crockery and the door opening was too short to even consider a bedroom-farce dash to the wardrobe. McLusky had carefully elbowed open the door, carrying a heavily laden breakfast tray. All she could do was shake Louise awake and hold her breath. Louise frowned, squinted at McLusky as though she needed glasses, and sat up. 'Ah. Bum. Is it that time already?'

Fairfield had grabbed all the available duvet to cover herself up, and from its dubious protection she looked from Louise, who was leaning back into the pillows with a look of resignation, to McLusky. He stood at the foot of the bed, holding the tray very still. He was frowning down at it; then, after a moment, he set it on the bed beside Louise. 'Morning, Dr Rennie, morning, Inspector.'

Fairfield's mood changed from embarrassment to suspicion and anger. 'You two set this up. You set me up, didn't you? Is this the kind of games you like playing?'

McLusky shook his head. This was not what he had been looking forward to after a night spent under a flyover, and suddenly he felt deadly tired. 'No, no. If I had known, I'd have laid the tray for three. As it is, I think two cups is just right.' He turned and left the room, closing the door behind him.

'Oh hell.' Louise swung out of bed, but Fairfield lunged at her, grabbing her arm.

'You knew, didn't you? *He* didn't know I'd be here, but *you* knew he was coming all the time.'

'Katarina, I didn't plan this.'

'You let it happen, though. You knew it might happen and you let it.'

They both heard the front door of the flat being closed noisily, and both breathed deeply with relief. 'Well ...' Louise shrugged and let her head sink back, smiling cautiously over her shoulder, but Fairfield didn't return the smile.

'I have to work with him, Lou. I'll be seeing him at work *every day*!'

Louise held her angry gaze for a while, still smiling. 'You know that tiny tattoo of mine you liked?'

'Yes, what about it?'

'Liam never even found it.'

'Ha!' Fairfield threw her head back, eyes closed. Slowly a happy smile spread across her face and her shoulders relaxed.

Louise reclaimed her side of the duvet, then slid the tray up between them and poured coffee. 'Go on, eat your croissants before they get cold.' She decapitated one of the boiled eggs and folded back the top to reveal a creamy yolk. 'Oh good, he's got the eggs just right.'

Chapter Twenty-One

McLusky felt too tired to slam another door. He'd slammed the door of Louise's flat, slammed the door to her house, slammed the car door coming and going. He let himself quietly into his own flat, pushed the door shut behind him and leant against it. It was bloody cold in here. Something had to be done about it before he caught pneumonia in his own bed.

In the kitchen he lit the oven and the three gas rings, put the kettle on the hob and washed a mug from the collection sitting in the sink. Even before he lifted the lid on the jar, he remembered he'd used the last coffee beans days ago. Instant, then. He thought there might be a jar of it, or at least some tea bags, somewhere in his 1950s kitchen cupboard. Halfway through the tea-bag hunt his mobile chimed in his pocket. It wasn't Louise. He didn't recognize the number, so he answered it. 'Yup.'

'Is that Inspector McLusky?'

'Speaking.'

'It's Ben here.'

'Ben?'

'Benjamin Fishlock.'

'Ah, the woodsman. How did you get my mobile number?'

'You gave it to me. It's on your card.'

'So it is.' One-handed, McLusky continued his forensic examination of the mess in his cupboard, making an even greater mess of the confusion of tubs and packets.

Fishlock sounded doubtful. 'Perhaps this is a bad time; I can hear you're busy with something.'

'No, it's fine. I'm looking for a jar of instant coffee, I'm ashamed to say. You decided you'd tell me after all, then?'

'Tell you what, Inspector?'

'Whatever it was you failed to tell me when I saw you.'

'I didn't know then what I know now.'

'I know that feeling well.' He slammed both cupboard doors shut, making the glass rattle in the frames. 'Are you in your wood? You got any coffee there, Fishlock?'

'I am, and I have.'

McLusky was already on his way to the door. 'Okay, Fish, put the kettle on.'

The wind had changed direction; milder air was travelling up from Spain, and a thaw was promised. On the radio, the talk was no longer of ice but of flooding. Out here the air might be milder, but the ground remained frozen, though the lane up to Fishlock's wood showed the tracks of various vehicles. McLusky decided to try it and found that the tyres were coping well.

Fishlock's careworn Volvo estate, which he had first seen at Gooseford Farm, was parked next to the little tractor. McLusky put the MiTo behind it and got out. All around him the trees dripped with the thaw, while from time to time whole branchloads of snow sagged wetly to the forest floor. Yet there was enough snow left on the ground to distinguish tyre tracks, and the knobbly grooves left by a trail bike were clearly visible in front of the mobile home. Fishlock watched him from the open door. 'Good morning, Inspector.'

'Not so far, no.' The aroma of coffee roasting was as strong as on his last visit. McLusky sat himself down in the tiny kitchen and slapped his leather gloves on to the tabletop. 'Now if whatever you have to tell me means that I'll have to arrest you, at least let me drink some coffee first.'

'I hear the food at police stations is lousy. I was going to have some breakfast; care to join me?'

266

McLusky was halfway through his plate of fried eggs, mushrooms and smoked bacon before he spoke again. 'You should open a caff in here. Excellent breakfast, and the best coffee I've had since probably ever.'

'Bit out of the way; who'd come all the way out here for a fry-up?'

'I would. Okay, I'm nearly human now, so if you have stuff to tell me – now is the moment.'

'It's not easy,' Fishlock said, putting down his fork and leaning back in his chair.

'Start with the motorbike. Yours?'

'Friend of mine.'

'The one who came past the crashed BMW?'

'Yes.'

'And found what exactly?'

Fishlock became defensive. 'He didn't tell me at first. Well, he did, but he said it was just a bag of puff. I don't smoke so I didn't really care. He does but he said it was a lot and he was going to flog most of it. He's lost his job, needs the money, all that   '

'You didn't know about the heroin.'

'No. Honestly. I didn't know there was heroin involved. A lot of it, apparently. Ian's an old school friend. He didn't do very well, he had a crap job working for the council and now he's been laid off. He always wanted to do something like I have, even asked me if he could come in with me, but, I mean, look around. It just about keeps me alive. So he thought this was his chance: the guy is dead, take the stuff and flog it. If it was just weed I'd have kept quiet about it, but not hard drugs. And of course he has no idea about heroin dealing and I think he got himself into trouble. Said he needs to lie low for a bit. He came to see me yesterday and came clean. He wanted to hide here but I said no. I feel like a crap friend; first I turn him away, then I set the police on him, but I think it's best for him. I think he's scared. Got himself involved with some weird people and got ripped off too, by the sounds of it.'

267

'My heart bleeds. Did he take the gun as well?'

'No, he left the shotgun.'

'Shotgun?' The fork with the last speared mushroom hovered halfway to his mouth for a moment, then McLusky closed his lips around it. 'No handgun? Not a Beretta?'

Fishlock shook his head. 'He never mentioned it. He said there was a shotgun inside the car, sawn-off, but he left it.'

McLusky took out his mobile. 'Okay, you did well. What's his full name?'

'Ian Geary.'

'Address?' He called Albany Road and left a long message to be passed on to Fairfield. *Immediately*. The memory of seeing her in bed with Louise intruded and made him stumble for a moment, but he swallowed it down. He listened to the DC reading some of the message back, then added: 'I got an anonymous tip-off.' He folded his mobile, pushed his empty cup towards Fishlock and nodded at the enamelled coffee pot on the stove. 'If there's any left.'

At Gooseford Farm, McLusky left his car on the track, where it would cause the most obstruction. The Land Rover was in the yard, the tractor in the shed, and he could see the quad bike in the lee of the house. He should, of course, have gone by the book and brought some backup, since there was a firearm involved, but Farmer Murry would have had ample time to get rid of the gun if he felt like being difficult. McLusky didn't expect violence, and when the front door opened and Murry stepped out, he knew from his expression that he wasn't going to get any.

'Morning, Mr Murry. I've come for the gun.'

Murry just nodded, stuck his hands in his pockets and shrugged deeper into his jacket before leading the way across the yard. Inside a large storage shed full of plastic drums and sacks, he reached behind a stack of wooden fence panels leaning against the back wall and produced a three-foot-long bundle. He unrolled the dirty piece of cloth and let it drop to the ground. 'Look what they've done to it.'

Even with twelve inches missing from the barrel, and despite McLusky's loathing of all gun fetish, he could see why Murry had taken the thing. The over/under shotgun was the closest a weapon could come to a work of art. Its stock was polished walnut, the side plates delicately engraved, depicting hills and game birds, surrounded by intricate scrollwork. The birds were gold-plated, the trigger looked to be solid gold. 'Thank you, Mr Murry.' The farmer placed it into his outstretched hand. 'It's valuable, is it?' McLusky asked.

'Even needing the barrels replacing – about five grand. It's Italian.' He looked straight at the inspector, as though weighing him up. 'It's not as though he needed it any more. And it looked as though he was up to no good with it.'

McLusky broke open the gun. It was loaded. He checked the safety was on and began to walk away. 'We'll be in touch, Mr Murry.'

Murry came after him but stopped at the door of the shed. 'I know it was wrong, but ... it was just so ... Will I be charged, do you think?' he called.

'Almost certainly. I'm sure I'll think of something.' Theft, obstruction, wasting police time, greed and stupidity for starters. And selling red diesel to his neighbours. More than likely it was a puddle of Murry's diesel that had caused the crash in the first place.

McLusky stuck the gun under the driver's seat, then turned the car around in the yard. The temperature in the MiTo was still quite acceptable. All the other places he inhabited seemed to be cursed with heating problems: the Mazda, home ... *Heating.* A crystal-clear image appeared in his mind: his kitchen stove and three gas rings burning on full, with the kettle left sitting on top. He put his foot down and skidded away, wheels spinning in the snow, towards town.

'Not our usual hour this, middle of the afternoon, not a good time at all,' said the team leader. The drug-squad team had arrived at their assembly point near the Bishopston address, not far off the Gloucester Road. Fairfield and the team leader were exchanging last-minute notes, standing in the snow behind one of the two vans. There weren't many notes to exchange; it was a rush job.

The leader of the heavily armed squad looked as unhappy as he sounded. Fairfield knew the responsibility for the arrest was his alone and he could still refuse to go ahead. 'I knew you wouldn't be happy, but we can't wait until the early hours so you can ruin his beauty sleep. Forensics have finally decided that the heroin in the crashed BMW is the source of the pure heroin that's been causing people to over-dose, and the twit who's flogging the stuff lives at this address. The target's name is Ian Geary.'

'But nothing definite on the gun.'

'No. The crashed dealer had a shotgun in the car. That's accounted for, but we found a magazine for a Beretta, and that gun is missing.'

'I want my misgivings noted.'

'I share your misgivings, but we can't allow the bastard to go out on the street tonight and sell more of the stuff. He also told a friend he was going to lie low, so he might change addresses.'

'Right. In we go, then. Same routine as ever: you and your DS stay close behind and take instructions from me. Any gunfire – you don't wait to be told, just get to cover. And please remember that a car doesn't constitute cover. I had to point this out to one of your CID friends before: cars are made of tin foil, bullets go right through them, okay? Think brick wall, not garden fence.'

Yeah, yeah. Fairfield hooked her thumbs into her bullet-proof vest and nodded sincerely, and sincerely wished they'd get on with it. When the call that ruined her Sunday afternoon came, she had been a couple of worlds away from this dump, and from testosterone-flooded blokes toting MP5s and Glock 17s. The team leader thumped on the back of the van and Fairfield nodded to Sorbie, who had stayed in his car. Sorbie looked bored, but Fairfield knew that was for the benefit of the drug squad. The target lived at the third house on the left side of the street.

They charged around the corner in single file, holding on to each other, the man with the heavy ram near the front. The wooden front door offered little resistance and caved in after two hits, and the man with the ram was nearly trampled by his colleagues rushing inside. 'Armed police! Listen to my voice!' bellowed the leader while thundering up the stairs, as other officers shouted, 'Clear! Clear!' from the downstairs rooms. 'Show yourself! Keep your hands where we can see them! Armed police!'

Fairfield was third behind the leader as they reached the upper floor of the little house. MP5 levelled, the second man booted open a bedroom door. 'Police ... ah, shit.' He turned around and poked his gun around a couple more door jambs, but the search was over. There was no one else, and they'd found Ian Geary.

Someone else had found him first. Even the team leader looked uncomfortable; he probably didn't know he was grimacing. 'I think that probably comes under the category of *he suffered a sustained attack*. Jesus, he must have pissed someone off.'

For Fairfield, the sight confirmed that the first day off she had had in weeks was now irredeemable.

Sorbie looked over her shoulder in the narrow doorway. 'I'm glad he's still wearing his underpants. Not sure I want to see what's left under there.'

'Is that the bloke you saw at the back of the squat in Easton?'

'No, that bloke had a face.'

'DS Sorbie ...'

'I really can't tell, honest, Kat.'

'Looks like they tied him to a chair but the chair collapsed,' Fairfield said.

The body lying in a large pool of blood and the splintered remains of a kitchen chair was naked apart from one sock and a pair of boxer shorts. Both had probably been white

271

but were now saturated with darkening blood. Blood seemed to be everywhere: on the floor, the double bed, the walls, the flimsy curtains drawn across the window. Somewhere in the mess where his face had been, she could make out a blood-soaked gag among the exploded skin tissue and shattered teeth.

'I'm not going further in there, obviously,' said the drug-squad leader, 'but I can see the handle of a cricket bat poking out from that mess on the floor. Bet that's what did it.'

'We can safely leave all that to SOCO.'

'But it looks like McLusky got *something* right at last,' Sorbie said.

Fairfield whisked around and pushed past him towards the stairs. 'Shut up, DS Sorbie, and get on with something.'

Unaccustomed warmth greeted McLusky when he pushed through the door into his flat. The temperature in the kitchen would have been pleasant, even, had it not been for the fact that there seemed to be no air left. There was an unpleasant smell, too. The kettle, which had boiled dry a long time ago, sat above the flames, blackened, buckled and pulsing with red heat. He turned off the gas and, armed with oven gloves, carried the kettle to the sink. He managed to free the lid and opened the tap, and even while doing it knew it was a stupid idea. Superheated steam shot upwards and temporarily blinded him. He dropped the kettle; it jumped and banged and crackled and sent acrid fumes his way. 'Marvellous.'

His phone rang; it was Austin. 'We have an ID for the flyover guy. We traced the serial number on the wheelchair, easy-peasy; it's a Darren Rutts.'

'Good job.'

'And he lived not far from your place. Another council flat; Deedee already picked up the keys.'

'All right, what's the address? I'll meet you there.'

Despite the proximity, McLusky took the car. He passed the scorched community centre on the way. The burnt-out floor had boarded-up windows, and scaffolding had gone up outside. Austin and Dearlove had arrived before him. Dearlove handed over the keys and they entered the building in order of seniority. At the flat, McLusky rang the bell and knocked.

'He lived alone, apparently,' Dearlove said.

'That doesn't mean he can't have his auntie staying over.' McLusky used the keys and threw open the door. 'Yup, they've been. Same scenario; place is a tip.'

'Could be he lived like that?' Dearlove suggested.

'Not in a wheelchair, you nit,' Austin said. 'How was he going to get through that lot?'

'That lot' was a mess of papers and books tumbled off the waist-high shelves that ran around the sitting room. There was a desk that looked plundered, its door and drawer open, the contents of its tabletop swept to the floor. There was no computer. McLusky looked around for a telltale charger that would point to a missing laptop, but saw nothing.

'Deedee, go to the kitchen and open the bin.'

'That's what I joined for: the glamour.'

'See if there's house keys in there.'

Dearlove obliged. Half a minute later he reappeared, holding the keys aloft. 'Well, what do you know?'

'Not a lot,' Austin said, and snatched the keys off him. 'Definitely the same bastards, then.'

While waiting for the SOCO team to arrive, McLusky gingerly sifted through the papers strewn on the floor: bills, bank statements – no luxuries there – and correspondence with the hospital; no personal letters. A name caught his eye and he snatched up the dog-eared letter. 'Well, we were looking for something to connect our victims – how about Mike Oatley and Darren Rutts having the same social worker? I just found an appointment letter from Mr Justin Hedges.'

'They lived in the same area, stands to reason. I take it you want me to check if he had dealings with Deborah Glynn as well?'

'Discreetly. I don't want him prepared. In the meantime, I'll try and meet up with him and see how he reacts when the name comes up.'

'Stuff's melting everywhere. I hate slush,' Sorbie said as he got into the passenger seat beside Fairfield.

'It might be melting, but it's hardly balmy. It was *freezing* in that place with all the doors open all day.' What Fairfield craved was to sit by the fire in a warm, spacious room lined with books – and she had an open invitation to do just that – but the day wasn't over yet and their destination was Albany Road station for a lot of desk work. There could be a connection between Ian Geary's murder and the series of killings McLusky's team were investigating, but until there was any evidence of it, Geary was her case. It wasn't much, but it was better than scooping up dead junkies. The lack of sleep was taking its toll: several times she had called the dead man *Dreary* by mistake. It was exactly how the day had felt, and the dirty melting snow squelching under the tyres just rounded it off.

Fairfield instinctively avoided the Gloucester Road, forgetting it would be quite driveable on a Sunday night, and dropped south towards Albany through a network of familiar streets that took them close to her own neighbourhood. When she saw the lights of a large newsagent's at a street corner, she stopped opposite and jumped out. 'Won't be a tick,' she told Sorbie, leaving him no time to get in a request for a chocolate bar before she slammed the car door.

Five minutes later she emerged on to the street with a box of matches and a tin of small cigars. She paused by the side of the road to unwrap and light one and sent a blue cloud of smoke towards the sky.

'When did you start smoking? And cigars at that?' Sorbie asked when she slid back into the driver's seat.

She ignored the question. 'Open the window if it bothers you.'

'It's not that it bothers, me; actually, I quite like—' His airwave radio coming to life interrupted.

It was control, with a rare request. 'It's a burglary in progress, reported by the neighbour. Intruders still on the premises. We've no units near, but I can see you're only about a minute away. Montrose Avenue.' Control gave the house number and the name of the neighbour.

Fairfield was already pulling away from the kerb, her cigar clamped into the corner of her mouth. 'Bloody GPS, there's nowhere to hide. It's the bloody perpetrators that should be fitted with it, every sodding one of them.'

Montrose Avenue was a quiet residential street of large Victorian semi-detached houses, many of which had had their front gardens turned into off-street parking. There were no spaces left on the street, and Fairfield left her Renault double-parked several doors down from the address. The couple who had made the call lived in the next semi along. 'I saw them going round the back and I heard glass breaking too,' the husband told them.

'How many?' Fairfield asked.

'Two of them. Boy and a girl, I think, couldn't be sure. Teenagers, by the looks of them; I only saw them for a couple of seconds. One of them had a sort of shoulder bag.'

'Who lives there?'

'Single chap, young, trendy. Must have a few bob, drives a BMW. We haven't seen him for a while.'

'Okay, thanks. We'll take a look. Please stay indoors.'

They left by the front entrance and walked casually next door. Blinds were drawn on both floors. A narrow passage led past wheelie bins to the back of the property, where their way was barred by an old but substantial wooden door. Sorbie stuck his torch into his back pocket and easily pulled himself up and over. Fairfield followed with little more difficulty and landed noisily in the wet snow on the other side. Sorbie pointed his torch: footprints were clearly visible, leading on to the lawn.

Fairfield was wide awake now. She hadn't done this kind of thing since her apprentice days in uniform, and the prospect of catching someone red-handed gave her a thrill, until she realized with a start that neither of them were wearing their vests – both their bulletproofs were in the back of the car. Sorbie was stealthily following the footprints towards the back of the house. She laid a hand on his shoulder. 'We're not wearing our vests,' she murmured into his ear.

'I know.'

'I think we should go back and kit up.'

'They'll be gone by the time we get back. Got to do it now. I got my spray.'

'I haven't.'

Wordlessly Sorbie handed her his pepper spray and moved forward again. They could both now see torch beams dancing behind upstairs curtains. In front of them the kitchen door had its half-glazed window broken and stood ajar. Sorbie's shoes crunched on broken glass as he entered the kitchen. It was large, contemporary and cold. They crept forward, keeping the pools of their torchlight small and close to their feet. They could hear the creak of movement on the upper floor.

'We'll go up in torchlight, then hit the light switches,' Fairfield murmured to Sorbie. 'If they jump out of the windows, please don't go after them.'

'No fear.' Sorbie led the way, making sure of the Speedcuffs on his belt. The house was heavily carpeted throughout, muffling the sound of their stealthy climb to the top of the stairs. They could both now faintly hear a hissed exchange in the second room across the landing, where two torch beams danced. Sorbie tiptoed forward, keeping to the left wall, out of sight. He snapped his torch off. From what he could see by the intruders' light, they were in the master bedroom. He was nearly at the door, Fairfield close behind him. Door opened right to left; the switch for the ceiling lights had to be on the right. He'd have to reach across the open doorway, but it would be quick. Surprise them, rush them. He could see one of them, standing on the far side of the double bed, zipping up a holdall. *Now*.

Sorbie slammed a hand across the wall switch and the ceiling lights came on, dazzling after the darkness. 'Police, stay where you are!' Behind him Fairfield rushed into the room. Both the scrawny boy with the bag and the hard-faced girl swore in a continuous stream. Everybody's eyes went to the gun on the bedspread, but the boy got there first. He grabbed it with his left hand and pointed it at Sorbie, then waved it from him to Fairfield and back. 'Fuck you, f-fuck you. I got a gun. I know how to use it!'

Sorbie froze. Here it was, then. He had always known it was waiting for him somewhere along the line, the strung-out junkie with half a brain, and a gun, and a screaming, rattling bitch behind him. 'Calm down, there's no need for that; you don't want to use that.'

'I will if you make me.'

Sorbie tried to keep his eyes on the boy's face, but they repeatedly strayed to the gun. A Beretta. Was the safety off? He couldn't see it; the boy was shaking, terrified, waving the gun. 'Get behind me, Kat.' He wasn't being chivalrous. Kat had the pepper spray and her airwave; out of direct sight, she might be able to hit the panic button and get the spray out.

The girl was dancing on the balls of her feet, clearly as strung out as the boy, and shouting continuously. 'Col, they're trying something, don't let them fucking come near us, we got to get out of here now, fucking do something, shoot them, why don't you fucking shoot?'

'Col, you don't need the gun; put the gun away,' Sorbie heard himself say, while his mind raced and his insides knotted into a hard ball of fear. 'Just keep calm and no one needs to get hurt.'

'Go over there, get to the side,' the boy shouted, waving the gun towards the wall.

Fairfield and Sorbie did as they were told, slowly. Why hadn't Kat got behind him like he'd asked? *Is the safety on or not? Hold the gun still, you stupid jerk, just show me the button's on safe and I'll come and shove the thing up your arse.* 'Okay, Col, no problem, take it easy.'

'What's she doing?' Col said. The gun swept aside, pointed straight at Fairfield now. 'What are you doing?'

'Relax, it's just a cigar. I feel like a smoke, keeps me calm. Just everyone keep calm, okay.' Fairfield's hands were shaking as she touched the flame to the cigar and sent a few fragrant puffs towards the ceiling. 'Want one, Jack?'

'They're up to something,' the girl squealed.

'Maybe later,' Sorbie said. 'I was going to watch *Strictly Come Dancing* tonight. But I'm not sure if it's on.'

'I think it's on. Actually yes, it's definitely on.'

'Shut up, you two. Take the bag, Tam. We're getting out.' The boy moved around the bed, coming forward, his gun hand shaking. 'You two are weird, fucking weird.'

'We need to lock them up somewhere,' the girl said.

'We just go. Go now, I got them covered.' As the girl squeezed past him out of the room, the boy shook the gun like a wagging finger. 'Don't you come after us. If I see you come outside, I'll fucking shoot both of you.'

Fairfield nodded, took the cigar from her mouth and stabbed it on to the boy's gun hand. He pulled his hand back; Sorbie lunged forward, grabbed his arm and jerked it upwards. The trigger finger tensed, but the safety was on. Sorbie crashed his forehead against the boy's nose, which split in a spray of blood, then yanked the Beretta from his hand. 'Go, go, it's sorted!' he shouted at Fairfield, and threw the gun on the bed. It was premature. The boy was wiry and furious and struggled in his grip, lashing out at his face, then kicking his leg. Sorbie managed at last to twist the boy's arm to the point of no return and forced him to his knees. He got one cuff on, paused to get his breath back, then finished the job. The boy stopped threatening and started whining. When Sorbie had his prisoner securely cuffed on the floor, he cautioned him, told him to *shut the fuck up*, then kicked him hard in the back.

Fairfield came up the stairs, out of breath, carrying the shoulder bag. 'I grabbed the bag as she climbed the fence, but she got away. You've got blood all over your face, Jack.'

'It's his. Where's the fucking bathroom?' Sorbie stepped over the now quiet prisoner into the hall in search of a washbasin.

'*Strictly Come Dancing*?' Fairfield called after him.

'Yeah, sorry. It was all I could think of.'

Chapter Twenty-Two

At his desk, Dearlove bit into his sandwich, sending a small squirt of salad cream into his lap. It was a home-made sandwich, an economy measure he now regretted, since his mouth was bored with it almost instantly. With his free hand he clicked his mouse until the *Bristol Herald* website appeared. 'Shit, it's true,' he informed the CID room in general.

'Whatever it is, I doubt it,' Austin said to the kettle as he waited for it to boil.

'No, it's here in black and white: they had a fire at the *Bristol Herald*. Early hours of the morning. In the newsroom. Says here the fire service thinks it could be arson. No paper edition for a few days; damn, I was waiting for the next instalment of the mystery photo competition.'

'Haven't you got any work to do?' Austin asked as he carried his mug of tea past him.

'This is lunch.' Dearlove lifted his tattered sandwich as evidence for the defence.

At his own desk, Austin clicked the print button and sat back while the large printer across the room started churning out preliminary reports by scene of crime and forensics. His phone rang. It was social services returning his call.

'Wonders never cease.'

'Pardon?' said the female voice at the other end.

'Sorry, talking to a colleague there. Did you get a result?'

'I don't know what you call a result. I am now in a position to confirm that Mr Justin Hedges has had dealings with all three of the names you enquired about. I must stress that I think very highly of Mr Hedges and his work. That three of his clients have met with a violent death just shows that we are dealing with very vulnerable people.'

'I'm sure you're right; we simply have to follow every lead. I must stress again, though, that this enquiry has to remain confidential while our investigation is in progress.'

Austin hung up and, carrying his mug of tea, went to see McLusky.

McLusky's tiny office was still in chaos. The other day, he had managed to lose his telephone in the mess; today it was the wireless computer mouse that was missing. He remembered the way the office had looked when he first set eyes on it: small but bright and functional. Now it looked like a skip and smelled like an ashtray. How had that happened? 'Sit down, tell me something cheerful,' he told Austin while he rummaged through the drawers of his desk.

'Social services called back: Hedges dealt with all three of our unburied victims. Ugh.' Austin shot up again off the chair and picked up the computer mouse he had sat on. 'Not looking for this, by any chance?'

'Genius. Give it here.'

'Are we bringing him in?'

'No, I want him relaxed. I'm meeting him at Darren Rutts's flat. He's been there recently, so no chance of contamination; his DNA will be all over the place anyway and SOCO are done.'

'Then you don't really think he's involved?'

'Who knows? He doesn't have a van registered to him, I know that much, but then that doesn't mean a thing. He isn't known to us and none of the three had any drug involvement, yet they were killed by the same bastards who killed the two in Leigh Woods. And both of those are connected to heroin. There's only one explanation. They were in the way somehow. They were witnesses. They knew something. They saw something they shouldn't have. They heard something, they read something. And from what we know so far, Fairfield's body fits in perfectly. Let me rephrase that: even without an autopsy, I'm sure the amateur dealer she found was killed by the same bunch.'

'And five minutes later, she and Sorbie stumble straight into the BMW driver's house.'

'They did what?'

'You haven't heard? Didn't Kat tell you?'

As far as McLusky was concerned, Fairfield seemed to have turned invisible. 'I've not seen her. Tell me what?'

'They got roped into a burglary-in-progress in Montrose Avenue. Caught two junkies doing the place over. One threatened them with a Beretta he'd found on the premises. The place was rented by our late BMW driver. The junkies didn't just find the gun, though; they also found a wad of notes and an armful of heroin wraps all ready to go.'

'They must have thought they'd gone to heaven. Fairfield and Sorbie tackled them despite the gun? Good on them. Shots fired?'

'Nearly. Kid didn't know his way round the Beretta, though, and they took it off him. And neither were wearing their vests.'

'Bravery award in the post, surely. Well I'm glad *somebody* got a result.'

'I can't believe you didn't hear it earlier.'

The phone started ringing while McLusky was still wrestling with a tottering pile of files on the floor. 'I've been buried in here. Get the phone and tell them I left without a forwarding address. I'm due to meet Hedges in a few minutes.'

'DI McLusky's office,' the DS said as he picked up. 'No, it's Austin. No, he's just left. Yes, I'll tell him. No, I won't.' He hung up.

'No you won't what?'

'Forget to tell you Denkhaus wants to see you for a progress report.'

'Marvellous. Leave me a note, then, since I'm out,' McLusky said. 'I'm off to see a man about some murders.'

Twenty minutes later, he buzzed Justin Hedges into the building from Darren Rutts's flat. He watched him come up the stairs from the door. Hedges looked harassed, but when he spotted McLusky, he managed a serviceable smile. 'I hope I'm not late, Inspector. I have a very full day. And a peripatetic one. I'm sometimes hard to get hold of, apparently, but I did get your message.'

'Good of you to come.'

'Terrible business, this. Vulnerable people. Brutal murders. The violence in this town is definitely getting worse.'

'Violent crime is down. It doesn't seem like it at the moment, I admit.'

'So how can I be of help?' Hedges said, looking at his mobile for a time-check.

'Are you in a hurry?'

'I have time for this.'

'To start with, have a look around the flat. Tell me what's amiss here.'

SOCO and forensics had added to the confusion in the place. Fingerprint powder was in evidence on the surfaces; many things had been moved, papers taken away for examination.

'Well, it was so neat before, everything in its place. Darren was struggling to come to terms with his disability; he had a lot of anger in him, and quite a bit of self-pity, too. But he knew that with a wheelchair it was important to be organized. And he had started finding new interests rather than hanker after the ones he could no longer fulfil.'

'New interests like …?'

'Photography mainly. I got him interested in that to get him out of the house. He went for a course at the Hope Community Centre up the road.'

'Photography.' McLusky tapped his walking stick against the side of his shoe in a nervous gesture. Something was about to click, he could feel it. 'At the centre that just had a fire?'

'Yes, unfortunate, that. Just when the funding is getting cut to ribbons. That was arson, you know?'

'It would be,' McLusky said, thinking. 'This is digital photography we're talking about?'

'Oh yes, it's all digital now, isn't it.'

'That means you'd need a camera and a computer.'

'Well, yes. But even if you didn't have your own, they had a bank of computers you could use, all donated, at the centre. They were all destroyed in the fire, I hear.'

'So no more photography course?'

'Oh, that folded anyway. The tutor left to take a better-paid job and the funding cuts meant they couldn't find anyone else to run it.'

'Did Mike Oatley also attend this course?'

'He did. He was very enthusiastic. He said it was the best thing he'd ever done.'

'Did Deborah Glynn?'

Not a flicker of surprise. 'You know, she might have done. I may have mentioned it to her. She'd just been rehoused after leaving a difficult relationship, if you know what I mean, and needed new friends in the area. Mr Morris could tell you. He runs the centre. But do you think there's a connection?'

Mr Morris, when McLusky found him later at the Hope Centre, asked the same question.

'It's a possibility,' McLusky said.

'I was hoping you were here about the arson.'

'That might be connected, too. Tell me about the photography course.'

They were sitting in the café area, which was furnished with an array of non-matching tables and chairs. Information posters and No Smoking signs adorned the walls. Even here, the smell of the recent fire was strong. Morris scratched his salt-and-pepper beard and pulled a face. 'Not much to tell. It didn't last long.'

285

'How many people were on the course?'

'Five or six. A few more signed up but didn't turn up for it. Always happens. So I think Ellen just had a few regulars.'

McLusky had his notebook open, pen poised. 'Ellen is the lady who ran it? What's her surname?'

'Carrs. Not sure if you'd call her a lady if you met her. She was twenty-two, wore Doc Martens and swore a lot.'

'You have an address for her?'

'I did have. All our records died in the fire. Everything was kept on computer.'

'No backups?'

'Melted.'

'No problem, we'll find her.'

'I'm not sure she's back yet. When she left here, she went on an assignment with some nature guy, to take pictures in the jungle. South America.'

'Nice job if you can get it. So what kind of things did they get up to on the course? Was it just how to use a digital camera, how to—'

'Oh, there was more to it than that. There was some theoretical stuff, but also what to do with the pictures once they'd taken them and so on. They had projects where they went out to take pictures of stuff. They'd go out in the van and—'

'They used a van?'

'Yes, our van. That got torched too, and the insurance are mucking us about; they think it was worthless junk. Same with all our computer equipment. Mind you, that really *was* worthless junk, that's why we were given it.'

Back outside, McLusky stood on the pavement and looked up at the burnt-out first floor. Computers turned to junk every three years or so. If they crashed, they could take all their files with them. Or a fire might do the trick.

A Mini drew up beside him. Philippa Warren parped her horn and rolled down her window. 'Are you here about the arson?'

McLusky started to walk away. 'No comment.'

Warren kept pace with him in her car. 'We had a very similar fire at the *Herald*. Quite a bit of damage in the newsroom.'

'Go away.'

'There's something I've been wanting to talk to you about, something I want you to look at.'

'Warren, if you don't go away, I'll have you picked up for kerb-crawling.' McLusky's mobile chimed in his jacket pocket.

'Suit yourself.' She accelerated away. Of course at the *Herald* they backed up everything properly, and online. Every file, every archive, every photograph. Even *bits* of photographs.

McLusky watched the reporter drive off as he answered his phone. It was Austin. 'They found Darren Rutts's mobile.'

'That's something at least. Where did it turn up?'

'In the melting snow under the flyover. It was pretty dead when they found it, but digital forensics got it going, and there's stuff on it they think we might want to see.'

'I'll go there straight away.'

Digital forensics had passed the files contained on the phone to technical support, who were still working on them. McLusky drove to Trinity Road station.

The technician was perhaps twenty-five, with bleached hair and a silver ring through his eyebrow. 'We stuck all the usual gubbins on disk for you, mainly pics and some dippy music,' he said, 'but one thing we're still working on.' He had offered McLusky a creaking office chair next to his in front of a computer. The long desk, which held several monitors, was cluttered with gadgets as well as papers, crisp packets and empty soft drinks bottles. The technician swept some of it aside, apologizing. McLusky recognized a kindred spirit. 'Is his address book there?'

'It is, but there's only a few names in it.'

McLusky didn't recognize any of Rutts's contacts, apart from the Royal Infirmary. 'He was starting a new life, I think.'

'Judging by the amount of phone numbers, he hadn't got very far.'

'Can we look at the pictures next?'

'If you insist.'

A few clicks of the mouse brought them up on the screen. 'He was supposed to have been interested in photography; I'd expected more pictures.'

'If you're interested in photography, you won't use a mobile to take pictures. The camera on his phone was crud.'

There were thirty pictures. The most recent one was of snow, taken from a window. Several others showed hospital staff, self-consciously posing; one showed Rutts himself, wearing inflatable water wings in a small hospital swimming pool, frowning up at the photographer. The ones that interested McLusky most came last. They were shots, some taken on the move and all from the low elevation of the wheelchair user, of people with cameras. He recognized Mike Oatley, looking seriously down at the screen at the back of his camera, and Deborah Glynn, smiling, pointing at something outside the frame. In several pictures a young woman with short dark hair made an appearance; she appeared to carry the camera with the longest lens, which probably meant he was looking at the tutor of the photography group. One picture, though extremely dark, showed the group against a background of trees. In one corner, the back of the Hope Community Centre van was just visible.

'That's all there is by way of pictures. There's something potentially more interesting, though. A voice recording.'

'His own voice?'

'No. It's quite murky and muffled, lots of background noise. Two voices. I'll run it for you.' The first sounds were of scratching and crunching close to the microphone, then a constant drone and rattle took their place. Human voices were just audible in the background. The counter in a corner of the screen ran on into its second minute. 'That sounds like it's in a van. You can hear the gear changes,' the technician said. He watched the counter. 'Coming up now ...'

One voice came closer, and the words 'with car behind'. The other voice, presumably turning towards the microphone of the mobile, became only just distinguishable for the end of a sentence: 'out, then go find the bitch'. A loud noise obliterated everything and the quality of the droning changed.

'That's the van door opening,' McLusky said. The sound continued for a few seconds, then the recording stopped. 'Why has it stopped?'

The technician tapped at the screen. 'Three minutes. Factory setting on the phone was for three minutes' maximum recording.'

'I think what we heard there were Darren Rutts's last three minutes. He must have been alive to turn on the voice recorder.'

'He may have been trying to call somebody, maybe dial 999, and ended up launching the voice recorder instead. It's easily done on that model if you blindly tap the screen.'

'Okay, play it again. The first speaker has a foreign accent.'

'Eastern Mediterranean, we think, though not a strong one, and quite a fluent speaker of English.'

They listened to the entire sequence again. The last three minutes of Darren Rutts's life. The voices of his killers. The rage that had been rising in McLusky for the last weeks hardened into a fist in his stomach. *Bastards*. 'What about the other one?'

'From the rhythms of his speech, the bit we can't make out, the computer came up with nothing much, except it's native English, southern counties, quite educated. Personally I think it sounds like London.'

'Yes. That was my thought. It's only six words, though.' *Out, then go find the bitch.* A killer in a hurry.

McLusky himself hurried away from Trinity Road, talking incessantly on his mobile. Had they found an address for Ellen Carrs yet? And why bloody not? No, he was not coming into Albany Road now, he was too busy to talk to Denkhaus.

Because he thought he had recognized both voices.

Chapter Twenty-Three

The Boat House was still closed. Through the glass doors, McLusky saw bar staff moving inside, setting up, straightening, polishing. At the Boat House, leaning time was cleaning time, he had no doubt, if his impression of the management style was correct. Armed with nothing but the thinnest hunch, he was glad he'd had a run-in with the man the night he had taken Louise out; it gave him an excuse, equally thin, to follow it up.

He rapped his car keys against the door. It attracted the attention of a white-shirted teenager but wasn't enough to bring him to the door. McLusky rapped again. The kid tapped his wrist where a previous generation would have worn a watch, then flashed his open hands twice: *twenty minutes*. McLusky unfolded his warrant card and slapped it against the glass: *now*. The young man relented and opened the door. 'Anything the matter?'

'You should know, you're the one who works here. Manager in?'

'Erm, that depends.'

The two other staff, both dressed identically in black and white, minded their own business. 'Crew cut, leather jacket. *Unpleasant*.'

'He's in the office, downstairs.' The kid nodded towards a door marked 'Private'. 'I'll call down for you.'

'I'll find my own way.'

'Oh no, he won't like that.'

'That's the idea.' Then he relented; the kid would get into trouble. 'Oh, all right, get on with it then.' The place was full of CCTV anyway; if the manager didn't know he was here, he would have to be asleep.

Behind the bar, the boy spoke on the phone, then told him: 'You're okay to go down.'

The interior designer responsible for computer-designing the Boat House ambience had not been allowed beyond the door marked 'Private'. Raw concrete steps, scuffed white-washed walls and strip lighting kept McLusky company on the way downstairs. There were several doors, one marked 'Office'. He tried the handle but found it locked. A lock release buzzed and he pushed in.

The office was simply, even dingily furnished, apart from the leather swivel chair the manager occupied. He was wearing the same jacket as before. The collar was half folded over, as though he had only just put it on in a hurry. 'Where I come from, it is polite to knock.'

'And where would that be, Greece?'

'Now you are insulting me. The Greeks are a rude people. I am from Turkey. Now, what do you want here? I am a busy man.'

That was the voice. It was the accent, anyway. Three words, just three words. 'Oh, I just wanted to show my face. It's called neighbourhood policing. Letting you know we're never far away.' McLusky took a few steps to the side of the desk, from where he could share the manager's view of a split-screen CCTV monitor showing views of the door area, of the till and the rest of the bar. 'How old are those kids up there?'

'They're all over eighteen.'

'And all under twenty-one so you don't have to pay the minimum wage.'

'I think this is harassment. Can I see your card, your ID?' McLusky produced it. 'Mc … Lusky.' The man scribbled it into a corner of his open diary and nodded heavily.

'Indeed. And while we're at it, what's yours?'

'Kaya.'

'That'll be your surname?'

He rolled his eyes. '*Yes.*'

'And what's your first name, Mr Kaya?'

It was Ilkin. McLusky knew this was futile. He couldn't question Kaya without giving away his suspicions, and he didn't have a single lead that pointed to him. *Three words.* 'Just out of interest, what car do you drive, Mr Kaya?'

'Why do you ask about my car? Are you traffic police now?'

'I just wondered … You're sure you're not behind with your tax and MOT?'

'I am not behind with my tax. What is the matter with you? You will please explain what you want or go. Otherwise perhaps I can arrange transfer to traffic police for you.' He glanced down at his diary. '*McLusky.*'

'You must be quite an influential man, Mr Kaya, because that's been tried before, without success.'

Kaya just raised his eyebrows and tapped his plastic biro against his thumb.

'Well, thank you for your time, Mr Kaya. The bar looks ready for business and I must admit, I do feel like a drink. Goodbye for now.' When he pulled at the handle, the door was locked again. It took three heartbeats before Kaya buzzed him through.

At the bar, he ordered Pilsner and swigged from the bottle. 'What kind of car does Mr Kaya drive, d'you know?' he asked the barman.

'Not sure. A Japanese one, silver, I think.'

'How about a van? Does the Boat House have a van?'

'Not that I know of.'

Another barman, who was stocking a glass-fronted fridge with mixers, looked over his shoulder. 'I thought I saw Mr Kaya driving a van a couple of weeks ago. I could be wrong. It was really clapped out. Only saw it for a sec.'

'What kind of van?' But the boy had turned back to the fridge. McLusky looked behind him.

Kaya was standing in the door to the basement, sending a text on his phone. He called across: 'Benji, get me some cigarettes!'

McLusky drained the bottle and left.

At Albany Road, he collared Austin and shooed him into his office. He played him the recording.

Austin listened, staring a hole into the wall. 'If that's really Darren Rutts's last three minutes, then that's really creepy.' But he looked worried. 'He only says three words, though.'

'It's him. I talked to him earlier, apropos of nothing, and heard him say "behind" and "car", and it's the same voice.'

'It's thin, Liam.'

'I don't care how thin it is, I want to know everything about him, and about the Boat House; I want to know who he associates with and what he has for breakfast.'

'D'you think Denkhaus will authorize surveillance?'

'Probably not.'

Twenty minutes later, McLusky was proved right. DSI Denkhaus started shaking his head while he was listening to the recording, and never stopped. 'Because you heard someone utter three words on a muffled recording made on a phone? You didn't really expect me to authorize a surveillance operation on the strength of *that*?' Denkhaus ejected the disk from his computer. McLusky tried to interject, but Denkhaus cut across him. 'Every Turkish man in the country would have pronounced those words the same. Do you know how many Turks we have living in Bristol?'

'No, how many?'

'Well … a substantial number, I'm sure. First find something on the man. But I don't want you to neglect any other lines of enquiry just because you have another bloody hunch.' The trouble with DI McLusky's hunches was that some were inexplicably brilliant but most led to expensive nowheres.

McLusky limped back towards his office. He was perfectly capable of walking without the stick now but felt reluctant to let it go. It had become his favourite tool for expressing his impatience as he stomped along the corridors and in and out of the incident room.

Austin caught up with him outside his door. 'Well, he's here legally; entered the country two years ago in January. Drives a silver Toyota, address in Shirehampton.'

'How quaint.'

Austin noted that the DI knew it to be a northern suburb of Bristol and no longer needed to ask where it was.

McLusky lit a cigarette and tested his kettle for water, then flicked it on. 'Nothing else?'

'No phone registered to him.'

'Rubbish, must have if he owns a bar; you can't rely just on mobiles. And you'll need internet access.'

'Oh, yeah, I meant his home address. And he doesn't own the bar, he's just managing it.'

'Who's the owner?'

'A James Cullip. He's clean, too. Owns quite—'

'Wait, name rings a bell. Cullip, quite young, curly hair.'

'Yeah, he's thirty-four, though it doesn't actually mention hair styles on—'

'Shut up, Jane. I had lunch with him, at the Isis. When I got roped in by Denkhaus. You know, concerned business-men, et cetera. And Cullip's from London. So is the other speaker in the recording. Where's that disk ...?' McLusky played it again. *Out, then go find the bitch.*

Austin scratched the tip of his nose. 'That's so indistinct, it *really* could be anyone.'

'I know, I know.'

'And who's the bitch?'

'The bitch is Ellen Carrs. She ran the photography course they all attended. Have we found her address yet?'

'Oh yeah, no answer.'

'Why didn't you tell me?'

'I thought I had.'

'Why did it take so long?'

'She's not on the electoral register.'

'You sent someone round?'

'Patrol swung round there, no answer. Neighbours said she's not been back since going off on her jungle assignment.'

'No, I still don't like it. If I'm right, then she'll be next. Get Deedee to check if she's entered the country recently. Then we'll go and have a look at her place. Where is it?'

It was a sky-blue terraced house in Ashley Down, not far from the college. There was no answer to either bell or knock. 'Locksmith?' Austin asked.

'Not yet. According to Denkhaus, I am costing the tax-payer a fortune. And if we get the locksmith to get us in, then we'll have to change the lock, and when the girl comes back she'll find herself locked out because her key won't fit.'

The next-door neighbour opened the door. She had her hands full trying to stop a tiny dog from escaping the house while the baby in her arm tried to gouge one of her eyes out. 'Yeah, sure, go through the garden. Close the door so I can let go of the dog. You think there's something wrong at Ellen's place? We had the police around earlier asking about her.'

'Nothing to worry about. We just want to make sure she won't find any nasty surprises. Through here, is it?' McLusky walked ahead through the kitchen and let himself out at the back. From the centre of the little lawn a melting snowman looked at him with stony eyes, his carrot nose sadly drooping. At the fence, McLusky pointed out an upstairs window above the kitchen extension of Ellen Carrs' house. 'See that sash, Jane? It doesn't look fully closed to me. I think it's your turn for the acrobatics this time.'

'You want me to climb up there?'

'Well you can pole-vault if you prefer, as long as you get in. I'll wait out the front.'

'And what if the window isn't open?'

'Then open it, DS Austin.'

By the time Austin had pulled himself over the fence and escaped the evergreen shrub on the other side, he was already scratched and less than happy. At the back of the house, he stacked recycling boxes on top of each other, then used the drainpipe to pull himself high enough to get a knee on to the sloping tarpaper roof of the extension. Mindful of DS Sorbie's recent breakthrough, he proceeded on hands and knees. He could see the window had been levered open and not shut fully. It opened easily on to a small room. The telltale signs of burglary were everywhere.

'Someone was here before us,' he told McLusky when he let him in. 'There's an office up there that's been ransacked. No sign of her.'

McLusky made straight for the kitchen and opened the lid of the swing bin. It was empty. 'The window was forced? Then it wasn't them. I don't think they've got her.' Upstairs he looked in the bathroom, felt the soap, searched in vain for a toothbrush. Next door he contemplated the office space, squinting, trying to see what wasn't there. 'This was a real burglary. Looks like a lot of photographic stuff went walkies; there's plenty of space in that drawer, but there's filters left in there.'

'Perhaps she took all that with her.'

'You see those rectangles where there's hardly any dust? I reckon there was a big photo printer there; you don't lug that through the jungle. This is different from the others. Coincidence, I guess. She'll have a great homecoming, won't she? House burgled and a homicidal bastard waiting for her.'

'Are you convinced of that?'

McLusky stirred the mess on the floor with his walking stick. 'I'm not convinced of anything, Jane, I just have a crap feeling about this.'

'What about Kaya and James Cullip? Are we going after them?'

McLusky looked out of the window at the grey, dripping neighbourhood. '*I'm* going after them. But you carry on as if your DI was normal.'

They secured the upstairs window and left a note in the hall for Ellen Carrs to contact Albany Road police station as a matter of urgency.

*

McLusky was disappointed. James Cullip's house in Lower Failand was large and set in a fair amount of gardens, about half an acre, he guessed, but it lacked ostentation. Being only twenty minutes' drive from Bristol, it would probably fetch a million, but it looked quietly expensive. In his experience, drug-dealers loved to show off their money, drive flashy cars, impress people. All people, all the time. Cullip's car was a silver Mercedes S something-or-other. It probably cost several times McLusky's annual earnings, but it wasn't shouty. Right now it was sensibly parked on the slushy tarmac drive outside the double garage of this sober Edwardian house.

It was day two of his unauthorized surveillance. With his airwave turned off, McLusky had parked his own car on the verge of the narrow lane, close enough to observe the front of the house in detail through his binoculars. The more he thought about the place, the more his disappointment grew. He'd had a good look around, making sure anyone at the house knew he was there. There was a wrought-iron gate, yet it stood wide open. It was less than man height, so merely symbolic. The property was surrounded by hedges, not fences, and there was no CCTV in evidence and no goons patrolling the place.

Earlier, he had spent two hours sitting in his car outside Kaya's house in Shirehampton, a bland, unassuming place, and had followed him into town. Kaya had parked in a multi-storey close to the harbour and walked to work. Now McLusky had been freezing his toes off outside Cullip's place for three hours, sometimes in the car, sometimes walking about in the melting snow. A middle-aged woman in a little VW had arrived earlier and parked at a respectful distance from the Mercedes. She was dressed in jeans and a grey jacket and disappeared around the back of the house. The age of the car spelled poverty, and McLusky had her down as a cleaner. Another hour, and a man in a Vauxhall estate arrived. He carried what looked like sample books to the front door and was greeted and admitted by Cullip himself. He stayed for half an hour and drove off slowly the way he had come. McLusky noted him down as a soft-furnishings salesman.

Cullip ran his multi-strand business from home. McLusky could see blond smoke rising from two chimneys, and imagined the heat and fragrance of the log fires as he tried to fumble a cigarette from the pack without taking his gloves off. He managed to extract one with his teeth and lit it. Only one left. Cullip's legitimate business interests, as far as he'd been able to establish, included bars and restaurants in England, several fur shops in France as well as a second-hand car dealership in Wales. This was the only cheerful note McLusky had heard chime so far. Fur shops and second-hand car sales lent themselves particularly well to laundering money. Fur shops, especially, often did no business for weeks, then turned over large amounts in a short time.

The front door opened. McLusky picked up his binoculars again. It was James Cullip, wearing a black overcoat, scarf and gloves. McLusky got ready to follow his car, but Cullip walked past the Mercedes, came out into the lane and straight towards him. He stopped briefly a few paces away from McLusky's car, produced an iPhone and took a picture. When he got close to the car, he took another picture, shooting from the hip. He halted for a moment to sneeze, then stood close and rapped on the driver window with gloved knuckles.

McLusky let the window slide down. 'Mr Cullip, what a surprise. Is that your house, or were you just visiting?'

'Cut the crap, Inspector. What the fuck are you doing outside my house?'

Out, then go find the bitch. 'Freezing my arse off,' McLusky said cheerfully.

'This is the second day you've been parked up here. Limping about in the lane. Along the field behind the house. Sitting in your car.'

'You noticed. Well, I know how concerned you and your friends are about crime. I'm helping to keep Lower Failand crime-free.'

'I'll help you to a career in traffic management if you don't find something else to do.'

'Yes, Mr Kaya said something similar a few days ago.'

'You've been harassing my staff at work, you've been following Mr Kaya around; now you're harassing me at my home …'

'You feel harassed?'

Cullip bent down to bring his face close. It was flushed now, and his breath smelled of whisky. 'We can do this several ways, McLusky. I'd normally try persuasion first, but from what I hear, you're not the sensible type. I've already had a word with your superior, DSI Denkhaus. He was suitably apologetic, and if you go to see him now, he will tell you what he thinks of you making a nuisance of yourself. But if that doesn't prove sufficient, then I'll consider other options.'

'Like giving yourself up?'

'I don't know what you are talking about, Inspector.'

'You see, that's where the charade falls down: a normal person would have asked what he was suspected of.'

'Your DSI seems to think you frequently go off on absurd tangents. This is obviously one of them.'

'There'll be DNA, you know,' McLusky said conversationally. 'There always is. A hair, perhaps, or a sneeze is probably enough these days.' Cullip abruptly straightened up and walked away. McLusky called after him: 'Was it you who did the killing? Probably more Kaya's style, eh? Did you hang around to watch, though?' There was the smallest hesitation in Cullip's gait, but he kept going.

McLusky got out and considered following him up the drive, provoking him some more, but he changed his mind and just stood and watched Cullip disappear into the house. Then he got back into the car and lit his last cigarette. He wouldn't last long without buying more after this one, but he didn't want to give Cullip the impression he was leaving because of what had been said. He smoked slowly, planning to stay for at least another half-hour.

300

He had only just taken the last drag of his cigarette and stubbed it out in the ashtray when the patrol car pulled up behind him. McLusky pretended to ignore them but watched the two officers leave the vehicle and approach the driver door of his car. He didn't recognize either of them. One of them tapped on his window. McLusky slid it down three inches.

'There's been a complaint, sir,' said the officer, bending down, one hand on the roof of the car.

McLusky opened his ID wallet. 'I'm a police officer.'

'Yes, we know. The message from control is: turn on your airwave and return to Albany Road immediately.'

McLusky sighed. 'Okay, tell them you delivered your message.'

'We're supposed to follow you in, sir.'

McLusky used the drive back, closely followed by the patrol car, to formulate responses to the rocket he was likely to receive when he fell into Denkhaus's clutches, but he'd have found ample time for it in the superintendent's outer office. For once Lynn Tiery's eyebrows gave nothing away. Denkhaus kept him waiting for nearly half an hour, but remarks about wasting police time would probably fall flat. When he was finally admitted, he didn't get much time for remarks of any kind.

Either Denkhaus had used the last half-hour to read the relevant sections, or he was displaying a remarkable memory when he quoted at length from the Police and Criminal Evidence Act.

'You are *this* far away from a suspension,' he said, holding two fleshy digits a hair's breadth apart. 'In fact if DCI Gaunt wasn't off sick, I'd be seriously considering it, so count yourself lucky. As it is, you will receive a written warning. Even if your idea of James Cullip as the mind behind this killing spree wasn't completely unsubstantiated, your flouting of PACE would seriously jeopardize any chances of conviction anyway. Fortunately all it'll jeopardize is what is

301

laughably called your career. The ACC plays golf with the man, for Pete's sake. I'd have thought you'd have learnt when a bit of tiptoeing is required. As for turning your airwave off,' he held up a hand to cut off McLusky's prepared speech, 'and claiming no doubt that it was malfunctioning or whatever, that's the kind of nonsense I expect from a DC, not a detective inspector on my team.'

When McLusky was free to go, he used his stick to lever himself up and felt as though he really needed it. After a brief exchange with Austin in the incident room, he buried himself in his office.

He doubted very much that the ACC would oblige and ask Cullip if he awfully minded giving a DNA sample next time they played a round of golf. It was time to rethink the whole thing, to review the entire case, revisit every location, read through every report again, look at every photograph and statement twice. He stood in the middle of what little floor space there was in his office, took in the collapsed piles of files on the floor, the overflowing bin, the mess on his desk, the condensation on the window. The fan on his computer terminal had acquired a rattle and the radiator had started gurgling again. He gripped the handle of his walking stick hard. Smashing the place up wouldn't help, he tried to tell himself. It really wouldn't. But the urge remained strong. He sat down instead, blew the dust from a drinking glass and poured himself a large measure of Glenmorangie. He swirled it around the glass, inhaled the complex fragrance, then dribbled it back into the bottle, put it away and pulled the first file towards him.

It was mid-afternoon and getting dark in the office. He switched on the lamp, counted his cigarettes. Ridiculous, that had been a full pack only a few hours ago. The phone rang.

It was Sergeant Hayes. 'We had this phone call, sir, from an Ellen Carrs.'

'Why didn't you put her through? I said I needed to talk to her urgently.'

'Well it's like this, sir, she never finished the call. I think you'd better come and listen to the recording.'

'I'm on my way.' McLusky surprised himself with the speed with which he could move. On the way down the stairs, the stick never even touched the ground.

'That was quick, sir.'

'Go on, play it.'

Hayes and McLusky both donned headphones, standing next to the civilian operator who answered all calls to the station. The recording sounded tinny in their ears. 'Albany Road Police Station, how can I help?' 'Yes, hello, I've just come back after a few weeks away and found my place has been turned over and there's a note in the hall that says it's from Detective Inspector McLusky and I should call this number and—' A door bell could be heard, quite loud, insistent. 'It's all happening at once, there's someone at the door, can you just hang on for one second?' Retreating footsteps. After several more seconds there was a distant thump.

Hayes took his headphones off. 'There's nothing more, just the operator going "hello, hello". What do you think to that … sir?'

McLusky was already running through the door and towards the stairs. 'Send a patrol round there immediately!' he called over his shoulder.

'I already have,' Hayes said quietly. 'I'm not a *complete* idiot.'

McLusky took the stairs two at a time. 'Where is Austin?' he shouted into the CID room. He didn't wait for an answer and ran on to his own office, grabbed his jacket and car keys and turned round. 'Tell him to call me,' he shouted as he hurried past again, struggling to pull on his jacket without dropping his stick. He hammered down the stairs. *Not her place, it'll be too late.* In the car park he slipped in the slush, nearly lost his balance. If he got it wrong now, Ellen Carrs would be dead. She might well be dead already.

He started the Mazda and forced his way out of the car park and into the traffic. *Not Kaya's place: too small, too suburban, too overlooked.* If he got it wrong, he'd be kicked off the force. No doubt about it. Perhaps he should have resigned before he got in the car.

Traffic was awful and he had no siren on the rented MiTo. He flashed his lights, used his horn, waved his arms, shouted. He barged across lanes, undertook on the inside, knocked the wing mirror off a slower car, jumped the lights and bullied his way across a junction. The suspension bridge was slower than the southern route, but once across, he'd make up the time. The cycle path along the river … Leigh Woods … Lower Failand, it was all more or less in a line, it was all within easy reach, it was *convenient*. It was *lazy*, just like the burials. And Ilkin Kaya was lazy. *Benji, get me some cigarettes.* Just voices on a phone. It was thin, Austin would say. It was desperately thin. But it was Cullip who'd be behind it; Cullip employed Kaya, and in the recording it was him who gave the order. *Go get the bitch.* And they had got her.

Once past Leigh Woods, McLusky found an empty stretch of road and put his foot down. The road was wet but clear; there'd be no ice, there'd better be no ice. He overtook three cars at once, only just getting back in his lane in time before the car coming the other way whizzed past, horn blaring. He slowed down a little. If he lost it on the road, there'd be no excuse. He nearly missed the turn-off, braked hard. From here on, it was single-lane. He used his horn on every bend, parping an angry rhythm. If he met someone like himself it would be game over. A fingerpost whipped past, too quick to read; nearly there now.

A hundred yards ahead a car joined the lane from a side track, travelling in the same direction. It was a silver Mercedes S. McLusky stood on the brake, allowing the car in front to gain some distance.

Cullip. McLusky couldn't see the driver, but he remembered part of the number plate. It was him. It had to be him. It had better be him. Where had he just come from? He checked his mirrors. Nothing but grey hedgerows, bits of dark sky. He slowed a bit more, the Mercedes out of sight now. He could go back there, drive up that lane. She wouldn't be at Cullip's house; they wouldn't have taken her there. *Nineteenth-century brick dust.*

Grab Cullip. He speeded up, chased after the Mercedes along the narrow lane, not using his horn now, swinging through the bends with gritted teeth and diminishing faith. He took the right turn towards Cullip's house too fast, bumping through the shallow ditch, dragging the side of the car through the hedge without slowing down.

He caught up with him just as he turned into his brightly lit drive. He followed him in, driving inches behind him, finally scraping along the driver's side of the Mercedes as it came to a stop, blocking the door. Cullip scrambled across, sprang from the car on the passenger side and came around the back to confront his pursuer. He was dressed in a blue boiler suit, gloves and black rubber boots. McLusky waited until the man was close enough, then flung open his door hard. It caught Cullip on one knee and he took a staggering step back, shouting obscenities. McLusky levered himself out of the car. Cullip looked fit and probably went to the gym, so he wasted no time. He swung his stick and hit him on the shin.

'You maniac!' Cullip shouted and staggered back a bit more.

'Where is she?' McLusky shouted back.

Cullip reached into his pocket. McLusky swung his stick with force and hit him on the elbow. Cullip cried out in pain. 'Ow, you arsehole! It's just my mobile!'

McLusky hit him again, repeating his question, then flipped the stick around, hooked Cullip's leg up and pushed him to the ground. 'Where is she, Cullip!'

'Fuck off, you creep, get off me!'

The man's suddenly high voice surprised McLusky. He brought the stick down across his nose, splattering blood, breaking it.

'Whatever happens, you're finished, McLusky,' Cullip groaned, holding his face, lifting the other arm to protect his head.

McLusky thought he was probably right; he swung the stick high and hit Cullip's knee hard. 'I'm using reasonable force here, but I'm in a hurry. We're moving fast towards permanent injury.'

'You'll never save her if you waste time beating me up.'

He landed a crack on his wrist, eliciting a sharp cry and a stream of expletives, but the curses became more pleading. 'You broke it, you bastard, you broke it.'

'She's alive then. I had imagined you'd be watching.'

'Not the girls, McLusky.' He tried for a laugh, but failed. 'Never the *girls*. If I tell you the place, you'll let me go, agreed?'

McLusky lifted the stick.

'Otherwise why should I tell you? Come *on*. You can't beat it out of me. A bargain.'

The stick remained suspended. 'If you send me on a wild goose chase, I'll come after you and finish you off. I swear I will.'

'I won't. Okay, okay,' he added quickly as the stick started descending. 'She's at Hartings Farm.'

'How do I get there? Quickly now.'

'Back along the lane, third turn-off. Keep going.'

McLusky gave a grunt of grudging satisfaction. Then he dug his handcuffs from his jacket and clasped them around Cullip's unbroken wrist, quickly dragging his protesting prisoner by the arm until he could thread the other end of the cuff through the rear door handle of the Mercedes. 'I lied to you,' McLusky said.

'So did I,' Cullip spat. 'She's dead.'

McLusky pulled Cullip's iPhone from his pocket and lobbed it into the garden. 'Why? Why kill them all?'

'Blackmail. One of the bastards was blackmailing me. With a picture of how we killed Wayne. Fuck knows how they took that. One of them sent me bits of it. And bits to the *Bristol Herald*. We took care of the *Herald*; we took care of all of them.'

McLusky got into his car and reversed out of the drive at speed. Once back in the lane, he dialled Austin's number while he accelerated away.

306

'Ah, good thing you called,' Austin began. 'The patrol that went round Ellen—'

'Shut up, Jane, and listen. She's probably dead. It was Cullip and Kaya. Send someone round Cullip's place. I left him cuffed to his Merc; make sure they caution him, I didn't have time. I'm on my way to Hartings Farm, near here. I think it's where the killings were done.'

'I just found out that Cullip bought it. It's a derelict farm near Lower Failand.'

McLusky turned up the lane from which the Mercedes had emerged. 'I'm nearly there.'

'Be careful, Liam. If the girl is dead, why not wait for backup?'

'Feel free to join me.' McLusky terminated the call and concentrated on the way ahead. This lane was even narrower; the hedgerows looked neglected. Only a mile further on, he found it. As soon as the loom of its dark buildings appeared, he killed the lights, stopped and left the car in the lane. Even so, anyone at the farm might well have heard the engine or seen the lights approaching.

A wind had sprung up, curiously mild after the long wintry spell. There was only the faintest light in the sky now, and it took McLusky a minute for his eyes to adjust. He walked carefully towards the buildings. After some steps he paused for a few heartbeats, then threw his stick into the hedge and walked back to the car. Half hidden under the driver's seat and forgotten until now lay the confiscated shotgun, gold-plated and sawn-off. He was amazed at the confidence the heavy weapon bestowed as he moved swiftly with it up the lane.

Hartings Farm had not been derelict for long but had obviously been neglected for many years. The signs were everywhere. The five-bar gate to the yard stood open but hung on a single hinge; the yard itself consisted of mud and concrete islands in a sea of melting snow; the old brick-built farmhouse was shuttered and partially boarded up, its roof missing several tiles. A row of low, sagging outbuildings contained a profusion of junk and rusting machinery. Confused tyre tracks ran all over the yard, some leading straight towards the closed double doors of a large barn.

McLusky stopped just inside the gate. There were thirty yards of open space between him and the barn. If Kaya was armed and had heard him, then it would happen here, between the gate and the barn. He heard a faint noise from somewhere ahead, a dull thud followed by a thin metallic clang. It was probably the wind. It didn't sound like a man taking aim. He started to cross the yard in deliberate loping strides. With a loud splash his foot disappeared up to his shin into a black puddle. He stood still while the icy water flooded his boots. There was no more sound. Slowly he withdrew his foot and squelched on, shotgun pointing at the uneven ground, until he reached the wall beside the door. Backup. Should have waited for backup. He crept into the dark along the right-hand side of the building, but his feet instantly snagged on hidden debris among the weeds. He withdrew back to the door, listened. For the fifth time since entering the yard, he felt for the safety catch, making sure it was off. Then he stretched out a hand for the crude wooden handle on the left leaf of the door and pulled. After opening a foot's width, the wood gave a creak that sounded like a shout in McLusky's ear. He slid through the gap and advanced a few steps into the cavernous dark, then squatted down, shotgun levelled.

Death. It was faint, but McLusky could smell it. The metallic odour of spilled blood and the stench of bowels and bladder discharged. He held his breath and listened. Not a sound. He held his pencil torch as far to the side of his body as he could stretch and risked a short flash. A few feet away stood a blue van; beyond it McLusky got the impression of a dark bundle lying by a thick supporting beam. No gunshot was aimed at his flashlight. He stood up, clicked it on again and advanced, bent low, stabbing the thin beam into the dark spaces between mouldering junk. He rested the beam on the slumped figure on the ground. It was the girl, still tied and

gagged. Her hair and T-shirt were smeared with blood, her face destroyed. All around lay bloodied lumps of brick, concrete and wood. He felt for a pulse at her neck. She was dead.

The door of the van was open. He shone the light inside; it was empty. Engine noise erupted; not here, but close, outside. Bright lights pierced the dark through chinks in the side of the barn. The crunch of tyres as a car sped alongside. McLusky ran. He could hear the car skidding away. When he barged through the barn doors, the brake lights of the silver Toyota flashed at him as the car negotiated the gate and turned left. McLusky ran. Even as he splashed through the yard, he could hear the car braking as it reached the MiTo blocking the lane. As he skidded out of the yard, Kaya threw his car into reverse and screeched towards him. McLusky raised the shotgun and held his breath. No matter where he pointed the gun, he couldn't miss. His adversary was invisible inside the car but kept on coming. Ten yards, five yards. McLusky swallowed hard. Three yards. He leant into the gun, and when the car was nearly on him, he fired and jumped aside. The rear window of the Toyota shattered; the car slewed into the hedge and stalled.

Silence. McLusky picked himself up and approached the car cautiously. He opened the passenger door, poked the shotgun at Kaya and snatched the keys from the ignition. Kaya was bleeding from his cheek and was holding his shoulder. He looked stunned but wide awake.

'I'll call you an ambulance,' McLusky said.

Kaya looked straight ahead. 'Fuck off.'

From beyond the parked MiTo several sets of headlights approached. McLusky gently set the shotgun on the ground. His hands were steady as he shook a cigarette from the pack and lit it. Then he walked away up the lane into the dark, in the curiously mild air, smoking, enjoying a last few moments of peace.

They hadn't come. They didn't pay up. And he was alive. Three hours he had waited beyond the arranged drop-off

309

time, and they hadn't come. He had convinced himself that they would kill him. Kill him without paying up, or pay up and kill him when he went to claim the money. But not turning up at all, that he had never expected. There was no sign of them, no sign of the holdall full of money, in the agreed place or anywhere else. He took another turn of Queen's Square in the strangely mild evening air, strolling along in the dim light. Somehow, he found, he did not feel disappointed. He felt light. As though a weight had been lifted. They had just ignored him. And him with the ferry ticket bought and the car packed and waiting.

He'd go to Spain anyway. It would always be this mild there in winter; that was where this air was coming from, they had said on the radio. He would expose them, of course. Just as he had promised. The picture would get them convicted, no question about it.

He looked for a postbox and eventually found one close to where he had parked his car. When he pulled out the letter with the complete photograph inside, he saw he had stuck a second-class stamp on it but forgotten to address it. He found the biro in his jacket, but now he couldn't remember the proper address. It didn't really matter.

The Bristol Herald, he wrote, and posted it. It would get there eventually.